D0684896

SHE LINGERED BEFORE THE MIRROR, SHAPING THE SILK TO HER NAKED BODY . . .

The chamber door came softly open. "Vanozza? Look at this! Isn't it beautiful?"

"I assure you that the view from behind is quite as ravishing!"

The reply was warmly appreciative and did *not* belong to the housekeeper. Her heart plummeting in horrified recognition, she whirled to face the prince, who stood grinning in the doorway. Her eyes, huge above the bastion of the green gown, accused him of enormities.

"For God's sake, do not clutch the wretched garment to you as though it represented your much-vaunted virtue! I do not care for crushed and rumpled companions. Unless," he qualified genuinely, "I have rumpled them myself!" He sauntered in and lowered himself gracefully onto the chest where he sat swinging one well-shaped calf as he examined those portions of pale gold flesh that escaped their inadequate covering. . . .

THE SINS
OF
THE LION

Annette Motley

FAWCETT POPULAR LIBRARY   •   NEW YORK

THE SINS OF THE LION

This book contains the complete text of the original hardcover edition.

Published by Fawcett Popular Library, a unit of CBS Publications, the Consumer Publishing Division of CBS Inc., by arrangement with Stein and Day Publishers

Copyright © 1979 by Annette Motley

All Rights Reserved

ISBN: 0-445-04647-3

Printed in the United States of America

First Fawcett Popular Library printing: April 1981

10   9   8   7   6   5   4   3   2   1

THE SINS
OF
THE LION

PART ONE

ONE

The Lion of the Valenti bent an indolent yellow gaze on the girl before him. She stood perfectly still, neither trembling nor trying to cover herself with her hands as the others did. Her eyes were empty of tears and were concentrated upon the sculptured facade of the imposing palace that faced the teeming wharf. The graceful and fancifully decorative windows of the Riva degli Schiavoni stared vacantly back, as indifferent to scenes of human misery as to the ceaseless drama of cosmopolitan commerce played out before them.

The great, painted galleys of the Venetian State had sailed home from Constantinople, and the citizens were waiting to welcome them. The quayside was lusty with movement as the triumphant captains swaggered and preened, golden earrings and silver cutlasses catching the sun as they strode among the sober-garbed merchants and auditors, only matched in magnificence, here and there, by the scarlet silk of a senator's robe, lying familiarly across a seaman's arm as they stood in close conversation. Her gorgeous captains were the eyes and ears of the *Serene Republic* as they crossed oceans and were entertained in great cities. Acre, Sidon, Alexandria, Tyre, and the new Byzantium welcomed them and their ducats, and the cheap raw materials gathered into Venice from all over Europe: the hides, the rough wool and the tin from chilly England, copper and steel from the German Empire, raw silver from Bohemia. In return they sent them home with spices and silks, the exquisite work of gold and silversmiths, damasks, jewels, sweet-scented woods and incenses—and slaves, bought, taken, won in a thousand ways from a thousand places. The proud captains brought back their cargoes and their riches, and with them the gleanings of each of their ready senses, extended to the utmost. There was little that Venice did not know about the actions and intentions of her neighbors.

Il Captane Ibn al Farid, of the too frequent white smile and the equally frequent lash, was a spy, a trader, and a pirate. A follower of Islam, he did not hesitate to send a man to his reward of gardens and houris; however, his more particular specialty was to provide those still living with as close an approximation of the joys to come, as the stolen daughters of a thousand international households might be forced to offer.

Today's collection was especially fine. There were a dozen girls, chosen with an expert eye to the Venetian taste for oriental opulence and dusky piquancy. They had been well looked after. His crew had received orders not to mark them during any amorous encounters they might have cared to have with them. He had once had a man's skin neatly flayed from his back by the Turkish eunuch who acted as slave driver to the rovers of the galley. He was a perfectionist whether beating out perfect time with the iron hammer in his giant, capable fist, or delivering the punishment affected by his nation with a steady, painstaking concentration; so none of al Farid's girls were marked.

He hoped to sell all of them to the most celebrated bawdyhouse in Europe, where, from its favored and convenient position overlooking the busy money market of the Rialto, the most voluptuous harlots enjoyed the busiest professional practices. Some were cultivated courtesans, who had gravitated from Rome during one or another of the papal purifications of that unseemly city. All were the most beautiful examples of their physical type. Farid's cargo would be well-placed, he had no doubt of it. And he had something very special to offer them today; one of them, the very girl whom the nobleman was studying with such commendable interest, was still a virgin!

Covertly, he examined the man. Tall, with the bearing of command, there was an easy negligence about him that Farid had rarely seen in the tense, excitable Venetians. He was broad-shouldered and deep-chested, the waist narrow, hips slender as a boy's. The bones and planes of his face proudly belied his careless posture; the head was a noble one, the unusual, deep amber eyes matched by a sweep of red-gold hair that curled, rather too perfectly, upon the velvet-clad shoulders. He wore an apricot tunic over a shirt of fine muslin, which Farid's practiced eye traced to Flanders; his hose were striped in russet and blue-gray, and his half-boots were of a darker gray and suggested the traveler. The slashed sleeves of his tunic were hung with golden medallions. Farid recognized the craggy countenance of the young Lorenzo de'Medici on one of them. It was obvious, from his bearing, the richness of his dress and the following of liveried servants, the man was a patrician and no mere Medici minion. He could be judged then, to have powerful friends. A Florentine, almost certainly, perhaps even a member of the respected Signory, and, therefore, rich!

Farid moved forward, bowing, in the manner of Venice, his hand on his heart; he did not care to use the salaam in the land of the infidel. The sun caught the crescent that flashed in his cloth-of-silver turban and the young man's eye was distracted to him.

"Excellence! Your Magnificence finds such beauty tempting?"

The girl was the pearl at the center of his small, perfect collection; he would be saddened, almost, to let her go at such an early point in the morning's transactions. He had looked forward to watching the bargaining for her, to seeing her made naked and displayed for his discerning customers, to hearing the bidding rise with their excitement as they thought of possessing her, and, at the last, to the imperturbable voice of Serafin, the indispensable majordomo of Madama's excellent establishment, blasting all hopes in his purring, Greek-accented Italian. And yet—if this magnifico were but rich enough—

Prince Leone da Valenti was intrigued. Physically gifted beyond most men, he was unaccustomed to blank indifference in a woman, even in such circumstances as these. The blonde valkyrie with whom the gods had been so prodigal was rolling her eyes and hips quite desperately in his direction, while the girl in front of him continued, it seemed, to be unaware of his existence, and also of that of the repulsive sea serpent at his elbow! It was almost as if she were in a state of trance, such as that attained by fasting, monastic mystics, or the whirling dervishes of the Sufic religion, talked of by the merchant captains. It was her stillness that first attracted him.

All about her was a chaos of motion and hectic color, the flashing of arms and jewels and tongues, and she had become the calm center of the maelstrom, a pool of quiet, whose depths were unfathomable.

Hers was the perfect, Byzantine purity of an icon. Dark, deeply lashed eyes, slanted an insensible azure gaze out of an oval face, the bones delicately visible beneath pale, olive-gold skin. Her mouth was closed as if it were a door sealed forever upon a past existence; its shape was full-lipped enough to please any sensualist, but with a firm, determined rim setting its limits, giving it unexpected strength. A curtain of hair the color of mulberries fell over one shoulder to her waist, covering one breast. The other, resting in the flattery of his gaze like a golden apple in the sun, was bare. A long skirt of Persian design hung on her slender hips, curving below an exquisitely narrow waist. It had been pulled up on one side and tucked into its waistband to reveal the excellence of her legs. The Prince of Valenti noted that her feet were small and shapely, with long toes, and unusually attractive nails.

She was perfect—but she was a living sculpture!

Tulla, at the center of her stillness, was not, in fact, unaware of the man who looked at her. He was the only part of the jostling, exuberant scene that had reached her where she had taken refuge. She had chosen stillness over insensible, animal panic. It had been this way with her ever since the moment she had seen her parents die. Unable to bear so penetrating a reality, she had fled along the echoing passages of her mind until she had reached a place where reality and belief and death were mere additions of syllables, compounded of nothing but air—meaningless, safe.

She had stayed in this refuge throughout the sack of the city, stayed where she had been when they had destroyed the palace, high in the forbidden tower of the muezzin, where she had liked to climb because she could watch the life of the town beneath her and feel a part of it. So they had not found her, not until she had come down from her minaret and sought, like a homing creature remembering warmth, her own room on the southern rampart of the palace. There she had kneeled upon her prayer rug and called upon Allah and Jesus, both, to help her, to put back the sands in the

12

glass; if they were all-powerful, to take away this nightmare of blood and the ending of childhood.

It was there that the man with the cutlass had found her. He had laid hands on her body at first, and then, crossing himself in the Christian way, had drawn back, looking into her face. He had taken her down to the shore and put her into a boat and rowed out to a galley, waiting, ruddy in the Bosporus sunset. From then on she had been conscious only of the smooth motion of the ship and the knocking monotone of the nautator's hammer as they moved across endless, cerulean waters. There had been a night when men had come to her and stripped and held her and put hands inside her body. She had come to herself and fought like a tiger, but they had reluctantly left her alone. She had retreated once more into the cave in her mind, allowing only the blue waves into her consciousness.

Farid was becoming impatient. Had the Byzantine witch put a spell on his customer with her dark blue, sightless gaze and her motionless body? Then it was time the young lord saw some action! Stepping forward, he administered a sharp slap on the girl's olive cheek, at the same time catching the cloth that bound her hips and pulling it away completely. Her immobility seemed undisturbed. Nevertheless, he was suddenly very aware of her eyes. The pupils dilated into the dark irises, and her look was changed, feral, and beyond reason.

Then the somnolence returned, and she no longer looked at him. Making no move to pick up her clothing or to hide her body from the hungry eyes that were closing around them, she took a single, considered step backward, removing herself from the proximity of the Arab. The calculation of the move was as obvious as its dignity, and Farid was hatefully aware of the smiles that it provoked. Instinctively he raised his whip, careless of his profit. As the leather snaked toward the naked girl, Farid was astonished to find it suddenly coiled about his own robes as a strong grasp seized and drew back his avenging arm.

"I do not buy damaged goods, Captain," a deep voice observed pleasantly. "Now, if you will name your price, I will relieve you of the troublesome merchandise!"

Farid, his momentary rage soothed by the dulcet song of ducats in the offing, smiled and bowed, the whip falling,

forgotten, about his ankles. He named an extortionate price.
The dark golden brows flew upward.

"She is a virgin, Excellence!"

The Prince of Valenti regarded him severely. "She had
better be!" he said.

The Arab spread his hands in the age-old gesture of the
honest trader. "If your Magnificence cares to make a personal examination—?"

The Prince smiled. It was a smile of considerable charm.
"I prefer to do that in comfort and privacy."

Tulla, now as fully awake to her situation as even al
Farid could have wished, fixed somber eyes upon the man
who had, certainly, saved her from the lash. For a second,
almost, hope flickered in her, dying instantly as she saw the
warm appreciation in his observation of her.

"If you'll be so kind as to wrap her for me, I'll take her
with me," the prince said equably. "I am traveling to my
principality of Montevalenti tomorrow. Do see, my good
Captain, that she is *properly* wrapped. It is a long journey
and the spring evenings can be chilly!" He turned away and
strode off among his following. He did not look at Tulla
again.

A clerk in his crimson and gold livery stepped forward,
jingling in a manner that was music to Farid. "You are most
fortunate, my dear," the reprehensible pirate remarked as
the cold-faced Tuscan counted florins into his eager hand.
"This prince will treat you well. He is a connoisseur of
beauty!"

Tulla did not speak. She was trying to retrace her steps to
her refuge. It was impossible, however, with so much commotion going on; she simply attempted not to think, as
Farid threw a cloak around her and hurried her into the
counting-house opposite the quay. Here she sat until a panting woman appeared and dressed her in the strange, close-
fitting garments of a Venetian gentlewoman. She did not
reply to the dressmaker's admiration for the effect of the
deep burnt orange damask next to her golden skin or that of
the midnight velvet of the cloak in relation to her eyes.

Oh Allah, who knows all—or perhaps, Jesus, who loves
women—what would happen to her now? Or rather, how
soon would it happen—and was there any way, however
improbable, to avoid it?

Her rising panic frightened her, and she tried, once more,

14

to cast out thought, almost shaking with the effort. But she couldn't; her refuge was gone. She was aware and awake. She sought a stable point upon which to concentrate. There was a journey before her; that much was clear. Very well, she would think of that. The more she could learn of this accursed country, the more hopeful might be her eventual flight from it!

She touched, for comfort, the gold cross that hung about her neck. At least they had not stolen that from her, as they had her rings and bracelets. She was glad, for her mother had given it to her. Her mother had been a Christian to the end, even after nearly 20 years of marriage to the Turkish pasha who had ridden into Constantinople to conquer and kill in the momentous year of 1458—and, instead of raping and casting off or even killing the auburn-haired Greek woman who had hurled such defiance at him, had promptly and irrevocably fallen in love with her. Against all reason they had married and been happy—until the terrible reliving of that eventful sacking of a noble city in their own small provincial town on the shores of the Bosporus. At any rate, Tulla told herself, they had still been happy together the day they had died—and could have been so long and lovingly, in the peace and prosperity of the little city they had so carefully raised and strengthened. They had been attacked before. Her father was a pasha and a general, strong in war and certain in rule; but this time he had lost. He had died bravely, scimitar in hand, defending his palace and his wife. Her mother had taken her own life, despite the teaching of her church, choosing eternal punishment rather than dishonor her marriage. It was an act of will, almost, for Tulla to realize, as her body was pulled and squeezed and combed and scented into the epitome of Venetian fashion, that she no longer had parents. That there was no one and nothing but the tight, stifling chamber of her own memories, filled with pictures she could not bear to look upon. This and a strange land.

She trembled. But she would give in, neither to tears nor to the onset of madness, for that was the way ahead of her, she knew, if she did not turn her back on it.

She slammed a door shut in her mind, irrevocably, at last.

They brought her a horse, a gentle, white creature with a blue harness. She mounted it and held the reins loosely in

15

steady fingers while the animal followed the businesslike clerk in the Valenti livery.

Later, there was a candle-lit palazzo, where there were many faces, feasting, and dancing and music. And above all, there were books! Books were everywhere, lining the high walls of chambers, stacked in the embrazures of windows, laid out in piles upon vast tables. They were beautifully bound, in dark red leather, with gilded lettering, and they all bore the legend of the Aldine Press. Not just books, but *printed* books! Tulla had rarely seen such a thing, and she found herself transported to an old, personal homing-place as she turned the pages of the old Roman masterpieces she knew so well. Cicero, Livy, Seneca. Her mother had been an educated woman and had insisted her daughter be raised to be the same; she had allowed her to follow Islam, as her father had wished, but she had no intention of seeing her end her days in the harem of a practicing Muslim pasha. Tulla's father had never wished for a harem, being wholly satisfied with his lovely Greek, but her grandfather had had one, and she had pitied the almond-eyed odalisques with their lack of interest in anything beyond the pleasure of man. Her own interests were wide. She spoke many languages, Greek and Italian among them; she was well versed in the classical authors of Greece and Rome and in the religions of both her parents, which made her apt to approach each in the light of its own specialities, and preferring the kinder side of both. In a balconied chamber above the Grand Canal, where they had put her, watched by a gold and crimson guard, she traveled in familiar realms until the candles burned away and she was lulled by the slapping waters beneath into a deep, dark lagoon of her own, without waves, fathoms below thought.

In the morning she was awakened and told to dress in her new clothing again. There was a rich breakfast which she decided she might as well eat if she were to maintain enough strength to establish her survival in this unaccountable, new world. She wondered if the Italians suffered very much from diseases of the abdomen or the blood, so much meat did they consume at this early hour. Not to mention the wine, which she found altogether too heady for such a time. She was taken from her chamber, and they brought the horse again; and, amid the courteous clatter of a million farewells, the Prince of Valenti left his Venetian friends and set off for

16

his own domains, followed by his traveling steward, his personal body-servant, his hairdresser, his cook, his lutanist, his fool, his male and female dwarfs, his court musicians, his favorite poet, several friends who had joined him for the pleasure of the visit, and a small troop of gaily-dressed men-at-arms, none of whom had used their swords for anything other than a friendly bout or two for close to seven years. There were also several ladies and gentlemen of his court in attendance. The mood was gay. The day was hopeful, being as tearfully bright-eyed as only April can be. The celebration of spring was the order of the day, both in words and in music; as lutes and pipes joined with voices and bell-hung bridles jingled and clamored amid the ringing of hooves.

Tulla found herself riding next to one of the young men in the brave gold and crimson livery; he was very young, scarcely out of boyhood, with a cheerful, handsome face and a smile that the ladies had told him was very fetching. His name, he told his companion, who did not want to know, was Gianbattista Carmaggio, and he came of a great line of condottieri, powerful, mercenary captains, whose name had spread terror about the countryside surrounding Venice. His mother, however, was ill-disposed to seeing him die as his father had done, beheaded for the edification of the *buonpublico,* in the quayside square between the great pillars that hold St. Theodore and his crocodile and the winged lion of St. Mark. He had been, alas, a traitor to the republic. Accordingly, his wife had sent her son to Florence, to learn more civilized ways. There, happily, he had fallen in love with Art, and now had more desire to wield a brush than a sword.

"This is why I follow the Prince Leone! In his court I learn a thousand things. He is the most civilized man in Tuscany—even more so than the great Lorenzo himself—though not, of course, so rich!"

Tulla made no reply. Her informant did not appear to require answers. It was as well, for she was at present overcome by a sensation of total unreality. It was as though the naked captive on the quayside of yesterday had, in some convenient manner, been removed, and in her place rode this utterly different girl. She looked the same; she wore the same gold cross about her neck—but she was an unreal creature, sprung into being incomplete, without memories,

17

without reactions. She was simply a girl on a horse who half-listened to the prattle of a foolish boy.

"You are very beautiful, Madonna! All the ladies are envious of you. The prince loves to be surrounded by beauty. Are you a ward, perhaps, or a distant relative of the Valenti? Your coloring is not Tuscan—its tones are deeper and yet more delicate." He hesitated. "My Prince seemed to think that you might wish to leave our company. I cannot think why this should be! At any rate, I am not to allow it."

Had she, then, been contemplating escape? No, she had been contemplating the hills on the distant horizon across the flat, wet plain over which they rode. Perhaps she *should* attempt escape; it seemed that at some time, not far past, she had considered such a course. But where should she go, if she gave herself to this unfamiliar, flat wilderness? Even if she were, by some miracle, to reach Venice, she was without money or friends—and besides, in Venice was the Riva Sciavoni—and Farid.

No, she would not try to evade her gay companion.

He was smiling at her. It was plain that she puzzled him. He had asked a question. She would answer it. "I am the prince's—newly purchased slave," she told him coolly, her voice low and clear, the Italian faintly and enticingly accented.

Gianbattista was astonished. He was also embarrassed. No one had mentioned anything of the kind to him. "Madonna! You are unkind enough to mock me!"

She might almost have smiled. "Messere! I assure you I do not!"

Was it true, then? And if it were, how should he behave? He stared at her in confusion. She was so very beautiful and seemed so much a lady. How was it possible that she was a slave-girl? He sought in his perplexed mind for some helpful parallel. Should he, perhaps, think of her as he would of Messalina, the prince's dainty Catalan dwarf? The prince treated her in every way as well as any other lady of his acquaintance. Better than—. But on the other hand, if this lovely creature had been purchased from a bordello merchant, for the prince's *personal* pleasure, should he not think of her more as one of the Florentine courtesans patronized by Il Leone? And how did the prince treat a courtesan? Much in the way he treated Messalina! Or any other woman! All was well!

18

"Your beauty will make us all *your* slaves, Madonna," he told her rather self-consciously, his hand over his heart. "You will be the chief ornament of the Palazzo Valenti."

Tulla was aware of surprise. It was evident that this small peacock, at least, expected her to anticipate the end of her journey with considerable pleasure. It was a startling concept. In considering its novelty she found that the sickening basis of fear upon which she had held her being, was no longer present, and that it was only now, in its absence, that she had become aware of its existence at all. She had been afraid, how afraid!

Gianbattista observed that some of the tension had left Madonna's face. She was even lovelier now. A question occurred to him. "Bellezza—they did not tell me your name?"

She did not wish to speak, but he, it was clear, did not wish to keep silent. "My name is Tulla," she told him softly. "It is Greek; it means a kitten."

"That is pretty, Madonna Tulla—though, to me, it seems, perhaps, a little frivolous to belong to you. You remind me rather of a panther than a kitten, a lithe, dark panther—perhaps even dangerous." He was pleased with his conceit. "And—Madonna's other name, the name of her house?"

She stared ahead, her eyes darkened. "There is no other name," she said.

He did not press her. Her look did not invite it; and besides, he liked to entertain himself with mysteries.

The journey lasted for several days. During its steady, stately, and insistently musical course, Tulla, while giving very little in return for Gianbattista's tireless informative encomiums, learned a great deal. She knew now that the Prince of Montevalenti was a man of unusual dedication, for one of his substance, to the pure enjoyment of life in every aspect of the intellect and senses. She did not question the boy's evident hero-worship of his patron, but found herself wondering what other qualities he possessed that might be more deserving of it. What of leadership, good government, the incisive command of the military mind, the legions of enemies subdued, the rebellious cities and riotous peasantry quelled? Where were the lists of the conquered and slain that she momentarily expected to spill from the lips of her adolescent jailer?

They passed a night in the ducal palace of Ferrara, the

home of the legendary d'Este family, whose fame had spread as far, even, as Constantinople.

"In Ferrara, the local proverb tells us, no man is too poor to own a dagger!" Gianbattista said cheerfully. He then proceeded to edify her with the history of the admirable Duke Niccolo III, who had consolidated the vast domain that now belonged to the family; he had founded the renowned university; he had most magnanimously decreed that any money intended to be spent on his funeral should go instead to the poor; he had also personally ordered and overseen the execution of his lovely, young second wife, Parisina, and his youngest son, Ugo, who had had the misfortune, being much of an age, and constantly thrown together, to fall in love.

The reigning duke, Ercole, although nicknamed, for his icy temperament, "The Diamond" and "The North Wind," was a disappointingly mild-mannered host, and the chief topic of conversation in the sconced and glittering hall where they dined, was books! It seemed that the score of packhorses who followed the Valenti train carried a consignment from the newly imprinted house of that same Aldus Manutius with whom the prince had stayed in Venice, and whose crimson volumes Tulla had handled so lovingly. The prince made the duke several presents from their number. The duke was enraptured and presented the prince with a fine silver likeness of himself on horseback. They embraced as they made their farewells.

They rode on to Bologna, the realm of the Bentivoglio family. This city, Gianbattista told Tulla, with childish appreciation, had been all but extinguished on a number of occasions, so bloody were their customs and so numerous their enemies. And what was the most obvious concern of the men and women who led this pack of ravening wolves? Would the Prince of Montevalenti be kind enough to carry a personal message to Il Magnifico Lorenzo, of the exalted house of Medici, begging him the inestimable favor of a visit from his young protégé, the artist Alessandro Botticelli, to paint the portrait of the youngest Bentivoglio?

Tulla was becoming more and more intrigued with these princes and potentates. Books and paintings were wonderful things, in their place—but surely the entirety of Italy could not be wholly given up to their appreciation? Even the swords of the men-at-arms, she noted, were worn carelessly and seemed more decorative than useful. She remembered her father's great, curving scimitar, always upon his person, its gleaming perfection a symbol of watchful readiness.

The Prince Leone himself, upon the rare occasions when she had caught sight of him, wore no weapon at all. She wondered what would happen to all these pretty songbirds if the train was attacked by bandits, or by the enemies of the prince—for every prince has his enemies, even if they are not known to him. Perhaps a similar lack of readiness prevailed in the prince's palace? In which case, it should not be so very difficult to engineer a method of escape. She realized that she was almost herself again. Her spirit was reviving; she was beginning, at least, to consider escape!

"What are you thinking, Mona Tulla," asked a concerned, boyish voice at her side.

She smiled. Gianbattista's heart was ravished.

"I am thinking about—Montevalenti," she said cheerfully.

For the next hour they discussed his city. Tulla showed a great interest in its general geography and position.

When, that night, they made their last visit to the ultimate, book-loving and artistically inclined acquaintance of the prince, Gian made arrangements to have his charge locked in her chamber, with both door and window guarded. He awoke her himself, at dawn, with an offering of delicious figs preserved in syrup.

But Madonna did not favor him with another smile. He had, instead to endure her frown, and, although he rode close beside her all that day, they did not speak. The silence between them lasted until the early afternoon, as their cavalcade wound among the wooded hills of Tuscany and through the golden valleys spread with the stunted vine and the silver gray of the olive. If Tulla was willingly silent, and her ignored companion unwillingly so, the rest of the company more than compensated for this. When, a week ago, they had left Venice, the musical accompaniment had been sedate and melodic, the songs of the court, even the plainsong of the church; now, as they felt themselves nearing home, musicianship gave way to sheer exuberance in the energetic rhythms of their native Tuscany. The ladies shrilled an enthusiastic descant as the prince's personal guard, almost bursting out of their gold and crimson, roared the bawdy choruses of the *stornelli,* the *rispetti,* the vigorous peasant songs of the *contada.* The flutes, the crumhorn, and the serpent were played too rudely, and the lutes and viols plucked too harshly. There was a great deal of wine and goodwill abounding. Gianbattista could bear his punishment no longer. He fixed his eyes upon Tulla with a universe of entreaty as, his hand trembling with pride and delight, he pointed ahead.

"There it is, Madonna! At last! Will you look? It's Montevalenti!"

Tulla directed a stony gaze after his gesture. There rose before her a mountain of white rock. It reared its twisted crags where small, peach-colored houses clung with unlikely optimism among dense thickets of trees and bright yellow broom. Swimming dramatically upon its pinnacle, against a tide of rushing, tumultuous clouds in an azure void, hewn from the same white rock, and surrounded by the roofs and domes and towers of its city, was Castel'Valenti itself.

Tulla caught her breath as, against her will, she looked and found it beautiful. She had known only the cities of the plain and the shore, calm, well-planned and broadly laid out. This bizarre edifice belonged to the tales of genie and efreet, or of her mother's Grecian gods. The castle was large and strongly built, seemingly impregnable, its smooth, blanched walls offering no purchase, no opening. Higher up there were deep and broad embrasures and casements with the glint in them of precious glass. Higher still, the castellated battlements, towered and spired, finialed and crocketed, challenged each other in an architectural extravagance reminiscent of old lace.

A tear gleamed in Tulla's eye. Angrily, she dashed it away, fixing her gaze with determined dislike upon the gold and crimson banners streaming from the topmost towers. What if it were beautiful? It would be nonetheless her prison!

"We are nearly home, Madonna," Gian declared happily.

She glared at him.

Now, for the first time since they had left the quayside in Venice, Tulla allowed herself to look, voluntarily, at the man who thought himself her master. Leone da Valenti rode at the head of his train, the sun still striking fire from his bared head. He sang lustily as he rode, one arm sweeping the meter. She looked away. She would not think of him until she was forced to do so. However, when they wound up a deceptively impassable-looking path and passed, at last, through the city gates, their progress was immediately impeded by crowds of excited citizens whose expansive welcome of their prince threatened to smother him in flowers before he could reach his palace! Tulla heard his name on every side.

A camellia hit Gianbattista on the ear, and, delightedly, he caught it with a deft hand. He held it out to her with his most winning smile. "Take it, Madonna. Let us welcome you, also, to Montevalenti!"

It would have been too petty a gesture to refuse. She gave him the faintest wisp of a smile and tucked the flower between her breasts. It would, at least, do something to counteract the extreme impropriety of Venetian dress. She sniffed disdainfully as she saw a bright-eyed woman, her black hair falling down her back, lean dangerously from a balcony to throw a confetti of tiny, scarlet hearts over the prince. She was equally irritated by the profusion of silk banners and gonfalons bearing the figure of a golden lion, lying, watchfully, its backward look expressive of indolent hauteur.

"He is named for the emblem of his family. His father and grandfather, too, were named Leone," Gian told her reverently. "The Lions of the Valenti. It is an ancient and most puissant house."

The great iron gates of the castle stood open, the guard standing at attention on either side. The cavalcade rode into a courtyard large enough to encompass them all and thankfully descended from their horses, who were led away by an assortment of boys, clad in a less splendid version of the livery of the men-at-arms. Tulla, who had been unaware of the glances she had excited throughout the journey, or of the questions with which Gianbattista had been plied, realized as she stood uncertainly on the honey-colored stones of the courtyard, that she was the center of a considerable amount of covert interest. The curious eyes widened as the prince himself, his handsome face lit by a truly dazzling smile, made his way toward her. He surveyed her for a moment, renewing his acquaintance with her beauty. Tulla stared at the ground. Leone, finding her abstraction reminiscent of the marketplace, said hastily, his voice low and courteous, "I wish you to come with me. I shall acquaint you with the household to which you have come—and to which you are most welcome."

The ladies and gentlemen were puzzled. He had not saluted the exquisite lady by any title—And, despite the gentle speech, she showed no sign of accepting the familiarity with which she was addressed. How fascinating! And how like the prince to offer no explanation.

After Leone had led her indoors, they crowded about the gratified Gian, who, to his chagrin, found that although he had been her guard and guide for so many days, all that he could tell them was that the lady's name was Tulla, which signified a kitten—and that she called herself his Magnificence's slave!

In the wide, marble-floored hall which they had entered, the prince dismissed those of his train who were still with him, thanking them gracefully for their company on his journey.

Tulla stood alone, looking about her at a grandeur she had not expected, despite the arresting exterior of the castle. The hall was vast enough to accommodate 100 guests if necessary; the marble of the floor was veined in rose quartz, and unusual in that cold stone, appeared warm in tone. There were several great, carved doorways surrounding the hall, and the upper part of the palace was reached by means of a broad, curving staircase that divided into two graceful crescents before reaching an oval gallery which ran around the walls of the hall, with various chambers and passages leading off it. The very high ceiling was domed in the clear, Byzantine blue that reminded Tulla forcibly of her own home. The walls wore frescoes depicting the pleasures of various sportive gods and nymphs. There were several sculptures displayed to advantage in the light which fell from high, clerestory windows, just beneath the dome. One, the slender, almost attenuated figure of a boy with a sling, caught at her heart almost as soon as her eye.

"You have made the right choice!" She turned to find the prince beside her. Apart from servants, they were quite alone.

"It is the boy, David. You will not know of him. He is a figure from Christian mythology." He smiled. "It is by the sculptor, Donatello—perhaps the greatest of all our Florentine artists. We miss him sadly."

"Certainly I know of David," she said abruptly. "I know of the psalms he wrote, and how he gained his wife, Bathsheba." She turned and stared into his face and saw his look become faintly puzzled as she continued. "I know that he was weak

24

and small—yet he killed the man of power who oppressed him!"

The puzzlement turned to lazy amusement as the prince replied softly, "I congratulate you on your learning. We shall have to see that no one gives you a sling!"

She controlled her anger. She would wait. There would be a time for her. She must do nothing to endanger the amount of freedom she would be given.

"And now," the prince said pleasantly, "let us both go and present our respects to my lady wife!"

She was surprised; she had not thought of a wife; though, of course, it was obvious that there would be one; the scion of a noble house would need an heir. But why, she wondered curiously, had the eloquent and informative Gianbattista failed to mention her?

Other questions crowded, unbidden, to her mind, as they walked through the long, cool galleries and elegant passageways. How did Il Leone propose to present his latest acquisition to his lady? Was this the kind of purchase to which she was accustomed? Would she herself become part of a harem, such as her grandfather had kept? Or was she, perhaps, mistaken? Was that appreciative look he had given her on the quayside merely the disinterested judgment of the connoisseur—was she intended to be, in fact, a lady's maid? And how, in either event, would the princess treat her? Would she attempt to beat her? What kind of woman was she? Might one even appeal to her—

The prince had stopped before two wide, carved doors, one of which was half open. A man-at-arms stood, immobile, outside it. He did not, Tulla noticed, wear the Valenti livery, but more somber garb of black, relieved by silver.

"Announce me!" the prince commanded. It was done.

"Come!" She walked beside him, head held proudly, into the chamber.

A confusion of impressions took her then; the strongest was of sunlight, streaming in moted brilliance through long embrazures at the far end of the chamber, like a slanting fall of bright water. Then there came a strange, swift sensation of contagion, only half grasped, as a hurried, stooping, black-clad figure brushed past her to the door, so close that the flapping robes touched her gown and caused her hastily to draw back, sickened by the foulness of unwashed cloth and the reeking breath that went in its wake.

But now Prince Leone was drawing her forward with him,

down the long room to the other side of the waterfall of sunlight. There were three people in the chamber, two of them looking at her. On a long, softly upholstered daybed reclined a woman of great beauty in a low-cut green velvet gown. Her white and gold coloring were of a kind unknown to Tulla except in works of art. Her face was strongly-boned but delicate, the gray eyes almost colorless, yet peculiarly striking. Her face was pale except for the carmined lips, and her hair, which held the faintly greenish tones of ripening barley, was coiled about her head like a crown. Her body, though long-boned, languorous and motionless, did not express rest; nor did the arresting eyes hold any welcome.

Near her, seated magnificently upon a chair resembling a throne, was a tall, spare man in the scarlet robes of a cardinal. Taut, ascetic, aquiline, his features were too unquiet, the eyes too brightly burning beneath the deep brow, to be those of a man who has found peace in Christ. The finger which wore the papal ring tapped rhythmically upon the arm of the chair. In the well of the widest window, gazing out of it, stood a tall, broad-shouldered figure in violet jerkin and mulberry hose, his hand negligently upon the hilt of a heavy sword. At the sound of their steps, he turned around, a dark man, thickly though not heavily bearded, with unusually red lips, his eyes overshadowed by curving black brows which flew up into the oiled and glossy cowl of his hair. He wore one earring like a Venetian captain; his expression was one of curiosity. The prince, his golden eye having encompassed all present, made a deep and flourishing obeisance to his wife. It was exaggerated and Tulla was not surprised when it was ignored.

"You see me home, my dear, safely preserved, as I'm sure you have prayed, from all hazard. I may be sure you have known how to entertain yourself in my absence. I could not forgive myself if I thought you had pined!"

This, too, was exaggerated. Tulla, despite her own insecurity, was intrigued. It was obvious that the silky comments were blatantly insincere, and that the princess did not expect any better. Nor did she find his observations worthy of a reply. She picked up a tortoiseshell fan from her lap and wafted it before her far from heated features with a bored and insolent motion.

The prince, satisfied that his conjugal duties were complete, turned his attention elsewhere, inclining his shapely head with punctilious, and as far as Tulla could tell, sincere courtesy, toward the cardinal. That gentleman lifted an elegant, white hand with a languid movement that might have been a blessing, but was in some indetectable manner reminiscent of the princess's fan. The other hand still lay along his chair arm and did not cease its tapping. "I'm sure you have cared for your sister better than her husband could," observed Leone politely.

The cardinal smiled but said nothing.

Tulla saw it now, the resemblance between them. It did not lay in any feature, but rather in a shared lack of repose, a burning beneath the skin. She did not know why, but she felt, momentarily, afraid of them.

The prince's bright tones dispelled the fancy. "As nobody, it seems, is about to present us to each other, Messere," he said, addressing the silent occupant of the window vault, "let us introduce ourselves. You will know that I am the Prince of Montevalenti—and, as you are evidently my wife's guest, I make you welcome in my house."

There was the impression of a snapping of heels, or was it of two rows of unusually white and perfect teeth, as the bearded man returned the greeting. "Andrea Zorza, captain and condottiere, Magnifico." There was a slight hesitation. A sidelong glance at the princess. "A—member of the family of Biscaglia. At your service, Prince." The voice was harsh, overloud in the quiet room.

"Delighted. At least a kissing cousin, I trust, Alessandra?"

His wife drew her lips into a thin line. The captain reddened and cleared his throat. "I am the son of the princess's late uncle. I was born out of wedlock." The admission did not appear to please him, though Leone made no comment upon it. "And now," the voice of the princess entered peremptorily, with the clear and resonant authority of a chapel bell, "perhaps you will honor us with a fair exchange!" The colorless eyes fixed upon Tulla. "To whom have *we* the honor of extending our welcome?"

Il Leone smoothed back a curl that had fallen from grace. "I thought," he announced, with a bright and winning smile, "that you were never going to ask." Then taking the apprehensive Tulla by the hand and silently demanding appreciation for her beauty, he continued silkily, "Her name is Tulla. Her perfection of person speaks for itself. I bought her—on the Riva degli Schiavoni, for an unconscionable number of florins. I have brought her here, my dear Alessandra, to perform the nightly duties which you have so long refused me."

Those strange, cold eyes were no longer without color but flashed with an icy blue light; but the princess did not speak.

"I commence to tire of seeking my pleasures away from home," Leone continued equably. "Tulla will share my bed—and our board. That is all."

There was a gasp from the swarthy captain, and in the cardinal's chair the hand had ceased to tap. Tulla stood at the center of a circle of hate-filled eyes, unable to speak, unable in any way to express the humiliation he had made her feel. To speak thus, here, before those who should be her peers—was worse than anything that al Farid had done to her. Inwardly reverberating with the pain of it, her calm look revealed nothing of what she felt.

"How dare you?" The low voice was heavy with loathing and disgust. "How dare you bring your filthy whore beneath this roof? If you have no sense of the honor of your own name—I insist that you show respect for mine!"

Alessandra had half risen from her seat, her fury lighting her whole body. Leone regarded her coolly, his head on one side.

"Alessa dear, the honor of the Biscaglie is much of a piece with that of the Valenti—in other words, non-existent! The vendetta waged by our two houses, I fear, has quite worn out our honor. It hangs in shreds from our battlements, together with the remains of some of its champions!"

Alessandra gave a smothered gasp, her hand flying to her mouth. The cardinal laid a protective hand on her arm. "Do not distress yourself, my sister. And you, Prince! I would remind you how our father died!" The burning eyes were intense.

"My dear Silvestro," Leone said with a fine patience, "surely I have just reminded *you!*"

There was an exclamation of sheer excitement from Andrea Zorza, whose hand feverishly caressed the hilt of his sword. He made a motion toward the princess, then thought better of it, contenting himself with a scowl in Leone's direction.

"Take your putana—and leave my apartments!" Alessandra flung at her husband, who had just caught sight of a fine silver inkstand and was weighing it admiringly between his fingers.

Tulla, abandoned and adrift in the middle of the room, found her voice at last. "Whatever may be the case concerning the honor of your families," she began, her tone a little too high, but steady and clear, "there is no question as to mine!" She raised her chin and gave Alessandra stare for stare. "I come of a house as noble as your own, princess—and I will have no one call me whore! My honor is perfect, and will remain so—unless your husband robs me of it!" Desperation crept into her tone along with the pride.

For a second, Leone's amber eyes betrayed surprise. When he spoke, it was with nothing more than regretful courtesy. "I assure you there can be no satisfaction in throwing yourself on my dear wife's mercy. For one thing, she has no such concept. For another, also, you do not belong to her, but to me! I have the disposal of your person—I and no other. I am delighted to learn that you come of good family. I had supposed that you had had a certain amount of education. But, please, Mona Tulla—" he begged, as though embarrassed by some faux pas on her part, "let us not discuss the more intimate details of our arrangement here and now. I assure you there will be a time and place for that, very soon!"

He spoke as though she had entreated him for just such an interview. Tulla nearly choked with her hatred of him.

"And now, putana," he finished, his smile loathsome to her, "shall we find more congenial surroundings?"

He strode from the room and there was nothing she could do but follow him, conscious of the contempt of three pairs of eyes at her back.

When they returned to the vast entrance hall, she found herself summarily dismissed into the care of a smiling, middle-aged woman of elephantine proportions dressed in black.

"Vanozza, this is Madonna Tulla. You will please look after her. She is to have her own chamber. One overlooking the gardens, I think. The one with the blue hangings will suit her coloring. Oh, and put something of Donatello's in the room—Mona Tulla likes his work!"

He wandered off down a long gallery without a further word.

Vanozza Grazzi was left to contemplate her new charge

with a mixture of puzzlement and admiration. His Excellence had given her no clue as to the young lady's status in the household, and it was hardly politic to inquire of Madonna herself. The prince had shown an interest in her esthetic welfare, to be sure, but this was by no means unusual. Il Leone would, upon occasion, permit the clash of words in his palace, had even, very rarely, been pleased to referee the clash of swords; but a clash of colors never! If she had put this black-haired, blue-eyed beauty in a room of dusty pastels, she would never have been forgiven!

The chamber was delightful. Tulla was even constrained to admit this, for Vanozza wished to be sure she was perfectly comfortable. "The hangings of the bed are blue like the sea at night and like your beautiful eyes—and the walls are tender gold like your skin. It is perfect, no?"

"I think," Tulla said acidly, "that you have been much influenced by your master."

She was complimented. "He is a very great gentleman, my prince, and very, very handsome, no?"

"No!" Tulla cried fiercely. She bit back further words. It was not dignified to argue with servants.

Vanozza shrugged. The little madonna had a problem with regard to the prince. It was natural; many ladies were in love with him; she was a little in love with him herself despite her 45 years and the fact that she had rocked his cradle. As a man, he was perfect, there was no doubt of it; as a Valenti, there were certain elements that were not in keeping with the family tradition— However, she must hasten to do his bidding and see that this lovely girl's visit was a pleasant one. Who knows, perhaps, since she *was* so lovely, and also, it seemed, of some spirit, perhaps the prince would take pity on her and love her a little!

"I will send you water and a maid," she murmured gently. "And you will want to change into another gown. I shall find something for you. The household dines together in an hour's time. The girl will show you the way to the great hall."

"Thank you. I shall be glad to wash, but I will not dine," Tulla said politely.

Vanozza threw up her hands. The problem was more serious than she had realized! "But you must eat!" she declared. "After a journey—"

30

"I am very fatigued," the girl said faintly, hoping that Vanozza's motherly instincts would awaken and save her from further public humiliation that day. "Perhaps if I could have something here, in my room—?"

"The very thing. Of course you must rest. There are delicious small birds in pastry and such apricots, preserved in wine as you have never tasted—from our own trees!" She kissed her fingers in the direction of the cloister-like windows. Through them, beyond the vines which clambered round the balcony outside them, Tulla saw the tops of many trees beneath the peculiarly optimistic blue of the Tuscan sky.

When Vanozza left her she went out onto the balcony. She was in a part of the castle, or palace, that faced away from the city. She was overlooking a wide, walled garden where delicate scents were sending their sweet notes upward through the soft, spring air. There was a pretty little arbor with a seat; a decorative pool where the presence of a white cat, pretending sleep, betrayed the likelihood of fish; and exquisite, pleached and tunneled shrubbery where many colors mingled to form a shady alley shaped like a horseshoe. The walls were covered in vines and trained fruit trees, and it was there that the apricots were already climbing and would ripen in the summer. But Tulla would not be there to eat them, neither in the summer, nor yet tonight, for her supper! Because, before supper was ready, she proposed to be on the other side of that sun-caressed wall, with the aid of those well-trained vines!

She stared down over the green-clad parapet of the balcony; it appeared that there were two floors beneath her; another, broader balcony, a loggia almost, ran along the length of the floor below. She would have to jump onto that before she could attempt, by a second jump, to reach the ground. She scanned the length of the walls visible to her, seeing no sign of life. The garden, apart from the cat, was empty. It was that hour when Italians slept, dreaming of their dinner to come.

Satisfied, she bunched the russet skirt and twisted it into her belt. Then she swung herself onto the parapet. Legs dangling, she doubtfully contemplated her first jump; it was farther than she thought. Then, with a swift twist of her body, she was hanging by her hands from the taut creepers. She let herself down as slowly as she could until she came to a jarring halt, her support given way at last, on the harsh stone of the lower balcony.

"Well, well! A small gift from the heavens! If you are looking for someone, Madonna, perhaps I can help you? I am, I assure you, most discreet in matters of the heart!"

"Allah!" There was no way in which she could have foreseen the figure sitting there at the back of the loggia, at ease in a deep and splendid chair.

"By no means." The voice was grave and polite though tinged with amusement. "Merely Francesco da Valenti, brother to the prince—and yours to serve in any way I can. Perhaps, firstly, you will allow me to offer you my seat?" He rose, holding out his hand. "You have had a somewhat uncomfortable descent."

As she took the proffered hand, Tulla saw that there was, indeed, a resemblance to Leone; the same amber eyes looked out of a brown, intelligent face, and his smile was similar to his brother's less ironic offerings. Francesco was a slightly smaller man, wiry and keen-bodied, with none of Leone's indolent posturing. His eyes were serious above the reassuring smile, and there were tiny lines of a light, permanently perplexed frown between them. His clothes were pleasant but unremarkable; he affected the loose-bodied gown that older men more often wore, in a warm shade of brown wool, trimmed in coney. Tulla sat gratefully back in the chair, still trembling a little with shock. There were tears in her eyes, of surprise and disappointment. She was unaware of this, but Francesco noticed them.

"You wished to leave without being seen," he said gently. "You are welcome to pass through my rooms if that would help you." He gestured behind her to the open doorway. She shook her head. A tear dropped onto her breast, surprising her. Despite his friendliness, she felt nothing but desolation. How absurd, how childish she had been, to think it possible to escape in such a fashion! Even if he had not been here and she had reached the garden, there might well have been a hundred eyes upon her from behind the rows of half-closed shutters and glassed windows! She would almost certainly have been seen before she had gained the vine-covered wall. The prince would have given his instructions. A cold fatalism overtook her as she sat staring out over the greenery.

"I will not go. It is not written that I should," she declared somberly, leaving him to make what he could of her Muslim

32

sense of necessity. "Not, at any rate," she added as her mother's doctrine of Free Will nudged her instinct, "today!"

"I am delighted to hear it! And now that you have so concluded, will you not tell me who you are?"

Tulla sighed, shaking her weary sadness from her, and, for the first time willingly, since the change in her fortunes, told him. "I am Thalia, called Tulla, daughter of Qara Rashid Pasha, a prince of Turks, and of Evanthia Tallianos, of the ancient family of the Commenos emperors," she said proudly. Then, emptying all emotion from her voice, she continued, looking straight ahead of her, "My father's city and palace were sacked by Arab pirates and my parents put to death. I was taken aboard a Venetian galley and sold as a slave on the quayside. Your brother bought me."

"No!" Francesco's exclamation held pity and shame. "For what purpose?" he asked. "Surely he can only have wished to help you?"

"He has told his wife, in my hearing, that I am to replace her in his bed—where I understand she no longer cares to be."

Francesco frowned. "Does he know who you are?"

"I think he has a very fair idea—but it does not concern him," she added bitterly.

"Then it must be made to concern him. Or do you favor the arrangement?" The vigorous shaking of her head convinced him. "I was trying to—avoid it, when we met, Signore!"

"Ah—I see! You were running away." He smiled as one would at a foolish child. "Then I am very glad we did meet! You have nowhere and no one to run to. It would have been an ill-chosen and perilous course."

"I have no other," she returned stubbornly. "I am a captive. I wish to be free."

He looked at her with sympathy. His brother frequently went too far, in all manner of foolhardy directions—but this deserved a papal medal for insensitivity. "Don't despair quite yet. I'll talk to Leone. Perhaps he can be persuaded that one does not treat the daughter of a pasha in the same fashion as those of the peasants out in the *contada!*" His tone was tight with disapproval and Tulla felt a small prickle of hope arise within her.

"Stay here if you wish." He indicated the room behind them. "I have a small amount of work to finish, and then—"

The chamber was furnished with chairs, tables, and numerous books and ledgers. It was a busy, lived-in room without any of the luxurious elegance of the rest of Castel'-Valenti. It had a comfortable, everyday reality about it that Tulla found reassuring. There was a similar quality in the man who inhabited it. He had about him none of the prodigal display that characterized his brother; his movements, as he swiftly read, wrote, signed, and sifted through the bundle of papers on his broad table, were those of economy and purpose.

Finished, he gave her a brief, encouraging smile and took his leave. "I promise nothing, Madonna, but I will do all I can."

Her answering smile, a fleeting, uncertain shadow across the strained perfection of her features, woke in him a sudden tenderness that took him by surprise. He admired her courage as much as her beauty. Many a girl would be weeping uncontrollably in her circumstances. Her spirit deserved a better fate than to become Leone's plaything. He quickened his steps as he neared his brother's apartments.

A wave of music and laughter reached his ears as he came to the magnificently carved doors of Il Leone's private pleasure domain. The bas-relief of the heavy rosewood described the Garden of Eden in the terms of a master craftsman; every imaginable form of life was represented in a universe of tiny and intelligent detail. The birds and beasts coupled and played among the leaves and branches; Eve walked with Adam, her head on his shoulder. They had not, as yet, seen the serpent coiled about the vast tree that was rooted at floor level and formed the entire framework of the great double doors.

Within, the scene was one to which Francesco was accustomed.

Beneath a ceiling stretched with striped silk to resemble a Saracen tent, his brother lounged in feline contentment upon a pile of cushions in shades of velvet, varying from deep rose through russet to brown. He wore an Arab *djellaba* of a striking black and white pattern. His musicians were collected near him, and several ladies were present. One of them, a bold-looking redhead whose gown appeared to have been slit to the waist without the usual addition of laces, leaned provocatively over him as she combed and perfumed the layers of springing amber curls she had just washed. Her expression was deeply amorous.

34

Beside them, the lute player swept his strings and sang softly, a new song he had learned in Venice from a gondolier. Francesco recognized young Gianbattista Carmaggio in the small group who were trying to help him remember it. He had promised the boy's mother that he would keep an eye on him. Perhaps he ought to give the lad something to do with himself, other than whiling away his hours in imitation of his master.

The song was a bawdy one and there were little spurts of laughter.

"Marcellina! If you dangle your apples over me any longer, I just might take up the invitation—and a large bite!" the prince threatened, showing teeth well equipped for the purpose.

Marcellina flashed black, adventurous eyes and wriggled her hindquarters like a preying cat. "It would be an honorable scar, Magnifico," she giggled.

"Ah—so there has to be a battle?" Leone yawned with exaggeration. "Then, alas, they will have to drop, withered off their branch for lack of plundering. I do not fight battles—not even with women!"

"Sword gone rusty in Venice, has it?" the lady suggested, directing curious eyes toward the approximate center of the prince's garment.

"For that," Leone answered, rolling swiftly over onto his stomach and slanting a threatening gaze into her inviting eyes, "you shall be punished!" Whereupon he thrust his hand into her open gown and carried the tempting, rosy breast to his mouth, nuzzling and biting at the nipple until she cried out with pleasure.

"Now, shall I lift her skirts and take her here and now?" He appealed to the rest of the circle. There was a unanimous roar of approval, which died away instantly, leaving several faces wearing the look of guilty children. Il Leone's brother was amongst them!

"Franco! How glad I am to see you! How have you been? You should have come with us! Venice was marvelous! I have brought home all we could carry of Aldus Manutius! He plans to print all the Greeks next year!" He was on his feet, his hands on Francesco's shoulders, his yellow eyes alight with pleasure.

Francesco sighed. It was almost impossible to find Leone in a mood for serious talk, unless on the subject of his beloved books and paintings. And, the disgraceful matter of the Byzantine girl apart, there were several matters about the management of their estates that needed attention—

"Leone." His gesture pleaded. "Could we perhaps speak alone?"

Leone shrugged. "We *are* alone. My popinjays have ears for the music alone. We need only move a little down the room— Isn't that so, my dulcet birds?"

Smiles and trills answered him, and the group returned to their quest for the words of their new song. Marcellina, who didn't know if she were glad or sorry for her escape, pouted a little.

Franco seated himself upon what he regarded as the only sensible chair in the room, though even this was an exaggerated affair more akin to a church pew than a serious piece of furniture. Leone selected another pile of cushions, ranging from clear citron to deep gold this time, so that the amber eyes of the Valenti came into their own.

"Well, my brother, life is grave? There is plague in the city? The cardinal has ordered us all into penitential weeds to weep for our sins in the marketplace? The well water has all dried up? Or my wife's pet ermine has died?"

Francesco waited. He was, of necessity, a patient man. He sometimes found it difficult to believe that he was two years younger than his brother.

"No," Leone moaned, now wearing the mask of utter tragedy, "it is a matter of florins and ducats. It always is when your face is as long as it is now!"

"Not money," said Franco briefly. "There is something that has come to my notice—a certain girl—"

"What girl? Don't say you're contemplating matrimony at last. I should have thought my example was enough for you!"

His brother raised an impatient hand. "No. Please. It is the Turkish girl. The one you bought in Venice."

Leone's smile was delighted. "You *have* been swift, little brother! Well, if you want her for yourself, you're going to be unlucky. I have no fancy to give her up. She's exquisite! Also, she intrigues me. There is something in her I have not met in a woman. I do not know what her quality is, but I shall take pleasure in the discovery!" His voice lost its bantering tone as he continued. "You should have seen how she stood on that quayside, Franco, in the midst of that cacaphony of trade and trickery. It was as though she stood alone beside a calm lake in her own gardens. She simply took no part in it. Even her own nakedness did not affect her. At the center of all that tawdriness and greed, she was something fine. I could not let them take her to the bordello."

"So that was it. That's what I thought. You'll set her free, then?" Franco was pleased and relieved.

"Free?" Leone was puzzled. "Why should I? A beauty like that. Certainly not!"

"So you only rescued her for your own private debauchery?" Franco was angry.

Leone lifted a finely-shaped brow. "Perhaps she will not view it that way."

"I think she does," his brother informed him with satisfaction. "I just found her trying to escape. She planned, it seems, to climb out of the walled garden and take her chance in the city."

Leone was interested. "Did she indeed? Then I had better set about persuading her that life could be enjoyable in Castel'Valenti—very enjoyable!"

Franco, disinclined to subtlety, said abruptly, "Leone—I don't think she should be treated this way. She's of noble birth, not a slut like Marcellina." He gestured to where that lady still hopefully displayed her charms.

"I disagree. She's also a woman, which is why I want her. As for her own inclinations—a challenge is always stimulating!"

"I thought I heard you say you didn't fight women. You may find, in this case, that you have to!" He was losing, he knew. He tried once more. "If you bought her, you can sell her, no? Then, sell her to me. You are right. I want her for myself." He was not certain that, in that respect, he lied.

Leone only smiled his pleasantest smile and said, "No, and for the last time. Don't be a bore, Franco!"

"But surely—"

"I have spoken. No!" the prince said, and Franco saw the fine, sensual mouth harden into the scarcely curved line that said he meant it.

Tulla saw at once that it was hopeless. "You tried. I thank you for that," she said, grateful for the concern in his quiet eyes.

He held out both hands, palms upward, in a gesture of defeat. "There is nothing I can do to help you," he said wearily. "My brother is the ruler here."

She sighed, knowing what that would mean to her.

Knowing, too, he did not embarrass her by speaking of it. He thought of the provocative *contadina* he had seen in Leone's room, and then looked again at this dignified girl; suddenly he hated both his brother and himself. He bowed very low as she left him.

A guard stood outside her door when she returned to her chamber. Another lounged on the balcony.

Tired, angry, and afraid, she lay crushing the dark blue velvet of her bedcover and watched the deepening, darker blue of the skies outside. Now and then the ghosts of music and of laughter crept up to keep her company. They were feasting below.

An hour went by. Two hours. Three. Four. Six times she turned the glass beside her bed. Then, just as her weary body insisted that she forget vigilance and drift into the sleep she so desperately needed, she heard a step outside her door. The pounding of her heart was almost frightening in its intensity. For a second she stared, mesmerized, at the massive door handle with its hateful lion's head. Then she had flung herself across the room, as far away as she could be from the bed.

When Leone entered he found her seated, bolt upright, in a tall, high-backed chair, facing out across the balcony. All he could actually see of her was the top of her head and the whitened knuckles of her hands as she gripped the chair. He stood for a moment, considering these signs of evident tension. Then he snapped his fingers behind him. Two servants brought in wine and a tray of food. They retired, closing the door behind them. The prince strode across the room and went out onto the balcony, where he dismissed the guard. He re-entered the chamber and inspected the pure profile now presented to him at a distance of some few paces.

She ignored him as successfully as she had done on the Riva Schiavoni, staring out between the convoluted columns that separated the row of wide windows, ranged like delicate clerestories between the room and the balcony walk.

"The night is very lovely, Tulla—and you are indeed right

to admire it so wholeheartedly! But I myself would prefer to look into the dark night of your inestimable eyes. Who knows," the lazy voice continued lightly, "it may even be possible to pick out a star or two!"

Stepping out over the threshold, he made a tour of the length of the room, firmly closing every shutter until she was left in darkness, contemplating a black wall. A candle flared behind her, then more; new shadows were cast about the peach-gold walls.

"I trust you do not intend to look at the wall all night. That would be both tedious and inconvenient." The voice lost its light tone and became more peremptory. "Madonna! Will you please address yourself to me!"

Her cool voice came to him as if from a great distance. "I do not need to look at you to do that. What do you wish me to say?" She hoped he could not hear as clearly as she did the desperate volume of her heartbeat.

Leone drew in a slow breath. He was becoming impatient. What was appropriate in the marketplace was by no means so in the bedroom. He had thought of her all evening as he had supped and drunk his fill. He was not going to allow her to erect her invisible barrier against him here. He had meant to be gentle with her, to let her see that he meant only well by her. But this behavior could be bested only by physical methods!

He reached toward her refuge and, seizing her by the wrist, pulled her sharply out of the chair and dragged her unceremoniously across to the bed. There he made her sit, pushing her backward a little so that she fell against the mound of satin pillows at the head. He saw with pleasure the now turbulent motion of her breasts, caught and pushed upward by the fashionable Venetian gown. No longer a sculpture, but living, fast-breathing flesh!

Her eyes enormous in the candlelight, Tulla watched as he poured wine into ruby glass goblets. His sudden movement had shocked her, and she felt much at a disadvantage. He had not been violent, but she had not expected the action, relying on his indolence.

He came to her and sat close beside her on the bed, handing her the cup. She drank the wine, hoping it might halt the draining of her small courage. She realized suddenly that he was wearing the dress of her people, the loose, flowing *djellaba*, caught at the hips by a silver cord. There was even a tiny, jeweled scimitar, a plaything merely, thrust into one of its loops. She felt at the same time a deep homesickness and a loathing of him for traducing something familiar. She drank the wine quickly, gasping, almost choking on its sweet, fierce fire.

"Steadily, my icon-eyed delight! I am not at all fond of making love to drunken women!" His voice was amused again, almost affectionate.

He took the cup away from her and put it aside with his own. Then he unslung the silver belt from his hips and cast it aside. He drew himself near until he was resting on one elbow, his face close to hers. She was aware of the scent of sandalwood. He raised her hand and carried it, palm upward, to his lips; his eyes, deliberate, did not leave hers. They were bright yellow, feral. She could not look away.

And then his lips were upon hers. She almost cried out at the strangeness of it. She felt naked, invaded, laid open as she had been that night upon the galley when they had thrust her thighs apart and sought to discover if she was a virgin. A man's mouth had never before touched hers. There were no stolen kisses for the pasha's daughter, unless a man wanted to risk the loss of life or manhood.

His lips were swollen, pressing, bruising upon hers, moving, rubbing against them like a cat that rubbed its back against her legs. And now he had forced her lips apart and his tongue was inside her mouth, flickering, pushing and exploring like some sightless, fleshy animal with its own separate existence. She made a sound of terror, fighting for breath. He kissed her lips gently again then and began to move his mouth across her neck and her shoulders, pulling down the neck of her gown. His lips were no longer cool but hot and urgent as they moved down toward her breasts. His fingers were working somewhere beneath her back, and then she gasped, the tears beginning to flow, as she was naked to her waist, her breasts filling his eyes, his hands, and his demanding, demented mouth! She shuddered as unknown sensations raced through her body like a current through swiftly flowing water. He kissed her lips again, and then buried his face in her hair.

He rested his head upon her breasts, caressing them softly with his long, delicate fingers. Shaking, but with increasing determination, she began to struggle; he gave a low, delighted chuckle and fastened her down more fiercely, looking down at her helpless motions with a blazing amber eye that held nothing in it save pure enjoyment. She lay quiet for a moment, trying to think, trying to get her bearings.

He raised her skirts with a soft, swift movement, so gentle that she hardly noticed it until she felt his fingers slide between her thighs. She pressed them together, trying to prevent it, but he parted them easily, and rested one of his own, surprisingly hard thighs between them. All was hardness, muscle and masculinity, unknown and feared. Something gleamed in the corner of her distracted eye. On the edge of panic, she drew back. Think!

His tiny, gem-encrusted dagger had fallen from its scabbard and lay, winking in the candlelight, a bare meter from her hand!

His kiss was deep and, though she did not know it, tender, as his hand invaded her. It was not now, as it had been before, when the animal stink of the Moorish sailors had made her retch as they crudely enjoyed their task. Yet his caresses brought that scene unavoidably to her mind and with it, a renewal of courage. She cried out unintelligibly and reached out for her last chance!

The dagger came to hand at once, sliding toward her along the smooth velvet. She raised it above his shoulder and caught the surprise in his widening eyes as she brought it down with all her strength. She felt it make its sickening contact. She had a brief, dreary premonition of what would happen to her when they found him dead.

But perhaps she could, after all, escape? They would not expect him to leave her till dawn.

He had slumped away from her. He lay, quite still, on his stomach, the dagger fallen at his side, bloody, oddly small. There was blood seeping through the coarse silk of the *djellaba*.

Tulla felt cold. She had never expected to kill a man. Although she hated him, she did not relish her action. Shame lapped at the shores of her mind. There was a deep groan.

The prince's hand descended swiftly and determinedly upon the tiny weapon, and he rolled over, gasping with pain, and sat up. Tulla cowered back against the pillows, certain that he would turn the bloodied blade upon herself. To her amazement, she heard a low, somewhat difficult laugh. "You are full of surprises, my inestimable houri," Leone remarked. "Some of them," he gasped, directing a hazy but still insolent gaze at her near nakedness, "extremely pleasant ones!" Then he frowned, his eyes darkening. "But this," he motioned with the dagger, "was most ill-conceived. And should not go unpunished!"

Rising slowly from the bed, he stared down at her for a moment. Then, with a single swift motion of one arm, he turned her over on her face. He tore the russet velvet upward, revealing her legs and buttocks; then, reaching for the fallen belt of twisted and looped silver wire, he brought it down upon her. Six cuts he gave her and she cried out savagely with the pain. And then the humiliation overtook her. This was what it was to be a slave!

The Prince of Valenti stood for a moment, silently regarding his handiwork. Then, with an expression of weariness and discomfort tensing his features, he walked from the chamber.

A member of his guard caught him just before he fell. As soon as he came to himself he gave orders to the doctor who hovered above him that the Byzantine girl's wounds were to be attended to at once.

TWO

It seemed to Tulla that she must surely lie awake all night, restless with pain and misery, endlessly rehearsing the fear and humiliation that this insolent prince had written into her fate. Bitterly she regretted her failure to kill him. Her father's daughter should have known better how to wield a dagger! And yet, it had been the puny instrument itself that had confounded her, edgeless, bejeweled and useless, betraying her swiftly-honed purpose. However, that was of no importance now; whether or not she had succeeded, she was certain that she would die for her attempt. She hoped, as she groaned involuntarily and turned again onto her stomach, that the manner of her death would not be too painful, but that hope was not strong. If only the end might be swift—and that she might not have to suffer a renewal of this night's indignities. Surely, he could not want her after this? And yet, since she had shown him that it was what she most feared, might he not think she had also shown him the best punishment?

When the doctor came to her she almost cried out, thinking her torment was to begin at once, but the vast form of Vanozza Grazzi, uncorsetted and flowing dangerously over the streaming basin she carried, brought her an unreasoned temporary relief.

"Such wickedness!" challenged the housekeeper, shaking an angry fist, and much else besides, at the small, candlelit occupant of the bed. "Who has sent you here to seek the life of Il Leone? Believe me—you shall tell us tomorrow! Do not mind if you hurt her, Doctor!"

Tulla remained mute, conscious with an odd regret, that she had lost a friend.

The doctor was a small, fair man of middle age in a dusty robe, his few remaining hairs on end about a strange, elongated cap that she would have found comical under other circumstances. He was mercifully quick and able in his trade. His touch was feather-light as he washed her wounds and brushed on unguents, and Tulla caught the reassuring tang of healing alkanet before he tied the dressing about her burning buttocks. Despite her fear, she was also conscious of a strong sense of ridicule in being thus tied up like a baby.

"Tis an herb ruled by Venus—and will cool your Vulcans' fires, both inward and out!" the man grunted as he washed his hands.

"Later, give her an infusion of poppy, Vanozza. She may as well sleep if she is able. And see that our master has taken the draught I left for him."

His tone was that of a man who was dedicated to his profession, making no distinctions between the object of it. His reply was an affronted snort, as Vanozza made a splendid and expressive exit, leaving the little surgeon to follow like some ruffle-plumaged duckling behind its mother.

She did not speak to Tulla when she brought the prescribed potion, only watched with a glare while it was drunk down. Behind the glare her patient sensed a certain disappointment and wondered, with exasperation, how it was possible that she should feel an answering second of shame. By the Hand of the Prophet! what was there in that perfumed despot that could inspire such devotion in his servants?

Neither knowing nor wishing to find the answer, she dug her chin into her pillow and prepared herself for a sleepless vigil. She did not pray before she slept, as had been her childhood custom. She had, despite the opiate draught, no expectation of sleep. And since it did not seem that her mother's God was about to snatch her from the jaws of death (her father's did not habitually perform such favors) she expected drearily that there would be ample time to prepare her soul for the world to come.

At any rate, she slept, deeply.

When she awoke Vanozza was again standing over her, an expression of puzzled disapproval still distorting the cheerful lines of her face.

For a moment Tulla thought it must still be night; then she saw that the room was filled with sunlight. The weight of nausea sank in her stomach.

Vanozza saw the fear come into her eyes and sniffed. A bundle of silks hung over her arm. "Get up. It is late. You are to wear these."

She threw the gown onto the foot of the bed. Confused, Tulla saw the soft sheen of plain gray, edged with coney, the flash of white muslin.

Slowly, she sat up, the fear replaced by contempt. "I am to wear penitential gray, then, in order that all may appreciate more delicately the fine, rich color of my blood?"

Vanozza clicked her tongue impatiently. "Certainly—if Il Leone was not blind to his own best interests! However he is inclined, instead, to ignore the ugly little incident, and treat you in a manner far better than you deserve." Diving toward the bed, she energetically pulled back the coverlet, "Now get up and get dressed—and if there is a certain stiffness in your walk, *Madamina,* give thanks to God, and remember that there are many who would say you merit a more lasting punishment than a bruised backside!"

Tulla stared at her, digesting the fact that she was not to die. "What will happen to me?" she asked, bewildered.

"Holy Spirit, the girl's a simpleton! Have I not said that nothing will happen? His Excellency, in all mercy and lenience—and I'm bound to add, in all foolishness—sends orders that you are to be dressed as befits a modest young lady and set to your lessons."

"Lessons?" Tulla accepted the gown that was now thrust toward her and hastily shed the remnants of her crushed and torn velvet, pushing away memory. She also removed her bandage, preferring the abrasion of silk to swaddling bands. Vanozza repeated her unappreciative sniff, nostrils curling above pursed lips.

"You are to be instructed in music, in dancing, in the skills of reading and writing—"

"I can do these things. I am the daughter of Rashid Pasha."

Vanozza was not surprised; her instincts had been correct. She knew a lady when she saw one. However, this lady was also her beloved master's would-be assassin, and young enough besides to require a firm hand.

"And was it your father who taught you your barbaric ways? We will leave the matter of your scholarship to those qualified to judge its excellence. Meanwhile, you will be so good as to pay close attention to your looks and deportment. That hair resembles a hank of sheared wool!"

Her distaste for her unprincipled charge overcome by her love for order and the perfection of a shining tress, she attacked Tulla's head with a metal comb. It did not occur to her victim to protest. Such, after all, was the proper work of a servant. The long gold-framed mirror upon the wall told her that the effort had been a rewarding one; also that the gray silk gown, with its pleated muslin insets at the bosom and beneath the sleeves, which were opened down their seam and laced with blue ribbon, was one which offered a quiet complement to her dark coloring.

Vanozza was adding a small blue-embroidered cap to the neat coils of hair when her task was interrupted by a peremptory knocking on the door.

"What is it?" Vanozza cried through a mouthful of pearl pins.

"It's Margarita! The Byzantine is to go to my mistress at once!"

"Just a minute!"

"Hurry! I don't want a beating so early in the morning!"

The pins went in vigorously, and Tulla was hurried into

45

the corridor where the impatient maid beckoned her to follow. The girl swooped nervously along the echoing corridors and up and down the broad stairways until they stood outside the carved entrance, still flanked by its black and silver guards.

A feeling of desolation overcame her as she was hastened into the apartments of the Princess of the Valenti.

No one was present in the long sunbeamed salon this morning. A door lay open on the left, and it was through this that the breathless maid steered her companion. They were in the magnificent bedchamber hung with white and silver. Upon tables and coffers, exquisitely carved, a wealth of silver objects caught the eye.

Alessandra da Valenti was seated before her mirror, her pale gold hair streaming down her back. It had been recently washed and had the color and texture of that of a very young child.

The face which it framed, as also did the glass, was by no means that of a child however, though the fine skin and the soft mouth were deceptive. The eyes, clear, intelligent, so barely gray, were those of a controlled and commanding woman. She did not turn as Tulla entered but halted her approach as their reflected gazes met.

"They tell me you have tried to kill the prince." Her tones were light and measured, without emotion. If the consideration of her husband's death brought her any distress, it was not obvious. Tulla said nothing. The lucid eyes studied her, revealing nothing of what they learned.

"You have not the look of a murderess. Indeed, wearing that mole-colored gown and that passionless face, you resemble nothing so much as a young novice, all eagerness to give herself to Christ." The eyes narrowed, very slightly. "But you were not, it appears, similarly eager to give yourself to your new master. Why?"

It was impossible to guess at the thoughts that lay behind the impassive beautiful face. There was neither enmity nor amity in the calm voice.

Keeping her own tones as free of color, Tulla replied, "He tried to take my virginity. I defended myself."

The princess smiled. "It would have been most resourceful of you, had you been still in the bosom of your family. However, I would remind you that you are a piece of goods, fancied and picked up in the marketplace, a slave, a being

46

without rights or personal interests. Your duty is to your master, the prince. He bought you to serve his lusts—until such time as he should tire of your body."

"My duty is to myself alone," Tulla interrupted, trying to maintain her cool tone, despite the disgust that the words had aroused in her. "Only a father may sell his daughter—and my father is dead," she added flatly.

The princess was amused. "A quaint view, if a barbaric one. We in Italy are not apt to sell our daughters. However, make no doubts that *you* have been sold and likewise bought, and that, whatever may be your attitude to the matter, your circumstances are as you find them—and not otherwise. You are my husband's plaything—his whore." She dropped her head to one side a little, considering, "But you are scarcely dressed for your profession. We must see that you enter more into the spirit of things. Margarita!" She snapped suddenly at the little maid who stood, mouse-quiet, near the wall.

"You are to find Marcellina. Ask her for a more provocative costume for Mona Putana—something which leaves nothing to the imagination."

"Immediately, *Excellenza!*" She hurried away.

Tulla stared in front of her, ignoring the lovely satisfied face in the mirror. She did not seek to understand this princess who did not sleep with her lord, yet who showed such a lively interest in the clothing of another woman's body to excite him.

A wave of hopelessness made her weary. She swayed a little. Recovering her proud posture, the princess's next words took her aback.

"Undress. I wish to see the quality of my husband's purchase."

"Lady—?"

"I did not ask you to speak. I told you to remove your clothing. Do so, at once."

"I will not."

Alessandra laughed unkindly. "Very well. My guard will soon accomplish my wishes—with enjoyment."

"You are vile."

"Indeed. The dress if you please."

Slowly, Tulla unlaced the gray silk and let it fall, rustling, to the floor. Her body could be clearly seen through the thin muslin of the shift.

47

"That too."

When she stood as naked as she had done upon the Riva degli Schiavoni, the princess swung deliberately around upon her seat and examined her as thoroughly as her husband had done.

For the first time, Tulla saw expression in the glass-gray eyes, gone before she could recognize it.

"Turn around."

She did so, slowly.

"Very well. You may put on the shift."

Burningly conscious of the other woman's eyes upon her breasts, her thighs, her scarred and discolored buttocks, she felt a humiliation that was entirely new to her.

"You say you are still a virgin? This is the truth?"

"The thing is easily proved," Tulla said, her acid tone covering her embarrassment as she picked up the fallen garment and pulled down its folds thankfully about herself.

The princess was thoughtful. "True. And yet I would not have thought the prince so easily deterred." A lively malice lit her face. "However—this may be all to the good," she murmured, musing once more into the mirror, a faint smile suggested in her eyes.

"Can you dress hair?" she demanded then.

"I have seen my maidservant at work, when I have been seated before my own looking glass," Tulla returned.

She made no motion toward the ebony table where the silver-backed brushes lay.

"Do you, I wonder, imply that I lack the intelligence to make use of my own powers of observation?" the princess asked with unpleasant silkiness. "I would counsel you against such subtleties. Must I again remind you that you are now a servant? Take up the brush and dress my hair as you have seen me wear it. If you do not, you will be beaten. I'm certain your own intelligence will immediately reveal your best course."

In silence, Tulla reached for the brush, despising the princess for her small triumph and hating herself for betraying the pride that suffered because she must stoop to be a servant.

Yet, as Alessandra had said, it would scarcely have been sensible to refuse. Another beating would do nothing to improve her situation.

She had drawn the hog bristle brush only three times

through the fine, soft swathe when there came the sound of footsteps, outside in the salon. They were slow, arhythmic, half-dragging. Then there came a scratching at the open door.

"Principessa. You permit me?"

The voice was harsh, ingratiating, and Tulla shifted a little so that her gaze embraced the doorway.

There stood in its ornate and unsuitable frame, the most unattractive caricature of a man she had ever seen. His face, sunk deep into his misshapen shoulders, resembled that of a malevolent ape, the glittering awareness of hot black eyes derided by the lugubrious sensuality of heavy lips and jowl. Alessandra made a brief impatient gesture and the creature scuttled hurriedly into the room with the sideways gait of a disturbed spider. His black rusty garments exuded the same miasma of the unhealthy and the unclean from which Tulla had recoiled yesterday. This, then, had been its object. His curious gaze was like an obscene touch as it rested upon her pale face and slid down her thinly clad body before veiling itself in respectful attention as it was directed to the princess.

"Why do you stop, girl?" she continued. "Well, Atroviso—you have the information I asked for?"

"I have it, *Excellenza.*"

"Then dispatch it."

But the simian eyes, hot and prurient, had returned to Tulla who now attended her task with a determined application, which her mistress noted, drawing a private satisfaction from the fact, not wholly connected with the appearance of her hair.

"You like my maidservant, Atroviso? You find her body appetizing?"

"Principessa—" The man held out thin, claw-like fingers in a gesture of embarrassment.

"No, tell me, I beg you, *Maestro.* Your opinion is of value to me. The prince has brought the girl home to be his whore. I'm interested to know whether you approve of his choice. How do you find her? Does she arouse you to lust?" She eyed him sardonically, noting the moist lip, the avaricious eye.

Atroviso had endured her mockery many times. It no longer troubled him. He wondered why the princess should suddenly evince an interest in one of her husband's mistresses. They had, Satan knew, been many and various in the course of the four-year-old marriage. What was different then about this one? Certainly, as to shape and coloring, she was one to set the loins itching, and there was no man who would wonder that he could not keep his eyes from making their own imaginative excursions beneath that shift—but what was it about her that could possibly concern the princess?

He smiled. His smile, unfortunately, was hideous. He knew it, for he'd often been told by friend and foe alike, but there was nothing he could do about it; and how, otherwise, was he to make known his slavish admiration for the sister of his patron and master, the cardinal. Alessandra shuddered, out of habit, as he made her a present of his array of decayed and yellow teeth.

"Do not waste words in flattery. It is not worth your time or mine to observe that she is less than the dust beneath my feet. We will take all such flourishes for granted. Also the fact that she is unusually beautiful. Does she, do you think, have the look of a whore?"

Atroviso's long forehead became a thousand alarming furrows over which his brows rode like crows resting, unlikely, on troubled waves. In the midst of the turmoil his round eyes glinted and schemed, piercing Tulla with sly precision at chosen points of her thinly obscured anatomy.

Then he came close to her and squinted into her face, his foulness creeping into her nostrils so that, sickened, she held her breath. She gripped the cold silver of the hairbrush with all her strength, concentrating upon its hard irregular textures in order to keep at bay her repulsion for an ugliness that she sensed was not merely physical.

Atroviso carefully examined her features. He was, he considered, as excellent a judge of beauty as any man, and certainly here was a beauty as rare as innocence. He noted the sweet curves of cheek and chin, the warmth of skin, its fine texture, the promise implicit in the fullness of the closed mouth, the pride (and the present discomfort) of the delicate nostrils. Then he raised his gaze to the eyes and found in them, miraculously, the one thing he sought in a woman. It was not beauty. He cared not if eyes be crossed, aslant, or parti-colored—only that they contained the deliciously arousing signals of disgust and of fear.

Perhaps it had been a kindness, as well as an irony on the part of the Devil who, he was very certain, had begotten him, that he, who was formed to be an object of revulsion

-50-

should require exactly that condition in any object of his manly lust. If a woman was willing—and there had been several who, pampering his profession and powers as a master of astrology, had offered themselves for his use—he could not, alas, be less interested; but if she found him loathsome, if her flesh cringed beneath his exploring hands, if she cried out in horror at his deformed and reeking body—then his enjoyment was rich, his satisfaction guaranteed. So now, as he looked into the blue, Byzantine eyes of Il Leone's whore, he was happy, feeling the old dance begin anew in his hollow loins.

He smiled at her amicably, charmed by the trembling of her soft mouth.

"She does not look like a whore, Principessa," he replied in answer, "but, speaking for myself, as you have so graciously asked me to do, I find her peculiarly attractive."

Alessandra smiled. "I am glad to hear it. And now, the other matter on which you came. You have a message for me?"

Hesitation sat uncomfortably upon the astrologer's unlovely countenance. "Indeed I have, Excellenza, but I must counsel you—"

"I do not desire your counsel, only the address."

"I am bound to warn you—my duty to your brother (may God ever prosper his Eminence), as well as to yourself, demands that I do not conceal from you that this woman you seek is a source of great possible danger. She is a powerful and notorious witch of considerable ability. I will prefer that any dealings you may wish to have with her should be through my own emissary. Pray, use me as your ambassador, Principessa—but do not, I beg you, seek to meet La Sventura yourself."

The princess regarded him with cold amusement. Atroviso's curiosity was a legend among the Biscaglie. It gave him pain to be ignorant of a single move made by a member of the family he served. With good reason, her brother had once remarked; thus he would be in almost as good a position to predict their fortunes as God himself. An astrologer who did not find himself in this comfortable position with acceptable frequency was apt to go without his dinner.

"Leave the address, and then you may go, Atroviso. But tell me, can this woman read or write?"

"She can read well, Principessa, and write clearly enough, though her hand is not elegant."

"Thank you, Atroviso. That is all for the present."

The astrologer shrugged his shoulders, one after the other as his anatomy dictated, and made his arachnid's exit from the room, muttering softly about his master's probable wrath if any whisper should come to him of his sister's interest in this unusually well-educated witch.

In the doorway he encountered the maid Margarita, returning with her arms full of gaudy materials. Almost cannoning into him in her hurry, she crossed herself fervently and automatically. Atroviso scowled at her and limped away, his dragging steps echoing along the marble floors.

"And now," Alessandra said with more warmth in her voice than Tulla had yet heard, "we will see whether or not you can look like an accomplished putana!"

An imperious wave of the hand deposited Margarita's burden upon the bed where its lurid colors insulted the purity of silvered satin. The girl held up several gowns, one by one, for her mistress's approval.

"Not that particular shade of blue, idiot! It has been popularly ascribed by our artists to the Blessed Virgin. Nor yellow, too rich, too reminiscent of the cornfield. It is the decadence of the bordello we seek, not the animal innocence of rural lovers. Ah, we progress! Scarlet—the exact color of a cardinal's robes—an insult to God and to virtuous womanhood. It is perfect! Show me no more. Here you are, putana, let us see you in your true color!"

Margarita held out the glowing garment toward Tulla, a furtive and swiftly extinguished pity in her eyes. Without taking it, Tulla turned toward her tormentor, her face filled with questioning.

"What am I to you that you should treat me with so much dishonor? I have not chosen to come here, nor to have your husband lay his hands on me. You have called me whore and will now dress me accordingly—but neither words nor clothing can alter the fact that I'm no such thing. I do not behave like a whore—and you, madama, do not behave like a noblewoman!"

The next instant she was reeling from Alessandra's blow to her face.

"Filthy Turk! Moments ago you called me vile, and I gave

52

you no punishment. I was too kind. Know that you will be called as I wish. You will be dressed, or undressed, as I wish. You are a nothing! Your life has not the importance of a single brief candle. If you wish to live, you will humble your pride. Now, put on the dress."

Then she was seated once more with her back to the mirror, her face calm and composed. Tulla, her eyes still watering from the physical shock, reached out to take the red dress. It fitted so tightly beneath the breasts that it took all of Margarita's exertions to lace the bodice. The stuff was velvet, old and thinning in places but newly re-dyed and its color more compelling than ever.

"Pull down the shift so that men may see what they are offered," ordered Alessandra coldly. The maid obeyed, so that the tips of Tulla's breasts could be seen through the muslin that scarcely covered them.

"Better—but I think a little carmine will improve the picture."

Margarita opened a drawer in the ebony table and chose from the selection of paints and powders.

Tentatively she rubbed the crude red coloring into the generously displayed aureoles while Tulla stood still as if she were willing herself to become marble.

"Excellent. And now her face. It needs a bolder look—and the hair—it is too severe. She should appear wild and tousled, as if she had recently left a patron's bed."

"Si, Principessa. If madam—if the girl," she corrected hastily, seeing her mistress's brows draw together, "will sit upon the chest here." Gently, she pushed Tulla into place, her face toward the windows with their folds of framing white drapery. Her fingers, too, were gentle as they did their work. This girl was beautiful, and nothing the princess could do would alter that; she was also young and sad and far from home and Margarita, who had left her father's farm in the contada all of four years ago, still remembered her home with a sweet sickness and found it in her heart to pity this quiet stranger of whom her mistress was so contemptuous.

The princess, though just in her cold fashion, and rarely cruel though often unkind, was not a mistress one could love; but Margarita, in common with most of her peers in the household, bore her a steady respect, and did not in general speak ill of her outside the confines of the castle. It was known that her marriage with Il Leone was no longer happy, though at first it had seemed that all augured well, despite the indubitable fact that the princess had been part of the spoils of war, rather than a courted and cossetted fiancée. The burning feud of the Biscaglie and the Valenti had died out with the terrible old men whose hatred had been its fuel, and for the first six months of the marriage, perhaps for a year, the young couple had done well together. But there had been no children, and then the prince had become restless, and there had been the women, many women—ah Maria! How Margarita wished that she could have been one of them—and the journeys and the books and the music and the hawking and hunting and God knew what else with the young Medici who, commoners though they were, lived and ruled like princes in Firenze. Il Leone had gone his own way, and his wife had been forced to go hers. Small wonder if she was not the gentlest of ladies. The Biscaglia blood was still warm in her veins if not hot for her husband, and as any woman might, in default of his company she chose that of her brother, the cardinal, Silvestro Biscaglia, to whose enigmatic and impressive presence the household was becoming more and more accustomed. Margarita concentrated. She enjoyed the opportunity to use cosmetics of such quality and value; though sorrowing that the effect was not for herself. The girl's eyes were vast liquid and now sooty with kohl, their slant exaggerated so that it seemed that they must take wing from the glossy reddened cheeks. And for the lips, see, here was a paint stick the exact shade of the dress!

"No, no—remember your aim. You are acting as a whore-mistress, not as an apprentice to young messer Botticelli! Choose a more strident shade!" Sadly Margarita selected a bright garish orange and turned Tulla's mouth into a livid gash.

"Bene! You have done well. As for the hair—brush it up the wrong way. That should give the required effect."

Soon Tulla's hair stood out about her shoulders in a stiffened bush, at which point Margarita clapped her hands and cried out, "Like a gypsy!" in uncontrolled admiration.

"Precisely," observed Alessandra, pleased. "You may add a flower behind her ear, Margarita, if it amuses you."

Gypsies were, as far as princesses were concerned, very much like whores.

"Look at yourself." The voice was chilled, triumphant.

Tulla stared into the mirror. She saw the painted figure from some outrageous masque or play, its hair in a state of shock, its face and breasts an obscene invitation.

She turned away.

The princess regretted this lack of reaction. There were, however, other ways to provoke one. She rose and came close to the girl, who stood as if she were some inanimate puppet waiting for her master to pull the strings.

"Listen to me carefully, putana," she began softly, "for your welfare very much depends on it. My husband has brought you into Montevalenti. He has announced his use for you, and I have aided him in his purpose by providing a suitable working dress. However—I find that *his* purpose does not accord with mine. It is not my desire that the Prince of the Valenti should thus defile his house and his blood and the blood of the Biscaglie by consorting with you under this roof. Therefore—" the clear eyes, washed of all color swam into her own, "therefore, you will *not* give him your body. You will continue in your refusal. If it brings you death, that would be unfortunate—for you. If he should have you held down and take you by force, that too would be unfortunate. However, such an act is not, I assure you, in his nature. He has never been a man of violence." She said this as though she almost regretted it. "One thing I promise you," she added, smiling, "if you do not do as I have ordered—your punishment is easily determined. I will give you to Atroviso!"

If she had wanted a reaction, now she was satisfied, for Tulla could not restrain a gasp of horror.

"Think how it will be to lie naked in his arms and have him take what you so greatly prize," Alessandra murmured. Then, yawning, she returned to her seat and addressed herself once more to her glass. "You may go now. Remember what I have said. Margarita—you may dress my hair. I have a fancy for the new Venetian style today."

It was as if Tulla no longer existed. After a second of blank confusion she turned and left the chamber, noticing abstractedly that her feet were bare and must have been so since she had left her bed.

She heard the door shut behind her as she found herself in the long salon, where the sun again conferred its shower of gold upon the morning. She sat shakily down upon a wooden settle and put her head in her hands. She could make no

55

sense of the motives of the Princess of the Valenti. First she was got up to look like a whore, then she was threatened horribly if she did not behave as though determined to die a virgin! Although she did not understand the paradox, she knew that it must have its roots in the strange relationship between the princess and her husband. Did Alessandra seek to humiliate that affable golden giant by destroying his pleasure—as a child breaks another's toy in pique? If so, poor toy, for she must eventually be broken indeed. Sighing she raised her head and looked dully about her. Despite the sunlight, the long chamber was a somber place, hung with much black and silver relieved with flashes of scarlet and azure. Everywhere she looked, on curtains and tapestries, on cushions and footstools, there appeared the inimical emblem that must belong to the Biscaglie—the doubleheaded wolf, with tongue as bright as blood, thrust from open jaws, its jagged outline stark black against a silver field. It was a fitting device for those who had to do with the wolves among mankind, the vile astrologer and his accessory witch. She looked at it and despaired. How was she to survive, poor petty prisoner, whose life was of value to none save herself, tossed helplessly among drawn claws in this incomprehensible game played out between the lion and the wolf?

THREE

The Prince of the Valenti was in high good humor. He spilled homeward down the mountains with his comrades, singing lustily about various delightful and doubtful pastimes, in several of which he had just been engaged. He rode his favorite horse, Brigante, and paced his most preferred of companions, Lorenzo de'Medici, known throughout Italy by his Signorial title of "Il Magnifico." At 27 he was the supreme arbiter of the Florentine Republic in matters both economic and artistic, as had been his father and grandfather before him. These cares sat remarkably lightly upon his satin-clad shoulders at present as, his harsh voice caroling a barely tuneful bass to Leone's clear baritone, he urged his damson-colored stallion on to beat the prince through a slim opening where the path narrowed into a small gorge.

There was a clash of spurs, followed by a clatter of obscenities and a cacophony of feathered and equine outrage as ruffled hawks flew up from the weaving wrists and two elegant figures sprawled in the surprised and pawing path of their mounts. Both Morello and Brigante were too well-bred to tread upon their masters and neatly stepped over their rolling bodies with a delicate disdain, to stand, swishing their tails expressively, a little way beyond. It is to be doubted that their conversation was flattering to frivolous mankind, Morello having sustained a nasty bruise to the shoulder from the gold-encrusted Valenti harness.

Lorenzo Il Magnifico sat in a puddle, feeling himself tenderly for broken bones. In high summer the gorge would be the course of a flashing torrent; already its floor was distressingly damp and dewy to the coccyx.

"I'm not sure," he grated lugubriously, lifting his arresting and irregular countenance toward the muddle of violet silk and blond leather that purported to be the Prince of Valenti, "but I think I have sustained a mortal injury, to my manhood at the very least," he amended painfully as he attempted to rise from the insolent stone that was penetrating his hose at an important point. Then, "My God, Leone! Are you still living?"

"As this seems too wet, though certainly uncomfortable enough, for the Inferno, and is therefore also unlikely to be the Paradiso, I conclude that I am," Leone achieved between grunts of effort to disentangle himself from his new and excessively voluminous cloak. He had known it was unsuitable for riding, but neither hunting nor hawking had been the major pursuits of the day—and both volume and color had greatly enhanced his most successful catch—the sport being that of Venus rather than hawking. She had looked so fetching as she had lain in the rustling violet nest, her black hair flowing about her bronzed limbs: Antonella, the miller's daughter! And she had known well enough how to grind fine

57

and small! Any little stiffness from last night's fiasco had counted for nothing against such expertise. A good day, an excellent day well worth another new cloak, and even another new bastard to shelter under it if that was what God decreed.

With sudden energy the prince leapt to his feet, noting himself to be bruised in several places, most of them unhelpful to the little comforts of daily life, such as sitting down, resting on one's elbows, or scratching the back of one's head. He stopped among the fragmentary rocks to offer the hand of friendship to Lorenzo, who heavily embraced its aid as he struggled to his feet.

"How are your hurts, truly? Any real damage?"

The heir to the Medici millions produced a small pebble from his nether regions. "Only to my dignity—I have a most embarrassing hole in my hose, and I fear my doublet will disgrace your table. Having no valet with me, I have no other."

"Never fear, Bellerophon. At Montevalenti you shall be clothed as befits a hero, and Pegasus will have his oats—as shall we all!"

There was a brief explosion of laughter behind them.

"I thought we'd had them already. Or were those lovely creatures mere chimerae, up there in the hills? My loins will eagerly dispute the case!" The new voice, light, theatrical, and laced with satire was that of a very young man with a blue doublet whose most obvious characteristic was the quantity of black hair that curled about his face, surmounted by a scarlet cap of unstable jauntiness, the sure sign of a friend of the Medici—which was just as well, considering the unfriendly grin that split his face at the sight of the discomforted *nobilità*.

"Do not speak to me of lions," groaned Lorenzo trying vainly to cover what could not be covered with his fashionably brief tunic. "And kindly spare me your interested gaze," he added crossly.

The unseemly individual, whose name was Luigi Pulci, was not remotely abashed. "One, two," he observed, still staring, "ah, as the whole of Firenze has always suspected—a mortal man like any other! Only two—and not six as you so extravagantly claim upon every edifice from the Via Larga to Cafaggiolo!" He turned and whistled through his fingers with vulgar proficiency. "Hey Sandro! Come look! Il Magnifico has only two balls!"

It should have been a stale joke, as old as the Medici escutcheon where the said balls were supervised by the fleur-de-lis granted to Lorenzo's father, Piero, by Louis XI, he of the humán orchard, in recognition of the friendship between Florence and France; however, Lorenzo laughed, as he always laughed at Luigi, and Leone laughed too, because he loved to laugh and because Lorenzo was happy. It was still a good day.

"What—an anatomy class *al fresco?* I must say—I like it better than old Pollaiuolo's dusty studio—though his models more often have the advantage to be female, and both an equal number of globes to Il Magnifico's! More interestingly placed!"

A sturdy young man in his physical prime led his own horse and Pulci's carefully through the malicious rocks. "I think," Leone opined lugubriously, his heavy lidded eyes making it an open forum, "one of us should donate his cloak to Lorenzo—as his own seems to have been swallowed up by Mother Earth."

"I gave it to the lovely Lydia. I had to give her something, and I wear no jewels, except my father's ruby," Lorenzo said simply.

"Is this how you guard the interests of our state. Give away a cloak! You should have hired it to the wench at a fair percentage—she'd have been honored."

"You are a stingy fellow, Sandro—and alas I fear no gentleman!" Pulci said, having no such claims for himself either, being a frequenter of taverns and a factory of easy verses, some of them with greater merit than he recognized.

"Not so," Sandro declared righteously. "I pay my way, like any man—only I pay in kind, that's all. My payment may well be still valued when your florins are worth a tenth of today's rate and Il Magnifico's cloak has turned to dust!"

"Don't tell us—you made a drawing of the girl," Leone guessed, his eyes rolling hopelessly. "I sometimes wonder if you really know how to appreciate a woman."

"I don't think she felt unappreciated," said Sandro smugly. "We spent a good two hours in that village—there was time enough for a more energetic appreciation I assure you, but see," he drew a paper from the wide pouch at his waist, unrolled it, and handed it to Leone, "is she not a paragon?

That slanting eye, that stygian hair—and *mama mia*, those breasts! Which of you did better?"

Leone studied the drawing. The girl was beautiful, certainly; her young face exuded health and sensuality, her large eyes invited. Lorenzo's eyes widened. Pulci whistled softly. But the prince shook his head.

"She is well enough. A healthy young animal. Unmistakably a peasant. You waste your gift of immortality my friend. But if it's slanting eyes and midnight hair you want—then I have something at Montevalenti that will engage your interest. In fact," he laughed, "I will even guarantee to allow you to draw what you see—strictly upon your promise as a faithful friend not to touch!"

Having made his offer, he threw his violet cloak around the broad shoulders of Lorenzo and climbed swiftly onto Brigante's saddle. He looked round at the ring of intrigued eyes. "Who will wager? The shadow against the substance," he cried expansively. "A hundred florins to Sandro if it is decided that his bovine beauty wins the prize on the merit of his portrait, and fifty to me if you agree that my little surprise package excels. I can't offer fairer odds, can I?" he appealed to Il Magnifico, who had barely conquered his excessive borrowed robe.

"I can't *afford* a hundred florins," grumbled Sandro doubtfully.

"Oh, *I'll* pay," Lorenzo was long suffering. "Call it the price of my dinner—and my dignity," he added, swinging cheerfully onto the apprehensive Morello and settling his disgruntled merlin on his wrist.

"Then what are we waiting for?" Leone beamed. "Let's go and feast our bellies and our eyes. I promise you, Botticelli, you'll not be disappointed."

Tulla was sitting dolefully upon her bed when Vanozza Grazzi reappeared.

"Holy Mother! How are you dressed?" were her first horrified words.

"As your mistress would have me dressed," Tulla replied tartly.

Vanozza looked puzzled. Then she looked worried. "I don't know what Il Leone will say. There is no time. I have been long enough finding you. Where have you been all day?"

"Here. Where else would I be?" She did not add that she

had spent the day in virtual hiding, hoping that this room, however distasteful its reminders of the prince, was deep enough in the Valenti apartments to be out of bounds to the servants and followers of the Biscaglie. She had not wished to meet either the princess or the sycophantic astrologer again that day. Nor, ignobly, had she dared to alter her disguise in case she should be discovered and further humiliated.

"I thought you must still be with the princess," fussed Vanozza, rubbing hopelessly at her charge's rouged cheeks. "I can't send you to Il Leone like that. You look like a—"

"A whore. I know!" Tulla finished for her.

"That dress!" In her dilemma the large housekeeper seemed to have momentarily forgotten her disapproval of the girl inside the dress. "There is no time to change it. You must go to his Excellency now, immediately! He is waiting for you—and he has brought home friends—*miscericordia!*—and Lorenzo Il Magnifico is one of them!"

"Then by all means, let us go down to greet them!" Tulla said, tight-lipped, striding to the door. "I don't know why you should suppose your master would take exception to my being dressed for my work in this establishment—it was, after all, work of his choosing!"

Vanozza, suspecting an insult to her idol, glared at the determined figure, chin held so disconcertingly high. Then she shrugged. Let the prince sort matters out for himself. May she spend an extra year in purgatory if Vanozza Grazzi was going to be drawn into the quarrels of her master and his lady, especially through the auspices of the graceless little madam in front of her. She swept before Tulla through the door.

"Follow me!" she commanded heavily.

She thundered through the apartments of the palace at an alarming pace, coming to a somewhat stertorous halt outside the prince's favorite cushioned and comfortable retreat, Tulla equally breathless behind her. As was usual beyond the Garden of Eden doors, there was a great deal of laughter, today predominantly masculine.

Tulla scowled at an innocent donkey rubbing its nose affectionately upon the wooden flank of its mate and at the jolly pair of robins who threatened to fly right out of the confining carving. Then, since the doors were opened, she had, perforce, to march in. She had spent a lonely, confused and anxious day. She had traveled from despair through resignation to resolution and a fine degree of righteous anger, and the vision of Leone, reclining, graceful and gracious upon his cushions, his golden smile embracing all within its compass, did nothing to abate it.

The smile wavered and disappeared.

Two persons spoke at once.

"I demand that you treat me as—"

"Sweet, holy Mother of God, what have you done to yourself?"

A silence followed, born of surprise on Leone's part and the sudden awareness, on Tulla's, of the intense surveillance, across the rims of silver wine cups, of several pairs of interested eyes.

A harsh voice spoke, not unkindly. "So, Leone, this is *your* paragon? I think she is rather angry about something. Perhaps you should ask her what it is."

"I shall certainly do so." Leone was in full command of himself again. "First, however, I should like to inquire of her why it is that she finds it necessary to display herself before my friends and myself in a guise which would do justice to the foulest stew—but does the opposite for what is, I assure you gentlemen, beneath this painted vulgarity, a very great beauty."

He spoke quietly but with an edged coldness that was new to Tulla. She found herself affected by it despite her hatred of him. When she had entered the room she had felt no shame for her appearance. How should she? The shame was not hers. But now that he had spoken, her fine bravado fell about her in gaudy rags like those she wore, leaving her with the sense that she resembled a work of art that has not come up to expectation. She raised her chin and stared about the small circle of men. One of them, the one who had spoken, nodded at her, smiling faintly, a lopsided oddly attractive smile set in a face which none could call handsome. The nose was too long, and undeniably bulbous at its tip, underhung by the full jutting lower lip that would close upon the upper, the thrusting chin making a third, uncompromising step in this staircase of a face. Only the eyes were fine; clear, reflective and a little tired, as if they had already seen more than 27 years could warrant. Again Tulla had the impression of kindness. She found herself relaxing slightly under that crooked smile.

"Madonna—will you not sit down—and tell us your name, since Leone is so boorish?"

"Her name is Tulla. She comes from the realms of Scheherezade, I bought her in Venice," Leone was brief. "Oh yes, sit down child. And don't look so depressing. No one will touch you—no one would *want* to just at present. Now—" as Tulla knelt gingerly upon the nearest cushion, "please tell me what possessed you to get yourself up like that? Is it designed to inflame our lust or to send us after other game?"

Dark flecks moved in the golden irises. "I can only assume the latter, when I recollect your eagerness for my own embraces."

Tulla did not want to hear any more. "Ask your wife, Lord Leone, if you require an answer. It is she who is responsible for my appearance. As for her motives, I cannot speak for them."

"My wife!" The yellow eye was lively. "Do I begin to comprehend? An interesting mind, the Biscaglia variety, my friends. Ah, women," he expanded, grinning like a tomcat at Tulla. "Women!" He raised hands and eyes to heaven. "One wonders if they should even be allowed into a civilized house!"

"Come, Leone—I thought you were the one who so greatly appreciates them." Sandro Botticelli's grin appeared to indicate the enjoyment of his revenge. Leone beat upon his back like a dinner gong.

"Peace, Maestro—you have won the wager. I freely admit it. No one could call this sorry sight an esthetic pleasure." Tulla loathed the careless tone. She opened a mouth filled with imprecations.

"Not so fast." Botticelli was there before her. "You are too swift in your own overthrow." The painter rose and came close to Tulla, his sleepy eyes assessing what they saw. Instinctively, she knew that this was not the mere lascivious inventory of the voluptuary, despite the languid curve of the full lips, moist and sensual, that smiled upon her so encouragingly.

"If Madonna would tilt her head a little toward the light."

There was no reason not to do so. His careful, rather melancholy regard did not trouble her.

Sandro sighed and half reached out his hand toward her cheek. Then he shook his corn-colored curls in slow regret.

"It is I who lose the wager, Leone. I have to confess it.

Wash the paint off this girl and I will show you my next Blessed Virgin—with your permission, Excellence? And yours of course, Madonna!"

Leone grinned suddenly. "An appropriate subject as it happens," he said in self-mocking regret. "Go then, Byzantium—and join us at dinner—cleaned and scented and decently dressed! Tell Vanozza she is to attend you personally— and I will send you a guardian to attend you to table. It would not do for you to be molested and metamorphosized on the way."

"Allow me to attend Mona Tulla to her chamber!" Luigi Pulci had leapt up with alacrity, sweeping off his scarlet cap, his smile angelic, his motive clear as a mountain tarn and murky as its depths.

"Nor would it do, my dear Luigi," said Leone severely, "if the lady were to be ravished before the quails in aspic!"

With further flourishes and a murmured "Alas," Pulci subsided.

"I don't know what you are complaining about," he remarked to the room at large, when Tulla had stalked out of it. "That's *exactly* how I like them!"

The Valenti table was a legendary source of argument, both sober and inebriate. Which came first, the riddle went, the castle or the table? Composed of solid oak, thirty feet in length and five in width, with no seam appreciable to the naked eye, it could have come in through no door in the hall where it was lodged. The early Valenti having been predisposed to eating their meat in peace and warmth, had designed their doorways some two and a half feet wide, making enemies and drafts easier to exclude or extinguish. The cooks had cursed them for centuries as the causes of skinned elbows and cropped custards.

At the center of the mighty board, which groaned ritually in a gastronomic ecstasy aimed equally at the rolling eye and the salivating palate, sat the Prince of Montevalenti, in his second best cloth of gold doublet, the beatific lord of all he surveyed, with the obvious exception of Lorenzo de Medici in his best one, seated on his right. Opposite were Botticelli and Pulci, a space between them.

On the left hand of the prince there was also a space. Fifty people, their rents and profits heaped upon their backs, were waiting for it to be filled, so that they might stop dazzling each other and eat. Above the hall, in the galleria, the musicians played again the quiet complaints of lovers and the like, chosen to accompany those of the unsatisfied stomach. As was so often the case, the Princess of the Valenti was attempting to embarrass her husband by keeping an august visitor waiting for his dinner.

Leone had done what he could, upon this occasion, to teach her better manners. He had despatched a page to entreat her to honor them immediately. He had also sent young Gianbattista Carmaggio in the direction of his own apartments, with a similar message. His smile, as he awaited events, was not altogether for Lorenzo and his friends, who noted something of mischief in it. He clapped his hands toward the musicians, who obediently ceased upon a surprised howl from the serpent.

"Give us something 'alla Turca,' something with a Saracen beat."

The leader, a small swart man called Guiseppe Murano, had followed his muse through many lands and did not disappoint his master.

Upstairs in the blue and gold chamber, Tulla sat mutinously upon the bed, observed by a hard-pressed Vanozza Grazzi and an impervious Saint John in his Boyhood, an early work of Donatello's, whose outstretched arm signaled not the imminent arrival of the Savior, but the presence of a quantity of silk and lace of an immaculate whiteness and exceptional quality.

"Go away. Leave me in peace. I will not be dressed up like a child's toy at the whim of every ignoble decadent who cares to order it." The red dress lay limp in the corner where she had kicked it.

"Mona Tulla," Vanozza raised patient eyes to heaven, "it is a very beautiful dress and in perfect taste. You cannot eat dinner in your shift."

"Very well then, I will eat no dinner."

Vanozza sighed. She had had express instructions to treat the girl gently. She took her hands from her hips and picked up the gown, holding it beguilingly across half of her mountain of bosom. It was a narrow flowing garment, cut close beneath the breasts but with a high square neck, embroidered with tiny pearls. There were pearls, too, woven in knots about the long pointed sleeves, which were slashed to show gold embroidered sarcenet beneath. There was an intricately meshed girdle of miniscule links of gold and a cloak of white lace lined with silk. It was the dress of a young girl who is filled with hope, whose life is lived securely amid beauty and love. Seeing it, Tulla suddenly longed for home and childhood and all things that were past. It came to her cruelly how finally they were past. Vanozza saw the tears that were brought by this knowledge and her impatience evaporated in the warmth from her heart. She sat beside the girl and patted her hand. "Weep if you must. It is better so. But then you must put away tears, for they will not help you. You have much spirit. I have seen it. When you have finished your tears, you will stand up, and I will make you look like a queen!"

The tone was rigorous but it reached its object where gentleness would have failed.

There would be no more tears. Tulla nodded briefly and rose from the bed. "First let me wash my face, then I will dress," she said.

Vanozza beamed.

When, some thirty minutes later, Gian Carmaggio knocked and gained entry to the room, he was rooted to the threshold by what he saw.

"Madonna is that you?"

"Mind your manners, you loose-tongued urchin!" chided Vaozza, though a little half-heartedly. Her handiwork was having the desired effect. The lad, though callow, was a gentleman of sorts, or would be, and his sincerity was undoubted. Not that she required the opinions of such insignificant species to know that the girl before her must certainly be the loveliest in the hall tonight; if only she could so easily ensure the good sense that should accompany such beauty!

"Remember—the prince is not your enemy," she counseled as Tulla walked sedately past her. "He has shown you a patience no other man would have contemplated. You owe him your life. If I were you, I should thank him for it!"

Tulla met the boggling, curious gaze of Gian Carmaggio and answered it with the briefest of smiles. "If you were me," she said, paying due respect to Vanozza's broad shoulders and muscular arms, "you might have succeeded in killing him."

She waved Gianbattista toward the corridor, where he swiftly attempted to recover his equanimity and a fraction of the bold swagger he had lately been so carefully cultivating.

"Madonna is very brave," he tried with an affected carelessness based on his own estimate of Leone's manner. "To assassinate the prince is a thing many men might try, but to speak thus to la Grazzi! You have my admiration, Mona Tulla!"

"Are you sure you can spare it?" Tulla murmured, almost grateful for the boy's power to amuse her at this unpleasant juncture.

Gian dismissed the suspicion that she could be mocking him. "Madonna it is all yours—as is my heart!" He placed his right hand in the center of his tunic where he supposed this organ to reside.

"Beware," Tulla said smartly, increasing her pace in inverse proportion to the boy's desire to linger, "in my country we eat Christian hearts for breakfast!"

"Madonna," protested Gian, discomforted, "is there no romance in your soul?"

"I do not find anything romantic in my present situation—and I defy you to do so, Messere," Tulla declared impatiently. "Keep your compliments for someone who will know better how to receive them," she whispered more kindly, touching his shoulder briefly as they arrived outside one of the narrow doors of the Valenti dining hall. Gianbattista grinned broadly as he threw it open and preceded her jauntily into the savory-scented bustle and din.

The music greeted her like an unexpected friend. They were playing a song of the Kurdish tribesmen. It told of a girl who kills the man who says that he loves her because he has murdered her brothers. "First she cuts the love from her own heart and then from his!" The rhythm was fierce and wild, the nasal, bittersweet savagery of the shawm ruling the heartbeat of the great dull drums.

At first Tulla thought they meant to make mock of her, to make her move to her own music like a player in a traveling show. Raising her head she looked across the room and saw the prince. He was leaning toward the man who had spoken to her so civilly, the one with the kind, cragged face and the voice of authority. Leone's hand was on his arm, his expression affectionate, his manner filled with enthusiasm. He had not seen her standing in the doorway.

Two things happened at once.

Gian turned about to bow her into the room, excelling himself in his courtly flourishes. She stepped forward, and a door behind the prince, opposite to the one she now hesitantly entered, was thrown open, and a number of people came through it in stately procession.

The first of these, flanked and slightly preceded by two of her black and silver bravos, was the Princess of the Valenti, coruscating with all the brilliance that cloth-of-silver and her father's diamonds could show. She was carved out of ice, clothed in snow, decked in icicles, iron-bred beauty frozen for posterity. Her entry was magnificent; her outriders paced beside her, reflecting her glory, while behind her moved the cardinal in simple, gorgeous crimson, silken and sinful as luxury, his hand raised in negligent benediction of all who sat there. Behind him, conscious of having reached an epiphany in his brief, brutal career, strolled Andrea Zorza, in stark black, a silver cross weighting his broad chest, its diamonds winking wickedly into his seeking eyes.

Half the room gazed and were stricken with a nicely calculated amount of awe.

The other half, however, happening to face the other way, was presented with its own, separate and simultaneous opportunity to view beauty, as an unknown young woman came modestly into the room, preceded by a single handsome young equerry with an ingenuous smile, his velvet doublet and hose quartered in the prince's colors.

The room held its breath, and the music faltered as the two late entrants took each other's measure. Heads now waved shamelessly as corn. Zorza, watchful, noted that the princess's pale hand tightened upon the pair of jeweled satin gauntlets she carried at her side, but her steps did not falter as she completed her progress to Il Leone's side. Those who had the advantage of seeing her face had noted nothing. The other lady, seemingly, was unknown to her Excellence—even, was it possible, unnoticed? Alessandra sat down and smiled at Lorenzo and the murmur began.

"You are to sit here, please Mona Tulla." Gian ushered her firmly between Botticelli and Pulci. For a moment her eyes raced, but there was nowhere else. Keeping her lashes lowered, she took the seat. Instantly a hand was seized on either side, and Botticelli's voice was smooth in her ear.

"You have the beauty of the Blessed Virgin herself, Madonna. As you came into the room, men saw again the innocence and dignity of their wives or their daughters upon their wedding day, women sighed for their lost perfection. You have a rare gift, Mona Tulla. It is my sincere hope that you will let me give it to the world."

She looked at him mute, surprised anew by his evident sincerity. There was a tug on her right hand. Luigi felt ignored. "I cannot praise you in paint Madonna, but I am very willing to do so in verse. I shall make you a celebrated beauty in Florence. You will rival Sandro's precious Simonetta Vespucci—perhaps he will even give her up forever."

Botticelli, who now wore a rose pink tunic, felt his cheeks bid to match it. Pulling her hands away from both of them, Tulla spoke quietly.

"I do not fully understand what you say, Messere, but you must not think of me in such terms. I have not the freedom to walk the streets of Florence—let alone to win its praises."

"How so? Is this the truth, Leone?" Pulci's roar could silence an entire tavern in a second.

Tulla, gazing studiously at her plate, where reposed a pigeon, a breast of chicken and a portion of suckling pig, tried not to stiffen at the relaxed, cheerful accents of the reply.

"I always speak the truth. Test me, if you will, my singing birds."

"The lady complains that she may not walk the streets of Florence if she wishes."

Leone smiled lazily. "Why certainly not. If I require the company of streetwalkers, I do not expect to look for them beneath my own roof."

Pulci looked puzzled. "What a fox you are, Leone. An hour ago she could have plied her trade with the best of them, now she has the appearance of a Vestal Virgin. What's a man to think?" He made an uncomfortable virtue of outspokenness.

"He is to meditate upon the many faces of woman—a suitable occupation for any man, wouldn't you agree, my dear wife?"

He turned with an expression of solicitous courtesy toward Alessandra, but found only her silver shoulder presented to him while she engaged her brother and the swarthy Zorza in deep conversation. She had not acknowledged Tulla's presence by so much as a flicker of an eyelid. Nor had she spoken to her husband, though she had exchanged animated greetings with Lorenzo de Medici.

It was Andrea Zorza seated next to her, his dark face

already flushing with wine and the sense of social arrival, who caught at Leone's words.

"It seems to me," he stated, his eyes sweeping dismissively over the artist and the poet, though lingering on the girl between them, "that the occupation best suited to a man is that of the sword—though he may lay it at a woman's feet if he wishes." Here he looked boldly into Alessandra's face, a permissible compliment to his hostess, though less elegant than he would have liked.

Leone twirled the long, twisted stem of the glass he had brought from Venice. "There speaks the true condottiere— ever at war with his own best interests. For myself, Messere, I'd sooner lay my good sword in a woman's lap than at her feet—if she'll let me!" he added disgracefully, catching Tulla's eye in a lightning turn of his head. She had not known she was watching him. She swore in Turkish and turned away as a little clatter of ribald laughter rewarded Leone.

"You reveal an unexpected talent, Mona Tulla. What exactly did you say? It had a most expressive roll to it." Pulci was curious.

"It is an expression of the marketplace. It signifies that the person whom it describes is one wholly without the natural pride which distinguishes a man from an animal," she explained icily.

Luigi considered before he spoke, a thing he did not often do.

"It is always foolish—and sometimes dangerous, to consider only the surfaces of life—especially when one is in unknown country," he remarked. "It is also unrewarding."

"You are a philosopher, Messere," she suggested shortly.

"Not I." Pulci saw Leone's grin as he turned back to the Medici—also Tulla's mutinous look. He made a stab at distraction. "However I am the slave of one who is perhaps the greatest of all philosophers—Plato, who said that human behavior, Madonna, flows from three main sources, desire, emotion, and knowledge. Desire equals appetite, instinct, impulse. These are one. Emotion is spirit, ambition, courage. These are one. Knowledge—intellect, reason, contemplation. These are one. Desire, we share with the animals—it has its source in the loins—but emotion belongs to the heart and knowledge to the mind. If the prince spoke from desire, Mona Tulla, it does not mean that emotion and knowledge do not also hold sway on him. It is a feast at which we are present, not a marriage or a board of counsel."

"You quote your master correctly, messer Pulci," Tulla surprised him. Then delicately, "Did he not have something less hopeful to say about the poets and artists of this world? That they should have no permanent place in this new republic bēcause their words could never be more than their poor impression of the appearances of reality, never of the substance? Would he not have his philosopher king listen to your words, then pay you for them, and set you on your way out of his lands, heard but not heeded?"

"Bravo, Madonna!" Botticelli was impressed. "Where did you gain your learning?"

Tulla had an instant vision of the sunlit courtyard where she had studied throughout long afternoons, of the library furled in winter rugs.

"In my father's house. My tutors were Greeks," she said. "And Plato was my early guide. Therefore I shall take lightly the advice of a poet, messer Pulci."

She bowed slightly in Luigi's direction.

"Pricked with your own pen!" said Sandro delightedly.

"Does the lady speak from her heart or from her head?" inquired an interested voice. "I assume, of course, that her loins are *never* discursive!" Leone's regard was both supportive and challenging. She felt her anger rising and downed it, thinking quickly. She had thought him occupied with Lorenzo.

"I can recall no instance in Plato's writings, Prince, where we are bid to think well of our enemies—I believe this is what messer Pulci would have me do."

"Enemies?" Leone was truly puzzled. "Who among us is your enemy?"

"The man who holds me here against my will." She looked at him steadily. His yellow eye blinked innocently as a baby's.

He considered. "The man who took you from your home—him you might hate. The man who sold you into slavery—him also. But the man who takes you from that marketplace and gives you a place in his household—why should you hate him?" He sighed. "Lorenzo," he appealed, "surely this is ingratitude?" He seemed unaware of the number of curious ears and eyes directed toward them.

71

Il Magnifico smiled softly, placing his hand on the princely shoulder.

"Leone, I feel you must take the consequences of your action in—acquiring Madonna Tulla's company. Even if she must perhaps accept those of a cruel fate that has, as you say, become less cruel than might have been the case. In any event," he finished looking swiftly about the fascinated board, "you do not, I imagine, wish to make a marketplace of your table. It is a place for conversation not for gossip."

"I am suitably reproved," murmured Leone, looking not at all deflated. "But how shall we manage, my friends, if we may not even discuss Plato?"

Lorenzo made a brief signal, and the musicians played up, ensuring that, although speech was not difficult between neighbors, it would become more so across the table.

Luigi Pulci kissed Tulla's hand and begged for forgiveness. "For what?"

"For being the ignorant cause of your discomfort. Sometimes, alas, my big mouth beats my small mind to the conclusion."

She found to her surprise that she could smile at him. "I don't feel so very discomforted." It was true. It was only when the prince spoke to her that she felt her very bones dissolve in anger at the man who held her life so lightly in his hands.

"Then we are the happiest of men," declared Sandro Botticelli cheerfully, "and would be even more so if Madonna would be good enough to tell us something of her history. Being mere slaves of the arts, we are not above a gentlemanly curiosity."

They meant only kindness. She saw that now. But a rehearsal of her story might well prove her undoing. "You must forgive me, messeri, but no. We will talk," she dictated, "about yourselves, your work. You must not think I agree with Plato in all his judgments. And you must tell me about Florence though it is a city I may not see—"

"But Mona Tulla," Pulci protested.

"Luigi—gently. You're like a great carthorse stamping roughshod over the lady's tender lands. She requires a quiet palfrey to ride where she will lead it." Sandro similarly was reassuring. "Florence, as the name tells us, is the flower of all cities," he began.

Turning to smile her thanks, Tulla saw that she was

watched by Andrea Zorza, brooding between the chilly scintillating Alessandra and the inscrutable church militant. He turned away his head at once and spoke to the princess, his lips close to her ear, though his eyes slid back to Tulla. Yet, if he spoke of her to the princess, that ice maiden gave no sign of it. Forcing down apprehension, Tulla concentrated all her attention upon Sandro's eulogy.

"For all men our city represents the epitome of what man can achieve with the best in himself. We have abandoned war. Our government is less corrupt than any in Europe. We are favored in the beauty of the city and the talents of her citizens—and happiest of all in our rulers—in Lorenzo who was chosen by us and has dedicated his life to us. For me especially, Florence is a city where a man may turn his dreams into living stone, into singing words, into glowing color. There is nowhere else in the world, no other time in the history of man, where I would rather have been born."

"Then you are a happy man."

He acknowledged this with his shy smile. "I have been very lucky." He swept round a surprisingly workmanlike hand to encompass the brilliant board. "I was not born to dine with princes. The most I could have hoped for would have been a place as my brother's journeyman—he is a goldsmith and a pawnbroker." He grinned then. "He has done well enough out of it—he is so well larded that our family name of Filipepi is forgotten and even I am known by his nickname of Botticello—the keg. And, who knows, I may end up as barrel-shaped as Giovanni yet."

He was certainly a large young man, but as yet there was no sign of such an unfortunate fate.

"But you have a talent for painting."

"I did. I do. It took me first into the studio of Filippo Lippi, and then to Pollaiuolo. Soon I shall have my own studio. But it's Lorenzo who has worked the miracle in my life. Since he has become my patron my work prospers like the city herself. And he is more than my patron. He is my true friend."

"Don't sound so alarmingly grateful, Sandro—remember it cuts both ways. True, Il Magnifico has swept up the likes of us from the sawdust where we rightly belong and made us his companions in Christian learning. He has given you fat commissions and me fat purses—but never think that Lorenzo doesn't rely on us as much as we do on him. Who else would have taught him the true pagan delights of life?

73

Who would have shown him good wine and bad women and the fierce pleasures of the stronger, coarser tastes in life?"

Pulci waved his cup in enthusiastic emphasis, giving his green doublet a crimson shower.

"I had imagined," Tulla said with mock severity, "that your hours were enlivened only by the deep discussion of philosophy."

"Ah, well—we find some time for that too," Luigi admitted, with his disgraceful smile. "We are both accredited occasional additions to the hallowed numbers of the Platonic Academy, that learned circle founded by old Cosimo, Pater Patriae, Lorenzo's grandfather. You would greatly approve of us, Madonna, if you were to attend our meetings. The hours are dedicated to Plato and Plotinus and to the eternal search for ideal government both of the self and of the state." He sighed. "I must admit I have been known, most appallingly, to snore like Vulcan upon several such occasions!"

"You are a sad wastrel and always will be," Sandro said as Pulci absentmindedly mopped his breast with his sleeve.

"What matter? They will remember me in the taverns where I spent my life and my ten talents." For a moment the poet brooded solemnly over his goblet. Then he noticed it was empty and called voraciously for more wine.

Across the table Lorenzo smiled as if at a favorite child, while next to him Leone rose to his feet.

"Let us have the masque!" he called. He spread his arms and addressed the company, now well stuck into its fourth plateful and willing enough to be entertained between mouthfuls.

"*Magnifico*," he bowed to Lorenzo, "my offering is poor compared to your own talents, which are those of Orpheus himself—therefore, let none make such damning comparison. Only honor my poor mummers with your attention and after, my musicians with the lightness of your steps."

As he sat down again he leaned across toward Tulla.

"Watch this, Byzantium—it is stuffed with good advice."

She was aware of having relaxed more fully than she could have wished. She did not want him to think her in any way content. Accordingly she glared at him most unpleasantly—only to find him already deeply engrossed with Lorenzo. Alessandra had caught her scowl, however, and the frozen breath of a smile floated past her lips.

At this point there was an arresting fanfare from several

shawms, a slide trumpet, and some doom-defying drums while Guiseppe Murano worked his small frame into an exquisite ecstasy of pomp and pageantry on a peculiarly full-toned and vibrant Spanish bagpipe.

The six doors of the hall all flew open at once, and the entire pantheon of classical mythology tumbled, trod, rolled, raced, or were raucously drawn in rather slender carts through the ungenerous openings. Plump Pans chased nubile nymphs, and buxom Bacchante worried Dionysiac Adonises, their garments scant and their young bodies comely to behold. They cavorted for a while in what Leone insisted was an Attic measure, though antic would have been a more truthful description. All were slightly drunk—some more than slightly. The prince, as impresario, believed in lending courage to his players, most of whom belonged to the surrounding contada and had never been inside the castle in their lives. The principals, however, were urban sophisticates from the savory end of the city and at least on scraping terms with the august personages they represented, as indeed with many of those who watched them. Soon the skirmish settled into a pattern, and the music into the recognizable form of the *canzone di ballo,* with its repeated refrain and interspersed verses in variation of the theme. The assorted nymphs and shepherds became silent, and the pride and joy of Montevalenti's choir of San Jerome stepped forward in the gallery, his flawless soprano swooping out over the gratified assembly like a swallow amusing itself. His song was in praise of love, which he personally found about as interesting at the age of 10 as praising God, but it formed a pleasing accompaniment to the cheerful charade now enacted below.

Botticelli and Pulci murmured explanation into Tulla's captive ears as a gilded youth, divinely slender, his copious curls as golden as his painted body, clothed in a strategically placed garland of acanthus leaves, was drawn, striking a noble pose, upon a wheeled platform by six puffing cupids. An owl sat ruffling its feathers upon his shoulder.

"The sign of Athena—the boy represents Wisdom," muttered Botticelli.

"He'll be wise to keep quite still, otherwise he will come to represent Embarrassment," remarked Tulla, averting her eyes from the thickest part of the boy's sartorial brushwood.

Having heaved the hero once, shakily, around the hall,

the stertorous putti drew up before the coy gathering of sylphs and satyrs, who parted explosively to reveal a flowing bank, ingeniously constructed, where reposed a true Tuscan beauty, white and gold and deliciously rosy, clothed in a couple of gauzy scarves and holding a golden apple, Aphrodite's prize.

"Beauty!" enthused Pulci, "and fresh as a newly plucked virgin, saving your blushes, Madonna!"

He did not see, so enraptured was he, that Tulla did in fact blush, though Sandro, who was watching the faint changes cross her careful face, did so.

Wisdom descended, rather gingerly, from his chariot and was wafted by his cherubs toward the lady who pretended to look alarmed. He made subtle but unmistakable advances. The lady looked more alarmed. Wisdom insisted; Beauty resisted. Wisdom enthused. Beauty refused. This tedious state of affairs was solved at last, to everyone's satisfaction by the cupids, who seized handfuls of bright red arrows in their little fat hands and dispatched them from miniature bows. Few of them sailed in the right direction, but this had been foreseen and the lady's golden apple, held as far as possible from her apprehensive breast, was at last dispatched by a shot from the gallery where one of the guards' most celebrated archers was concealed. Beauty then opened her arms and Wisdom was enfolded to her roseate bosom, the prurient view being sadly masked by the ubiquitous nymphs and satyrs.

"So, Beauty is ravished by Wisdom. What is gained?" demanded Tulla, irritated by the playfulness of it all.

"If you do not know, Madonna, then it has not yet happened," solemnly declared Pulci, raising his cup to her.

Tulla made an impatient sound.

But the masque was not yet done. After a suitable interval, during which the forgotten song soared to new heights, the press of lesser beings, hooved and horned, floreate and flimsily clad, yielded their company once again and behold, the golden lad and his tasty lady were gone, and in their place, was, of all things, a plated wicker cradle, weighted with acanthus, apples, and a certain amount of excess matter, which must be laid at the door of the owl, still as ruffled, which sat scruffily atop the lot.

"What prodigy will they raise?" wondered Luigi, one eye

on the wine jug which was circulating in the wrong direction.

"The marriage of Wisdom and Beauty? Wit—if they are lucky. Conceit if they are not," Botticelli opined.

But the figure that rose, unsteadily, from the cradle, was that of a very small girl not more than three years old, and already showing signs of a fragile beauty based upon fine bones and delicate coloring. She was crowned with laurel, Lorenzo's personal emblem, and dressed in a tabard upon which was quartered the arms of the Medici and of the city of Florence, golden balls and golden lilies on an azure field. The young chorister doubled his effortlessness, and she stepped down, assisted by the cupids, who were all at least twice as old and prominently solicitous and superior. The child then ran across to where Lorenzo sat and bowing gracefully, thrust a small casket into his hands. Lorenzo, who had children of his own, scooped her onto his knee and allowed her to open it. A jewel was revealed, a ruby of such vast proportions as to be quite vulgar, set in gold and pearls. Into the lid of the casket were engraved the words, "Montevalenti salutes her friend and neighbor."

Lorenzo appeared overcome.

"There now, next time you have to pay your little forfeit to a lady, you won't have to give her your cloak!" Leone grinned like a hyena.

"Thank you, my friend—and when you have, very soon, impoverished yourself with your own generosity, you will know where to come for a loan!"

The Medici was possibly the richest man in Italy, apart from the Pope, yet he was renowned for the quiet simplicity of his dress and his habit of failing to carry money on his person. He took the joke and the gift as they were intended and allowed the child at once to pin the jewel on his breast, where it shone magnificently against his borrowed doublet.

The masque now developed into dancing for all, and Guiseppe's consort led them into the favorite basse-dance, with courtier and peasant shoulder to shoulder, while her husband displayed his muscles to a noble lady. Like Lorenzo in his city of beauty and wisdom, Leone governed, if he could be said to do anything so strenuous, in a democratic fashion. His people loved him because he knew their names and he spoke to them man to man, and man to woman! Without being particularly aware of it, he loved them too.

77

He watched for a moment as Il Magnifico wove through the crowd to return the little spirit of Florence to her mother, touching a shoulder here, returning a smile there, then he himself rose to his feet and disappeared into the crowd. Tulla, who could not help being aware of his presence, whether she wished to or not, heaved a relieved sigh and turned animatedly toward Botticelli.

"I hope your mouth is open to say that you will dance!"

The appalling tones were behind her. Before she could reply she was pulled urgently to her feet and swung against a solid, cloth of gold chest.

"You may not know the measure," Leone said nicely, "but with your swift wit, you will learn as quickly as you learn to dissemble with Plato."

"I don't wish—" she pulled at the hands which held her.

"Will you never accept it? Not thy wish, but mine! And my wishes are barbed with little scarlet arrows." He purred, cocking a lascivious golden eye.

"You can't force me to dance. You will scarcely be content to drag me inert, about the floor!"

The prince sighed, releasing one of her hands.

"You lay claim to a certain breeding I understand. You would therefore scarcely be contended by the discomfort and embarrassment of all here present—who are innocent of any harm to you and probably think of you as one of my relatives, if the gossip hasn't yet got to them. Besides, my lady wife is favoring you with her frostiest gaze—if you would have your revenge, you will look at me as if you thought I was a human being and dance with me. At any rate, I shall not let you go. If you fall on the floor, I shall say you have fainted and have you undressed and put to bed like the unpleasant child you are." Then, "My dear girl, there is no need to blush at the mention of a bed."

Frustrated and confused, she allowed herself to be drawn into the dance. They took their place among the moving couples, and she forced herself to concentrate upon her part. Neither the music nor the steps were like those of her own country, but they proved simple enough and curiously chaste. There was plenty of goodhearted enjoyment in the weaving, bowing, and twisting of the pattern, but nothing of passion. These Italians were very strange. A man and a woman could dance together (a thing never permitted in Turkey, except among peasants), and yet there was no recognition of this advantageous fact in the leisurely movements. If, however, she was a little contemptuous at such bloodlessness, she was also more than grateful. Even so, the touch of Leone's hand on hers provoked an uncontrollable flurry of rage each time it occurred. All went bearably, until the end of the measure. Then the prince, after bowing his thanks for her company like a ridiculous, courting peacock, she thought nastily, abandoned this innocuous pastime with shocking suddenness, seized her in his arms, and subjected her outraged, protesting lips to his kiss. Breathless and furious, she broke away only to meet the reckoning stare of Alessandra behind her husband's shoulder.

Seeing Tulla's look, Leone turned easily, all pleasant affability.

"Alessandra dear—will you not emulate my excellent example?" He raised his voice, deep and sure above the throng.

"Let every man honor his partner with his lips. Youth is brief. Seize the moment!"

There was a roar of pleasure. Then every woman, young and old, found herself soundly saluted. Just before Leone enfolded her again, Tulla saw with a faint shock of surprise that, watched by the enigmatic gaze of the cardinal, the antarctic splendors of the princess were wrapped about by the dark, pressing form of Andrea Zorza. The gallant condottiere's lips had engulfed hers with all the pent-up passion unreleased by the dance. One white hand rested negligently upon his heavy neck, and as the other briefly caressed his hair the thin lips of the interested prelate tightened into a faint, surprising smile. This remarkable sight was abruptly blotted out by a golden doublet. Tulla held herself quite still and stiff as the prince bent to her once more. Then, "Devil take it, I'll kiss no corpse!" he declared disgustedly and, tossing her away from him like, she thought angrily, a half-eaten apple, the overgrown infant stalked away after more palatable fare. She stared as half a dozen eager women surrounded him.

"I give you a warning, putana—the first. There will not be many." There was a scent of roses, heavy, compelling. Alessandra stood at her elbow, her voice a wisp of raw silk, her eyes executioners. Zorza glittered some distance behind her. Tulla, caught in their glare, felt suddenly the desperate injustice of it all.

"Why me?" she cried impotently. "Why not one of them?" She gestured toward Leone's crowd of sycophants.

"He has made an exception of you. So, therefore, do I."

"But *why* do you torment each other so? And what have I to do with your quarrels? Believe me, if you would let me, Principessa, I would gladly leave your house!"

The words were rung out of desperation.

"Have you never heard of the scapegoat, Madonna?" This time the new voice was mild and filled with concern. It belonged to the prince's brother, who had so far been absent from the feast, having work to do which would have weighed upon his conscience, undone, as much as dinner might have done upon his stomach. He had eaten a guinea-fowl at his desk however, and was now ready to be pleasant among the company. He did not consider it a good beginning to find his sister-in-law adding Greco-Turkish mincemeat to her fare. He therefore minced no words himself.

"You are not kind to take the lady to task for Leone's lapses. God knows he can be irresponsible at times—but she is not to blame, and she is right to defend herself. Leave it, Alessa. It is profitless."

The princess smiled. "You do not know what you are talking about, Franco," she said. Then she turned to Zorza and wandered vaguely away on his arm. Franco sighed as he watched her go.

"She's right," he admitted to the disconsolate Tulla. "I don't. I comprehend neither my brother nor his wife and as for the relationships between them, it would take the Almighty himself to pronounce on that—"

"Please." Her hand importuned his sleeve. Her face was white and tense. "Please, take me away from here, back to my chamber if you will."

He saw that she could take no more of whatever treatment they had handed out to her. She was shaking slightly all over. Ever practical, Franco asked, "Have you eaten anything? No? Then you must." He spied Gian Carmaggio making a fool of himself over some girl in a corner. He roared. The boy was at their side.

"Fill a plate and a flask for Madonna. Then take her back to her chamber."

"Magnifico!" Automatically snapping his heels at Franco, and widening his smile for Tulla, Gian was puzzled. One brother had given him very specific instructions as to Tulla's entry to the feast—now the other was supervising her departure. And, it seemed, she had not even eaten. He knew better than to question Franco, however.

"I thank you, Signore." Tulla's relief was as deep as her gratitude.

"Promise you will eat it all," Franco insisted. "You have an hysterical look about you. Food will calm you, and wine will bring you rest. I would accompany you myself, but I have much to discuss with Lorenzo."

"Thank you, I am accustomed to Gian," she replied, realizing that this was in fact a surprising truth. She would not make him suffer, in Alessandra's fashion, for the sins of the Prince of Valenti. As she turned at last, to follow the boy with his loaded salver, Franco murmured one last word. "Do not fear any—intrusion—tonight. Leone will be engaged with his visitors until dawn. He doesn't think a feast a feast unless the last dish is of cockerel, crowing on the platter!"

She turned her gentle smile upon him. "You have made me the present of sleep. You are kind. I thank you again."

"It is nothing. Have courage. Good night." His bow was low and conveyed respect.

As she left the hall, with that wonderful unconscious dignity of hers unimpaired by her unhappiness, Franco made himself a promise that he would spare no effort to find ways to make her life at Montevalenti more acceptable to her. He also thought, as he did at least once every day, with accompanying emotions ranging from affectionate indulgence to incandescent fury, what a damned fool his brother was.

FOUR

Franco's present did much to improve matters. Tulla woke late next morning in full command of herself. Last night's fears had melted like djinns into their bottles and a consort of determined birds had taken their place. She decided, over a delicious breakfast of wine, fried chicken, fresh bread and oranges, brought by an almost smiling Vanozza, that she'd given way appallingly under very little real stress and that her father would not have been proud of her. Her mother perhaps would have understood the humiliation, the frustration, the challenge that was offered without honorable opponent, but even her mother would not have approved the loss of spirit that had sent her into retreat. To have run from that hall was to have disgraced her blood. She should have stood her ground against the prince.

What was now required was a return to the calm in which she had managed to close herself before she had encountered this thrice accursed prince. She bit hard into her chicken and hated Leone.

She was delighted, a little later, to find that both the Lord and the Lady of Montevalenti were absent from the castle, albeit in different directions. The prince had taken to the hills again with the Medici and the poet, their aim Vanozza said doubtfully, being hawking. The princess with her cavalier servant Zorza and her saturnine brother had departed on some mission of her own.

"Messer Sandro Filipepi is waiting to speak with you,"

Vanozza continued, as she assisted Tulla into the polite gray gown.

"Botticelli? Why hasn't he gone with the others?"

"I can't say. Madonna will find out for herself if she goes to the herb garden—I will show you the way."

So she was Madonna again; it was comforting, she would not deny it.

Castel' Valenti's herb garden was set at the heart of its absent-minded architecture, in justice perhaps, to the fact that herbs have a similar relation to a good meal. It was a cozy, comfortably sized courtyard, with the kitchen on one side of it, the library on two more and open air, leading to the stables and the fowl-runs on the other.

An assembled army of aromatics charged forth in olfactory onslaught so that Tulla's immediate reaction was a sneeze. Having thus repelled the invaders en masse, she took her time to deploy each separately so that thyme and rosemary, oregano and dillweed, costmary and rue and garlic and parsley and mint marched neatly through her nostrils in good order, followed, in the medical department, by alkanet and arssmart and stinking agrimony, nettle and wormwood, horehound and hawkweed, fennel and sage. Surprised on the flank by assafetida, she sneezed again and uttered a charm against the incubi who take advantage of such events.

"Here, what you need is marjoram. Sovereign against the sneezes!" The yellow head of Sandro Botticelli rose from behind an unidentifiable bush, and he presented himself upon the path before her, neat and nearly contained in blue tunic and gray gown. She acknowledged his bow and a handful of herbs which she bruised and held to her nose.

"Good. I doubt if even Verrocchio could get away with a Madonna of the Streaming Cold! For that is why I am here, Mona Tulla, to beg you to sit for me. Will you?" His request was persuasive for its undertone of urgency.

"How can I refuse? You have given up your day's sport for this, and what else have I to do?"

"Excellent. Then we'll start at once!"

"Here?"

"Certainly. If you would like to sit here, on this bench, you should not look at the sun—it will tire your eyes."

"How shall I sit?"

"As comfortably as you may."

83

The artist produced a heavy linen bag from beneath the bench. It contained sketchbooks, chalks, inks, brushes and a small array of colored pigments. He selected what he needed and, seating himself cross-legged in a bed of mouse-ear, set to work without further civilities.

There was a silence.

It stretched itself about them until both found it comfortable. Tulla let herself drift into a pleasant somnolence. Occasionally, when the luxuriant corn-colored head was bent over the drawing, she considered the purposeful figure before her. It was peculiarly satisfying to see so much power of mind and muscle gathered and controlled into one steadily moving hand, guided by the exquisite mechanism of the impartial, exacting, heavy-lidded brown eyes. Her tutor had once shown her a drawing of a section through a dissected human eye. She had found his tentative explanations of its workings miraculous and had spent minutes afterward, staring into the mirror into her own dark blue spheres, hoping perhaps for transparency to fall upon them from heaven! Dear Aristides, how wise he had been and how tolerant. Well, his finely tuned brain edified worms now; one of the invaders had solved its complexities with an axe.

She sat up straight suddenly and spoke to Botticelli.

"What is your main work, Messere, at present?"

Sandro grunted, squinting along his brush, and mumbled, "Venus and Mars," without further elucidation.

"In what guise?"

"The god sleeps. Venus has conquered him. His weapons lie beside him, no longer necessary, mere toys for insolent satyrs."

"How undignified. The god of war disarmed and snoring. I don't think I like the idea. Tell me about the composition."

Sandro sighed and laid down his chalk. "I want to turn you into the Blessed Virgin, not a critic of the arts. I require serenity of feature, not a bobbing of brows and a curling of lips." He opened his disreputable bag and dragged out another heavy sketchbook. He laid it upon the bench beside her and turned its pages. "Since you are so curious, Mona Tulla—there, that is my last cartoon for the Venus and Mars."

Even before the details of the composition had begun to imprint themselves upon her mind her vision was ravished by the sweet languor of the line. Within a frame two and a half times as wide as it was high, the immortals lay resting, bedded in silk upon sprouting grass. The God was naked apart from a cloth thrown over his loins. His head had fallen back, his eyes were closed, his mouth open. One elbow rested upon his abandoned cuirass, into which an impudent infant satyr had crawled for amusement. Another played with his lance, while a third blew impolitely through a conch shell into his sleeping ear. Venus, awake and gazing out of the picture with perhaps the faintest of smiles, was unexpectedly fully clothed, in a modest and flowing garment that revealed no more than one slender naked foot, to draw the eye compulsively to the base of the frame—though no compulsion on earth could have kept it long from that face!

"Who is she, your Venus?"

"She is—a Florentine lady." There was a reluctance in his reply and he hastened on purposefully to explain the drawing to her. "Marsilio Ficino, the renowned philosopher and tutor to the Medici, has given the astrological character of Mars as outstanding in strength among the planets because he makes men stronger—but Venus, when in conjunction with Mars or in opposition to him, or watching from sextile or trine aspect, often checks his malignance. She masters him. But Mars never, in any aspect, masters Venus. If you follow me, Madonna, you will see that I have placed my figures opposite to one another, top to tail as you might say, while their limbs lie at the angles mentioned."

"Ingenious, Maestro—but won't you tell me who she is? I think I shall never again see such beauty."

Sandro's sigh was fetched from his moss-gathering boots.

"Her name is Simonetta Vespucci—she is the wife of messer Marco Vespucci, a merchant of Florence."

"And that fact does not please you?" Tulla enquired artlessly.

The sigh was becoming a habit. "Even if it did so, there is a further fact, madonna, Mona Simonetta is also the mistress of Giuliano il Superbo—the brother of Lorenzo de Medici."

"Il Magnifico and Il Superbo—Imsh'Allah! And they mere merchants too! What title would the city of Florence have left for her princes if she had them?"

"It is a man's nature that makes him a prince, Madonna, not his title," answered the painter shortly.

"I am reproved, Maestro. The painting—is it to be for Madonna Simonetta—or for her lover?"

"It is in celebration of the great tournament that Giuliano is to hold—in honor of the city's most recent treaties of friendship with Venice and with the pope, in which the Prince of Valenti's recent embassy to Venice played a part. *Misericordia!* I am a clown, Madonna. Forgive me!" He looked quite comic as he realized his blunder.

"It's all right," Tulla said shakily. Then, "Oh! How clever!" Her slightly self-conscious cry was not certainly in recognition either of Botticelli's apology nor the ambassadorial talents of the Prince of Valenti.

"Vespucci—it signifies 'little wasps'? And I have just discovered them, buzzing about the head of Mars. You are full of surprises, Messere."

"Bravo, Mona Tulla—and can you also tell me, as a classical scholar, the meaning of these laurel trees behind the heads of the pair?"

She considered. "The laurel is the emblem of peace, of violence subjected by the higher powers of reason and of culture." A note of bitterness crept into her tone, but she banished it at once. "It is also, is it not, the emblem Il Magnifico has chosen for himself—and therefore implies that Mona Simonetta's beauty will conquer all comers at the tournament! I only wish I might see her. She has the face of springtime itself. I wonder you look elsewhere for your Madonnas, messer Sandro."

Sandro blushed uncomfortably.

"Variety is necessary to my work. And besides—"

"Yes?" there was sympathy in her voice for what she knew she would hear.

"I love the lady, Madonna," Botticelli said simply, his large form unutterably dejected, his curly head bowed. He dabbled in the mosses with his chalk until it broke and he had, perforce, to look up at her. "She is as far beyond me as the stars, as Venus herself, and as far beyond mortal beauty."

The humility in his good-natured face stirred her to pity. It lasted a moment only. Snapping shut the open sketchbook, she fixed Sandro with a severe and questioning gaze.

"Forgive me, Maestro, but I have much to learn about your Tuscan manner of thought. The lady Simonetta, however beautiful and however well-married, is," she hesitated delicately, "nevertheless a whore, is she not?"

"Madonna!" Affront sat bulging on his brow.

"The whore of Giuliano de' Medici?"

86

"That is not a term anyone in Florence would think of applying to Madonna Simonetta," he reproved frigidly.

"What is it then, I wonder, that makes a woman a whore?" Her tone sincerely sought enlightenment.

Sandro toppled into the trap.

"A whore is a woman who accepts payment for her offices—a woman of the people, a peasant—"

"Ah—then it is *birth*, is it, that makes a woman what she is? A peasant may be a whore, because she takes a man's money for her work, but a Madonna Simonetta may not be so described, though I dare swear she is hung about like a harem favorite with tokens of Il Superbo's love! How is it," she finished on a note of fine, high contempt, "that birth may make a whore of a woman, but it cannot make a prince of a man? You are defeated by your own definitions, painter!"

Botticelli groaned. If he had known that such distracting subtlety lay behind this dark-eyed, liquid beauty, now dangerously foaming, he would have gone hunting.

"I meant," he said quietly, "that it is not birth alone that can make a man a prince among men."

But Tulla was away on the tide of her argument. "I," she stated loudly and determinedly, "am of noble birth. I am the daughter of a prince in my own country. I am no whore. Tell that to your prince, and ask yourself where circumstances such as mine fit into your star-gathering, moon-struck, hypocritical philosophy!"

There was a mere suggestion of a tremble in her lip as she completed her diatribe, and seeing it, Sandro forgave her all of it.

He smiled at her with true friendship, then bent and took both her hands. "I will, Madonna of the Angry Countenance. I promise you, I will."

She looked into his brown eyes, and some of the torment died in her own. She exhaled slowly and held tightly to his hands. "You are patient, messer Filipepi—I don't deserve it."

"Call me Sandro—and you do!"

After this they spoke of many things. Tulla told him a little of her life on the shores of the Bosporus, of fierce horsemen and intricate scholars, of gentle, submissive veiled women and her determined, educated mother, who cast the whole of Europe's learning into her lap like a crop of ripe apples, enough for a lifetime. She talked too, of her father, exacting

87

in his rule and ruthless in his punishments, honored and feared by friend and foe alike. A harsh man, but never unfair and with a surprising, engaging vein of humor in his trenchant wit.

"And was there no other—no young man—a prince of your own people, whom you loved?"

Sandro asked this hastily to avert her recollection of what had happened to her family.

She looked at him flatly. "I have never known love of the kind you suggest."

He smiled ruefully. "If only I could say the same. And yet—no, I will not say so. It is suffering and a madness and bitter frustration—but I would not have it otherwise. I strive to love with my soul, to transmute my rough emotions above the mere, fumbling flesh. If I can succeed, it will not matter who possesses her—for I shall have gained the exquisite ecstasy of the spirit, the conquest of Venus over Mars." He finished on an excited note, "That is why my Venus is no woman of wanton flesh, but the very epitome of chastity and spiritualized love."

"I think I understand you," Tulla said, after some consideration, "but I'm very glad it is your problem and not mine. It seems an excessively difficult way to be in love!"

Sandro regarded his latest model with growing affection. "I should not be so certain that love will not be, in some guise, your problem also," he said, his eye alight with unusual mischief.

It became her problem sooner than Botticelli might have expected, though certainly not in any fashion that that delicate spirit would have recognized.

At sunset, seated as far as possible from the prince, they attended dinner, at which the digestion was again distracted by fierce music and exotically spiced foods, and persons who burst out of pies—for no conceivable reason surely, other than the discomfort of remaining inside them. One small infant, parboiled and suffering from an extreme emergency, had to be removed from under Lorenzo's sensitive nose. So did the pie.

Tulla lost her patience and her appetite and discoursed volubly upon the degeneracy of the Italian palate.

It took a stroll in the courtyard with her new friend and the discovery of an abandoned lute, which she played and played well, to restore her to temper. And then, after all Botticelli's good work, the prince sent for her to come to his apartment.

"I shan't go."

"He will have you fetched. Better to go with dignity." The artist smiled. "You never know. There may be some advantage in the visit."

She knew that he had spent an hour with the prince before dinner.

She reached tiredly for the worn garment of her equanimity and obeyed the summons.

In the bold pavilion of his chamber, bathed in approaching sunset, the prince was lolling on his elbows among his cushions, slack-lidded and loose-limbed, every inch the sybarite and an affront to serious thinking humanity. He was playing with a small and scruffy dog that did not know its own variety. Upon Tulla's entry this rushed toward her, possibly backward, one couldn't tell, in an exuberant skitter of unkempt fur. At her feet it bounced up and down as though on a string, emitting shrill, excited sounds in a piercing coloratura.

"I'm sorry. A recent acquisition. I've not had time to teach her manners."

She looked at him suspiciously but Leone's smile could have charmed hungry lions from Christians. He indicated his own superiority in such matters by offering her one of the straight-backed, throne-like chairs with which the castle glowed and bristled. She sat, equally straight-backed, upon its softly golden seat. The dog trotted back to its master.

"Your face is full of reproof. I don't remember insulting you today," the light voice puzzled. "I scarcely recall *seeing* you. It comes to mind that you might even have been avoiding me." A few notes down the scale to injured pride in parody.

"If I had the freedom to do so, be sure that I would use it," she answered calmly, ignoring this feigned ingenuousness.

"Ah, freedom." The prince pondered. "It might help you, I think, my Platonic dealer of dialogues, to remember the words of Marcus Cato upon this vexed subject. 'Good men only are free. The *wicked* all are slaves.' " The lift of his brow was more damnable than his silken smile, and Tulla longed for a weapon that would put an end to all such exquisite movements.

"You have no comment to make? You prefer to consider carefully the widsom of the truly wise. I applaud the instinct."

He twisted lazily amid his crushed luxury and leaned his negligent weight upon one elbow, throwing back his head for a moment so that the ruddy gold mane lay spread behind him on the pillows. Then, surprisingly, he heard the unlikely sound of his captive's laughter, deep, melodious, and undeniably genuine. He raised his head.

"Am I allowed to share the hilarity? Or is it a private joke with the dog?"

There was no chance that she was about to tell him that his last, self-indulgent posturing had irresistibly called to mind the vanquished and sleeping form of Botticelli's Mars—albeit unbedeviled by cloven-hooved imps and clothed in more than a sheet.

"I hope you are not laughing at Cato," he said severely, wagging a long finger at her. "I should not expect it of your mother's daughter."

"What do you know of my mother?" She was instantly on the offensive, glaring at him, the moment's humor fled.

"Nothing other than what Sandro Botticelli has told me, but I'm sure she was in every way a most gracious and well-schooled lady. I hear that she even attempted to ascertain that her daughter followed in her wake." He sighed. "However, we are all more or less a disappointment to our parents. My own father, for instance, would sooner have had me boil in oil as read Cato. An old-fashioned gentleman, though forceful in his way."

"I do not suppose I am here to discourse upon your family. And I prefer that you will not speak of mine." Her voice was dry as prunes.

"You set me a difficulty there, but I will try," Leone drawled reasonably. "I have already been forced to discuss your origins once today and have been brought, *Deo gratias,* to see the dreadful errors of my ways with regard to your inestimable and apparently highly elevated person." He hesitated, but she gave him no reaction.

"The overgrown cherub with the charmed paintbrush, who has made himself your cavalier, informs me that it is a grave mischief in me to take you for my concubine—always supposing that happy state of affairs to be physically possible without fear of instant execution! He says that your birth is as high and irreproachable as my own and that I am taking a dastardly advantage of your bad fortune." Again he left her space for comment which she did not make. His tone aban-

90

doned some of its bravura. "It occurs to me that I should like to hear of that unlucky fortune for myself, from your own lips if you would be so kind. Having been titillated with scraps from both my reprovingly practical brother and my embarrassingly romantic artistic friend, I hunger for some sort of mean, which I invite you to supply." He waited.

"Did my seller provide no pedigree?" Tulla inquired flintily. "He would have done as much for a dog." Their canine companion, recognizing part of its meager vocabulary, bounded a couple of times and wagged its preposterous feather-duster of a tail.

"It didn't seem to me that the opinions of Al-Farid, upon any subject under his grinning sickle of a moon, could have any sort of a value to a Christian and a seeker of the truth," Leone answered her with courteous patience. "I ask you again, Mona Tulla—will you not tell me your story?"

"What will it profit me to do so?" she asked abruptly, aware that he had spoken to her, for the first time, neither lightly nor dismissively—without in fact any trace of humor.

In the same even tone he said, "It will affect your future—as is always the case with the past."

A single, unwarned-against breath of hope sent her heart to her throat. Had Botticelli, simple and determined, caused genuine consideration in that butterfly mind? Could it indeed be directed to her good?

She did not speak for a moment, then, ordering hope away and patience to her aid, she found her wind and her pace and began to tell him the brief history of her years, the light and then the dark.

There were tears behind her eyes at the end. She kept them caged there, suffering their pricking.

The prince still leaned upon his elbow, his posture remaining a prodigal fall of long limbs and gilded silk, but he held his fine head alert, its angle accidently conferring an undeserved air of resolution upon its handsome planes. He listened without interruption until she had finished speaking, having reached again the havenless terminal of the Venetian quay.

Leone prolonged the silence for a term, then said delicately, "Thank you. You have been succinct—and remarkably unemotional for a woman, and one with such a tale to tell."

A stony contempt for his unnecessary thanks removed all possibility of tears. She stared in front of her, the graven

91

image of all those who are where they do not wish to be, and cannot be where they wish.

The dog, intelligent creature, sensed her position and whined in sympathy looking at her with liquid, sorrowful eyes. She dared it to jump into her lap.

Leone, observing that silence was his property's preferred state, called back elasticity to his limbs, untangled them and rose, stretching broadly, to his sandaled feet. He padded the chamber for a time, in the loosened, crepuscular glow of his rose-quartz windows, his white and gold blooming like a virgin's cheek, cinnabar, cochineal, madder, as he moved past the flawed crystals.

The sun, in unusual splendor even for the mountain top, was going to bed.

He stood at last behind her chair, and she felt his murmur, when it came, upon her skin, as though it had been his breath.

"What am I to do with you?"

It was unlikely that she would offer him a solution, but she did. It was not one he, seduced to esthetic ecstasy by the sheen of gules upon the crown of her head and the fine, particular bones of her clavicle beneath the thin, roseate and softly pulsing flesh, could have wished to hear.

"You could send me home." Her voice was harsh.

"To what? And how many shall I send with you? A hundred men to guard a disinherited lady in her cold hearth? I do not think that they would go—and small blame to them—even if you could pay them. No, Scheherezade," the lightness returned, "you have caught the Sultan's interest with your tale. You cannot now turn your fate about, but must stay and spin marvelous edifices with your tongue."

What seemed to her nothing but empty mockery caught her on the raw. She half turned and drove her fist into his face. Ducking, he parried the blow, his laughter freezing her pride. Her wrist caught in a steel grip, her eyes blazed, cannons of hatred, and received only more amusement in return.

"Softly, my Saracen. We come to the movement later, first let us finish with the words."

"I have nothing to say." She felt bruised, depleted by his imperturbable good spirits. The dog, unnoticed, scrambled into her lap and settled with one eye half-open.

"No, but I have. That you are a woman of exceptional

beauty, I did not need Botticelli to tell me. That you are of noble birth you've proclaimed without the aid of my brother's trumpet. That your education has been excellent has revealed itself publicly." He relaxed his grip upon her arm but only a little, sliding his fingers absently up and down the slender wrist, passing and repassing the tiny throb of the pulse. "The princess, my wife," he continued surprisingly, "is also possessed of all these qualities—though I do not expect you to appreciate them in her—however, there are, as you have noticed, others which she lacks—and for which I have a need. No. Do not act like a cornered hind. I'm not speaking of the bedchamber. I'm simply saying that there is work for you in Montevalenti—work that you might enjoy. I have heard you play the lute. Have you also mastered the keyboard? Is your French good? And your Latin as good as your Greek?"

Tulla was nonplussed. "I am acquainted with all these things," she admitted coldly, her pride conquering her vow of silence.

"Excellent!" The long fingers now blatantly caressed. "Then matters will improve for you, oh Moon of my Delight—and if my lady wife proves incapable of containing her pique at your continued presence, do not be too proud to make me aware of it. All you need do is to speak of it to Vanozza."

But nothing would make her speak of that.

"What would you have me do?" she asked, her mouth filled with the ashes of stillborn hope.

"You will be pleasantly surprised."

"Then," she pulled at her arm which was beginning to be numb, "if there is nothing further—"

"Oh but there is. We have dismissed the business—the cold words. Now for the pleasure—the sweet, warm, delicious movements—"

Before she could know that he had moved he was standing before her seat and without losing his hold on her, had drawn her up against his taut body, the little dog tumbling untidily to the floor. There was a soft pillow of white silk at her cheek and her hand was trapped beneath his upon his breast. His smiling lips played in her hair. His voice suggested an agony of intimacy as he swept his fingers up and down her stiffening back.

"Can I provoke no chords of thunderous joy upon this delicate keyboard—no Gloria in Excelsis? No Te Deum? Not even a tiny, private Angelus? And they say I have the touch of a master of the organ. I obviously need practice."

He swung her adroitly about until she rested against his supporting arm, her chin tilted and held by a hand gentle as lace, exactly where it should be to receive his kiss.

And yet he did not seek her mouth at once, but surprising, shocking her almost, sealed her eyes with his lips instead, so that blinded, disoriented, her weight no longer her own, in seeking stability she found his waiting mouth, still smiling a little at the trick but not for long. The subtle, wickedly mobile lips came to their serious celebration of her beauty and the prince, for once, was silent for a long space. His kiss was unashamedly expert, as were his fingers which brushed her body lightly, surely touching upon half-known passions, mysteriously and decadently sweet.

As it might occur to a non-swimmer, seduced by the soft caress of the water, suddenly that he is drowning, it came to Tulla what was taking place. Desperate for escape her body plunged wildly, her balance thrown to fate. The little dog barked shrilly about her unsteady feet as she bit fiercely into Leone's loving lower lip.

The prince aired an oath, and hastily let her go. He raised an exploratory hand to his mouth and observed the brightness of his blood.

"A healthy shade," he said chattily. "I think I shall christen the little bitch Daphne—she too was hard to hold." He gazed thoughtfully at the living representation of Outrage before him, then remarked softly, "Pray excuse me any further courtesies, Madonna. You have given me the oddest wish for my own company. It is less painful. Go! Fly the ogre, and seek your narrow bed, Byzantium! Virtue has conquered once more! However, we progress. Your present weapon becomes you better than a dagger."

Then with the faintest inclination of his head, he strolled toward an inner door through which he disappeared, leaving her stupefied with anger and a half-awakened sensuality. She stood rooted in the middle of the decorative chamber for a full minute before she abstractedly followed his instructions to leave. The dog had trotted amiably after its master. This made her feel strangely alone, as though, *Kyrie elesion!—she* were somehow in the wrong!

Moving, dreamlike, to the door, she realized that he had allowed her to go free once more. Still angry but increasingly perplexed, she went as directed to bed. There, couched and cossetted by her blue, soft silks, she lay awake for some time, musing upon the various natures of man's passions. She knew it to be a fact, blown her way during one or other of those interminable meals, that Sandro Botticelli and Pulci and the prince himself, even the magnificent and magnanimous Lorenzo, moral tutor to universal Italy, were sworn comrades in regular escapades that concerned ladies of the profession in which she had so generously included Simonetta Vespucci. How then was it, since these were their appetites, that they were all, so Sandro had told her, famed as gifted and excellent poets, whose sweetest songs were those of love—love of the exalted nature which the painter himself had tried so excitedly to define—the pure love of spirit for spirit, surpassing that of the body?

For a long time she gazed into the dark.

Illumination, when it came, was only partial. "They are all hypocrites!" she decided.

FIVE

The prince's brother requested the presence of Madonna Tulla. This, on a morning clear and bright and crisp as new grass shoots, was a summons which, unusually, brought no accompanying apprehension.

In Franco's company she would be safe from the exotic attentions of either prince or princess.

Franco was seated at his desk amid a choppy sea of paper, his head resting on his hand as he wrote.

"It would have been considerably quickly, Signore, to have

arrived as I did the other day," Tulla said, unaware that for the first time, she had spoken to an inhabitant of the castle willingly and before she was addressed herself.

Franco turned and rose at once. He had almost forgotten how lovely she was. Smiling, he held out his hand. Since the pen was still in it, she touched his fingertips only, then arranged herself on the settle.

Franco offered wine. "Tell me—are you any happier among us?" he inquired softly, his brother's eyes complimenting her appearance, though not in his brother's terms.

"I shall never be content to remain a prisoner," she said slowly, "but I have to thank you—and messer Botticelli—for your interventions on my behalf."

"Have they been successful?"

She blushed. "Up to a point, perhaps, though it is hard to say."

"Where Leone is concerned it is generally hard to say," Franco admitted. "But let us not speak of that—I have a favor to ask you."

She was startled. "I hadn't thought I was in any position to grant favors, Signore."

"You are fluent in Greek. That places you in exactly that position. Here," he waved a bundle of papers, "I have the long overdue accounts of one Emmanuele Stefanakis, a merchant of Candia, living in Constantinople, with whom we have certain dealings. As you may know, Montevalenti is known for its gold and silversmith's work, and we trade with this man as both buyers and sellers. It has seemed to me lately that he has been cheating us, but I cannot trace the error. He does not balance his books as we do, by the double-entry system. The merchant has written this letter, perhaps in explanation, but it is couched in the language of his own people, while my Greek is that of Homer only."

She took the letter and surveyed the spidery writing. "The Cretans do not speak or spell in the manner of mainland Greeks, but I think I can help you. If you would give me ink and paper, I will try to translate it."

A space was cleared on the other side of the broad desk, and Tulla settled herself to her task, her spirits rising involuntarily at the prospect of having something specific to occupy her after so many fallow days. Franco returned to his ledgers, and their pens scratched companionably through the morning though they seldom spoke. If he allowed himself the circumspect pleasure of looking at her from time to time, a wistful expression in his eyes, she was never aware of it.

The merchant's Greek was deplorable, and Tulla soon began to suspect that it was as Franco had suggested; the man was cheating the house of Valenti by the introduction of certain other men acting as agents—mentioned in the letter but not in the accounts, whereby they became merely itemized in the "cost" columns. Their services, even if they existed were unprecedented and unnecessary.

Franco was delighted with her discovery. "You are a jewel, Madonna! You have saved us many thousand of ducats. How shall I reward you?"

"Help me to make my escape from Montevalenti!"

He turned away from the clear challenge of her look. "I've already said I will not. I will do all in my power toward your happiness here, but I will not set you free for the wolves to prey upon. You are protected by my brother, however ill you may think of him."

Her answering laugh was oddly wild. "From whom does he protect me? From his wife and her whole clan of wolves—or from himself?"

"He has not, so far—ill-treated you?" He was delicate.

She looked down. "He has not treated me kindly."

"How unkindly?"

What was she to say? That the prince had spared her life when she could have taken his? That he had mocked her, denuded her of her dignity? That he had promised her better days, that he had kissed her and left her alone?

"It doesn't matter."

Franco was satisfied. "Leone has many irritating qualities. He is lazy, prodigal, luxurious—mischievous, sometimes foolish—but rarely unkind. Indeed, he is frequently too lenient when he should be severe. A friend to all the world, he thinks little of enemies." He smiled. "You are not the only one to have attempted his death, Mona Tulla. Only a month ago he escaped the dagger of a more dangerous assassin."

"I wish he had not! He would not then have seen me in Venice!" Her cry came before thought.

"But you would have been on the Riva della Schiavoni just the same," Franco said quietly, "and by now, it is almost certain, would have been earning your keep in the bordello. Try to be a little thankful, Madonna, for what is not the case. It is good counsel."

97

A short impatient sigh and then she nodded. "You are right, my lord, but it is hard to accept." She wanted suddenly to be rid of the subject of herself, her past.

"It is known who wished to kill the prince?" she inquired.

He smiled at her quaint air of politeness. "No," he said gravely. "Leone, typically, had exchanged his clothing with a companion of, shall we say less than noble birth. Both were masked. The assassin killed the man in the scarlet cloth with the gold lions on it. His reasons, or those of his principal's, were never discovered. Another of Leone's companions killed him at once."

He saw contempt flame in her face. "Why did he not cut him down himself? My father would have run his sword through such a man before his own blade was drawn from his victim!"

Franco sighed. She looked magnificent, regal in her pride. "We are a line well enough steeped in blood. Our title, like so many others, was won by it. Kept by it. Leone is disposed to even the balance a little. He does not shed blood if he can help it."

She stared coldly. "One cannot even the balance. One must protect what one has."

"Certainly, if one values it."

"And your brother? He does not value his principality?"

Franco felt older than his years. She saw it all in clear black and white, this strange, strong girl. If only it were as simple as that.

"He values the land, its people, the city, its skills, the beauty of the countryside—but not, I think, because our father won what must have been the tenth bloody dispute over it with the Biscaglie."

"Whom he hung in tatters from your battlements."

"Just so. My brother, unlike our father, and your father, Madonna, is a peaceable man."

"Then he will lose his land and his title," she declared simply.

"Not while I may prevent it. I am not myself, a man who goes out to seek war, but I know how to tend my brother's vineyard. Never fear, Mona Tulla, Montevalenti has a well-trained guard—and no mercenaries either. My troop, though not over large, is loyal, permanent and when possible, regularly paid."

"Then I need fear no rescue by the prince's enemies," Tulla said sourly.

"If he has enemies still, they are as yet unknown. He has many friends. I wish for your own sake, you could become one of them. Now if you will forgive me," he added hastily, seeing the light of battle glinting once more in her remarkable eyes, "I have to ride out to see to a matter of rents overdue."

"He makes you his steward?"

"No. I make myself so. There is much to oversee. Our net of wealth is spread wide. There is the land and the mines—precious alum for the dying grounds of Florence—our smiths, our weavers, our fine tailors. All are in the balance here." He indicated his piled volumes. "I ensure such a balance exists."

"A prince who can neither handle a sword nor understand a ledger! A poor excuse for a man."

She could not hurt Leone, but she sensed in some queer, intuitive fashion that she could hurt the image of him in his brother, who all too evidently loved him.

Franco sat down again. His morning was proving more difficult than he had foreseen. He considered swiftly, spoke slowly. "When we were boys together, there was no one I admired as much as my brother—not even my father, who, rugged warrior and stern man of justice as he was, lacked humor to the last. Leone had the golden touch in those days, for everything that came his way. He was a hero to all of us. A champion of arms, no one in Tuscany could match his skill in swordplay or at the quintain. He had an archer's eye and a duelist's wrist and he practiced and polished his art like a veteran until it was well nigh perfect. In learning he was the equal of our tutors. His mine is swift and elliptical, endlessly inventive. He could paint, make poetry, had himself taught by our best goldsmith, and he is an excellent musician. Women did, and do, Madonna, think him incomparable. His wit you will not deny—his charm you may not see."

"What happened to his sword arm, signor Franco? Did it become sodden with lifting and spilling too many cups of wine?"

She had cut off his eulogy. He had gone, he saw, too far in his praises. And anyway, Leone had changed, the girl was right.

"He exhausted it," he said shortly, "in the struggle with the Biscaglie. He did his share of killing, if that pleases you.

And then, after our father died—and our mother—he said to me one day that he had done with the sword."

She did not speak. She saw how he had looked when he spoke of their mother.

"And now, Mona Tulla," he rose and bowed with grace, "if I am to persuade the tenant of the Valacci farm that he owes us a tax on his wine—" Then he smoothed his forehead with his hand. "I had forgotten! I offered you a reward for your kindness. What will you have, a jewel, a lute?"

For a moment she was about to refuse. There was nothing she wanted of the Valenti. He had denied her the only thing she needed. Then a thought cut across her mind. "Yes," she said, forcing her voice to a lighter tone. "I will take something from you, signor Franco, if you can obtain it. Sandro Botticelli has told me of the great tournament to be held by Giuliano de Medici. If it is not too much for a prisoner to ask, I should dearly love to see it."

He saw that she had allowed her face to blossom with appeal. He pondered an instant and decided. "I do not think there can be any harm in it. The entire household of the Valenti will be there, certainly—and I think I could ensure your—safety amid the throng." He met her eyes.

She smiled at him with a clear innocence. Let him try as he would. Even were he to manacle her by wrist and ankle to his brother's side, she would somehow contrive a way to gain her freedom at Giuliano Il Superbo's tournament.

Later, finding herself unaccompanied in the long corridors of the palace, Tulla, her mood lightened, was inspired to explore further into its eccentric spread. Castel' Valenti had been conceived by an adventurous spirit in the early *quattro cento* for the equal purposes of admiration and defense. Inpregnable by design, it had never been taken, although the Valenti had been twice forced to cede it to the Biscaglie after mixing blood with mud in iron struggles along the river bank below the mountain of the town. That first Valenti architect had been a romantic as well as a man of war, and outwardly his castle belonged to those few fine edifices of the imagination celebrated in song and legend—it was Camelot, Lyonesse, the Chateau d'Ys. On a more practical level it was Krak des Chevaliers, Castel' St. Angelo, the fortress of Kublai Khan Its dungeons were legion, as were its windows and its towers, its stairways and its passages, both aerial and subterranean.

The original core had possessed a satisfying symmetry, but each passing generation of Valenti had been inspired to add its own idiosyncratic variation, and the effect was now one of a randomness quite beyond the reaches of a tidy mind. The dungeons, the cellars, the storehouses demanded ghosts as the turrets and eaves and battlements demanded nests.

The corridors, as Tulla found, demanded an excellent sense of direction—better in fact that her own, which would have taken her easily back to her room, but it took her only five minutes to lose herself completely. She was now at least one level, perhaps two, lower than Francesco's apartments and the passageways were increasing in dampness and darkness as they decreased in height and width. It came to her that these dingy ways, ill-lit by tiny gratings under the sweating roof, must be those of the dungeons—which caused her no alarm nor even pity. It seemed unlikely that under the present enlightened incumbency there would be any languishing denizens in the dark cells. She was disconcerted, therefore, as she stopped at yet another division of the way, to hear the unmistakable, slightly distorted sound of voices, rumbling about the stonework to the right. Aware of her heartbeat, she stood still, listening. A rat skittered passed her ankles.

There were two voices, one dark, one light. Their discourse was not smooth. Presently, as Tulla stood frozen, undecided, a door was flung open and Andrea Zorza, his walk and features energetic with anger, exploded out of it. It was slammed behind him.

He saw her at once. "Well now! First one now the other! Your looks are modest today, my beauty."

She hesitated, did not speak. Should she attempt to pass him or turn and try to retrace her steps? The moment's confusion brought him to her side, his smile only half pleasant.

"I have foolishly lost my way, Condottiere," she said hastily. "Perhaps you will direct me to the domed hall. I know the turnings after that."

"Perhaps." He came closer, his black eyes snapping with interest. He laid his hand on her arm. Instinctively she pulled away. The eyes narrowed and he showed his white teeth. "Why so timid? I mean you no harm. Indeed, I would gladly assist you to perform these domestic duties mentioned by the prince." The hand was more insistent, the brooding

101

face hovering near hers. There was a heavy scent about him, of roses, perhaps, not in their first dew-sprinkled freshness but toward the end of their life. There was a rottenness at the heart of the perfume.

"Let me pass, Messere," she said quietly.

"Certainly—but first, a forfeit! Your body was made for love, Madonna. Do not be niggardly with it!"

Swiftly, brutally, he thrust her back against the cold, seeping wall, all the weight of his trained soldier's body holding her still while he ground his mouth upon hers and his big square hands worked knowledgeably to free her breasts from their coverings.

"You are even more delicious. You are enough to provoke a man to excess!" he muttered, and setting his arm like an iron bar across her naked chest, he began to pull up her skirts, excitement glistening wetly in his rutting eyes. "I am not too proud to take the prince's leavings—if I am not to have the main dish, why then the side platter! Often they are the sweeter—damn it!"

His curse flew above her head as there came a sound from within the cell he had just left. He dropped Tulla's skirt, and she found herself thrust roughly away from him as he listened, alert for any further noise. He frowned, lust contending with discretion.

"Alas! Not now, after all, I think! But we will make merry music together, very soon. Believe it, little Turk!"

With that he released her and hastened off down the passage, running swiftly on soundless feet. Weak with relief, Tulla leaned against the dank wall, taking great gulps of the fetid air.

"Holy Mother of God," she prayed fervently, "thank you for your intercession!" She was shuddering and she felt unclean as though the man's hands were still upon her. A small sob, mostly of rage, escaped her. She felt sick. He had been abominable, repulsive, far worse than—her cheeks blazed. Was every man in this barbaric country going to throw himself upon her like a stallion at stud? It was hideous, unbearable! She must wash herself, she must get the stink of him off her.

She had half raised her hand toward her disordered dress when she was frozen by a sound from the nearby cell. This time the footsteps clearly approached the door, and the iron handle began to turn.

It would have been difficult to determine which of the two women who now faced each other across the dark passage was the further taken aback.

In front of Tulla, framed in the heavy doorway and lit from behind like the jeweled figure of some richly patronized saint upon her altar, stood the pale shape of Alessandra Biscaglia, her alabaster features changing from tones of simple shock to those of surpassing contempt as she deduced what must have taken place. Her fine brows rose almost with humor. Standing still, the blond silk of her gown reflecting the rushlight and outlining her in cold fire, she allowed her aristocratic gaze to travel slowly over the disheveled hair, the flushed and naked breasts, and the even more naked face of the girl whom her husband had so insolently set up in mockery of herself. She saw more mortification in that proud Turkish face at this moment than there had ever been when she had forced the creature to undress before her or when she had made her clothe herself in the humiliation of whore's scarlet.

There was pure pleasure in her voice as she spoke. "It seems you have learned your duty excellently well for one who made such proud proclamation of her virginity! Indeed I think you have exceeded duty. I do not think the prince will be best pleased to learn that you have given yourself with such concupiscent dispatch, nor that the shameless avidity of your lust forces you to lay in wait for a man in dark passage-ways like some female animal when her season is upon her." Her eyes narrowed faintly as she reflected who that man had been. "Cover yourself. You disgust me."

Tulla was only too glad to do so. She tried, too, to gather her scattered defenses with the ragged edges of her dress. She could not hope for dignity but she would not let herself be further maligned.

"If the sight displeases you, you may sue to your cousin, the condottiere, since it is he who is responsible for my present appearance. And you must know that what you say of me is untrue. I still have my honor, though if you wish me to maintain it, you should inform Messer Zorza of your wish. He would have relieved me of it but a moment ago, had you not been so close."

A sudden realization arrested her. That heavy, corrupt perfume of roses that had hung about Zorza; she recognized it now, for it was about her still. It was the cloying, personal miasma of the princess herself. "If not the main dish—" he had said.

So. It had not been entirely her own attractions that had excited the military ardor! Rather it had been a splinter of ice that lay, mordant, at the center of his desires, an irritation beyond his control.

"He lamented his inability to secure your own favors," she announced with a cool insouciance. "You may be sure I am a mere second choice, fallen upon by chance."

An iron control was Alessandra's chief aid in life. Nothing revealed the extent of her anger or the loathing that was growing within her for this peculiarly unsuppressable girl.

Andrea had been too pressing, too clumsy in his attentions. When she had reprimanded him he had accused her of coldness, of an immunity to passion, insulted in his manhood. Even after he had been forced to beg her forgiveness for this, he had again attempted to overwhelm her, swearing himself crazed with love—and when she had at last demanded that he leave her, he had come upon this insignificant slave, this nothing—and found her good enough.

And the girl knew it. It was insufferable. For a second, it was as though their positions were reversed. The Turk's damnable air of dignity seemed to reproach her, despite the disarray of her dress, and her last words had claimed a near equality that Alessandra could not countenance. What if the slut was high-born in her own accursed land; she ought to feel all the more keenly how despised a thing it is to be a slave.

As she stared at the lifted, challenging features, all their customary gentleness in abeyance, she longed above all things to call her guards and have them whip every inch of that tawny skin from the straight, voluptuous body and give them what was left for their plaything. Some day, she promised herself that this should be—but meanwhile the girl lay too securely under Leone's protection, his living reproach to her for her own coldness—though God knew she had been within her rights with him. She sighed slightly, her eyes raking Tulla, regretting the prince's prejudice against physical cruelty. Although he might turn a blind, even an amused eye, upon such counter-taunts as the affair of the red dress, he would not brook the breaking of the flesh. Abruptly, she rescued herself from these thoughts.

"You do yourself no good to accuse my cousin," she remarked with perfect equanimity. "You would not be believed. A nobleman of the Biscaglie is above the petty spite of household slaves. You must try to accustom yourself to your station in this place. Otherwise it may become necessary to demonstrate it to you more clearly." Her threat was not quite empty. The shadow of Atroviso lurked behind her words.

Tulla made no reply. She was more than glad when, without a further word or look, the princess turned away from her and descended once more into the lighted cell.

As the door closed, she stood for a terrible moment in the sudden, suffocating darkness and knew herself hated. Then the faint light found her eyes, and she gave a sob and began to run. She fled down the corridor and turned the corner into another, then another, then up a staircase and along, flying directionless up and down until she stopped, weeping against one of the ubiquitous works of art, a small statue in danger of toppling.

Dazed, she realized she was in the vicinity of the main entrance hall. Thankfully she slowed her pace and went toward it.

Safely there, she was greeted by a glad "There you are. I thought I had lost you!"

"You are to come with me if you please," cried Vanozza Grazzi, as Tulla stood beneath the welcoming blue dome.

She had no breath left for questioning, so, sighing, pushing at her untidy hair, she followed the swaying mother-duck down yet another corridor.

"No—*this* way, Mona Tulla!" Vanozza's chick had taken another wrong turning. "And Madonna will please to take that disagreeable expression from her face!"

She did so, replacing it with one of straitened patience, as they hurried upon whatever errand this novel and familiar servant had in mind.

They soon came, through the barrel-arch of a lion-crested doorway, into a courtyard reminiscent of the herb garden. It was filled with light, and she felt her soul lift in relief after the darkness, both human and natural that she had left behind. Its dense greenery was strung with vibrant color like daylight lanterns and hummed with bird song, and something else—

It was the laughter of children.

There were two of them, two gilded heads pressed close

together over something that occupied their attention where they lay, chins on elbows, on the ground.

At a word from Vanozza they looked up sharply, presenting two bright faces that were as like to each other as they were to the less innocent but no less remarkable features of the Prince of the Valenti.

"Hey, Vanozza! Come and look!" It was the boy who spoke. He would be about ten years old Tulla thought as she watched him discover her own presence and saw how the girl, younger, her face still rounded in babyhood, followed his eyes at once as though he had spoken.

She followed Vanozza, conscious of their inquiring gaze. On the ground between the boy's slender fingers quivered a small brown bird. It was very small indeed, a quail, the species that is apt to end its brief span as a half-noticed savory morsel somewhere between the baked meats and the fruit tarts.

"Look, Vanozza, he's hurt. I think his leg is broken, but I've made a little splint. If only he wouldn't struggle so. He doesn't seem to know that we are trying to make him better. Good afternoon, Madonna," he added tardily, his smile, bright as a ducat, offered in expiation of his forgotten manners in the presence of a strange lady.

"Nardo! Lucia! Get up and make your courtesies at once." Vanozza, her eyes soft, chided only gently.

"This is Madonna Tulla. If you are good, you're to have some of your lessons with her in future."

The children scrambled to their feet, the boy tenderly lifting his tiny patient. The girl, sturdy and round and fresh as an apple, dipped into an unsteady curtsy, her rosy cheeks breaking into dimples as she said cheerfully, "I shall like that. Madonna is very pretty."

"Thank you, Lucia," Tulla returned gravely, touching the chubby hand which instantly curved about hers and remained, warm and confiding, while the Valenti eyes, a lighter gold than the adult variety, subjected her to the customary thorough scrutiny.

The boy Bernardo favored her with a brief inclination of his shoulders, concentrating upon the comfort of the bird.

"What will you do with him?" Tulla asked, pitying the frightened, feathered scrap.

Recognizing her concern, Nardo gave her again the swift

shining of his smile. "I'm not sure what is best. I think I'll have to make a cage for him."

"Oh no, not a cage. You must not make him a prisoner!" She had spoken before she had thought.

"If I do not—a cat will have him, or a larger bird. I must cage him to protect him, Madonna." The boy spoke gently, as if he sensed that her words had been mere confused flutterings, such as those he now held between his hands.

She thought of Franco's similar strictures upon her own imprisonment, and a smile that was almost a grimace steeled her mouth. Looking at the boy, she thought she saw something of Franco in his thin, alert features—more certainly than there was of the other.

But the girl, certainly, with her long lashes and her mobile, laughing mouth, was all Leone.

So then, if she was not, for the present, to be forced to act as the prince's concubine, she was to be given the honor, instead, of becoming tutor to his bastards! She supposed wryly that if she was to take signor Franco's advice and be "grateful for that which is not the case" she should regard this as a promotion, of a kind. At any rate, the children were enchanting.

She took Lucia's hand more firmly and turned to the boy. "If you'll show me where we should go, I'll help you with the cage," she offered. "I used to keep gerbils in Soraya."

"Soraya?" Bernardo carefully copied her pronunciation. "Where is that, Mona Tulla?"

"It is on the shores of the Bosporus, in the region of Constantinople," she told him.

Vanozza, seeing that the eyes of both children were widened at once to let their imaginations look out, nodded approvingly at her older charge and marched ponderously off toward the doorway, leaving her to call new worlds into the quiet courtyard.

"That is where the Turks live, the sultan and his terrible janizaries who took Constantinople from Christian hands." There was awe in the boy's voice.

"The sultan, yes—Mehmet the Conqueror, Supreme Lord of the Ottoman Empire—and my father's friend," Tulla replied firmly.

"But the sultan is our enemy, the enemy of Christendom. Are you also our enemy, Mona Tulla?"

She considered. The moral problem *was* considerable. She

107

did not believe in telling lies to children, however uncomfortable their questions might be.

"I am a subject of the sultan, and our countries are not friends," she said diplomatically. "My fortunes have brought me to your country and into your household—but I do not count you, Bernardo, or you, Lucia, as my enemies. Indeed, I hope you will be my friends."

Lucia smiled her willing agreement, not much occupied by the sultan or his empire, but Bernardo frowned thoughtfully, much resembling his Uncle Franco, before he reached a conclusion that would satisfy both his own honor and that of his family.

"If we are truly to work together, there *must* be friendship between us," he reasoned seriously, "or we shall make no progress. And then," he added, "you are a guest in our house and must be made welcome as such."

Tulla did not know if she was touched more deeply by the girl's open-heartedness or the boy's deliberate gravity. She knelt impulsively and took both children into her arms.

"We shall make wonderful progress—all of us," she said, "and you will teach me surely as I shall teach you."

"That is what my uncle believes," Bernardo interrupted. "But only those who are constantly learning are fitted to teach others." He grinned in appreciation of her newly obvious credentials.

"Your uncle Franco is wise in many ways," she acknowledged in return.

"It was not Uncle Franco, who said this. It was Uncle Leone."

"Indeed," her voice lost its color. This must be the customary "courtesy title." Surely they were not unaware of their parentage. Poor innocents. What a pity it was that they had not been born in wedlock. But then she thought again. No children born of the unspeakable Alessandra Biscaglia could ever glow with such obvious health of mind and body as these. No, they were better off as bastards, even *his* bastards.

"Come," she cried, rising briskly to her feet, "let's go and attend to the making of this cage. There are strong reeds in the kitchen brooms, no doubt, which will suit our purpose exactly!"

"Bravo, Mona Tulla! I wouldn't have thought of that." Bernardo was admiring.

"You shall stay here and guard your patient, while Lucia shows me the way."

The kitchen, a vaulted immensity of shadowed walls and smoldering fires, blackened iron and polished copper, throbbed with a movement that was never stilled until midnight, and often not until dawn when a smuttied turnspit would conjure the last flames from the warm depth of the three broad hearths. The fires were not extinguished in winter or summer. Neither was the great stone oven that stood outside the door. Now, at the hot end of April, most of the twenty men and women who worked there had stripped off much of their clothing. Even the chief cook, Egrigio, an astonishingly attenuated Florentine whose dedication to his profession dictated that he would eat personally only that which he considered perfect (which was very little), wore a linen headband to prevent beads of sweat from dropping into basins and pans from a brow permanently furrowed in concentration. There were several moments of waiting while Tulla's modest request clambered up a kitchen hierarchy as immutable as that of the great hall.

"A broom! San Rocco! What have I got to do with brooms?" The master, interrupted at a moment of crisis, was not pleased. The eyes of the little pewter-maid, caught between two authorities, implored Tulla to intercede. But it was Lucia who put all to rights as she wiggled through the busy throng of bodies, smells and talk, pulling her new friend after her until they were at Egrigio's side.

"What are you making? Is it for tonight?" An accustomed childish thumb made an expert excursion around the basin. "Mmm—it's good, Egrigio! Is it for a *dolce?* Will you cook it, or shall we have it as it is?"

Egrigio, whose temper was generally uncertain, had happily, a deep love of children. "We shall put it into little pastry coffins, my pretty bird, and cook it until it is crisp and golden on top and a delicious melting mixture of eggs and cream and honey inside. It will be very good." He kissed his fingers to the basin.

"And can it be colored, please—pink or yellow?"

"Certainly. It shall be golden like your hair."

He condescended at last to notice Tulla. "It is a dish for the angels, Madonna, *when* it consents to stiffen to the correct consistency."

He glared at the shamefaced boy who had measured the

ingredients, then thrust the mortar upon him, his eye encouraging improvement.

"It is you who wishes a broom?" he tried to remember who Tulla might be.

"This is Madonna Tulla. She is my new teacher," Lucia said helpfully so that their relative positions of command should be quite clear. She further explained her need for a broom, lest Egrigio should think her tutor about to demean herself with menial labor. An urchin brought the broom with a scrambled courtesy and Tulla was amused to recognize the contents of a certain evening's pie, seemingly none the worse for the experience.

"*Ciao*, Paulo!"

"*Ciao*, Mona Lucia." The exchange was cheerful.

Then, "Come and see! Nardo and I have found a quail. It is hurt."

"A quail?" The half-naked and very greasy child was mystified. "My father has dozens of them already prepared. We don't need any more."

Lucia sighed, and they left the lower regions, chins in the air—Lucia's to express a superior caste of mind, Tulla's to discourage the grin that threatened her dignity.

"It is a happy place, the kitchen. I like it," she confessed as they regained the garden.

"A happy kitchen makes happy stomachs," Lucia said seriously, patting her own small rotundity.

"Is that an old Tuscan saying?"

"No, a new one. I made it up."

This time Tulla let her laugh ring free, only to cease uncertainly at its highest note, as she caught herself in the forgotten sensation of pleasure. A tear followed swiftly as she reached out to caress the golden head that bounced beside her. She was aware of a moment of pure happiness. Its surprise was total after the early terrors of the day.

She was not sure whether or not she welcomed it.

The cage was made with a great deal of love and concentration according to a design which Bernardo had thoughtfully sketched in the sand of the garden path. The tiny bird, its leg bound to a splinter of wood thinner than Botticelli's slenderest brush, was made comfortable within upon a nest of feathers thoughtfully provided by Lucia after a second visit to the small Paulo. She hoped it wouldn't know what had happened to their previous owners. At any rate it soon closed its pin-prick eyes and settled its minute head into its breast, and all three felt a suitable satisfaction with their efforts. Tulla sat down upon a stone seat, the children remaining at her feet.

"He will recover now," pronounced Nardo with certainty. "So, Mona Tulla, would you, very quietly, so as not to wake him, tell us a story from your own country? My uncle said we should be sure to ask you for the story of the Princess Scheherazade?" .

"Your Uncle Leone I presume?" she asked.

"Yes. He is best at stories. Uncle Franco is best for military affairs and arithmetic—and for the sea—he loves the sea."

Tulla did not wish to discuss the relative merits and skills of their uncles.

"I will tell you the story of the fisherman and the djinn," she said firmly.

"Please?"

"Yes, Lucia?"

"Who was the Princess Scheherazade? Could we have her story first?"

"Very well," Tulla sighed. "She was a lady of surpassing beauty, great courage, and unparalleled ingenuity who was abominably treated by a tyrant without a heart or a soul."

Her voice, becoming gentler as she gathered together the threads of her tale, wove its bright, barbaric colors into the soft green and gold background of the afternoon with such skill that the children's eyes never once left her face. However, it was no longer her face that they saw, but the subtle beauty of the sultan's silken-tongued favorite, while the peaceful garden became uneasy with the barbed luxury of the court of a cruel potentate. Time fell away from them, so intent were they all, and it was as though they awakened from a long, dream-tossed sleep, when a shrill note of alarm reached them. The quail, unaware of its perfect safety, stood upon one leg in the center of its cage, its eyes bright with fear, its beak opening and shutting upon one demented note after another.

"Poor little thing!" Nardo said. "He doesn't understand. It is only Annibale—and he can't possibly get hold of him."

The cause of the commotion was a large and very solid white cat, padding purposefully toward the cage. Lucia had scooped him up and turned him upside down in her arms just as he was within a yard of his objective. He made a sound

111

midway between complaint and pleasure as she tickled his well-filled stomach. "No, Annibale, you must be friends with the quail. He is a guest," she admonished, settling back at Tulla's feet. "You see," Bernardo said gently, "I told you a cage was necessary."

Tulla smiled patiently. *Pace* Franco!

It was then that she became aware that another pair of eyes were watching them as closely as Annibale had studied the bird. At quite some distance, behind the backs of the children, still half in the shadow of the mulberry tree that guarded the entrance to the courtyard, stood Cardinal Silvestro Biscaglia, his crimson robe militant in the sunlight. Something in his stillness brought his sister inescapably to mind, and Tulla felt a flutter of fear. Seeing that he was observed he raised his hand in a blessing and strolled toward them.

"Good day, my children. I see you are engaged in a defeat of Nature," he observed with amusement. "No, do not get up, Lucia. I should not like you to disturb the cat on my account."

"Thank you, my Lord Uncle. You had better bless him too, for he was just considering committing a mortal sin."

The cardinal sat down upon the stone seat beside Tulla and surveyed his adoptive niece calmly. "It is you who are near to mortal sin, my child, in imputing the concept of sin to an animal. In order to sin, your cat would have to possess a soul, and our Holy Mother the Church has taught you, has she not, that he cannot do so. Only man has a soul, and therefore only man may sin, if that is any consolation to you," he added with the faint compression of thin, ascetic lips that passed for his smile.

"I don't *feel* sinful," Lucia decided. "And I always do when I've been naughty. I didn't *know* Annibale had no soul, poor thing. How horrid to be like the wicked sultan in the story."

Tulla, dismayed, damned the literary minds of children, but the cardinal came to her rescue. "The sultan had already lost his immortal soul through the evil he committed upon earth. He had no hope of heaven. Is that not so, Madonna?"

"You put it well, my lord." She would not discuss comparative religions before children, as he obviously realized.

"So I should hope."

"I thought," Bernardo said, puzzled, "that all infidels had no souls, the sultan was a Turk, and Turks—" He broke off, his face as crimson as his uncle's gown as he gazed at Tulla in an agony of embarrassment and genuine distress on her behalf.

"That of course is nonsense. All men have souls, although in the case of the Turks, it is not likely that they will be shown the path to heaven. This is for those who follow Christ alone."

The cardinal's eyes were of a deeper and less elusive gray than his sister's, and humor came and went within their depths like a swift-changing tide. They were restless eyes, as his hands were restless. He looked delicately at Tulla. How would she extricate herself?

"Have no fear on my account, Bernardo, nor you my lord," she said serenely. "My mother was a true Christian, as you are."

"I am relieved to hear it, Madonna," Silvestro said silkily. "You will understand that I am responsible for the spiritual welfare of all who live within these walls."

"Especially of these children of your brother-in-law. It would never do for them to be taught by a heretic," Tulla said amicably, sensing herself to have won some small victory. She was surprised by his dry laugh.

"Not his children, Madonna, only his godchildren. In truth he, as much as I, should be the keeper of their souls."

"I do not understand."

Bernardo, released from his embarrassment, was eager to assist her. "My father is dead." His young face became serious. "He died in battle. He was the uncle of Prince Leone, who is really my cousin, but I call him my uncle."

"So many uncles!"

"Yes, Madonna, and also the prince is my godfather. He has taken the solemn seven-year oath for me and for Lucia. He has sworn to keep us both for seven years, from fire, from water, from horse's foot and hound's tooth. He has done so for four years already," he finished, smiling at his sister.

Tulla looked down at the small, straight figure, greatly perplexed by his revelations but feeling unable to question the children more closely.

"Why do you and Lucia not take the bird into a small dark corner in your apartments? I believe he will recover more quickly if he has silence and darkness to aid him." The cardinal's smile was one of affable but unassailable command.

"You are right, my lord, of course," Bernardo said, and both made their obeisances and took their leave.

"It is sad that their father is dead. But what of their mother?" Tulla murmured as she watched them walk carefully away, carrying the cage between them.

The cardinal looked thoughtfully at the pure profile presented to him. "She died when Lucia was born—happily." Then, "Hear me, Madonna, it is time you learned something of the history of the household of which you have become a part."

And so for the first time the several fragments of her knowledge of the city and the family of Montevalenti were drawn together and set in their full perspective. As the curiously detached and unambiguous voice made its revelations in tones devoid of rhythm and color, it came to Tulla that this prince of the Christian Church was presenting to her a world that belonged as much to the realms of dreams and nightmares, of the feared, the recognized, yet scarcely credible, as did the tales of the *One Thousand and One Nights*. The voice that spoke the words of God now spoke imperturbably of horrible violence, of an inhumanity beyond comprehension. The generations of the Montevalenti and the Biscaglia, were each conceived and nourished in one sole desire, that of eating out the other's heart. Their swords were sharp for each other from the cradle, and it was but a short distance therefore to the grave. Tulla did not interrupt; neither did she cover her ears. If she had done so she would have heard a light voice reminding Alessa Biscaglia that her father had hung in tatters from these battlements. Her father: and also the father of this man who sat beside her telling his appalling tales with such frigid clarity. Perhaps in some measure the cruel nature of the princess was, in the light of such a history, understandable?

At last he had done and she was free of the relentless words, if not of the horror they had contained.

She said nothing for a moment. There was no comment that could have been fruitful. Then she remembered the children and the question that had gained her cruel enlightenment.

"And it will end, now that their father has died in reparation for your father's death? Will not the Montevalenti seek revenge in turn?"

Turning, she caught the bright flicker of his stone colored

114

gaze. "They have done so. We have a brother dead, Alessa and I." And then the cardinal smiled at her, with kindness in his look, his long unquiet fingers touching her shoulder momentarily. "Have no fear for your new charges, Madonna. These are old tales now, history merely. There has been peace between us for seven years."

"Cemented by your sister's marriage to the prince?"

She let him sense her doubt.

Silvestro sighed gently. "Marriages are made in heaven," he said, smiling still, "but there are those which even God must take a long time to make."

Tulla did not doubt it.

He had distanced her with his reminder that he was a leader of the Church, rather than of the Biscaglie, but she found, now that he was about to leave her, that she retained no sense of holiness in the man.

There had been the imams, at home in Soraya—one in particular had seemed to her all that a man of God should be, selfless, humane, and deeply kind. She sensed none of these qualities in the cardinal, no matter how he smiled upon her.

He rose and gave her his blessing. "Do your duty as well as you can, my daughter," he admonished her, "and the children will enrich your days."

This at least was true. Indeed, all he had said had been true. Where was it then that she felt a lack of truth? "I will do so, my lord," she acknowledged.

He was about to leave her when he turned back toward her. "And if anything should trouble you, my child—do not hesitate to come to me. Anything."

She bowed her head. "Thank you, my lord."

Was it on his sister's account, she wondered confusedly, that her heart cried out "Never!"?

115

SIX

The days that followed were ones that she was to remember as being extraordinarily free from any troubles. For the most part they were spent with the children in such a variety of activities, of both mind and body, that Tulla forgot, for whole hours at a time, that she was a prisoner.

Of her jailor-in-chief, she saw little unless at supper. The prince was much occupied away from the castle, presumably in pursuit of his many pleasures. It seemed that her attempted seduction was, for the present, no longer to be reckoned among these. Neither did the princess appear to have an immediate interest in causing her discomfort. When this pleasant situation had outlasted a week, she began to allow herself, very gradually, to relax a little of the tension in which she had been accustomed to exist.

It was impossible not to respond to the children. Their enthusiasm for all that surrounded them was inescapably infectious, as was their evident pleasure in the process of learning. Their education it seemed had been far from neglected. Their multiplicity of uncles had surrounded them with tutors from the day that Bernardo first began to talk. They were eager to tell her about them. First there was Fra Bartolemeo, the grave and learned Franciscan sent to them by the cardinal. He was a renowned "Master of Grammar," and with him they studied the *Donatello,* the indispensable late classical textbook of the Latin tongue, written by the grammarian Donatus. Then there was uncle Franco's friend, messer Nero Balbo, who taught in the Abacus School in the city, a free establishment where any who wished might enter into the mysteries of arithmetic and simple bookkeeping. Bernardo attended this school, in company with most of the youth of Montevalenti three afternoons a week. Messer Nero also gave him extra lessons in mathematics when he came to the classroom to teach Lucia. Uncle Leone's contribution was one Vitruvio di Sestri, a brilliant and impecunious student in his last year at the University of Florence, where he was studying law. He had taught both children to write in a very creditable script and was endeavoring to insure that they grasped the essentials of history, poetry, and ethics. When he had time, Giuseppe Murano laid the foundations of their musical education. And when *she* had time, which was rarely, Vanozza would attempt to introduce Lucia to the onerous responsibilities of the lady of a house. These last two were content to abandon their duties to Tulla. The other tutors would continue their lessons, though less frequently, while Bernardo attended the city school two days only.

"It is a heavy responsibility we give you, Madonna," Francesco da Valenti informed her upon one of his frequent fleeting visits to the schoolroom, a light comfortable chamber placed conveniently next to the prince's magnificent library. "As Bernardo has no doubt told you, we expect him to enter the university." He lowered his voice, leading her toward the open window and leaning slightly over the sill so that his words should not reach the boy, deep in his problem about men filling baths.

"It is not simply that he will be a nobleman and bear his father's name. If matters continue as they have between my brother and his wife, and it seems unlikely at present that they will change, then Bernardo will be his heir. You are helping to educate the future Prince of the Valenti."

"I am sensible of the honor you do me," Tulla murmured. "Am I to include hawking, drinking, and whoring in my curriculum, or does the boy apply to the more obvious master?"

Franco smiled, equally dulcet. "For the hawking, certainly. If you think you can manage the rest—"

"Signore, you put me to shame," she acknowledged, laughing at her momentary ill humor.

"You must not call my uncle 'Signore,' Mona Tulla. He is a count." Lucia was well informed on matters of protocol and loathe to let slip such a glaring infringement.

Tulla frowned. "You have never said so. And everywhere you are known as signor Franco." It was true, though there

117

was generally a greater respect in that "signore," than many a count might count upon.

He shrugged, gazing out and down the precipitous, blooming hillside across the fields and woods.

"Montevalenti is a small principality. There is not enough of it to belong to more than one man. And what is a mere hollow title if it has no land attached? No, I prefer to be known as plain Francesco da Valenti, brother of the prince."

"But do you not feel envy, you who do as much for the city and the land? Would you not wish it to belong to you, rather than your brother?"

Franco fixed her with a cold eye. "Never think it," he said abruptly. "I am my brother's man and always will be. As for Montevalenti, I live it as he does, and I work for it from love of itself and of its prince. It does not seem to me less my own because Leone has the title to it. It is love that creates the bond between a man and his place in the world, not empty titles."

Tulla felt an uncomfortable desire to change the subject. She noted somewhat ashamedly that signor Franco harbored very similar ideas to those of messer Sandro Botticelli. And although they might be expected in an artist and an eccentric, they came strangely from a nobleman. Happily there now came a voice from beyond, vibrant with release.

"It would take four men one and a half hours to fill the bath, uncle. It was a very large bath, bigger even than uncle Leone's Roman pool. And now, if I may finish doing sums, can I ask you a favor?"

"Are they all correct, Bernardo?"

"I think so. Will you check them, Mona Tulla?"

Arithmetic was not her favorite subject, but she reached for the boy's paper with good grace.

She was so deeply involved with buckets of water and units of time that she only half heard Bernardo's plea.

"May we have the whole day off tomorrow, to go Maying—and not just the afternoon for the procession. We want to show Mona Tulla the city. She says she may not go out, but surely that is not possible?"

At this Tulla looked up to find Franco's eyes steadily upon her.

"It does sound possible," he said slowly, holding her gaze.

"What do you think, Madonna? Surely you could find it possible to bring in the blossom to the city with the children

118

and myself? And of course, you will ride in the procession later. I should be honored if you would be my companion in welcoming the summer."

She smiled slightly, understanding that he was offering her a freedom delicately qualified by his protection. It would not, unless there were a miracle, be an opportunity for escape, but it would be a chance to stretch her legs, her eyes, and her spirit.

In the morning a green dress lay spread across the painted chest opposite the foot of Tulla's bed. There was a note pinned to its damask folds. "May it bring you the gaiety it possesses." There was no signature. She picked it up and held it against her; it was obvious that it had been made for her. Its color was the happy shade of spring leaves, and she smiled as she looked into her mirror.

Franco. It must be his gift. There was no one else. For a whole day she would wear it and rest in his kindness. Easy, therefore, to be gay. Today was for enjoyment. She would not allow herself a single dark thought.

She lingered before the mirror, shaping the complaisant silk to her naked body. The chamber door came softly open. "Vanozza? Look at this! Isn't it beautiful?"

"I assure you that the view from behind is quite as ravishing!"

The reply was warmly appreciative and did *not* belong to the housekeeper. Her heart plummeting in horrified recognition, she whirled to face the prince who stood grinning in the doorway. Her eyes, huge above the bastion of the green gown, accused him of enormities.

"For God's sake do not clutch the wretched garment to you as though it represented your much-vaunted virtue! I do not care for crushed and rumpled companions. Unless," he qualified genuinely, "I have rumpled them myself!" He sauntered in and lowered himself gracefully onto the chest where he sat swinging one well-shaped calf as he examined those portions of pale gold flesh that escaped their inadequate covering.

Whole dictionaries of contumely suggested themselves to Tulla, which her disadvantage advised her to dismiss. She summoned, in their stead, something of her distant demeanor upon the Riva degli Schiavoni, being at this moment inescapably reminded of that occasion.

"If you wish to speak with me, I shall be glad to present

119

myself to you when I have dressed," she said neutrally, keeping her voice steady with an effort.

"No doubt," he smiled, "but there is more gladness to be gained, speaking for myself, from the present charming prospect. I had almost forgotten why I had purchased you in the first place. I am most pleasantly reminded."

"This visit is not courteous in you, my lord," she said tightly.

He considered, reluctantly removing his eyes from the pleasing swell of her hip to the uncongenial storm in her face. "Madonna, I imagine I am at liberty to go where I will in my own palace. I cannot help it if one of my household is late in rising and is therefore forced to greet its master without the civility of wearing clothes!"

He had neatly turned her complaint against herself. The reversal conspired with her nakedness to make her feel foolish as well as vulnerable.

Leone caught the hint of desperation in her taut stance. He did not want her dissolving into tears. "By all means, get dressed, if it pleases you," he offered generously. "I must confess to a desire to see how well the gown will suit you. I had your measurements from Vanozza, but the seamstress grumbled, as they will, that she could produce only a poor thing without a proper fitting."

"The dress is *your* gift?" Her surprise almost betrayed her into dropping it.

"Whose else?"

She blushed, shaking her head. Her mortification increased tenfold.

"Well, then—since you do not care to be naked before me, do me the honor of putting it on," Leone suggested reasonably, drawing up one knee and circling it with his arms in the manner of one who anticipates some pleasant entertainment. He was wearing several shades of green himself, in honor of the day, which with the additional touches of white silk at his throat and wrists lent him an air of fresh innocence.

What was she to do? She could hardly continue to stand like the unfinished exercise of some sculptor with the green silk shrinking, as it seemed, beneath her fingers; on the other hand it would be even more humiliating to have to go, stark naked before those hungry eyes, through the inelegant motions required to cover that nakedness!

If she were to lower the garment to the floor and step into

120

it, however modestly, she would present him with a full view of everything he wished to see. If instead, she attempted to throw the dress over her head, even supposing she were fortunate enough to find it easy of access, her lower quarters would still be available to his eyes—and at a moment when her own would be shrouded in cloth; the possibility seemed to contain even more indignity than the former. "I would prefer to dress in private," she hazarded with small hope, excluding the note of pleading from her tone.

"And I prefer that you do not," he insisted, smiling and firm.

She hated him and thought again. Almost as much, she hated herself for feeling shame before him. She had not done so upon the Venetian quay, nor yet when she had found the courage to plunge his own dagger into his side; why, therefore, should she do so now? An inspiration came to her; small but sufficient. She too would turn the insult upon its maker. Looking dispassionately into his expectant face, she held his eyes for a space and then turned her back upon him. The insult was evident; also, this way, he would see nothing he had not seen when he first entered the room. She lowered the gown and sought desperately for its opening.

"Allow me."

She gave a low moan as his hands came suavely about her from behind. As she cursed her own naiveté she felt his wrists brush against her breasts, their touch delicate but insistent. A strange and disturbing ache was awakened, frightening her into stillness.

Imperturbably the prince's fingers traveled among the green and the gold until they found what they sought—the laces of the dress, which were at the front of the bodice. He gathered the garment into an enticing ring of cloth and, kneeling, held it for her to step into. She felt the weight of his hair tickling at her flank and obeyed with alacrity. Before Leone rose again, drawing the soft silk caressingly upward over her body, he planted an impudent and unexpected kiss upon that part of her anatomy which was thrust, much to his pleasure, against his face. No mere tickling this, but a full-blooded and sensual salute to beauty.

She exclaimed in outrage and failed in her stab at the sleeves. Thrusting her hands into them, one by one as if she were a late developing child, Leone clicked a teasing tongue and reproved her indecent haste. At this, the small fires of

121

trepidation and shame coalesced at last in an unreckoning blaze of anger. She flung around within the circle of his arms, her nails seeking his eyes, his thrice-accursed mouth. She heard his low chuckle as he threw back his head to avoid her, and then, somehow, he had contrived to have hold of the laces that should close her gaping bodice and now held at the length of the ribbons, like a child once more, this time in leading strings. He held them daintily apart so that the bodice offered him her breasts as though in proud proclamation of their perfection.

Her fury left her with no weapon; her impotence threatened her with tears. Her arms fell to her sides as slowly he pulled in the strings and she was inexorably drawn toward him.

He looked carefully into her face. He spoke to her gently then, an odd regret in his tone. "You are very beautiful, Tulla. Your body is most distracting."

"Use it then! You have paid for it!" she raged, driven by an overwhelming sense that the trap had closed about her forever. "I am not armed, and you have strength enough!"

For the length of a breath she knew her true danger as his eyes clouded and he drew a finger lightly across her breasts. Then he stepped back from her and the amusement returned to his face. "It is a most generous offer, Madonna—and one which I wish you had been disposed to make before you scarred my poor heart. But I regret I must refuse, for the moment." Then he came close again, only to begin, expertly, to lace up her dress. "My purpose here is merely to take you a-maying," he informed her, as, tongue between teeth, he wove a neat and complex pattern with the ribbons more quickly than she could have done herself. "However—just to show that I appreciate the offer . . ." He pulled her into his arms and kissed her with a thoroughness that shocked, after the leisure of his speech and movements, every part of his exuberant body communicating his fierce joy in the exercise. He stopped after a time, feeling her heart beating beneath it, wondering whether, perhaps after all—? Then he saw the fury in her eyes and shook his head at himself, grinned gracelessly, and kissed her soundly again. He did, however, allow himself the immeasurable felicity of caressing her newly-imprisoned breasts. True, the laces were chastely fastened, but he had ordered the dress to be made with a very low decolletage.

For a beatific moment he stood in fervent and grateful prayer to the God who had seen fit to fashion a woman's breasts to a man's hand; then he felt her stiffen in his arms and reluctantly withdrew the hand.

Tulla, a battleground of breathlessness and rage, scarcely knew any longer what was happening to her, so successful were Leone's efforts to confuse her. Her mind wandered dizzily about the possibility of a miraculous dagger from Heaven, while her body overrode this hopeful vision with its insistent remarking of novel and extravagant sensations in parts of it that did not normally aspire to anything more stimulating than the caress of cloth or the wooing of water. She noticed that her mouth was open under his and closed it with difficulty. Suddenly he stopped kissing her and sat her considerately upon the chest to recover. "Now, pray brush your hair and let us go. Your horse is saddled and we are waited for."

His effrontery sparked a fresh blaze. "What kind of woman do you take me for?" she demanded. "I would not go with you did you hold out the last ladder to Paradise! I'd sooner sup with the Serpent."

His objectionable grin, if anything, was increased by her outburst. "Then you had better take him a long spoon," he advised. "But in all truth, Madonna," he added quite soberly, "it would be a pity if you were to miss the festivities. Will you not reconsider?"

"I have no need. I am promised to your brother for the day," she told him coldly. Surely now he would leave her?

Leone raised a quizzical brow. "Indeed? Sits the wind in that quarter?"

"I know nothing of winds, my lord," she replied irritably. "Like you, we go Maying with the children for company."

"Then I am the loser. I wish you joy of the May and the morning, Madonna, and will sadly seek another companion." His brow bordered on the ironic, but as it indicated the end of the interview Tulla was not inclined to fault it. He strode off, seemingly as cheerful as when he had come in. When she was sure he was quite gone, she sank on her knees before the chest and, mouth set, hammered with her fists upon its hard wood until their flesh was red and swollen.

She knew that this could not relieve her of the fact of his unnecessary and profane existence, but it promised her a purely temporary relief from the anarchy of her thoughts by forcing her to concentrate upon the pain!

When she rose at last, her mind quietened and her hands smarting enough for her to regret the coming need to hold her horse's reins, her immediate desire was to tear off the now loathsome green gown. She knew, however, that there could be no time for such a satisfying gesture if she was to meet Franco after breakfast as she had promised. Accordingly she gritted her teeth and brushed her hair as had recently been suggested, wound it up beneath a little scarlet cap and hurried down to the dining hall.

Tulla had just taken her place between the children at the end of the long head table when the prince made his entrance, his green doublet now set against a shining golden cloak. As he passed he beamed upon his household like their personal sun, letting the blessing of his countenance fall upon each one alike so that they cried out his name and wished him joy.

Tulla was mortally embarrassed when he interrupted his resplendent progress to the seat, wreathed in hawthorn to an alarming degree, that awaited him, to lean and murmur, "Enjoy our festivities, Byzantium, and do not lead my little brother into evil ways!"

The meal began with a generous quantity of fine red wine from Burgundy, served with exotically spiced boar and partridges stuffed with larks. "No, Nardo, not quail. You may eat in good conscience."

Afterward the cheerful Franco, oddly surprising in emerald instead of his usual modest brown, escorted them to the stable yard and extricated their horses from the milling crowd, animal and human, that were setting off to plunder all corners of the contada for blossom and greenery in the name of the divine Maia, beloved of Zeus, Mother of Hermes, harbinger of blessed, fervently welcomed summer, and conqueror of the long darkness.

Many, children especially, had gone forth at dawn and the castle was already bristling with green wherever the eye fell; in a few hours it would be transformed into an interior forest. When they had mounted and were riding out in good order, the children behind the adults, Count Francesco offered a shy compliment. "I see that you have decided to honor our custom and wear green for the feast day. It becomes you admirably."

Her response was curt. "I am glad you think so, Signore. It was rather your brother's decision. The gown is his gift."

He sensed some disharmony in her but merely nodded approval. "A thoughtful one, Madonna. It makes you one of us."

Seeing her frown openly and her cheeks begin to burn, he was swift to make amends. "I confess, Madonna, that I find the dress to be well chosen, the more particularly because it will look even more attractive with the addition of the small gift I have for you myself."

He leaned toward her and held out a small leather box. "Do me the honor to accept it with my deepest admiration, and respect." His words banished the mockery of the early morning and her face lost its strain as she smiled at him and took the box.

Inside it was an enameled pendant in the same verdant green that throbbed everywhere about them; it was in the shape of a leaf, watered by two flawless emerald raindrops.

This time nothing stood between the donor and his deserved thanks. So perfect was the manner of his giving that for an instant she, who had received so many gifts in her short life, felt herself back in the reception chamber of her father's palace, graciously accepting the tribue due to the pasha's daughter. "Thank you, my Lord Count," she said gravely. "It is delightful." And she stretched out her hand to be kissed. Formally he pressed his lips upon the imperious fingers.

"I am happy that it finds favor with you," he said quietly. He did not smile at her dignity, though doubtless Leone would have done so.

When Lucia, after clamoring, was shown the pendant, she swung it for a joyful second on its golden chain and remarked approvingly, "Oh yes, it is just the thing to go with Uncle Leone's dress. I suppose there isn't one of these for me, too?"

Franco laughed, while Tulla pretended a deeper examination of the jewel. "No there is not. But there is something in my purse for both of you, when we reach the mill—and not before."

"Can you eat it?" demanded Bernardo.

"You can."

"Good. Shall we race for the mill, then, all of us?"

Franco hesitated, then, "Why not? But wait for my signal!"

Both children rode as though centaurs and were champing with their horses.

Franco leaned toward Tulla who seemed to have frozen in her saddle.

"This is a mere formality, Madonna, but you'll understand. I must have your word."

She sighed, her fingers plucking distractedly at her green gown.

"That I will not attempt to escape you? No." She sighed again, somewhat angrily, he thought. "Not today."

"You have my word," she said brightly, shaking her reins. "Now, I believe I shall find the mill at the foot of the hill, to the left?"

"Follow me, Madonna!" As he leaned forward and spurred his horse she caught sight of a face from which all responsibility had fallen, leaving it that of the boy he had perhaps never had the opportunity to be.

"Follow you? This is a race!" she cried, and leaned low along the neck of her chestnut.

They flew for the gate, in the wake of the children, all four scattering through the cobbled streets amid a welter of evading feet and joyful curses. Cries of "Viva Francesco" bounded between tall houses, soared across squares. Banners streamed everywhere, gold upon red, whole prides of interested lions regarding their progress. The city was dressing for the festival. But this was not the time to look about. Indeed to have done so would have been dangerous. They erupted out of the city's gates and down upon the plain like a small, contained volcano, the nimble hooves picking their swift, accustomed way down paths surely traced by goats for their own particular use. A small avalanche of creamy rock accompanied them. In four minutes they were on the plain, and the race, until now a mere suggestion, was a fiercely competitive reality.

There was no question of holding back on the children's account. They rode fully grown horses and rode them well. If Lucia's stirrups were somewhat short, she made up for that by the determination with which she plied them. Soon they were stretched neck and neck, shrieking like a band of marauding brigands, Tulla adding considerably to the quality of the tumult with her ululating calls upon Allah, beloved of Turkish janizaries, in battle. She had taken the lead, almost sure of her victory, when her mount half-shied at a bush which had no business being where it was. It was only the faintest check, but it allowed Bernardo to overtake her, skidding in the dust before the mill-house with a hoarse cry of triumph, Francesco and Lucia so close behind as to create equine pandemonium as they collided with the other two.

Tulla was aware of a relief and an exultation she had not known in a long time. Riding fast had always been her joy and release, and though the green Tuscan plain was far from offering the unending reaches of her native desert, the effect had been as welcome as if it did.

Stefano Bossi, the miller of Montevalenti, having ears, had come out to greet them. He was a huge man, reminiscent of an elderly oak, gnarled and weathered but with a strength that would outlast storms. Today was a proud day in his life, for this feast-day was the occasion chosen by his second son, Rico, apprentice to the baker, Sardi, to present to his master and to his city and his prince, the masterpiece that indicated his full accomplishment in every intricacy of his trade. Indeed, the baker's masterpiece was to form the centerpiece of the evening's palace banquet.

"Good morning, Ser Stefano." Franco dismounted and tied his horse to the fence that was there for the purpose. "We'll come in and have a drink with you. Racing is thirsty work in the heat."

The miller backed swiftly into the doorway of his sturdy stone house. "Don't trouble yourselves. I'll be glad to serve you here myself, if you'd care to sit down." He waved a hand at a rough wooden table and chairs in the shade of the elm whose roots were entwined with the foundations of the mill.

Franco shook his head. "Inside I think, don't you?" he appealed to Tulla.

Tulla, who had not had occasion to visit a mill before, was intrigued. "Certainly. It is very hot."

Ser Stefano shrugged and stood aside, an expression of embarrassment on his seamed features.

They stepped inside the cool building. The miller, who was a rich man compared to the neighboring farmers and laborers, kept a comfortable home. There were terracotta tiles on his floor and even a small oriental rug on the wall, a present given to ensure that no sand found its way into the donor's flour. A broad table was already set with wine, fine-grained bread, and soft cheese. Behind it sat a woman of indetermin-

127

able age with the black, oiled hair, prominent, slanted cheek-bones and glittering strong-browed dark eyes of the wandering tribe of the Zingari. Franco checked himself as he saw her. She did not rise in respect but fixed him with a heavy, sardonic gaze, nodding as though to an equal.

"You here? We had not expected to see you again in these parts."

Franco's tone was mild but Tulla knew instinctively that his feeling was otherwise.

The woman spoke coldly. "I go where there is work for me to do, where I am called for." Her voice was deep and fine.

The count turned to the miller, "And you have work for her, Stefano?"

The big man shifted his weight from his left foot to his right one, distressingly conscious that the tenancy of a mill, though entrusted for three centuries to a single family, lay nevertheless in the gift of the owner of the land. He held out his hands, huge palms begging understanding.

"A small thing only—a little mixture—to—to—" Embarrassment won the day and his mouth hung open, wordless as a fish.

The dark woman lifted her cup to her lips and drank deeply, ignoring him. Franco looked thoughtfully at the children, standing beside him, their faces alive with interest. He reached into the pouch slung behind him. "Here, you two! Take the sweetmeats, and eat them outside. You shall have a drink shortly."

A small war was waged between greed and curiosity, to be won by the former. Since she had been forgotten, Tulla remained, as curious as either child. For a moment there was no sound other than the muffled thunder of the grinding stones in the adjacent milling chamber. Then Stefano snatched at his manners and poured wine for his latest guests.

"Well then, what is your purpose in Montevalenti? You have been asked to leave our lands. I was not aware that anyone had recalled you."

Her calm was as imperturbable as his own. "You cannot know all that takes place in this domain, Lord Count, diligent though you are. I was invited, be assured of it."

"By whom?"

"I am not answerable to you." Her perfect ease was somehow disturbing.

He turned to the miller. "You, I think, will not say the same?"

"No, my lord." Stefano had found his tongue and the words burst forth. "It was only a matter of a potion or two. 'Tis Theresa the milkmaid, Signore—I have the itch for her. It affects me grievously. Can't sleep at night. So I do plan to put a little something in her wine next time she's past here—only herbs—do no harm?" He appealed to the gypsy who ignored him still. "And then—she has given me a spell—only short—to repeat so that my boy will make a success of his masterpiece. No harm there either." He sounded more sure of himself now that confession was over.

"And what does she take in payment? Not simply wine and cheese?"

"No." The hangdog look had returned. "I have ground off some little pieces of the millstones for use in her remedies. 'Tis well known such can cure many an illness."

Franco nodded impatiently. "It's equally well known that millers are in league with the Devil, who delights in grinding the souls of men. Have a care, Stefano, for your reputation. La Sventura is not an acquaintance to foster."

Tulla's face lost its recently acquired expression of enlightened superiority to such woeful ignorance and ceased to contemplate the probable words of her mother's own physician upon millstones in the bladder. So this was the woman, the witch, whom Alessandra Biscaglia wished to consult; a friend of the unspeakable Atroviso, who had said that she was to be feared.

As though sensing her sudden alarm, the gypsy gave her a slow considering look. Then she grinned as though at some private joke and rose to her feet. Moving with an impressive, almost ceremonial grace, she halted before Franco, her eyes level with his as she fixed him with a stare that brought basilisks to mind. "The Devil has need of more puissant auxiliaries than Stefano Bossi," she murmured, her voice melodious in its softness, "and be assured, Count Francesco, he knows where to find them. However, you do right to fear his power. It is unconquerable." Then, peering closer into his face, she nodded slightly, as if in confirmation of some previous thought. "You will know, for it will not be long before you meet him. He will prove your master."

Franco's gaze flickered an instant before he drew back with a look of contempt. "Did I wish my fortune told, I'd not ask it from such as you. Be damned to your predictions and to your presence!"

La Sventura shrugged. "It's all one to me, Valenti. Ask of a priest, or the pope if you will. If he has the sight, he'll say the same." As Tulla opened her mouth to join in Franco's ridicule, she found the disturbing ruminative gaze of the gypsy upon her own features.

"You stand proud, though you are not free," the low voice told her. "That is good, for in pride lies strength. One day, if you have the strength to dare greatly, you will be offered your freedom."

"Are you an oracle that you are so generous with others' days and minds?" Tulla demanded lightly, casting off the near-hypnotic dark gaze with an effort of will.

"Many have found it so," was the reply. And yet, Tulla sensed, she spoke the simple truth. There *were* those who possessed the gift of future-sight. Certainly such a gift would explain the weight of this extraordinary woman's presence. It might be well to treat her with respect.

But Franco, it seemed, had no such qualms. "You've done your business with Stefano. You have none with us. I'll thank you to leave us without further benefit of your doubtful wisdom!"

"My words can alter nothing," she stated with an iron smile. "Nor can yours." Then, as though it were she who had pronounced the dismissal, she flung a sharp command to the miller agog with tremulous curiosity behind them. "My horse, Stefano."

The miller was torn between fear and fealty. La Sventura strolled to the door, her dark red cloak brushing Tulla as she passed. "We shall meet," she murmured, looking into her eyes.

With a strangled apology, Stefano lumbered in her stately wake. Through the open door they saw him cup his hands for her to mount. Still she did not speak to him, though he mumbled a farewell.

"There is undeniably a *power* about her, and she is very handsome in her way," Tulla said, staring after her. "Do you not feel fear when she threatens you with the Devil?"

Franco snorted. "She has threatened the Valenti with the Devil ever since he spawned her," he said shortly. "But she does a great deal of harm among the peasants. I thought we were rid of her."

An unquiet thought nudged her. "I know who has a use for her."

"You do?" He was surprised.

"The princess." She explained the source of her knowledge, flinching at the memory.

"What is Alessa thinking of? Oh well, let her meddle. She's likely to get nothing worse than a bellyache out of it. It's probably that accursed astrologer of theirs who's responsible. He and La Sventura are old friends—lovers, if you can imagine anything so unlikely."

Tulla could imagine. She remembered the burning behind Atroviso's eyes; eyes that were in some way very similar to La Sventura's.

"I don't like her presence here today. Last night was the feast of All Hallows, the Great Sabbath of the witches. And even the Mayday festival remains to us from pagan times. Her kind like to take advantage of such opportunities."

"She is truly a witch?"

"She has been known to practice certain ceremonies that the Church has forbidden."

"Why has she not been arrested?"

"It was long ago, before the peace between the Biscaglie and ourselves. La Sventura has always been attached to their family. Alessa's father held her in some respect. Some say she was his mistress. You have seen that she does not love the Valenti. I could wish her gone."

"Then why do you not attend to it?" It seemed a simple matter.

"I will. And be damned to Leone's wife."

Tulla hoped he would carry out his word. It seemed to her that he was altogether too casual in his attitude to the undeniable powers that rested within that dark, commanding woman. If they were not, perhaps truly those of Darkness, they were certainly those of Mischief.

The miller reentered and began a shamefaced ramble of apology. Franco clapped him on the back. "Enough of that— tell us where the best blooms are left. We've come Maying, not to tryst with a witch."

And so, after the children's questions had been swiftly and truthfully answered, though with scant information, they got down to the real business of the morning. The exercise was conducted among the thickets of hawthorn, blackthorn willow, and rowan along the river bank, with the continuous groaning of the mill for encouragement. It was a prickly and strenuous occupation, but it yielded copious armfuls of blossoms and greenery, with clumps of wild bluebells and lilies for good measure.

"Why do we *do* this?" asked Lucia at one point, sucking a bleeding finger.

Bernardo gave her the benefit of two years further education. "Perhaps for Maia—the nymph who, with her six sisters, became one of the Pleiades, the constellation which appears this month. I will show you when it is dark. Or it may be in honor of Flora, the Roman goddess of the spring. The Romans," he continued enviously, "held the Ludi Floreales, their feasting and games, from April 23rd to the 3rd of May—not just one measly day like ours!"

"Oh. What did they play?" asked Lucia humbly.

"Well, they pelted each other with flowers and held all kinds of sporting competitions."

"Then," Lucia pronounced practically, calling out of her bush with an air of finality, "it is *just as well* we have only one day. Otherwise there would be no flowers left for summer!"

When the demented bells announced the time for the great procession through the streets of Montevalenti, it became clear that the minds of its citizens were far from dwelling upon fashionable classical deities. Flora and Maia could look out for themselves; their chief interest was their prince! Crowned somewhat tipsily with a garland of hawthorn, his leaf-green cloak sewn with living flowers, he rode tall upon a white horse, also caparisoned like a garden, weaving and smiling his way through crowds who did more to impede than speed his progress. Shrieks of "Il Leone!" hammered the ear from all sides, and blossoms filled the air. Tulla riding with Franco, just behind the prince and his entourage, noted without surprise that her own invited place had been filled, to overflowing, by the voluptuous charms of Marcellina the whore, an arrangement that appeared excessively popular with the crowd. "Bread and circuses," she muttered self-righteously as they turned into the street of San Jerome, averting her eyes from the spectacle of Marcellina's disgracefully exposed breasts, offered rather than confined by her tightly laced bodice.

"Madonna?" Franco had observed the movement of her lips, but hearing was impossible in the throng. He was having difficulty in keeping close to her and was worried both by this and by the fact that Leone, despite his own earnest strictures

132

to the contrary, seemed to have shaken off the dozen officers of his guard who had instructions to cling to him like a second skin. In such a crowd as this it was impossible. Franco swore. If only the people would all consent to move in one direction? It was simple enough, God knew. But the fact that *everyone* wanted to walk alongside the prince *all* the time, turned the occasion into an annual purgatory for those who had his safety in their keeping. As for his subjects, the most cheerful of them at this moment were probably the physicians, the bone-setters and the women skilled with herbs, for tomorrow would see the greatest number of broken bones, cracked heads, trampled limbs, and devil-possessed hangovers since the year before.

Tulla spent a great deal of time wishing she had stayed in the castle; the rest she spent anxiously turning round to see that the children were safely moving behind them, amid their own, determined guard.

"Isn't it wonderful?" bawled Lucia ecstatically upon one such occasion.

Tulla smiled numbly and held fast to her reins. Her ears buzzed with bells and yelling. She was suffering from claustrophobia and nostalgia for her father's slow, dignified processions, where he sat serene and resplendent on his golden platform carried by a dozen bearers. He would look neither to left nor right, and the folds of his jewel-encrusted robe did not stir. When he passed, his subjects bowed to the ground and were silent.

Also, there had always been the certainty of arriving home whole.

She was so surprised as to be almost piqued when after three hours of this sweating, jostling, screeching torment, Montevalenti's May procession was brought to a similarly satisfactory conclusion.

By chance, Franco assisted her from her horse just as his brother, wreathed in smiles and hung about with praises, also dismounted.

Leone grinned at them and plucking a wild orchid from his belt, tossed it toward Tulla. She let it fall, disregarded, to the ground.

"Well, Franco. Here I am, you see, neither assassinated nor deposed by a peasant revolution. How are your bruises, Byzantium? And how do you like our festival?"

She raised her chin. "I find it lacks dignity, my Lord."

"As does the master of the revels?" His grin increased. "This is the people's day, Madonna. They are poor for the most part and cannot afford dignity. They do, however, know how to enjoy themselves."

He bowed cursorily and left them. Tulla, though knowing herself reprimanded, did not feel chastened. The citizens of Montevalenti were an undisciplined rabble and their unprincipled prince their fitting champion. She was tired and yes, bruised and out of temper, and though she had enjoyed the morning immensely she had now had enough of the first of May. However, there was one more function to complete the celebration.

The dining chamber, heavily disguised as the May King's forest region, was in extreme danger of consuming itself in its own ashes before the guests could consume their food. The green and bristling walls were hung with their vulgarly excessive number of candelabra, while numerous garlands were drying out nicely about those which hung over the tables. Franco's eye seemed to Tulla a little feverish as he surveyed the prospect and spoke seriously to Vanozza and the chief steward of the house. Shortly a long line of urchins appeared, each carrying a slopping pitcher of water. By way of insurance it was scarcely the most encouraging of sights.

"Has there ever been a fire?" Tulla inquired of Bernardo, wondering which of the two-foot doorways would make their best exit.

"Oh yes—when I was seven," the boy replied cheerfully. "It was great fun, but I don't suppose there will be another," he regretted.

There was not. However, Bernardo was to have his entertainment, as were all the diners, and in an even more spectacular fashion than that provided by the tumblers, jugglers, and enthusiastic country dancers and singers beloved of the burghers, guildsmen, and well-to-do farmers who shared the board with their betters. It was still the people's day. This was made clear with the fact that the chair beside the prince was occupied by the baker's wife Gianna, a pretty, blushing girl whose dazed happiness in coming so close to the object of her dreams vied with her agony of ignorance over how to use a fork. A more savory choice, at least, than a whore, Tulla thought. She glanced disparagingly at Marcellina who now held court at the foot of another table. On Leone's other side there was an empty chair which she supposed to be for Alessandra. She had just settled herself comfortably on her cushioned bench between the children, had insisted that Lucia's doll sit beside the child rather than in her lap and that Bernardo make some attempt to hold his knife elegantly rather than hunter style, when the portly majordomo tapped her shoulder respectfully and whispered in her ear.

The children saw her soft mouth become a thin line of displeasure and rolled their eyes at each other. The majordomo waited. Mona Tulla did not move. He spoke again, reproachfully, it appeared. Mona Tulla shook her head.

"What is it?" demanded Lucia.

"His Excellency requires that Madonna sit beside him, little mistress."

"Lucky you! You'll get all the best bits!" was the reaction.

"I would really prefer—"

Ferrucio waited more heavily. Like his master, he was unaccustomed to question. "Hurry up, Madonna! Everybody is waiting for you!" Bernardo implored. She looked about her. It was true. The prince would not give the signal for the night's entertainment to begin until she had taken the seat on his right. There was nothing for it but to obey. She would not spoil the evening for the guests. She took her place with her back straight as a tent pole.

"I am glad to see you again, Madonna," Leone murmured sweetly in her ear, "but I would remind you that you are not assisting at a funeral. Your elevated position requires you to smile. Court etiquette. I'm sure you remember."

"I cannot imagine why you should want me beside you, since I find *your* company detestable," she muttered, looking straight ahead of her.

"I told my wife you would share my bed and my board," he explained, "and since you will not take the former—I thought I would make up for my mischievous behavior by offering you the place of honor at the latter."

He sounded so completely sincere that her suspicions were immediately aroused. As though he read her thought, he filled her cup, smiling his most feline smile. Then, to her relief, he turned his attention to the baker's wife who was without doubt more appreciative of both wine and smiles. Tulla turned her shoulder as much away from him as was possible without provoking public censure for rudeness, and concentrated upon the entertainment to drown the doubts

135

that had begun to afflict her upon the subject of the princess's thoughts upon her present position.

The main entertainment was of course the meal itself. The baker's trade encompassed far wider crafts than the mere making of bread. Upon this occasion Rico Bossi had become an artist, a sculptor—he had let his fancy roam in its native, bucolic regions. There were herb dumplings in the shape of small animals, complicated loaves disguised as sheaves of grain or flowers, pie-crusts molded into the heads of the creatures whose meat they contained; there was a wondrous pastry model of his father's mill, complete with working wheel, set beside a wobbling stream of apricot jelly; a representation to scale, of the great bell of San Jerome, dyed an inedible looking bronze and carved as intricately as the original; and most highly applauded of all, a stupendous lion, couchant, regardant, the length of a man's arm, wearing a collar of marzipan jeweled in jellies and angelica, fastened with a shield bearing the arms of the city. There were dozens of attendant minor fantasies, pastries, tarts, cakes and custards delivered by the urchins of the fire buckets. The larger pieces were presented with a great deal of pomp by other apprentices to the trade, being piped in by reed flutes accompanied by the large flat tambour.

Tulla was diverted despite herself, as she looked about her at the surrounding tables. There was no doubt that the prince was right. These people knew how to enjoy themselves. Dressed in a style and grandeur that often surpassed their betters, in boldness of color and cut if not in good taste, they seemed every bit as much at home as did the residents of the castle. Especially at home were their parrot-voiced, magpie-jeweled wives who chattered and gestured with unceasing animation, their chins, single and double, dipped in more cream and honey than they had ever dreamed of. Their eyes, like their tongues, were everywhere, and Tulla knew herself the subject of many a sticky conversation. She found that she did not mind in the least. There was a peculiar innocence about the proceedings that made her smile. Without knowing it she relaxed her Spartan posture and lay back in her seat, enjoying Montevalenti's enjoyment.

Leone, relinquishing Gianna's conversation to messer Buonavia of the Arte della Lana on her left, regarded his prickly purchase in silence for a while, relishing an unguardedness that he had never seen. Her beauty struck him again as it had when he had first seen her; so uncompromisingly pure and yet so tuned to the arousal of the senses. As he looked at her, smiling serenely at some burgher's floreate salutation, her full lips more amused than polite, he wondered at his own patience. What was it in her that stayed his lust, changed it, even, into something near respect? He did not doubt that, given time enough and a little wine to damp her fears, he could arouse her. Why, then, did he allow her the dignity of her anger, the self-respect of her refusal? Did he want more from her than the simple surrender of her body? Then *what* more?

She saw that he watched her and sat up at once in her chair, her look distant and severe once more.

"From goddess to governess in the flick of an eyelash." Leone mourned. "I can think of no one else upon whom I have this disastrous effect. Not," he added urbanely, "that you do not make an excellent governess. It was, however, quite delightful to see you smile; I wish that it lay in *my* power to make you do so."

"What in the name of Mahomet does he expect me to say to that?" Her thought was made obvious by her look of disgust.

He sighed. "Madonna—if you only possessed a little more humor, I believe we should get on together very well."

"And if you possessed a little less of it, your vision might extend beyond your comedian's nose!" she flashed, indignant at such unjustified criticism.

"So intent are you upon the surface of life that you do not care whether the smiles of those about you have as little life in them as that of Lucia's painted doll! I am not your puppet, Prince. It may please you to consider you have bought my body," her contempt told him that even this was his delusion, "but my mind and heart you have no power to pay for—and it is from these that smiling comes."

"Then am I to understand that you have opened your heart a little to the citizens of Montevalenti, if not to her prince?" he inquired with relentless pleasantness. "I distinctly saw you smile when messer Vincenti the goldsmith raised his cup to you."

"Messer Vincenti was courteous and represents no threat to my privacy or to my—person."

"If you will have the goodness to overcome your natural revulsion and look at me for an instant?" His purr suggested churlishness in her.

137

She turned a marble face toward him.

"Thank you. I dislike addressing an averted profile, however noble. Now listen well, Madonna, for it is to your advantage. I see that I have offended you by behavior which, perhaps, another woman would find—However, if it is so, I am sorry, for the offense if not the behavior, which gave me a certain piquant pleasure. I admit it." Even in the midst of his apology his eyes glinted with sulphurous diversion so that it became simply a refined form of insult. She wondered what would happen if she upended the wine jug over his epicene curls.

"If it is privacy you desire," he continued lazily, "then you shall have it. I swear I shall make no more unexpected visits to your chamber. There—now please relax that frozen face. If I had wanted to sit next to an iceberg I should have invited my wife."

Both promise and barb flew to their mark so that she was startled into the smile she had so determinedly denied him. True, it was a mere quirk at the corners of her mouth, but it satisfied him, for the present.

Confounded by the ease with which he had offered her the secure solitude that was what she most longed for in her present circumstance, she searched his face for a sign that she could place trust in it.

"You don't believe me?" he said shrewdly. He shrugged. "I keep my word. You may sleep and wake without fear that the ogre will leap from behind the curtain."

She did not know what to say. Thanks stuck in her throat, but what else was there? She said nothing, resenting his power to make her feel ungracious. He touched her cheek suddenly, his fingers cool as silk, and shook his head at her. There was nothing but kindness in his eyes.

As his hand lingered she remembered how he had caressed her naked body with the same delicate contact, as though he swept the responsive strings of an instrument that was worn to his touch. She gave an involuntary shiver, though she was not cold.

It seemed that he would speak again, but he did not. Instead he turned away to give a signal to the musicians, whose gentle efforts had so far been scarcely noticed by the company. They set to work at once to remedy this condition, pounding into an energetic peasant *stornello*. The company looked up, sniffed and refused to be bested. Conversation rose at once to an amicable roar, and everyone became scarlet in the face. Tulla sat back and drank her wine so that she might have something to which to attribute the sense of well being that was insidiously creeping over her.

Under cover of the general orchestration, Gianna Bossi, whose husband had entrusted her with a small civic duty, seeing that the prince was disengaged, blushingly seized her opportunity. "My Lord Leone!" she bellowed in his ear, tumbling toward him in her low-necked gown in a manner that brought ripe apricots to his fruitful mind. He grinned wickedly and pondered happily on the *droits de seigneur* as she leaned dangerously over the table toward the pastry effigy of the Valenti lion, which sat neatly before them, its amiable features streaked with melting orange glaze. Dimpling, Gianna detached its marzipan collar and laid it before Leone's plate. Then she pulled off the little coat of arms from its center. It was a pretty confection, so strongly colored with golden saffron and the brilliant crimson mixture of extract of sandlewood and blood that one doubted its edibility. Gianna held it out to the prince and indicated that he should open his mouth.

Leone, who had already eaten more than he wanted, was aware of a distinct disinclination to accommodate her, lovely as she was.

He threw her his most engaging smile. "What, consume my own blazon? Not I! I am no cannibal, Madonna!"

His words had attracted attention, and a cheer went up at the center of the table, though no more than half a dozen could know why they cheered.

Leone then took the tiny bright shield from his companion and held it delicately between finger and thumb. Catching up Gianna's hot little hand he rose to his feet and lifted her with him.

"The prince salutes the beauty of his city!" he cried and popped the gaudy morsel between her open lips. Confused and flattered, and as deep in love with Leone as if she had never laid eyes on the handsome baker, the girl took the foolish wafer upon her tongue as if it were the blessed host. She closed her eyes and bit into it with a sensual reverence, its bitter taste unimportant.

When she had consumed it she opened her eyes and smiled gloriously upon Leone. He leaned to kiss her cheek, and the cheer went up once more. He held her by the hand and

139

signified that it was all for her. It was the crowning moment of her young life.

It was also almost the last.

Suddenly Gianna caught at her throat, her eyes wide with incomprehension. She staggered and fell back into her seat, her breathing fast and shallow. Horrified, Leone bent over her urgently. "Little one, what is it? Tell me. Have you a pain?"

She moaned in fear, and he gathered her into his arms, taking her across his knee like a child. Tulla leaned to take her hand at once, stroking it and murmuring reassurance. Beads of sweat broke out upon the girl's pale forehead, and her hands contracted into taut little fists as pain made a fresh onslaught. Her eyelids fluttered erratically as she tried to focus upon Leone's face, the strained eyes filled with question and a terrible trust. She twisted and arched her body in his lap, her fingers wringing Tulla's hands with a desperate strength. All about them there were whispers and questions; someone called for the physician. The music dwindled and died. The great concert of pleasure had quietened to an uneasy muttering bass.

"*Poor* little bird. Try to be still," Leone begged softly, smoothing the damp hair from the brow that was creased with pain.

"She cannot get her breath. Raise her a little." Tulla's eyes, leaden with pity, met and found the same compassion in his. Together they attempted to make the panting Gianna more comfortable, but it seemed that she could not draw breath without pain. She was restless and feverish, hardly conscious, unaware when Tulla held a cup of water to her lips, or when Leone gently spoke her name.

All at once it was over. Gianna opened her eyes, gave a little moan and died, her head fallen back upon the prince's shoulder. Leone gave a cry of disbelief, then gazed urgently into her face as though he must be mistaken. He looked up at Tulla, but she only shook her head. They were alone at the center of a great silence that spread outward in waves to quell even the ragged edges of conversation in the great chamber. And now the little doctor panted in, cap askew, but he could only pronounce what was already known, murmuring his swift, sad diagnosis in the prince's ear. In the wake of the silence now began the whispers, rippling swiftly through the sea of astonishment and shock.

140

"Poison! She is poisoned!"

"Can it be?" asked Tulla, still stroking the dead hand held soft as a bird in her own. Leone said nothing as the doctor bowed his head, but nodded gently to her to release Gianna's hand.

Down in the great kitchen, at the rocky roots of the castle, the Bossi, father and son, faced each other in anguish. Both were torn by tears and neither cared.

"I could not have known, my son. How could I?"

The boy who had been Gianna's husband beat helplessly upon his own breast. "I should have done it myself. It is all my fault, all. What you begged me to do was an evil thing. God has shown it by His terrible punishment. We are damned souls for this and will burn forever!"

The miller's only reply was a stricken groan.

His son looked at him without pity. "I will leave Montevalenti tomorrow, Father. There is nothing for me here."

Stefano lowered his huge head. It was best, perhaps, for everyone.

It was argued for many days afterward about the town; had the baker thought to kill his wife because she was the prince's mistress? Or had he thought to kill the prince? Or was it possible, even as Il Leone himself averred, that the sweetmeat had been colored with blood that had long since gone bad?

The baker could not have told them, for his father had found him hanging from a beam in his cold hearth, when he had gone at dawn to bid him farewell.

SEVEN

The effect of this disastrous feast day was to plunge the whole citadel into a deep, lightless tunnel of gloom. The prince was not seen to smile and his brother threw himself into a desperate search for the truth behind the poor girl's death. He went about looking pale and tight-faced and was shorter tempered. The children, who had observed the event with just a shade more interest than horror, were quieter than usual, chastened by the evident heaviness of all adult hearts. Tulla was utterly bewildered. It had been said in Soraya, that the Italians were a nation of poisoners, but it was also said that the Greeks were untrustworthy and the whole world knew *that* for a lie. She shared in the general disposition toward misery, truly sorry that a young and hopeful life had been cut down in the midst of happiness.

And yet she thought once—what if it *had* been the prince who had died? Would Franco have let her go? She was ashamed of the thought. Although natural, she felt it to be unworthy of her. The poor girl's death had in some way served to demonstrate to her that she and Leone da Valenti were, after all, occupants of the same universe. There had been a brief closeness between them which, though she had no desire to repeat it, had rendered her hatred of him too extreme an emotion to be sustained at its earlier pitch. She did not dwell upon this odd, subtractive factor in their intermittent relationship, but was aware of it nonetheless.

In order perhaps, to distract his own mind from the tragedy, as much as his brother's, Franco decreed that now was the time for Leone to make a tour of his dominion. There were various taxes and dues still to collect and even some princely debts to pay—to Lorenzo, for instance, who had recently subsidized Montevalenti's alum mining interest in return for a percentage of the valuable proceeds. Alum was used as a fixative in the process of dying cloth, and although the Medici controlled a virtual monopoly of the mineral in Tuscany, Leone's mines were still his own—for the present. Lorenzo was not greedy, but he possessed an exceptionally tidy mind.

It was Franco's opinion that his brother's rural subjects saw too much of their prince at play and too little of him at work. It did not occur to him that not a single one of them expected such an unlikely view, or even desired it. However, Leone did not have the heart to hunt and hawk, at least not until after Gianna Bossi's funeral, which would be held the day after tomorrow. Therefore he would accompany Franco with good grace. If Franco privately thought that they might discover, in their travels, some clue as to the hand that had offered poison, he did not confide in Leone. His other thoughts he made known to all. "You should be seen. It will reassure those who have heard rumors even more terrible than the truth. Also, you should be seen to sorrow. There are always those who will turn a prince into a tyrant at the first whisper. And then," he finished with satisfaction, as they entered the region of his paper-filled apartments, "I will be able to keep my eye upon you for a couple of days and upon others who may do the same!"

"Oh—I am sorry, my Lord—I did not know—" a confused voice greeted them on the threshold. Tulla stood beside a bookcase, holding a small unsteady ladder for Bernardo who scanned the gold-leafed titles.

"We wish to borrow your Dante," she exclaimed keeping her eyes determinedly upon the count. "Bernardo tells me you have an excellent copy—and since you were not here—"

"You are welcome to any book upon my shelves, Madonna, as Bernardo must surely have told you. I think you will find Dante to the left on the top shelf, my boy."

"Ah, the divine Alighieri," murmured the prince, intrigued by this demure reception. "You must read the story of Paulo and Francesca, Mona Tulla. How does he put it? Ah yes—'Love is the necessity of every gentle heart.' Is your heart gentle this morning, Madonna? Does it make known its necessity?" His humor, then, had returned; but it was not of the wounding kind. Her reproof, therefore, was similarly mild.

"You are trivial, my Lord. I am well acquainted with the story you mentioned. It is not one, however, that I consider suitable for children. You may take the book and leave us, Bernardo."

The boy did so, bending his head a little to conceal a smile. He wished he might stay. He found the strange relations between Mona Tulla and his uncle Leone most interesting to observe.

"You should not speak so before Bernardo, Leone," Franco reproved calmly. "It will hardly assist their tutor to maintain discipline."

"I never said I wanted them disciplined," the prince replied mildly, wandering over to the open window and gazing out over the sunny garden. "There is a white tomcat lifting his leg over the apricot tree. I'm exceeding fond of apricots," he observed somewhat sadly. "Perhaps if I were to hurl a paper-weight in his direction?"

"No! Don't hurt him—he is Lucia's favorite!" Tulla was at his elbow.

Leone made an impatient noise. "You really are a most extraordinary creature! Why on earth should I hurt the animal? Franco help me! Disabuse her. She obviously sees me as the worst kind of bully—causing heart stoppage to innocent tomcats with brutal thrown implements, demoralizing small boys with Dante—"

Tulla, sensing that he was attempting to disarm her with his teasing, and also that he had half succeeded, made a sudden movement to leave. She found herself held firmly by the upper arm.

"I wish to go, my Lord," she insisted frigidly. "The children are waiting for me."

"Of course. Certainly you may. But not before you have forgiven me for embarrassing you before Bernardo. Come, then, let us kiss and be friends?"

Franco clicked a disgusted tongue behind them.

And although she turned her head away, Tulla did not quite evade his lips which only fell gently upon her cheek before he released her arm and allowed her to leave him to the stern admonishments of his brother.

Not one of the three had noticed that, from a window in an opposite efflorescence of the castle's flamboyant architecture, the astrologer Atroviso was watching, his cavernous nostrils flaring as if at some savory morsel. His princess would be interested to learn of her husband's attentions to the Byzantine.

She was indeed, and so, while Tulla introduced her pupils to the more improving aspects of "Il Paradiso," rather than the condemned lovers endlessly whirling through the much more interesting "Inferno," and while Franco led Leone upon a grueling expedition into the nether corners of his principality, those with less laudable aims also applied their influence to the fortunes of the Valenti.

It was while the prince was gingerly accepting the hospitality of his overseer at the alum mines—alum is a taste that tends to get everywhere—and Tulla was reading a good-night story from the "Golden Legend of the Saints" to a snuggled Lucia and a restless Bernardo, that the latter were disturbed by the arrival of one of the sable and silver guards of the Biscaglie.

"You do not knock upon entering?" demanded Tulla angrily.

"You are required by the princess in her rooms," was the unimpressed reply.

"Us too?" asked Bernardo. He did not feel like sleeping.

"No."

"Good," murmured Lucia, who did. "My aunt does not really like our company—but perhaps she will like yours better."

Tulla did not think so. "As you see, I am occupied at present," she began.

The young man, who was of the peculiarly faceless variety common to soldiers who are without ambition, marched woodenly back to the doorway and waited, heavily. Not wishing to argue about it before her charges, she bade them as cheerful a goodnight as she could muster and followed him out of the room. "You are to go to sleep. I'll see you in the morning," she ordered from the door although suddenly she had lost the ability to envisage another calm awakening.

She marched resentfully after the stolid guard. She had heard Leone call the somber brigade "a joyless set of bastards." For once, she agreed with him.

Joy, however, was unusually present in the Biscaglia apartments, or if not joy precisely, a degree of mirth. The undeniably funereal decoration of the grand salon was softened by candles and warmed by a dozen or so brilliant gowns and

145

doublets. There were the frequent flashes of jewel light. Most of the illumination was centered about the small group that included the principessa and her attendant cavaliere, the brooding Zorza, resplendent in gold lace. The black hung walls seemed to have receded into infinity so that all one felt was a thick, surrounding darkness, not sensible to touch.

It appeared, Tulla thought, like an assemblage within the confines of a suitably spacious tomb.

Alessandra, in sepulchral white, held her preferred pose, reclining upon her sofa. Zorza stood at its head, his air confident and proprietary. He gave her all his attention, while she gave most of hers to a small gray monkey with long limbs and a curly tail that perched upon the cushions next to her while she fed it expensive Cretan pistachios, intended for Leone's personal consumption.

A quartet of lutenists stood at a distance, just within the friendship of the candlelight, softly retuning their instruments. Their exaggerated dress and their sharp intelligent faces suggested French origins. France, beginning to lick her greedy lips on the northern boundaries of Italy, was already her master in musical matters. Il maestro launched into a delicate motet by the Flemish Dufay.

Tulla stood before the door until she was signaled in. She noted the absence of the cardinal. She regretted it, for he had offered her friendship, a commodity she did not expect to find in this room. She was filled with foreboding.

His sister looked at her with carefully judged distaste, a look that recalled her instantly to the subterranean location of their most intimate meeting.

"You are dressed with unusual modesty tonight," she observed sardonically.

"I consider it suitable for the governess of your nephew and niece." Tulla was mocked by an echo from earlier in the day.

"Ah yes, there has been a rise in your status in the household. I wonder why that should be." There was no malice in her face, neither was there any other human emotion. She turned her head, fragile beneath its crown of plates and curls, to the condottiere. "Why do you suppose, dear Andrea, should one who, so she would have the world believe, has so roundly and righteously refused to part with her virginity to the man who is her master, be now thus exalted amongst his servants? Not only does he put her in charge of the children, he also has her beside him at table.

146

Why is that, I wonder?" The tone was one of honest desire for enlightenment.

Zorza squared his manly shoulders and thrust forward one hip after the fashion of the Venetian dandy. He was a man who, after years of being overlooked, had been offered his element. Today the princess had allowed him to embrace her; his lips had rested upon hers; he had begun to know the secrets of her body. Not for long it was true, but she desired him—he was sure of it—as much as he desired her; though at present he was forced to revere her for the aristocrat she was. It would be, he considered, a wonderfully fortunate man who might, one day, be a real husband to her. As for her question, it was simple. "It grieves me to speak so of your wedded husband, my lady," he murmured, head bowed a little, then, raising it to meet her bravely in the eye, "but it would seem that her master has overcome her claims to righteousness."

"That is untrue." Tulla spoke quietly, knowing herself for a fool. She was already taking her allotted part in their game. Zorza shook his head at her, a mournful reproof sitting precariously upon his unpracticed features. "I fear not."

"But I insist, Condottiere," Tulla replied, hating his hypocrisy, "and you will doubtless remember how successful was your own attempt on my virtue?"

Alessandra delicately raised her brows as though a pig or a peasant had untowardly entered her salon. Zorza laughed in as hollow a fashion as was necessary and looked at Tulla as though she *were* that pig or peasant. Then he stepped forward and slapped her face, once, resoundingly. "Let us have an end to your lies. You insult the principessa."

Alessandra waved him back. "Enough. The girl thinks of her skin, as well she might."

Tulla had staggered slightly but had shown no other reaction to the blow. The princess saw that it had not shaken her dignity, a quality she was loathe to recognize in her. She had sent for the girl because her presence preyed inexplicably upon her quiet. She found that she wished to know what it was in her that had attracted her husband and how deep that attraction was. Surely this cool Byzantine was of more importance to him than his several other lights of love, or he would not have brought her into the house to be a permanent insult to his wife? Or was it simply another of Leone's unpredictable whims, of no greater import than the camel he had brought home last year that had died? She had neither

147

the gifts, nor in their estrangement, the opportunities, to thread the mazes of the prince's sensibilities, and yet, restless, she wanted to know them. She *needed* to know them. The girl's presence had become a canker at the heart of her serenity. She gave herself no reasons for this; they were not required. She and Leone had ceased to be lovers before they could begin (against their history) properly to become friends. By now she felt him to be her enemy. She had found it impossible to wound him with words or with coldness. He responded like a light-minded, unaware child. One might wound a child, however, by the destruction of prized possessions. She smiled at Andrea Zorza. She had attracted other admirers in the course of the last few years but none so passionate, so tenacious as he. She found him attractive enough in his brutal fashion, but by no means expected to yield to him. He passed the time; he was personable—and her brother had intimated that he found him useful in the convoluted scheme he was presently engaged in. Silvestro, like any ambitious churchman was always wrapped about in intrigue; it suited his nature as the cardinal's crimson suited his person. She was never made accessory to his machinations but was always aware, through the peculiar understanding that they shared, when one of his enterprises was coming to fruition. It was as though they were tenants of a single skin, so that their moods were matched even when they were apart. If she was dull all day she would discover him angry at sunset; if her flesh tingled and her mind snapped and she felt a nervous restlessness in all her faculties, as she did now, she knew that he was bringing himself to some great point of culmination. At such times he would embrace her fiercely, and they would stand close together, allowing the excitement to flow through their veins. But she never questioned him; the politics of the Vatican were not to her interest. If he wished to inform her he would do so. It was sufficient that they had been born under the same constellation of Capricorn, were ruled by the same planet of Saturn, shared the same blood of Biscaglia. It was good to love and to know herself loved without reserve.

If Silvestro therefore, approved of Andrea Zorza, as far as was possible, so would she. It happened that she had thought of a manner of pleasing the bold condottiere this very night, while also pleasing herself. She summoned one of her servants and whispered carefully in his ear. She expected the events that followed to achieve the various effects of removing Zorza's pressing attentions from herself for a time, while gratifying a certain desire of her own; of wounding Leone and of breaking utterly, the ill-conceived pride of the pale, possessed girl who stood before her.

Tulla thought that the princess smiled as she said, without any noticeable unpleasantness in her tone, "I wish to satisfy myself as to the curriculum my young relatives will follow. Perhaps you will enlighten me. Begin with Latin texts you read with them."

There followed a thorough catechism of her tuition which revealed that her education had been broader and more selective than Alessandra's own—a thing she had not expected to learn and did not welcome. The girl was setting herself up to be her intellectual equal even as Leone had set her up to be a physical reproof. Color tinged her fine features as she reflected how soon and how sudden would be the reward for such insolence. "Let us have refreshment," she ordered, "and, perhaps, a little amusement. I understand you sing, Madonna Putana? If you will instruct my musicians, we would like to hear you."

Tulla had the sensation of walking, alone, upon a rope stretched across a cavern—and yet, she was merely required to sing, a thing she now did daily with the children. If she should refuse, her fortunes for the evening could only deteriorate.

She turned to il maestro. "You will know the 'O Rosa Bella' of Ciconia?" She had chosen a charming ballad by the Liège-born composer who had written in the Italian style. The musicians both knew and approved her taste.

Distancing herself as far as possible from her present circumstances, Tulla raised her light contralto, soon conquering a faint, unwanted tremulo. Her voice was excellent and the musicians responded to its quality.

Alessandra, leaning slightly to her left to catch a murmur from the condottiere, allowed her right hand, lying loosely upon her couch, to come into sharp contact, complete with its many-faceted rings, with the rump of the little gray monkey, which had been dozing beside her. It leapt up with a squawk and dashed, scolding, about the room. The musicians, naturally, did not falter, and neither therefore did Tulla, though her pleasant melody had been rendered quite ridiculous. She ignored the amused faces and the ripple of talk among the guests and held faithfully to the thread of her song. Then Zorza, thinking to amuse his mistress still further, tossed a handful of nuts in the singer's direction so that several of them showered about her head and neck. Before she could take her next breath the monkey had bounded into her arms and was energetically seeking its treasures. She smiled inadvertently and hesitated.

"Continue!" snapped the princess peremptorily.

Tulla attempted to do so, though it was evident that she sang only to be mocked. She picked one of the nuts from the neck of her bodice and threw it a little way before her, hoping to distract the little creature from its earnest delving between her breasts. Unsuccessful she wavered on, while the impudent ape, having satisfied itself that there was no more to be found, transferred its attention to her hair and sat upon her shoulder determinedly pulling down its coils and combing it with clever fingers for possible vermin. Zorza, finding this a less entertaining sport, threw another handful of nuts, whereupon several others did the same, the women tinkling with laughter and the men loudly encouraging the ape.

Tulla was now quite unable to continue and abandoned the attempt. She wrenched the wretched animal from her dress and held it at arm's length by the scruff of its neck; it squealed with rage and frustration. Almonds and filberts fell from her like a broken necklace as she strode over to Zorza and flung the gibbering monkey against his chest where it clung like a burr while he tried to detach it.

"I trust you have properly enjoyed the song, Princess," Tulla said, "though I imagine you found it difficult to appreciate, since you have respect neither for the music nor for yourself and your guests."

Again Alessandra felt the warm color flood her face. She must not be angry now. Let all come as she had planned.

"Humor our levity a little—we are hardly to blame for the antics of an ape," she observed calmly. Then, "Perhaps you will take some refreshment with us after your labors. I assure you that you sing very sweetly."

Tulla was thirsty, and drink was offered. Why not take it?

A further diversion, it seemed, had been prepared for the entertainment of the guests. A line of black-clad flunkeys, mere shadows outside the circle of light, had brought in an assortment of dishes which they offered to the members of the company where they sat. Others, members of the guard, stood still against the wall, their silver blazons flickering occasionally, as also did something jeweled upon their lifted arms.

An enormous pie was brought in and set upon the central table. Warily, Tulla sipped at her wine, standing back near the musicians, waiting to see some gravied infant clamber forth. The stupidity of this preoccupation aroused tired contempt in her as a serving man stepped forward and ripped open the vast, disposable crust. To her astonishment the air was suddenly filled with throbbing, beating movement as perhaps a hundred, tiny bewildered birds flew upward to an illusory and speedily curtailed freedom as the shadowy guards lifted their wrists and loosed a dozen hungry hawks. The entertainment was brief and bloody and most heartily enjoyed. Tulla stood clutching her wine cup, her mind amazed by the movement, the cruel laughter, and the cheeping, desperate cries. A scrap of blood and feathers hit her breast, and she swayed, stunned and sick with nausea. The room expanded and contracted before her eyes, and all its hideous sounds and sights rushed toward her. And then, abruptly, there was nothing.

"You see—it is all there already—even in the *major arcana!* Judgment, reversed—revealing the foolish concentration on pleasure, the lack of foresight, the troubles ahead. Then the *death* card, also reversed, bringing illness, disorder, war, frustration in all aims and efforts! And lastly, the *tower of destruction*, the fall of a monstrous pride—a revelation that the subject's vaunted security is an empty illusion—the Hand of God, poised to bring him down!"

The speech was low, booming, resonant, unseparated.

"And the *minor arcana* bears it all out. Oh excellent, excellent! My friend, you should be jubilant!"

"You are sure? Read it to me. I know nothing of the *tarot*."

"No need to cross yourself. The cardinal himself reads the cards regularly, and one supposes *he*, at least, is guaranteed to reach heaven!"

"This is not a time for joking."

"Learn to take your amusement where you find it, young man. You'll wait a long time till Judgment Day, and worms are not eloquent. Look there, where the three of *swords* sits between the six of *cups* and the three of *clubs* reversed. He is to suffer separation and disappointment, loss of love. He will

151

attempt enterprises with no certainty of outcome and will be offered help he cannot trust. He will be alone in his tribulation, quite alone. And yet not quite! See! The queen of clubs at the center of the second line. A dark woman, part of his household, who would befriend him—but to no avail. She is rendered powerless by the queen of swords upon her left, the woman of malicious intelligence who will help to encompass his downfall. The nine of cups ensures that he will make a badly mistaken decision. He will perhaps—doubtless—be wounded.

"It is a truly beautiful reading! The cards could not be more strongly in your favor, Magnifico!"

"Then let us trust that they do not lie."

The booming had receded, and a human voice was discernable, a voice that was recognizable to Tulla as she hung, suspended in the darkness that had overtaken her—when—how long ago—a moment or an age, she could not tell.

The voice continued. Now she could distinguish the words.

"The king of swords there—this is the great man, whom we know, do we not, whose energy and resource is most dangerous to the prince. See how he is aided by the seven of cups, which will dash the ambition, conceived too late, and the ten of clubs, which will bring him to hopelessness and despair, utterly to be overthrown in body and spirit."

The meaning forced its way into the confused and fuddled press of her mind long after the words had made their imprint.

It was Atroviso who spoke with Zorza—and they spoke of the prince, of some harm the tarot predicted for him. Coming completely to her senses, she realized that she was lying, blindfolded and, yes, bound, upon some hard surface nearby. They could see her, then, though she did not share this advantage. She longed to ease limbs that now signaled cramp, but did not wish to draw their attention toward herself. She felt chilled as well as cramped. This was more than half due to apprehension, for, now that she was fully awake, she was also mortally afraid. The nausea that still lurked in the pit of her stomach told her that she had been given some drug, perhaps poison. The wine had been a Greek gift after all, though whether from Zorza or from the princess herself she did not know.

"What about the horoscope? Is it equally definite? Is there

good news there for me?" The soldier's voice was sprung with greed.

"The opportunities are there. See here is Mars in excellent aspect to your constellations. An Arian is a great fighter. You have chosen your profession well."

"And is Aries equally proficient as a commander of men?"

The astrologer hesitated. "When he has first learned to command himself."

"Damn it, one might say that of any man. It is enough for me that I can rule my troops. But mark me, if they are left to roam the country without work for much longer, they are likely to take what they want before it's given them. We must make no mistake. Are you certain of your date?"

"Perfectly," the harsh voice grated. "Il Superbo chose the day of his tournament precisely because it is so well aspected. That the stars which smile upon his festivity might also smile upon our interests is not something that will have concerned his astrologer!"

"The baker's masterpiece was well-aspected also," grumbled Zorza "And look what happened there! Poor girl! So unnecessary!"

"The influences were by no means as strong. Unnecessary, as you say—and a foolish waste. I detest waste."

Tulla sensed Zorza's shrug. "A peasant girl."

There was the sound of uneven padding about the stone floor as the man's restless feet belied his resignation. Tulla heard them come and go in a repeated pattern that brought him near to her and then took him away—approach, retreat; approach, retreat; she felt her own heartbeat begin to attune itself to the steps. There were other noises, the chink of some weapon or implement, an occasional hiss like that of boiling water falling upon a stone, and the familiar pounding of a pestle in a mortar.

The discomfort was increasing. She lay upon her side, with her arms bound behind her, her ankles tied so tightly as to reduce the circulation to her legs. Worse, now, than the pain was the waiting.

It occurred to her that it would be better for her, should she be intended to survive whatever use they would make of her, if they were unaware that she had overheard their conversation. She moaned softly and tried to move her limbs, as though she were just awakening.

"Ah hah, the little virgin is with us again." Atroviso's

153

harsh notes were increased in their roughness by pleasure. Hands fumbled at her blindfold. The odor of stale sweat hung about her. The focus returned to her eyes, showing her a dark, cavernous room walled and floored half in stone, half in the rock from which the castle was hewn. The roof was low and crossed by beams hung with a motley variety of objects; brass pans, clouded glass vessels, strangely shaped alembics and retorts, a broom, a bunch of drying herbs, several dried toads, a bologna sausage, a pail, a cage containing some small creature, three lanterns, and a skull suspended, motionless, by a thread. Almost level with this, cocked to one side and alight with good humor, appeared the unfortunate features of the astrologer who had stepped back so that he might fully savor the fear and revulsion he expected her entire figure to express.

He was disappointed, for she kept quite still, her face composed. Zorza came to her and bent over her, his grin triumphant.

"Ah, Madonna, this is a grave situation in which you find yourself! Your body bound and at the mercy of men, your cries muffled by these sturdy walls. You shall not leave me so soon this time, by Saint Rocco! I promised you that we should make merry music together, and so we shall."

His dark face swooped, and she was engulfed. She kept quite still, her body as lifeless as bread, as he showed her how his hands were now her master. Lips, breasts, thighs, in none did he find a response, so that at last, intemperate and disappointed, he struck her in the face as he had done before. "Slave! I will rouse you soon enough, you will see!"

"Magnifico?" The astrologer, who was enjoying the small drama, coughed as delicately as his phlegmatic chest would permit. "If I might make a suggestion—?"

"Well?" The condottiere swaggered away from Tulla, breathing heavily. "I hope it is to the effect that you will be out of this chamber for the next hour! As you see, I have business to perform." He was removing his lace-encrusted doublet.

"It has just come to me," lied Atroviso, who had thought of it as soon as the principessa had asked him for a draught to remove the young lady's consciousness, "that on Saturday I shall celebrate the mass of the *old religion*."

"If you must, use your filthy practices—but don't let the cardinal hear of it. Well?"

"Surely you must know that in such ceremonies the effi-

154

cacy of the sacrifice is a hundred times greater if it is performed upon the body of a young virgin?"

"So I have heard. What of it?" Zorza wished the astrologer would remove his unlovely presence and leave him to his pleasure.

Again a humble hesitant cough. "We have with us a very satisfactory example of such a creature."

Zorza frowned and took a threatening step toward the astrologer. "Oh no, Maestro! And let you have her first, not I!"

Tulla closed her eyes, wishing she could lose her senses at will.

Atroviso's grin was pleasantly insinuating. "That is, I believe, what our illustrious and thoughtful principessa had in mind. After all, Condottiere, in view of your own ambitions in certain directions, it would perhaps be as well if you did not—er—sully the vessel of your worship with the body of a slave, particularly one whom Alessandra Biscaglia has personally found offensive."

Andrea's face was almost comic in its indecision. He took the drift of this repulsive practitioner of God knows what black arts (or the Devil knew, if God did not) that he was to hold off from his delightful captive, lying trussed and waiting for his lance, because the princess, of whom he dared to have more lasting hopes, might be put out by his quenching his steel in these particular waters. He glared at Atroviso.

"Who's to know of it?" he asked.

"No one. *If* I may have her for my mass." They glared in unison. Tulla thought of prayer, but it seemed a foolishness in the circumstances.

"But—Saturday. She will surely be missed before then. The prince—"

"I do not wait until Saturday. I have everything ready. I shall prepare for the mass tonight!"

A weakness ran through Tulla's limbs like water. They did not, then, at least, intend to kill her.

Atroviso resumed his energetic activity with the pestle and mortar, adding some powdered ingredient from the row of jars upon the table where he worked. Zorza brooded resentfully upon the problem posed. Should he risk the princess's coldness by satisfying the present moment's itch—and taking the girl's virginity *if* she still had it, which was something he had intended to discover for himself immediately. Or should he wait until his repulsive collaborator had taken his pleasure of her?

"What are you doing?" he inquired irritably. "You promised my complete horoscope but all you have given me is the kind of advice I could have gotten from my grandmother."

Atroviso poured over his mortar, humming softly as the mixture took on the color and consistency of sewer slime. "All in good time. I am engaged at present in business for another friend. I promised this—er—potion to La Sventura for today. She will soon send for it."

"What is it?" muttered Zorza, sniffing fastidiously at the bowl. "Smells like a mixture of blood and shit!"

"You are not far out," admitted the master of astrology. "The preferred recipe contains, I believe, a consecrated wafer that has been fed to toads. These are then burned and ground and added to the powdered bones of a hanged man and the blood of a newly-born infant. I find however," he added modestly, "that the two ingredients you mentioned, together with anything else I happen to have handy, will do equally well. It is also rather less expensive and less likely to endanger my liberty if I should be discovered."

"But what on earth is it *for?*" The condottiere was entirely ignorant of the arts of the Magus.

"It is to smear upon the broomstick, which a witch will then grip between her naked thighs. It will, she believes, enable her to fly." Tulla caught the dry amusement in the fractured voice.

The condottiere gave an impatient snort. "I thought La Sventura was a sensible woman who confined herself to killing cattle and love draughts and the like. What does she want with this rubbish?"

"Influence."

"Of what kind?"

"She is to initiate a novice. They will attend my mass. Afterward the novice will smear this concoction upon her loins—"

"—and it's up and away? Don't make me laugh!"

"Certainly not, Magnifico. She will also imbibe a certain draught which contains an amount of *this!*" He indicated a jar of desiccated mushroom. "It will bring her waking dreams that will include a sensation much like that of flying. That is—since no human being has ever flown, a sensation guaranteed, to *persuade* her that she has done so! However, I do

156

not like my secrets known too far. Not even by La Sventura. Let them believe it is the unguent, if they will."

Zorza grinned. "You're a wily old fox, Atroviso. You always have to be one step ahead."

"True," observed the astrologer, resisting the urge to chuckle. If he was one step ahead of La Sventura, he was ten ahead of Andrea Zorza.

The soldier, who was more impressed with the esoteric novelty of his surroundings than he wished to be, strolled back to Tulla's pallet and glowered down at her. He was already beginning to lose his hold upon her future. Atroviso's was not a comfortable friendship, and he did not wish to find himself in the old devil's debt. Italy was full of virgins.

He sat beside her and began to amuse himself by caressing, not gently, the most sensitive parts of her body. He sighed for the waste of such loveliness. "Think of it," he said conversationally, favoring her with his canine grin, "such a perfect, fresh blooming rose—to be given over to yonder burrowing worm. Tell me, Mona Tulla, the truth now. Would you not greatly prefer myself?"

He evidently expected no reply, for he now bent and fastened his mouth upon hers. She locked her teeth in a death's-head grimace so that his lips bruised themselves against them. Furious he raised his head, his hand lifted to strike her. Then he thought of a better punishment. "Then I'll go where you have no teeth, you slut!" He wrenched up her skirt and transferred his attentions to her thighs, sliding one hand between them to shame her while he savagely bit into one of them so that she cried out with pain.

"You like it as much as I, then, Madonna?" he mocked. "I have traveled a great deal, putana," he added, "and have learned many things you will like even better. In good time, you shall know them all."

Suddenly he drew away from her, his face darkly suffused. So aroused had he become when he thought of the things he would do to her that he had almost lost his control.

It was at that moment that they heard a sharp tattoo upon the iron-barred door.

"Who disturbs me?" demanded Atroviso testily. His mushrooms were on the point of boiling.

"Open in the name of Biscaglia!" came the cry.

As the astrologer made no move, Zorza sprang, somewhat stiffly, to his feet and removed the bar from its socket. He

157

peered around the door at two of the Biscaglia guard and at the decidedly impatient, scarlet-clad figure between them.

"Is there any need to go to such lengths for your privacy, maestro Atroviso?" the cardinal demanded drily, sweeping past Zorza and gesturing him to shut the door. The guards remained outside. "I assure you there is adequate protection in your very locality. None other than a convicted felon is likely to find himself in these dismal cellars. Why man, you are a very troglodyte. No wonder you cough. Zorza, my friend, you should not remain here too long; it will not do for you to take chill—" Silvestro Biscaglia stopped speaking abruptly as he caught sight of the figure upon the bed.

"Why, Mona Tulla!" he frowned. "What is this?" his air of bonhomie fell from him instantly. It was clear that he must be answered. Zorza cleared his throat.

"Untie Madonna," Silvestro ordered and was obeyed.

"The condottiere has taken a fancy to her," offered Atroviso with his caricature of a smile. "She refused him. What would your Eminence?"

"I would he might display a more subtle intelligence!"

Tulla, sitting up and gingerly flexing her newly shrieking muscles, tried to shut off the pain enough to enjoy the soldier's discomfort.

"But surely, my Lord, she is of no account? A whore from the Riva Schiavoni!"

Zorza did not like to be in the wrong. A curse on Atroviso for laying it all upon his shoulders!

"She is tutor to the prince's heirs. As far as you are concerned, Condottiere, that is *all* she is." His look and tone lost a little of their steel as he admonished softly, holding Andrea's unwilling eyes. "It would be exceptionally foolish, I am certain you will agree, to arouse Prince Leone's enmity while you are a guest in his house. It would hardly be convenient, at this present juncture, if he were to ask you to leave Montevalenti. Consider, my friend, consider."

Andrea gritted his teeth and considered, one hand fondling the pommel of his sword. "You are right, my lord," he acknowledged solemnly. He did not look at Tulla again.

"You are free to go, Madonna," Silvestro told her kindly. "I am desolated that your position should have been so greatly misunderstood." He placed a slender hand beneath her elbow to help her to her feet and guided her gently to the door.

"See that Madonna reaches her chamber, and send Vanozza Grazzi to her," he ordered his waiting guard.

Tulla found her voice in time to thank him. He nodded and raised his hand in blessing. "Go in peace, my child."

She heard the door clang behind him as he re-entered the cell. Even in her present self-preoccupation, she found time to ponder upon the nature of the errand that had brought him to the place.

Later, after Vanozza, her face a volume of unspoken questions, had fulfilled her demands for a hot bath and a soft robe and had personally rubbed dry her recovered limbs and soothed her insulted skin—and all without mentioning the obvious bite on her thigh. She lay drowsing upon her bed, one of the prince's guard outside her door to aid her relaxation, and reflected again upon the strange nature of the relationships of the inhabitants of Montevalenti. One of the many questions that gnawed at her desire to sleep was this: did she owe her evening's experiences to Alessandra Biscaglia, who had once threatened to give her to Atroviso, or to the man upon whom that lady chose to leave her perfume? Or to both? Also, why should the cardinal, known to be as close to his sister as any man had been, act in Tulla's interest? And, most insistent question of all—what were the intentions of the astrologer and his brutish fellow conspirator with regard to the prince?

For an hour or more she lay awake but could find no answers.

Nonetheless, before she slept, she had reached the conclusion that the evening's events, appalling as they had been, might yet be turned to her own advantage.

EIGHT

During the following day Tulla kept very close to the children, sensing that this was where her safety lay. No Biscaglia guard should command her presence again. This was made doubly sure by the insistent though discreet attentions of a smiling young man in reassuring scarlet and gold, a fellow of the sentry who had watched her door all night. For this she must be grateful to Vanozza who knew her duty to her prince.

A further day of such surveillance was passed, much to the diversion of the children. There was also a certain amount of curiosity, not alas about the Virgil that they read in their favorite courtyard.

"Why does he follow you, Madonna?" Bernardo asked forthright.

"I expect he has fallen in love with her," Lucia decided, smiling her blessing upon the suggestion. "Do you like him too, Madonna?"

Tulla smiled gravely. "I have no objection to his presence," she admitted, "but if you are going to stare at him so rudely, Lucia, we shall have to go indoors where you may better concentrate."

"Oh no, that would be cruel." Lucia resolutely placed her stool so that her back was toward the grinning guard. She had a very loud voice.

It was not until the next afternoon that the castle became aware of the sounds of hooves and voices that proclaimed the return of the brothers da Valenti. Tulla was demonstrating the finer points of Tartar horsemanship to the children in the outer bailey when its gates were flung wide and she found

160

herself deserted in mid caracole as her pupils ran to welcome their uncles. This was not how she had hoped matters would be; she would have preferred a quiet interview with Count Francesco. However, so be it. This way would perhaps save time.

The children were already examining the interesting packs upon the small train of sumpter mules that was entering the gates at its own erratic pace. Their faces vivid with the excitement that the thought of the outside world always aroused in them, they plied the steward, the accountant, and the merchant of minerals with questions. Where had they traveled? What had they seen? They had visited Florence? Was Il Magnifico Lorenzo in good health? What was in this package? And this barrel? Had the prince brought back any gifts—?

Tulla waited until both brothers had dismounted before urging her own horse over to where they stood.

"Signor Franco—"

"Madonna Tulla! You are a most refreshing sight. Have your rascals been biddable?"

"The children have borne themselves well. It has not been so with others. Count, I have news of the gravest kind. Will you hear it? I would prefer to speak before you enter the castle."

"What's this, Mona Tulla?" The prince joined them, smiling mischievously. "Are you so enamored of my brother that you importune him before he can cast his spurs?" He spoke with the faintest rueful resentment, which neither caught.

"Madonna has news," Franco said briefly. "Let her speak if you please."

Leone shrugged and was silent, his golden eye sardonic. It had pleased him to see the girl riding out in her gray dress, even if it were only to amuse her charges. It pleased him less that she preferred to ignore his presence beyond the small, stiff nod of the head she had just given him.

"I do not know if it will surprise you, Signori, especially after such events as those of the May feast. It has come to my knowledge that messer Atroviso has cast the prince's horoscope, and at the behest, it seemed, of signor Andrea Zorza. The terms of their speech did not indicate an interest in his welfare."

Franco's look encouraged her. "Continue. How do you know of this?" Leone displayed no reaction. Encouraged by

161

the count's friendly and alert attention, she began to tell her story, stumbling a little with occasional embarrassment but leaving out nothing she considered relevant. When she had finished the brothers exchanged looks of dismay.

"Zorza! Under your very roof!"

"The man's a fool and a braggart. A dreamer of idle dreams. But I do *not* like it when he mishandles my people. He shall be brought to account for that, Madonna."

Tulla stared at him, disbelieving. "Did you not *listen* while I spoke, Prince? The man may perhaps be plotting against your life, not merely seeking the borrowed use of your imagined concubine!" Her face flamed. Words had been the forerunners of thought.

"I doubt if that is true." Leone regarded her gently. "You were drugged, and you say yourself that what you heard was not altogether clear to you. And even were it true, you must know that there are few ways in which he could harm me in my own citadel."

She exclaimed aloud in anger and astonishment so that her horse shook its head and stamped a little. "And if it was he who would have given you poison, killing that poor girl in mistake?" Only now did *this* suspicion fully raise itself. There had been something more than mere callousness in Zorza's attitude to Gianna Bossi's death. But Leone only laughed shortly.

"Then he did not succeed. But I do not believe it was he. It is said in the city that too many men had cast eyes upon poor Gianna Bossi, her husband killed her. He was mad with jealousy, poor fool. Why else would he have killed himself?"

"Is it certain that he killed himself?" Franco asked quietly.

Leone was tired of the subject. "Certain? The one man is dead who knows for sure! However the opinion is that he died at his own hand, and I believe it was so. And now, let us leave this depressing subject and we will show you all manner of marvels from Florence. Bring the children to my chambers."

"Leone!" His brother was terse. "Will you not at least speak to Atrovisò, demand to see this horoscope? He had no right to have cast it. There is mischief enough in the man, God knows. If you act now, he will take the warning. He is intelligent as well as malicious. If not—"

"Then Andrea Zorza will topple my castle about my ears, singlehanded but for a lunatic old warlock who has amused himself at his expense? If you believe this, Franco, you are as weak in the wits as Zorza himself! I thank you for your solicitude, my brother, and you, Madonna Tulla, but I am quite sure it is unnecessary. There is only one thing of mine that touches the interest of the handsome condottiere. That is my wife. Good luck! He may have her with my blessing, if he can get her!"

His laugh remained with them as he strolled off, shouting instructions to the servants upon the disposal of the baggage.

Tulla's face was set. "I thought you told me your brother was a proper man, Signore," she said fiercely. "It is clear to me he has never been other than a child and a foolish one at that. Bernardo is more fit to rule than he!"

"You called me, Madonna?" The boy came toward her, smiling.

She controlled her rage. "Go with Lucia to the prince's apartments. He wants to show you his new toys!"

Bernardo threw her a searching look. It was explained to him later by Lucia that Uncle Leone must have been angry about the amorous guard. It occurred to him that he had preferred his sister when she had thought of nothing but horses.

Franco looked with sympathy at the angry girl on her restless mount, sensing her humiliation. She had expected to be taken seriously and well she might. Her experience must have been terrifying as well as unpleasant, and yet she had spoken little of herself in her brief, careful attempt to warn Leone of real danger.

"I apologize for the prince, Madonna. He is lighthearted because he has enjoyed a pleasant trip and—"

Her words spilled out, the contemptuous product of her disappointment.

"He is *always* lighthearted! And his head is lighter even than his heart. Let Zorza kill him if he will. I care not."

Franco smiled. "Do you not? Then you were doubly generous to give him your warning." He reached up and took her hand in his, looking steadily into her face. "Remember that *I* have listened to you also, and my nature is light neither of heart nor of head. I will take heed for Leone, Mona Tulla, even if he takes none for himself." He pressed her hand and then carried it to his lips in earnest of his words.

Tulla found herself trembling, overwhelmed with the sense of steady reality she obtained from this man, in a world that had become increasingly peopled with such nightmare crea-

163

tures as might appear to a fevered or defective fancy. His cool touch restored the precarious balance that Leone had carelessly toppled and she marshaled her courage to broach the matter that lay now at the center of her thoughts.

"I have given the prince this warning in good faith, signor Franco. I owed him nothing. His death indeed, might be my gain. I ask you again then, in the name of all you hold dear, to be my advocate with him. Beg him in return for my honesty, to let me go. I long for my own country, my lord. My heart is heavy among strangers." A wave of homesickness had engulfed her, so strong that she forgot, for the moment, to what manner of home it was she would go back.

Franco still held her hand in his. He gave it another gentle pressure before he loosed it, for she would not think his next words to be kind. "It is not usual for honesty to ask for a reward," he observed softly. "It surprises me that you seek to bargain with me when I have always shown you my interest. I have put your request to the prince and have twice been refused. There is no point in a further suit. And do you sincerely suppose, Madonna, that if Andrea Zorza were to overthrow my brother and myself as you suggest, that your fate would be anything other than the one he had already designed for you?"

He saw shame flood her face and hastened to banish it. "And is your heart, in truth, so very heavy here with us? Am I still a stranger to you? Are the children strangers? And even Leone, whom you profess to loathe so deeply—can he yet remain a stranger?"

At this last she raised her head, stunned, as he had intended her to be. "I will never allow it to be otherwise," she flashed. It was almost, he thought, as though there might be some danger.

But at least he had driven the lost, wan look from her eyes. Congratulating himself upon this he prepared to follow the prince, indicating with his outstretched arm that she should accompany him.

She was about to turn her horse's head when it was born upon her with a sudden cruel stab of clarity that her new and fragile hope had never been within a hairbreadth of fulfillment. Even had he been remotely affected by her story, Leone would not have let her leave Montevalenti. And Franco, who, it seemed, gave it some credit, would not give her aid. Very well—if none would help her, she must help herself!

Her plan was conceived and brought forth all in the same instant, arriving as malformed and incomplete as might be expected.

Instead of turning her horse toward the stables, where Franco had raised his arm to lead it, she snatched the rein from his grasp and uttered a sudden sharp command to the surprised animal, in the direction of the still open gate where the last of the sumpter mules were ambling in.

There was no outcry behind her. Exultantly she thought that Franco, after all, had let her go. Though where she would go and how she would pay her way, she had not, of course, had time to consider. But even as she reached the open gateway she saw that two of the mules stood across her path, two more behind them. She screamed at them to move, putting all her will, all her strength behind them. But mules, alas, are celebrated for their imperviousness to suggestion; and certainly when they have just turned around to suit one perverse member of the human race, they are unlikely to perform the same service in reverse for another. Tulla's mare, whose intelligence was far better than Asinine, saw the trap and ignored the desperate drumming at her sides. She raced up within an arm's length of the unamused beasts of burden, then caracoled spectacularly, curvetting on delicate hooves toward the left, then resuming a more refined progress. The discomfort at her flanks had ceased. It should not, however, go unpunished. At her chosen point she halted abruptly, threw up her heels and tossed Tulla neatly over her head.

Franco, whose signal to the muleteer had barred the escape, now bit his lip and raced toward the fallen girl. She lay upon her back, her eyes closed, her limbs disposed untidily about her. Franco knelt and began, in the informed manner of the experienced soldier, to search for damage. She stirred at once and opened her eyes. "There is no need, Signore. I have broken no bones," she said hazily, imagining her tone to be one of icy servility.

"Can you sit up?" He raised her tenderly, supporting her back against his shoulder. She groaned inadvertently and closed her eyes again.

"Where is the pain? You fell upon your head, I think."

"My head is perfectly clear, I thank you."

He sighed. "Nevertheless, I shall have my men carry you to your chamber."

"You will do nothing of the sort!" She did not wish her ridiculous attempt to be publicized. "I am quite able to walk." She would never admit to him that her head felt as though the wretched mare had kicked it.

Understanding, he smiled, admiring her foolhardy courage, even now. He searched her tangled hair with gentle, probing fingers. They became sticky. "You have a nasty gash. It is clean enough and will heal well, but I fear you will lose a small amount of your beautiful hair."

She did not reply, and he helped her to rise and walk slowly back into the castle and up to his own chambers, where he washed the wound and applied a soothing ointment.

"What is it?" she demanded sulkily, sniffing at the fresh pungent scent.

"It is called Clown's Woundwort," he observed, somewhat drily. "And now you must be quiet and rest upon my couch. None will disturb you here."

"I have no need of rest. It is a small hurt. The bruises on my limbs will cause me the greatest discomfort tomorrow. Thank you for your care of me, signor Franco," she offered, still subdued.

He thought that she was holding herself off from his friendship. He smiled kindly. "I could wish that you had a better care for yourself." He considered what he might say to help her. He had thought her more resigned to Montevalenti—and perhaps indeed she had been so. Small wonder if that had been reversed by Zorza's brutal actions. Poor child, she must feel that she had no friend in the world, apart from the children. Perhaps indeed, they in their innocence were her best company just at present.

"Come, if you are certain that you will not rest, I will take you to Bernardo and Lucia. They will want to show you their presents. We have been quite prodigal with our gifts."

In his haste to reunite her with the uncomplicated affections of her charges, he had quite forgotten his brother.

The room resembled the decks of a pirate galley that had just taken its richest prize. Every possible surface gleamed with booty. Tables, couches, the floor, even the balcony rail were hung with shimmering stuffs in clamoring jewel colors, spiked with the wonderful objects to which they were acting as brilliant foils: a small dagger set with turquoise; exquisite tiny shoes in scarlet leather leafed in gold; a spinning top gilded and set with faceted colored glass to catch the light; an almond-eyed doll dressed in Chinese robes of painted satin. A lace fan; a fine leather belt.

"Ah, Byzantium! How slowly one may work if one is truly determined," Leone observed from where he sat enthroned at the center of it all, a length of Asia silk draped about him after the fashion of a Roman toga. "Enter the cave of the djinn and choose your heart's desire!" He beckoned Tulla with a finger that wore a ruby and a great pearl, and she moved obediently forward. Her mouth was, however, half open to say that she would leave and return later for the children, when she caught sight of Lucia, sucking blissfully upon a striped sugar-stick and wearing a white gown sewn with pink rosebuds that had brought her to ecstasy and made her look like a newly fledged angel. It would have been impossible to walk away from such a smile of pure happiness.

"Look here Mona Tulla! *Prende guarda!*" Bernardo, a finely tooled Florentine sword belt around his slender loins, was flourishing a sword exactly suited to his height and weight. "It has a Toledo blade and a Tuscan pommel. There is none better. And messer Julio of the Guard is to teach me the positions, the strokes and ripostes. I already know some of them. Uncle Leone, give me a *'coda lunga'*."

Leone seized upon his own sword, which lay where he had cast it off atop a pile of books and leapt gracefully to obey his nephew's request.

"See! The *becca cesa!*" Obligingly, Leone let his steel be beaten down.

"Ah, but do you know the *cinghiari di ferro altro against* the *becca cesa?*" he asked, demonstrating the stroke. "Remember, for every stroke you learn, there will be an opponent who has learned one more. And it will be that one which is the only one that counts!"

"Then I shall learn all there is to learn," said Bernardo with optimistic simplicity. "Messer Julio says that *you* know everything already. Will you also give me lessons sometimes?"

"I will examine your progress from time to time if you wish," the prince agreed. "And now get you gone, you and your sister. I wish to discuss a private matter with Mona Tulla."

Lucia giggled outrageously and ran to be kissed before racing happily off with her booty, her embarrassed brother, even more heavily laden, in her wake. Franco, from his vantage point near the doorway where he had been studying the company, gave a delicate cough. "You will find me in the study should you need me, Leone." And with a respectful bow to them both, he left the hopeful runaway with her master.

Tulla would have given much to follow him. Alone with the prince, she was a prey to a confusing and disagreeable jumble of emotions. Apart from that chaste whisper of a kiss in Franco's library, he had been true to his word and had not molested her in any way since the May banquet. There was no reason in the world why she should feel any gratitude for this; on the other hand such a *lack* of insult and humiliation did nothing to feed the necessary fires of her hatred. And her hatred was important to her. It maintained a simple opposition of the main forces of her life—her interior wishes and the exterior powers. She had already exempted the count and the children from this easy equation. If Leone himself were to show even the faintest sign of beginning to slip away from it also, then the confusion that constantly threatened her margins would be total.

"Do not hold yourself so stiffly," counseled the object of her fears with a harmless amiability. "I wish only to make you a present also. It comes to you from one who cannot be with us today, but he sends you his kindest wishes and hopes you will set some value upon his work."

Mystified and more than a little disconcerted, Tulla watched him take up an oblong shape covered in a dark cloth. A mirror perhaps, but from whom? And why for her?

With the legerdemain of the mountebank magician Leone effected the disappearance of the dark cloth. Facing her was her own image, its truth deeper than any mirror could reveal, made with the hard, sweet line of Alessandro Botticelli. She recognized its fineness at once, though she did not mistake its beauty for her own. She made no attempt to speak but stood and looked and was humbled by so close an approach to perfection.

Tears stood in her eyes when at last she said quietly, "The followers of the Prophet believe that no man should attempt to imitate the creation of God's creatures, whether human or animal. Only Allah, they say, can make them in their blessed wholeness. When I look upon this, it comes to me that they say this because it is a fearful thing for a man to come near to emulating God. Perhaps they fear His jealousy. If it is true, I think He may well be jealous of Sandro Botticelli."

"You do yourself credit, Madonna," the Prince said gently. "I sense your meaning, though I believe in no jealous gods. Nor, I think do you. As for the painting, it is as fine a thing as Sandro has done. He tells me he could not concentrate on his Venus and Mars until he had completed it, so great was his pleasure in it. He begs me to say that any merit it has is purely that of its subject, though you, Madonna, have recognized where its true excellence lies. Sandro is one of those who make Florence great."

Tulla nodded, surveying the portrait wonderingly. Her face looked out in three-quarter profile, the head bent a little, giving her an air of gentle contemplation that Leone found revealing in its novelty. There was no challenge, no alertness to danger in the beautiful, dreaming face, only a secure serenity and a kind of latent expectation as though the dreamer might look up at any moment and see the prospect of her dream made flesh. It was timeless, enchanted, eternally fresh.

Leone, looking from the portrait to its inspiration, knew that upon the canvas he had seen her true nature for the first time. It had taken Sandro's art to show him how she should look—warm, confident and unafraid. This was how she must have appeared to her family, her friends and her people in distant Soraya, before fortune had taken her for its innocent plaything. He experienced an overwhelming desire to see her regain this truth that was before them. More than once he had wished to see her smile—out of selfishness perhaps, he could not tell.

Now it became important to him to see her not only smiling, but truly happy. He wracked his brain to see how it could be accomplished. "It seems as much of the spirit as of the flesh," he heard her say hesitantly, as she shyly followed her own contours and recesses with astonished eyes.

"Sandro loves to wrap himself and his work in the mysteries of Plato," he offered. "He seeks to portray a woman's beauty in terms of the soul as well as of the body. It is the quality of *desio*—the soul's longing for the Ideal Good—that he looks for in a face. I think he has found it in yours, Madonna Tulla."

She moved away from him a step. His words disturbed her. She preferred his mockery; it did not bring him so close.

This gift, although it came from Sandro himself, the fruit of their morning together in the herb garden, was too precious a thing for her to accept without difficulty. It was no such trifle as a green silk gown. Yet its very greatness precluded petty refusal. Though she did not wish to be beholden, she knew she must disregard her doubts.

"I give you thanks, Prince," she said quietly, "and I beg you to convey my deep gratitude and admiration to messer Botticelli. I hope," she added uncertainly, "that I may perhaps soon have the opportunity of expressing them in person."

Here at least was a small thing he might give her. "Assuredly. You will meet Sandro again at the Medici tournament. I believe you wish to see it? It will be my pleasure to ensure that you do." It gave him satisfaction to see her surprise.

"I—shall be glad to see it, my lord." It could not be more strange, more ironic; would he hold out the key to her freedom with his captor's hand?

His eyes narrowed. "A brief word of warning." He smiled. "My young heirs will doubtless be cluttering your skirts on that occasion. Keep your eyes on them as closely as you may. Children are notoriously apt to lose themselves at such festivities."

It was quite clear to her that he was not, in truth, discussing the children. "I will endeavor to do so," she murmured. She would not look at him.

"Indeed I hope no member of my household will be so inconsiderate as to lose himself," Leone added firmly.

She smiled a little at his insistence. "If he did so, my lord, I am sure that he would afterward find his way—home."

"Home being where *he* has left his heart?" he enquired sardonically, wondering if he were a fool in this matter. He thought of her risk, not his own. "You understand me, I think?" he concluded gently.

"I do," she admitted, still looking anywhere other than at Leone. Her promise to such a man could mean nothing of course, and yet how she would hate to have him know her forsworn. Better not to swear. Her confusion was increased when the prince caught up a bolt of pale golden silk from a table, and another of heavy Venetian lace.

"Here. Gild yourself for the tournament like the rest," he cried cheerfully. "Tell Vanozza she is to use the very best seamstress. Giuliano gives the joust to honor Beauty. Can the Prince of the Valenti do less than honor it also? Your loveliness will enhance this poor silk so that even the keenest merchant will rather kiss his fingers to you than use them to work out the price of your gown!"

PART TWO

Quant e bella giovinezza,
che si fugge tuttavia!
Chi vuol esser lieto, sia;
di doman non c'e certezza.

Fair is youth and void of sorrow;
But it hourly fades away—
Youths and maids enjoy today;
Nought ye know about tomorrow.

NINE

She could not believe her ears. Without any semblance of mockery he was making speeches to her that the most hopeful of her former suitors, all of them satraps with tongues of honey, would not think unworthy. Her thoughts were like blown leaves. How does one deal with a man who will not acknowledge one's enmity, when that enmity is all that still attaches one to the rags of one's pride?

He had placed the shining bolts upon a chest. She shook her head, gesturing toward them. "Your Excellence is more than kind, but I cannot take them."

He smiled. "You will take the greater gift, but not the lesser? Come now, Madonna, surely that is less than gracious."

Her head was beginning to ache. His speech was as full of traps as a game tract. "It is not that—"

"Then what?"

She wished herself a million miles away from him and his unsolicited kindness. "I do not wish to take gifts—personal gifts—from the man who keeps me captive," she achieved with difficulty.

He made a gesture of impatience. "You do not scruple to eat at my table. And you will easily admit that you must have clothes as well as food. So—?"

Her instinct for flight became unbearable.

He came closer, stretching his hand to touch her shoulder. "I think I understand," he said, his voice low and newly harsh. "It is the personal element you dislike." He raised the hand to her hair, cupping the back of her head gently to draw her nearer to him. The throbbing in her temples increased. She felt hot, almost feverish. "It is because of this dislike that

I have not pressed you beyond what you can bear—though you can bear rather more than you might think." His eyes demanded honesty of her, but her gaze fell and she bent her head to turn his hand aside. She succeeded only in shifting it to her neck, where the sensitive fingers gentled and stroked as though he comforted a horse or a child. She trembled, her pain pressing on her, though less than the burden that she sensed he offered her.

Again she was swept by the strange currents that his fingers could conjure, as though her body had developed an errant imagination of its own. At any rate it would not obey her clouding mind.

"My lord, I *cannot* bear it!" she cried, her voice attenuated with misery, her eyes imploring at last.

To her amazement, Leone, after looking into her tormented face for a dragging moment, nodded slightly as though he were well satisfied, and let her go.

To her chagrin she reeled as though she had relied upon the support of his hand.

"You are not well?" Instantly she had it again, her arm in his firm grip, his face solicitous. It was enough! She *must* have an end to this mummery. She clapped a hand to her beating temples and, tearing herself from him, ran from the room without the formality of farewells.

It was as though they rode through a field of flowers, to whom God, in sudden divine eccentricity, had given voices. Florence had been brought to the perfection of her blooming at the loving hands of her young merchant princes and today she exhibited—for them, for the world at large, and, since Narcissus was not least among her blossoms, for her own satisfaction, the fullest expression of that perfection.

Even as they wound down among the soft green and golden hills that cradled the city, shawled in a translucent amber light, it became clear that this was no ordinary day. The broad, curving ribbon of the Arno carried a traffic that was Venetian in its density, as every manner of small craft plied on busy self-important journeys, transporting the merchandise out of which carnivals are made. Flags and banners flew from bowsprits and masts, and lined each of the four bridges; the Ponte Vecchio especially, with its crammed and crowded houses and shops, bristled like a hedgehog stuck with millefiori, with the gonfalons of its artisans' guilds, the banners of the

174

Medici, and the bright flags of the children. Feudal towers displayed the devices of ancient families. The splendid new palazzo of the Pitti flaunted an insolent challenge to Brunelleschi's magnificent dome of the cathedral, vaulting high and bold as ambition itself to astonish the eye and give wings to the spirit.

Tulla caught her breath as they descended into the joyful streets. To set eyes upon Florence for the first time must be unforgettable whatever the day, but to see her thus, veiled in sunlight and gowned in her own flowers like a bride dressed for her lover, was an experience beyond the limitations of a mere five senses.

Their cavalcade was pelted with blossoms as it steered an erratic passage across the Ponte Alle Grazie, finding itself swept along by a crowd of masked dancers wearing ingenious costumes of paper and buckram, simulating various flowers. Their multicolored banner proclaimed them to be the Arte del Profumo, the guild of perfume makers, who accompanied their dancing feet with the song that Lorenzo had written for them:

"Girls, we've bottles as long as your hand.
If you don't believe it, feel them, they're grand!
To warm them must be your intent;
Then soon they will spill out their scent!"

They swept the Prince of the Valenti and his train, half suffocated by a cloud of their own wares, along the broad Via de' Benci and into the Piazza Santa Croce, where the tournament was to be held. Only the most illustrious members of their party might enter the cordoned-off area, massively guarded by the Bargello di Città, whose unhopeful duty it was to police the occasion. Tulla could not repress a smile of pleasure in return for the many admiring cries as she left her saddle and, with an exultant and popeyed child upon either hand, made her straight-backed, silken progress into the enclosure behind the prince and his brother. They were quite alone. The members of the Biscaglia clan had, as was their habit, formed their own cortege, traveling ahead of the Valenti, so that Tulla, after the initial embarrassment that recurred each time she came into Leone's company, was able to look about her with pleasure in both the journey and the country-side, unadulterated by apprehension.

Her first impression had been that Florence was unexpectedly small; she realized that she had been comparing it not with any other city but with its own reputation, which had indeed outgrown that of any town in Italy at this time. She was delighted to find it so compact and complete. It spread like a circle of lace upon the plain, displaying the open work of the broad squares and palaces, interlaced with the thread of the river's blue, and the cobweb of intimate streets about the great cathedral at its heart. This last was as small and intricate in design as little Montevalenti, wrapped close to the clouds about its parent rock.

The Piazza Santa Croce was accustomed to public spectacle. When the graceful little thirteenth-century church at its head had become too small to accommodate the numerous faithful, the Franciscan friars had preached *al fresco* before its door. The great St. Bernadino of Siena had been the most notable of them and the most popular. "Italy is the most intelligent country in Europe," he would begin his sermon, "and Tuscany the most intelligent region in Italy, and Florence the most intelligent town in Tuscany." In case such sentiments should go to the heads of his intelligent congregation, he was careful to add, "But where noble gifts are allied to malice, you find the most evil of men."

Upon less holy occasions the piazza became the people's playground. The four quarters of the town challenged each other to games of *calcio,* the football beloved of the male population and thundered dangerously around the circumscribed course of the *palio,* the horse race which, if anything, caused an even greater amount of feminine impatience.

Everyone, however, loved a tournament. Long ago these had been held annually in the square, and Lorenzo had recently revived the tradition, celebrating his twentieth birthday with a splendid joust in honor of his forthcoming marriage to Clarice Orsini (who happily could not be present) and of his beautiful mistress, Lucrezia Donati.

If it was doubtful on that occasion, that anyone had remembered Clarice Orsini, it was certain that, upon this, no one spared more than a passing thought for the treaty between Florence and Venice. The day was dedicated to Love and Beauty, personified with exquisite fitness by Giuliano I Superbo and the transcendent Simonetta Vespucci.

The lists had been erected during the night and took up the greater part of the square, separated from the impatient, jostling crowd by painted wooden partitions bearing the arms and devices of the participants. It was usual for the younger members of the society to occupy the stands behind this barrier, while their elders watched from the more civilized vantage points of windows and balconies. Il Magnifico, however, had elected to join the politer element of the crowd upon the coveted central stand, and Leone, as his invited guest, would do the same.

"Wonderful!" exclaimed Bernardo, as they thrust their way to the space delineated by the Medici banners. "We shall see everything and yet be a part of it too!"

"Remember, you are not to stray!" Tulla counseled with a certain amount of regretful irony. The crowd was vast and restless enough, it was true, to swallow up a whole regiment of determined small boys, but would it so easily accommodate a single, foreign woman who would be totally lost the moment she left the square? And if she, while present, would do her duty in keeping a severe eye upon Bernardo and Lucia, might not one of their party, equally, take note of her own disappearance?

Yet this day presented, perhaps, her only chance. It was imperative that she take it. But it was not, had she ever imagined it, going to be easy. There had been small possibility of planning the details of escape. It seemed now, as she climbed to where Il Magnifico waited to greet his friends, that there was even less.

A roar of acclaim went up as Lorenzo embraced the Prince of the Valenti. It seemed that Leone was both known and loved in Florence. Everyone was dressed to be seen that day and the prince was no exception. His doublet was flame-colored, stamped with golden lilies in compliment to the city. Soft boots of gold-dyed leather covered scarlet-clad calves, and a totally unnecessary cloak of pure white, gilded with couchant lions and lined with the expensive fur of some spotted creature from a colder climate, was flung elegantly from one shoulder. As he bent his tawny head to Lorenzo's dark one and clasped him affectionately by the shoulders, he looked like a peacock "displaying" before a crow, Tulla thought, amused. Lorenzo, content to leave color and *éclat* to others, was dressed in his favorite black, imposing it was true, in taffeta and quilted velvet, but his jewels, as always, were sparse and his manner collected. In the midst of such a commotion of color and cries, where each man

177

attempted to outdo his neighbor, he drew the eye like a target.

At his right hand stood a woman who now stretched out her hand for Leone's kiss. Above middle height, she had a fair skin and a tinge of red in her light brown hair. Her face was too round for beauty, though her expression was serene and pleasant. Her neck, which she held bent slightly forward, was well shaped, however, and the hand which Leone held was long and delicate.

"God give you good health, Prince. We have heard news of you which has concerned us. I hope all is now in order in the matter of the baker's masterpiece?"

"Ill news and idle chatter travel fast, Madonna Clarice. As you see I am in excellent health and spirits and propose to remain so—as long as my lady does not intend to scold me throughout the day."

Clarice Orsini smiled gravely. "There's no gain to be had in that, my friend, as I know to the cost of my time and my temper."

It was obvious that she spoke quite seriously, and Tulla was intrigued. She had heard from Lucia, as great a gossip as any of her elders, that Lorenzo's marriage had not been popular in Florence. Chosen by his mother, the gifted Lucrezia Tornabuoni, whom his grandfather Cosimo had once sourly described as "the only man in the house," for her good sense and the robust health that might help to eradicate the family curse of gout from the Medici, Clarice came of a noble Roman family, replete with cardinals, generals, and condottieri. The Palazzo Orsini in Rome was the first in a long line of fortresses leading north to Florence; nothing could be more secure for Florentine trade. But as every Florentine knows, no Roman, however noble, can hold a candle to the lowest Tuscan peasant, and they looked upon Clarice's bent head and unremarkable features with superior distaste.

Now Franco too had greeted her, and she had turned toward the children. "But here is another to be welcomed! Why have you not presented the lady, my friends? Is she one of your cousins whom you have been hiding until she was grown up?"

There was a spurt of unforgivable laughter from Leone, and even Lorenzo was provoked to a slow smile.

"Madonna, it is this way. The children—"

"Allow me, signor Franco. It would be my pleasure to present the lady." The harsh voice of Il Magnifico was pleasantly firm. "This is Madonna Tulla, my dear. She is a

Venetian connection of the family. Is that not so, Leone? She now makes her home at Montevalenti and has taken Bernardo and Lucia under her gentle wing." He held out his hand, and Tulla moved up two or three steps to make her curtsy, the children beside her.

"I am glad to see you, my dear," Clarice said kindly. "It is time you two ran less wild about your mountainsides." But she sugared her words with comfits taken from her pocket, and her smile was especially warm for Lucia.

All were now gathered into the Medici circle and the next minutes were a confusion of introductions and courtesies, names and titles, which Tulla did not hope to remember. She was full of gratitude to Lorenzo, however, and doing her best to behave like a visiting Valenti, soon found that she had relaxed until she was nothing more or less than herself.

"I do not see the principessa, your wife," she heard Clarice murmur as they took their places upon the cushioned benches set down before the lists.

"She likes to look down upon me," Leone observed cheerfully. "You will see her, should you care to look, dear Clarice, across to the third balcony on the right. As ever she is in better and holier hands than mine!"

Tulla also looked up, without moving her head, and saw them at once.

Alessandra Biscaglia sat, like the waxen image of the newly dead which one finds in a family church, still and cool and unaffected by the rising tumult beneath. She seemed not to see the riotous square, the waving pennants, the popinjay clothes; not to hear the bawdy songs, the bellowed greetings, the snorts of impatient horses behind the lists, the provocative clatter of steel as the first contestants laced on their armor; nor to notice the mingled warm sense of perfume and sweat, fruit and savory sausage that climbed upon the bright air. She sat, in her white gown, beneath her wolf's head banner, her brother's scarlet sleeve resting upon her shoulder, and conversed with him as intimately as if they were in her closet at Montevalenti. Behind them, gorgeous to the point of discomfort in aquamarine and rose, Andrea Zorza surveyed the scene with a practiced disdain, underlined by the negligent manner in which he tossed his orange peel over the finely wrought railing. Beneath the careful insouciance, excitement raged in him as though he were about to take a coveted woman. The enforced hours of foolishness ahead would pass so slowly as to be a refined form of torture.

Something of the quality of a leashed animal in the man communicated itself to Tulla, and she turned away, not wishing to court the memory of his hands upon her body. She found that Franco, seated at her side, was watching her.

"A strange man, Madonna," he mused. "So much the soldier and the courtier and yet so ill at ease in his own skin."

"He will doubtless be comfortable enough when he has flayed your brother and wears his hide instead," Tulla replied tartly.

"You do him too much honor, I assure you. His powers are a great deal more circumscribed than his desires. Do not mistake me. I believe that he intends harm to Leone and will make some foolish attempt. I have, however, made certain dispositions of my own. We are for instance quite surrounded by our own men and have been so since we entered the city. All are men for whose loyalty I'd go surety with my own life."

"You are wise, my lord."

"Why thank you, Madonna." His tone was urbane.

"It is a pity your brother is a fool," she could not forbear to add.

He sighed. In some ways he agreed with her. "Do not let it concern you further, Mona Tulla. Enjoy the tournament. They say God looks after the fools of this world."

"They also say," she replied grimly, with a lethal glance in the direction of the third right balcony, "that the Devil takes care of his own. Though in this case, surely he must be hard put to it to know how to choose!"

There was a tug at her sleeve. "You must look, Mona Tulla! You must not miss the beginning!" Lucia and her brother, incapable of sitting down or even keeping still, raced up to warn them of the opening of the joust, then fled back to hang over the barrier before they could be ordered otherwise.

Those who were lucky enough to possess seats now left their groups of friends and took them, the Prince of the Valenti in the place of honor on the right of Lorenzo de Medici at the center of the front row of benches. Behind him, a little to his left, sat his ever-watchful brother, with Tulla upon his left. On every side were crowded the perfumed, chattering members of Lorenzo's following. Many were both sumptuously clad and muscular young men so that Tulla began to realize that the watchfulness was not Franco's alone.

There was a commanding blare of trumpets, and her attention was claimed by the lists. There was a swelling rumor of anticipation as the gate at one end of the arena swung open. This crescendoed to an earsplitting roar as a single horseman rode into view; then every breath was exhaled upon a current of swooning admiration. Giuliano de Medici wore his armor of pure silver as lightly and gracefully as his twenty-one years. A helmet of the same metal, fantastically carved and molded into the interwoven forms of animals and flowers and surmounted by a small winged cherub blowing a horn, sat splendidly upon the dark curling hair which touched his straight square shoulders. His horse, caparisoned in dozens of *"palle"* and whole fields of lilies, was white, male, and mettlesome, its eye glossy, its step high. In his right hand he carried a standard. Necks craned to see. It bore neither the Medici arms nor those of the city, but a painting, a portrait of a beautiful woman accoutered with the helmet and arms of Pallas Athene, sprung from Jove's brow into a green Tuscan meadow sewn with flowers. Her beauty was as instantly recognizable as was the work of the artist who had captured it. It was the portrait of Simonetta Vespucci by Alessandro Botticelli.

The crowd threw its sanity into the resounding air. This was their best beloved son, their paragon, their Giuliano! They gave their respect and yes, a great measure of love also, to Lorenzo who was their prince, the first among them, but they kept the greater part of their hearts for this younger brother—for his rare beauty and proud accomplishment, and above all, for the charismatic charm and hopeful promise that symbolized, for each and every one of them, the superlative nature of their triumphant city.

Il Superbo made a single, meticulous circle of the arena and then came to a halt beneath a balcony directly opposite the Medici enclosure. The group of bright faces and rich materials thereon parted like the well-trained members of a dance, and there was a sudden, almost impossible fall of silence as the hundreds hung upon a single breath and waited.

Her beauty was that of one who has already been marked out by the gods and was the beauty of their world, not of ours, not even of the sublime Florence. Speak of golden hair and an oval countenance, of perfect proportion and a gentle mien, a shape to stir the heart and a smile to spring tears—this is not to speak of Simonetta Vespucci. Her quality was one so universal that all men recognized it, though few could have given it a name. What they saw in her was the reassurance, that the body and the soul would at last become one, that all lusts will become love, that all desire will be fulfilled. And so, although they did not know that this was what they felt, they sensed, in part, what Sandro would one day apprehend wholly, and stood for a moment before this modestly smiling young girl in silence; and a few, perhaps, also sensing the jealousy of the gods, in tears.

And then she had thrown him a scarlet lily, and he had caught it and kissed his fingers to her and stuck it under his helmet. His horse had caracoled appealingly before her and raced off down the lists. The gates opened once more, and a stream of brilliantly clad men and horses careered after their leader. The spectators rediscovered their voices and the trumpets sounded again. The contestants circled the piazza in a fine show of bravado and expensive clothing for horse and man. The jousting would now begin.

Tulla, who had followed the mood of the Florentines with her understanding if not with her uncommitted heart, had been very near to tears herself at the sight of the adoration of Botticelli's platonic ideal of beauty made flesh. She was smartly dissuaded from any such softening by the ensuing spectacles, all much alike, involving half a ton of metal-clad horse and man crashing headlong into another at a combined speed that endangered the life and limbs of both. Few lances could or did withstand the impact, and the sanded square was soon streamed with shivered spears. Many of the splendid young gallants lost their composure and their helmets, though none, happily, their lives. Bruises and dishevelment were the order of the day rather than blood and dishonor. The tourney was no longer the place to air one's private grievance, and no man present rode against his enemy. Indeed after the first few contests, interest waned somewhat in all but the obsessed, and people began to walk about and visit their friends to show off their festive dress, to eat and drink, to pursue a love affair or share a joke. Among the wanderers were Sandro Botticelli, his face permanently rosy from receiving compliments upon his banner and Luigi Pulci, protecting a bottle of red wine carefully against careless elbows. In company, it seemed, with half the city, they came to present their compliments to Giuliano's family and to pass on and acquire the latest gossip. Lorenzo, at the time of their arrival, had his arm about the shoulders of a lad of about his brother's age, whose lank brown hair, aquiline nose, and faintly sneering expression did nothing to explain such obvious affection. Sandro went at once to join them, but Luigi with a muttered, "Hold me excused!" looked about for more congenial company.

"Madonna Tulla! I am more than delighted to see you here." He bounded toward her and seated himself upon her left. "Am I to understand that Il Leone has relaxed his strictures upon streetwalking?" he inquired, good humor depriving the question of insult.

"I rather think I may not walk. But I am permitted the run of this enclosure," Tulla replied. "I am glad to see you also, messer Pulci. This occasion should furnish you with a fine foundation for verse."

Pulci grinned. "Perhaps. My brother Luca may beat me to it. He has already got out his first line. And then there is Lorenzo's Sunday poet yonder." He bent a derisive thumb in the direction of Il Magnifico's companion.

"Who is the young man? He has not the look of a courtier—nor," she smiled, "in my slender experience, that of a poet."

Pulci comforted himself with a swig from his bottle. Then he wiped the top of it with his cherry red mantle, offering it to Tulla. "It is Agnolo Poliziano," he said as she shook her head, "Firenze's own living reincarnation of Ancient Greece—ancient Rome, too, for that matter. He speaks Greek and Latin better than he speaks Italian and is generally regarded as the finest classical scholar we have, which he is," he admitted, sniffing, truth overcoming envy.

"But you do not like him? Why?"

"Because he has no humor, and Lorenzo needs men about him who will ease his burden with laughter—men such as your prince. And because he has a perpetual hole in his pocket! As a student of seventeen he sent Il Magnifico a begging letter, asking for a robe and a pair of shoes. Lorenzo sent two robes and more! And young Agnolo, seeing his pasta well oiled, writes back his thanks in such sagacious verse that Lorenzo, taken with his scholarship no less than his cheek, invites him into the Medici household! And there he has remained, with Calliope and Melpomene chained to his elbow, ever since."

"And do you, therefore, seek to enlist Thalia in your own course, messer Luigi? I warn you—it is possible she was wrongly named."

"Madonna?" He was clearly puzzled.

She laughed. "Nothing, Messere; it is only that my parents,

inviting gladness to our house, as signor Lorenzo invites poets and scholars, named me for the muse of comedy. As far as I am able to tell," she added, "the invitation was refused. It is just as well that my father preferred to call me Tulla."

A sickening weariness overtook her as thoughts of her family came crowding in. The packed and seething square, the clattering knights and waving banners seemed suddenly to represent the meaningless, undirected, and patternless chaos that her life had become. Pulci spoke gently. She did not hear him. She sat staring into the milling throng before the enclosure, only half seeing, her mind in another world, the world to which she *must* return. And then, beyond all reason, part of that world was suddenly with her, materialized before her eyes as though her thoughts had conjured it. A troop of musicians was weaving through the crowd at the foot of the stand; dressed in hooded robes and outlandish masks with the faces of demons, they sent up a wild, alien strain on their instruments—a drum leading; trumpets, fifes, symbols, a bagpipe—and something which, passing before Tulla's glazed eyes, sliced through her inertia, to be instantly recognized. It was a short slender pipe of bone, used by the mountain tribesmen of her father's country—not as an instrument of music, but of death!

She could not have recorded the impulse which hurled her out of her seat and sent her reeling to the ground before the stands. Her own surprise was as deep as her disgust when she found herself, winded, confused, in total disarray, lying with her face in the dust with the greater part of her body thrown across that of the Prince of the Valenti! Swift hands assisted them amid a babble of voices. There came a louder cry. "My God! He is dead!"

Tulla stared at Leone, now on his feet beside her, his arm, though she did not realize it, supporting her.

"Then who—?"

But the wave of interest flowed behind them now, to the row behind Leone's empty seat. A young man lay thrown across the bench like a discarded effigy from one of the day's processions. He might have seemed asleep had his position been more comfortable. He was indeed dead.

"It was this that killed him." Franco, kneeling beside the body, held up a tiny, red feathered shaft. "Its tip is as fine as a needle. It took him in the throat. He can have known nothing of it, poor lad. I think we will find it carries poison." He

184

wrapped the dart gingerly in someone's kerchief and placed it in his purse.

He raised his eyes to his brother's. "It was meant for you, Leone."

There was quiet.

Leone coughed delicately and surveyed Tulla, his arm still steadying her for she still trembled. "It seems that Madonna thought so at any rate," he observed, his own composure as complete as though it had never been disturbed. Tulla could not believe that this was the truth of it. She pulled herself together.

"I am not certain what were my intentions, Prince. Events were too swift. I think that I simply understood where the pipe might be aimed and launched myself in that direction." She sounded ungracious before the craning court, she knew. But she could not bear to have him think—

"Whatever your motive, Madonna—and who can know the workings of the heart under such duress—you have saved my life and I give you my thanks." His bow, a simple inclination of his body, without flourish, no hand upon the heart, was perfect in its grace and humility, and she found herself bound to acknowledge it with her own lowered head. A sigh wafted about them. It was a moment that the onlookers would treasure, another bright jewel in a gaudy day.

Leone smiled about him a little and then took Tulla firmly by the elbow and re-established her in her seat, himself at her side.

A certain determined reserve in his countenance, rarely called upon, made it clear both to well-wishers and to the curious, that he wished to be undisturbed. Even Bernardo, who had raced up with eyes shining with excitement, was given a quiet, "Not now, my boy. Uncle Franco will tell you all about it."

Tulla kept her eyes in front of her, where the tournament still progressed. Only the immediate section of the crowd had noticed anything untoward, and they, together with the members of the Montevalenti guard, were desperately struggling among the watchers and other revelers in pursuit of the mountebank musicians. It was a hopeless task, for the masks and cowls had long been discarded, and the players, whoever they had been, now mingled in motley freedom in the best disguise of all, that of the tree amid the forest.

Leone too sought with a keen eye for a moment or two, then

185

shook his head and turned his attention to the girl beside him.

"You appear to regret your superb instinct on my behalf," he said experimentally, seeing her rigid mouth.

"I don't wish to discuss the matter."

"No? Then upon what subject shall we discourse? The relative merits of the knight of the banner of the bear yonder, and he of the three gold coronets—or are they hedgehogs—an unfortunate confusion. Or shall we speak of the beauties of Florence, the ebullience of her citizens, the generosity and wisdom of her ruler—"

"If we are to speak of the wisdom of princes, pray excuse me," Tulla said with all the court manners of a fishwife. "I scarcely comprehend how one who shows himself so lacking in that quality, can be capable of recognizing it in another."

He studied her without obvious reaction, rather as if he wondered whether she too might not turn out to be a hedgehog. "I suppose if a lady saves one from death she may be allowed a brief lecture," he sighed settling himself more comfortably, though failing to remove the arm that lay innocently along the back of her seat. "Pray tell me in what respect I lack wisdom."

His utter insincerity of tone added to the unmerciful discomfort and invidiousness of her position. She wished, how fervently she wished she had not noticed the man with the blowpipe, or having seen him, that she had stayed in her seat. And then since he had asked her, she answered him.

"Does it demonstrate wisdom for the ruler of a state to dedicate himself to his own pleasures and leave ruling to his brother? Is it wise for a man to allow his wife to live a life of her own, among preferred companions who are his enemies? Is it wisdom or weakness always to seek the love of your people, never their fear? Has it been wise, after there have been two known attempts upon your life, to court another knowingly? Was it wise, was it kind," and here she rounded upon him, her whole being rigid with contempt, "being aware that this attempt would be made, to endanger the lives of your heirs, of your brother, your friends—of Il Magnifico Lorenzo himself?"

He regarded her silently for a space, his look unfathomable.

His words, when they came, were calm, and he appeared unaware of opprobrium.

"I will take your points one by one, Madonna, and answer them with questions of my own. First, does it seem to you

186

that a man must follow a profession for which nature did not intend him, simply because he is the older of two brothers? Especially when the same profession is so manifestly suited to the younger? Secondly, if a man and his wife have proved that they are sadly at odds in one another's company, shall they be forced to suffer each other like a cat and a dog tied up in a sack? And shall my wife, who cannot abide me, choose her friends from among my friends? As to the love of my people—I cannot answer for that. If I have it, I am glad of it. I am not aware that I consciously seek it. Certainly I do not desire their fear, nor that of any man, or woman! And if it is wise to seek it, I must admit, in this one matter, to a lack of wisdom. And if I do not want my people to walk in fear, neither in answer to your next point, do I wish to do so myself. All princes hold their lives in danger simply by the fact of their birth. It is an inherited condition. It holds as little fear for me as the fact that I have my mother's smile or my father's eyebrows. You say there have been attempts upon my life. Perhaps so, perhaps not. Possibly three, possibly none. Who knows? The result is that I remain upon this earth, seated comfortably—in a physical sense at least—upon this bench and can admire your very fine eyes." He grinned at the furious impatience that sentenced him from their indigo depth.

"As for your last accusation," his tone hardened a fraction, "my heirs are the children of a ruling family, as is my brother. My friends are the friends of that family. The same may be said of Lorenzo. I repeat once more. And you, who are yourself a daughter of a ruling house, must surely find it simple enough to understand. The ruler lives in danger. Even his brother cannot take that burden from him. The prince accepts the danger because he can do no other. Ask Lorenzo whether he would miss a tournament for fear of the threatened danger of an assassin! He will give you the same answer as mine. He will give you his presence because he is a prince."

His words had not touched her in her fastness of anger and contempt.

"Do you, then, compare yourself with Il Magnifico?" she challenged. "It is not he who plays the gallant with another man's wife and wastes his substance in empty entertainment. If you had been born a Medici, Prince, I think you would have been a Giuliano not a Lorenzo."

"To be either is doubtless felicitous, but I would rather be myself, with Madonna's permission. Certainly, however, if I were to choose, I'd prefer Il Superbo's existence—as you have noted, Lorenzo carries too much responsibility on his back for my liking. I, of course, with my complete lack of backbone, can scarcely support the weight of my doublet."

Before she could interrupt he added in quite a different tone, "One thing, Mona Tulla, you must not underestimate the value of public show. What you call 'empty entertainment' has its place in the government of a city within a state. A display such as we see today reassures the populace that their masters prosper, that the state is solvent. And in aligning themselves with a guild, or with a quarter of the town and indulging in competitions for pleasure, as they do upon all of these holidays, they lessen the likelihood of faction and bloodshed—and even of the assassination of a prince. It needs no wisdom to see the truth of this."

She could see that in this he was right, as also in his statement of the inherent danger of leadership. She had the unacceptable sense that, all in all, he had slipped from the noose of her argument. Since she would not reply, he offered her the magnanimous smile one extends to the empty-handed hangman.

"I will leave you now to the congratulations of the multitude," he said brightly. "I do hope that you will banish that unbecoming frown before poor Sandro Botticelli is ambushed by it!" He saluted her and sauntered over to rejoin Lorenzo. Relieved of his company, she would have liked to have remained alone, but she saw that the artist was indeed approaching and hastily summoned a welcoming smile.

"Messer Sandro! God give you good health! I have been looking forward to offering my thanks for your drawing. I shall always count it my greatest treasure."

"Do not mention it, Madonna!" He bowed awkwardly, his eyes shining. "I am delighted to have had the opportunity to set down for posterity the unparalleled features of so courageous a lady. Your action just now was one of which the most seasoned condottiere might be proud."

Tulla could have named one such, at least, whose pride indeed would have taken a considerable fall at the outcome of her action.

"May we speak of something else?" she asked Sandro abruptly.

"With pleasure, Mona Tulla." He approved her modesty.

188

"In the matter of the portrait, Madonna, I have a confession to make."

"A venial sin, I'm sure. You are forgiven in advance."

Sandro shuffled uncomfortably. "It is simply that your thanks are due to him who paid the painter. It was the prince who commissioned the drawing when he saw my small sketches of you."

"Mother of God! Does my whole life belong to him? Is not even my likeness to be called my own?"

Sandro was amazed at her outburst. He smiled uncertainly. "I think the prince wished to make you a gift that he thought you would value," he said. "At first I would not let him pay. It was not my original plan. But he was insistent and—well—I have not seen a whole ducat in a month," he confessed shyly. "I hope Madonna will forgive me?"

She was ashamed at once. "It is I who need forgiveness. Please forget my foolishness. It is simply," she added honestly, "that I have not, perhaps *cannot,* accept my new place in the world, and I seize upon any matter to lay blame upon the Prince of the Valenti."

Sandro shook his untidy head. "And yet you had no hesitation in saving him from death? I do not comprehend you, Madonna."

"I do not comprehend myself," she said. "Tell me, Messere, how goes it with your painting of Mars and Venus?" It was clear from her tone that the subject was entirely changed.

But he was disappointed. There was something here to be grasped, and he was unable to grasp it. He was only slightly encouraged by the fact that Mona Tulla did not appear to grasp it either.

He was further chagrined by the fact that they were not to be left alone for longer. Pulci, his eyes snapping with doubtful humor, was, as Leone had predicted, only the first in a long line of congratulatory visitors, each more unwelcome than the last. It was not until she had reached a point of desperation, where she considered standing up and screaming, that Clarice Orsini noticed her predicament, and putting it down to modesty as Botticelli had done, kindly moved to her rescue.

Gently dismissing young Gian Carmaggio who was pouring out his heart in a fashion recently acquired from reading Petrarch, she patted the tightly clenched fist in Tulla's lap as she took his place beside her.

"Do not distress yourself, my dear. It will be an hour's wonder. The Florentines are insatiable for entertainment. Soon Giuliano will take the day's prize, and you will be forgotten."

"You are kind, your ladyship," she managed a grateful smile for the tact that betrayed an understanding of others as instinctive as her husband's.

"There is no doubt, however, that someone must make it very clear to your cousin Leone that he is as vulnerable as other men are. Perhaps you may succeed where others have failed. Franco, I know, watches him like a hawk—but today even *his* eye was not swift enough."

"I have tried, your Ladyship, believe me," said Tulla faintly.

"I'm sure you have. Ah well, we can do no more. If only Alessandra—but that's another story. Tell me, Madonna, how do you find the children?"

This was a question which she found no hesitation in answering and a tranquil half hour was passed, despite the consistent noise and movement about them, during which Tulla learned of the problem of Clarice's three-year-old son Piero, to whom Lorenzo had appointed Agnolo Poliziano as tutor. The scholar had enmeshed the unwilling boy in the intricacies of the Latin tongue while all the child could hold in his young mind were the pleasanter prospects of his toy sword and his first horse. "He's so young still," his mother mourned. "A mere baby really. I think Lorenzo has been hasty. A mind like messer Agnolo's is too subtle for a three-year-old. And I'm afraid Piero is not going to be very clever—not like your little Valenti. They both have minds of quicksilver."

Tulla's lips betrayed her with a smile of pride. At the same time she thought crossly, "They are not *my* Valenti!" And wondered if she might burden her sweet-natured companion with the truth about her own birth and present position. She had not done so, however, by the time the tournament had approached its climax and all fell silent to watch Il Superbo dispatch his last opponent. This was a cousin by marriage to the Medici, and a member of the Rucellae, who would not have dreamed of attempting to overcome Giuliano upon his day of triumph. He received a roar of appreciation for his gallantry and was wreathed in flowers until he resembled the personification of Spring. Then he left the arena so that the two chief actors in the day's pageant could play out the closing charade.

Once more the hearts and eyes of the crowd flew to the Vespucci balcony and Simonetta came forward bearing the victor's crown. There was a flourish of trumpets as Giuliano removed his silver helmet, shook out his dark curls, and stood straight and proud, his eyes locked in those of his love, while she replaced it with a wreath of golden laurel leaves. Then there was a ruffle of drums, and the trumpets sang again for the victor.

The graceful ceremony over, the crowd cheered itself hoarse until the Medici contingent began to disperse. Then it took a blissful second wind and roistered into the streets to swell the numbers already occupied in singing and dancing and in endless processions of painted chariots overflowing with allegorical figures. There were grotesque giants on stilts, angels battling with scarlet-tailed devils; rich merchants dressed as beggars on horseback; harlots robed as virgin nymphs; men dressed as Gods, satyrs, and heroes; and women gowned as goddesses, bacchante, and legendary princesses. The streets rang with Lorenzo's lusty songs and ran red with wine in Giuliano's honor. Tonight every citizen would share in the feasting, and the most intelligent city in Italy would dance until she dropped.

TEN

As Tulla guided her horse behind that of signora Clarice, toward the Palazzo Medici in the Via Larga, where the Montevalenti party would celebrate the evening and spend the night, she occupied herself in bitter contemplation of the utter failure of the tournament in so far as her escape was concerned. Not only had she neglected to make an opportunity to lose herself in the vast crowd, but she had clumsily and ludicrously perpetuated the greatest obstacle to her freedom. She could not bear to think of it and scowled horribly in the direction of a dancing boy in an obscene mask who took it as a compliment. Perhaps it would have been impossible to have made herself invisible, seated among the Medici in the glare of the public notice; perhaps it was equally impossible now, nose to tail with Lorenzo's wife, with Il Magnifico and Leone close behind them. She might grant herself that. But it must not continue to be impossible! Tomorrow she would ride back to Montevalenti, and she would be a prisoner once more. Not, when she reflected upon it, that she was any the less a prisoner now—guarded as she was by so much hospitality and good grace.

The Via Larga seemed a great distance away. They made excellent progress when the flow of the jubilant crowd was with them, but it was as though they rode through a swamp when it was not. Often, when their identity was realized, the surging mass would obligingly try to change its direction, causing havoc further down the street. A certain amount of blood began to run with the wine.

The palace, when at last they reached it, proved to be a stout and rather forbidding edifice of gray stone, surprisingly unassuming in design. Its cool interior was soothing to their bruises. Tulla was given a room near Clarice's own apartment. It was clear that Lorenzo's kindly and unaffected wife had taken a fancy to her. As she removed her silken gown before taking a welcome rest, it came to her again that she might do worse than to throw herself upon that lady's mercy. Even if she were never to see Soraya again, she thought, she could bear her exile better if it were to be spent, perhaps, in some service in the civilized household of the Medici, rather than in the careless hands of Leone da Valenti. The more she dwelled upon this, the greater became her hope. She would speak to the signora the first opportunity.

She lay upon the wide, comfortable bed and tried to marshal the words she might use to express her need. She soon found, however, that she was unable to concentrate upon words; they seemed to fly up and become entangled with the wings and flowing hair of the angels carved upon the wooden canopy above her. Her thoughts became meaningless; mere vague shadows of emotions and fears. Reluctantly, she let them recede from her and drifted, murmuring, into sleep.

It was not until she awoke, much refreshed, an hour later

that she realized how tired she must have been. It had been the weariness of the spirit rather than of the body, despite the hot sun and a difficult ride. And its chief cause had been simple anger. She did not know, even now that her mind was quite lucid again, why she had come to the rescue of Il Leone; but she recognized that the root of the anger lay somewhere between that event and the prince's casual acceptance that he had remained untouched. This, together with the resentment and frustration of her captivity and the disappointment of her hope of escape, had exercised a pressure too great to bear. The result had been a slight fever, now happily quite dispersed. She was in command of herself again and would remain so.

She dressed with meticulous care in her other new gown. If the gold silk had been well chosen to catch and hold the sunlight in its graceful folds, then this was created for the enhancement of lamplight and candle. Fine lace in deep cream lay over thin silk of the same shade. The neck was low and curved about her breasts, the high waist tight beneath them. A sleeveless mantle of soft velvet, bound in sables, dramatized her darkness. Vanozza had done her work well. A momentary dismay, as she recalled the origin of this loveliness, was dispelled by the open admiration of the maid sent by signora Clarice to dress her hair. That she dressed it with a net of pearls was another mark of the Orsini favor. It boded well; Clarice, she was certain, would give her the help she would ask for.

It would have halted her growing confidence had she known that at this moment the lady of the Medici was sipping a restorative camomile tea with her exalted guest, the Princess of the Valenti. The two ladies reclined in loose robes among cushions and fanned themselves in a desultory fashion against the heavy, late afternoon heat. They had been friends throughout the four years of Alessandra's marriage. Their conversation, naturally, treated of the day's most interesting event.

"So you saw nothing at all, Car'Alessa? It is just as well. I know you and the prince have your differences—but to observe one's husband's narrow escape from death, cannot, in any circumstances, be good for the heart, particularly in this weather." She plied her ostrich feathers with energy.

Alessandra stretched and smiled noncommittally. "I regret to have left the tournament so soon. I fear it was not courteous. To tell the truth, such occasions fatigue me. One bout is very like another. I must confess that after we had withdrawn I engaged in a game of cards with my brother and messer Zorza and others among our company."

Clarice waved away her apology with a look of complete sympathy. "Believe me, my dear, I should have joined you had it been possible, but Giuliano would never have forgiven me. He looked surpassingly handsome did he not? And with Simonetta—enchanting! However, tournaments in general are not much to my taste either. I prefer a quieter form of recreation. However I was much enlivened by the company of Leone's little cousin, Madonna Tulla of Venice. A beautiful creature and surprisingly full of good sense."

Alessandra's lip trembled a little. "She told you she was his cousin?" she drawled flatly.

"That is how Lorenzo introduced her." Clarice frowned, seeing her guest's sardonic smile. "Why? Is there some mystery about the girl?"

"No mystery." She wafted a semicircle of carved ebony slats before features that did not appear even faintly warm.

"She is not his cousin. She is his whore. Though one might allow, I suppose, that she hails from Venice," she added magnanimously. "He bought her there—on the Riva degli Schiavoni. I believe she was expensive."

"My dear Alessandra! You cannot mean it!"

The princess shrugged. "It's true."

Clarice kept quiet and digested this distasteful information.

"She seemed such a pleasant girl," she said at last, her plain features deprived of their serenity.

"It is to be presumed that the prince thought she was that at the very least," murmured Alessa, "though not in the capacity of a companion for the tournament alone," she added indelicately.

"It is unforgivable!" Clarice's indignation was growing. "If he must take a mistress then he must!" It was every man's right if he could afford it. "But to bring her into the house, to flaunt her on his arm, right beneath your nose. I am not surprised that you do not care to sit with him also. Who would bear it?"

Alessa's smile was unperturbed, even cheerful. "Do not concern yourself on my account. I do not suffer. It is merely—a little embarrassing—" She allowed her voice to trail into silence. Then, with renewed animation, "But tell me about

194

the new baby, Giovanni, and Piero—is he any happier now with messer Agnolo?"

Fearful that this lightness concealed real distress, Clarice allowed herself to be drawn to this subject. "I think not. Messer Poliziano seems to think *every* boy is capable of translating the Iliad from Greek into Latin at the age of seventeen! Giovanni, however, is all my own for the present and the delight of my life! You should have children, Alessa. You cannot conceive of the comfort they bring—" She stopped abruptly, conscious of having again strayed into an unfortunate path.

"It is unlikely, in my present situation," declared Alessandra, her forthright tone not entirely lacking in dark humor, "that I shall ever meet with the conditions necessary to conceive a child—much less the comfort! The house of Valenti seems fated to pass into Bernardo's hands. I dare say he will acquit himself well enough as its ruler, as well, let us say, as any of his family have done," she added dismissively.

Clarice was indulgent. "Ah, you will always remain a Biscaglia at heart."

"When the Biscaglia held Montevalenti, the city knew their grip." The bantering tone was gone.

"Is there any need for a grip of steel, if the naked hand may do the office as well?" Clarice wondered mildly.

Alessa caught herself, then laughed. "You are right, my friend. It is an old argument and best forgotten." And, having pleased herself by her diplomatic airing of a certain matter, she sought among less personal areas for gossip to please her hostess. "They are saying in the city that the beautiful Simonetta is ill. Do you know if there is any truth in it?"

Thus it was that when the numerous guests sat down to dine at the Medici board, Tulla found herself seated at a great distance from signora Clarice and as far away as possible from Leone da Valenti. The prince was, unusually, placed next to his wife with whom he appeared to make tolerable conversation during the course of the meal.

As Medici fare was excellent but notoriously simple in its presentation, they were not kept long at table, but encouraged to disperse to the ballroom where various entertainments appropriate to the day would shortly be forthcoming.

Tulla was escorted hither by Gian Carmaggio, who offered himself with a flourish of his scarlet cap.

"Count Franco has bidden me to see that Madonna wants for nothing."

"Then I shall not want for conversation, ser Gian, I have no doubt."

"Nor for sincere admiration, Mona Tulla. May I tell you that your beauty is the talk of Tuscany?"

"Indeed? Then all Tuscan tongues must run as fast as yours. You may carry my wine if you will and let us admire the ballroom."

They entered a long high-ceilinged chamber hung with oriental carpets and tapestries whose patterns and great value Tulla instantly recognized. They contributed a warmth and luxury that was at present enhanced by the richly clad guests. These as yet showed no inclination for dancing, despite the very excellent persuasion provided by the consort of that celebrated master of music from Germany, Heinrich Isaac, more familiarly known to all Florence as Arrigo Tedesco.

Seeing that signora Clarice stood at the center of a small circle at the far end of the room, Tulla moved toward her. She was surprised to find her progress accompanied by several murmurs of friendliness and approval as Gian cleared a courteous path before her, every inch of him expressing Valenti pride. He hesitated on the outskirts of the group surrounding Clarice, waiting for the signal that Tulla had been noticed.

It did not come. Clarice let her eyes fall negligently upon Gian then raised them and let them pass over the straight figure in the creamy lace, as though she were no more present in the room than a figure upon one of the tapestries. There was none there who, seeing this, was unaware that it represented a studied insult. A discreet undertone began to flow beneath the bright babble of conversation.

Tulla alone did not understand. She glanced worriedly at Gian whose face was now a polite mask, his smile fixed, his ears reddening.

"If you would care to take a seat over here, Madonna—" he was leading her away from Clarice.

"But I wish to speak with our hostess!"

"Later, Mona Tulla. Her ladyship is—occupied—at present."

She was puzzled but she followed him obediently. There was something here that required an explanation.

Gianbattista, unfortunately for him, was quite unable to furnish her with one.

"I don't know *how* I know that the signora does not wish to speak with you at the moment. I just *know* it, that is all."

Conscious both of the offense he had given her and of the hurt she might otherwise have received, he was vastly relieved to be rescued, in part, from his predicament, by the entry of Il Leone and his lady, in the company of Lorenzo. Clarice came forward at once to greet them and a larger circle was formed at the center of the room.

Tulla was now quite content to subside into a chair, though still annoyed with the idiotic boy for spoiling her chance.

Before she could begin to remonstrate with Gian she was approached by a young man of superb looks and carriage whose green and gold garments demonstrated the epitome of fashion. His bow nudged elegance toward the limit of the absurd.

"Tarquinio Deodati, *gentil'donna!* I lay my heart and my sword at your service!" His sword was so brief and bejeweled as to be a toy; his heart he kept captive in his velvet breast, buried beneath a mound of gold chains and a medallion of St. George. "I have marked your beauty and heard golden reports of you from many friends. Sandro Botticelli had promised to introduce me to you, but alas, he is occupied with the masque we are to see. I hope you will forgive my temerity in presenting myself?"

"Assuredly, signor Deodati." He wore a fortune about him; it seemed likely that "signore" was more appropriate than the humbler "messere." "Will you not sit, and, perhaps, make equal the balance between us? You may furnish your own golden opinions of yourself, as there is no friend present to do it for you."

He grinned his appreciation and accepted the chair that Gian pushed forward for him, beaming with gratitude for this timely appearance.

Signor Tarquinio, who was tiring of his present mistress, and regarding any gathering as an open field, returned the boy's smile. It was always good policy to be liked by a lady's servant. One never knew exactly how and when he might come in useful.

"An attractive boy—he is your page?"

"My jailer." She smiled innocently.

He laughed. He liked humor in a woman. And with that face—and those breasts! "If he holds the key to your door, Madonna, I can see I shall have to speak gently to him. Though naturally, it is the key to your heart I should rather seek."

In Soraya, the daughter of the pasha was not subjected to such idle court flirtations. However the knack did not seem difficult to acquire.

"After such a brief acquaintance? Tell me, Signore, are you married?" His finely curved brow shot upward. Such a forthright question undermined the airy creation of compliment and suggestion he was planning to create.

"Madonna, until this day there has been no lady who could touch my soul so deeply." He saw her lips curve deliciously. "And then, I am too young for such responsibilities," he added with conviction. "Though of course, if my heart should dictate it—" The white courtier's hand flew again toward St. George. Was it marriage she wanted, he wondered. If so, being a Valenti, she could choose as she would. What was her fortune? Sandro had remained damnably uncommunicative about that. She wore only one jewel, and that a pendant of no special value. Still, the pearls in her cap were good.

"You are a native of Florence, Signore?" Tulla guided the conversation into safe, if dull waters.

"Certainly, though my family has property in Venice also, and I spend a great part of my time in La Serenissima."

"Venice!" She began to regard him as something other than a few minutes' amusement. "I too have—connections— there. Er—part of my family came there from the Bosporus."

"Indeed? Then Madonna is not from Italy? You speak our language so divinely."

She smiled and spoke it even more divinely. She was not at all certain exactly what use she proposed to make of this modish philanderer, but an admirer who journeyed often to Venice was to be cultivated. For from Venice, the only "part of one's family" that remained, might *return* to the Bosporus!

Therefore, when Lorenzo called for the dancing to begin, she accepted signor Tarquinio's invitation and did her best to remember the steps she had learned so unwillingly in Leone's arms.

Tarquinio found it charming when she failed to remember, not merely because she apologized so winningly, her sapphire eyes laughing into his, but because it enabled him to guide her movements with his hands, giving him the opportunity to clasp the curve of a hip and once, by accident of course, to cup a sweet, gently rising breast in his hand. He was enough of an expert in female anatomy to know, from this brief excursion, that he must have more.

When the time came for the dancers to rest and be entertained by a masque, Tulla found the signore's chair locked against hers. Gian was nowhere to be seen. The seats were narrow and it was impossible to escape either the arm thrown about her shoulders or the long thigh in smooth, tight hose that pressed against her own.

The masque represented the birth of Venus and her conquest of Mars. Madonna Simonetta herself had graciously consented to play Venus.

"She was born at Porto Venere, where it is said that she truly rose from the waves," confided Tarquinio, his lips nuzzling Tulla's ear. Although La Vespucci wore an ethereal creation of blue and green gauze, strategically hung about with seaweed and shells at certain points, and with her yard of golden hair rippling about her slender body, she was indeed the personification of divine beauty, though Guiliano de Medici, attired in not very much at all, displayed his athletic perfections to excellent advantage as the love-vanquished Mars; Tulla knew, as messer Arrigo's lilting melodies became more erotic in timbre and signor Tarquinio's jeweled hand stole slowly further down her shoulder, that she was going to have to get out of the room. If she remained, and wished to keep the signor's interest, she must not snub him; if she remained and submitted to the further invasion of his hands, she would probably scream. Such tasteless behavior being utterly unthinkable in the most civilized court in Europe, there was only one course.

"Signore—I feel a little faint. It is very hot. I shall go to my chamber for a time. No no! I insist that you remain." Allah, the man was already half out of his seat! "My lady companion is there, and will look after me," she whispered, inspired. To allay any suspicion she gave him her hand. "I will return, very soon," she promised, touching light fingers to her lips.

"Beautiful! Adorable!" he muttered thickly as she slipped away. He shifted to a position less constricting upon those parts that madonna had chiefly interested and contemplated a rosy future. He would have her tonight if it could be arranged. A pity about the companion, but all things were possible, Santa Madalenna, what a beauty! He stared at the smiling Simonetta, who might as well have been transparent for all he saw of her redoubtable charms. Truth to tell, he found masques, on the whole, exceedingly tedious. The tournament now; *there* had been a day of pleasure! And a man could stretch his legs at the same time and talk with a friend if he wished to, instead of ironing his cheeks on a goddamned hard chair and wearing out his mouth with polite smiles. The girl would be gone for half an hour or so. He might take a stroll until the masque was over.

Tulla, having avoided all eyes and escaped from the ballroom without hindrance, had inquired of a servant where she might find fresh air. Following him, she had come out into the central courtyard about which the three stories of the palace were raised. A continuous arcade of Corinthian columns gave it an air of the cloister at ground level, which was relieved by the row of mullioned windows upon the first floor and echoed again by the open loggia upon the second. The early evening coolness was rendered even more refreshing by the presence of two lightly spraying fountains. Each centered about an imposing bronze sculpture. Tulla moved to examine the one nearest to her and caught her breath in an astonished recognition. A slender boy of little more than Bernardo's age, clothed only in richly ornamented leather boots and a laurel-wreathed hat of the kind that the *contadini* wear to keep off the sun, stood with his left hand upon his hip as effeminately as any courtier, holding a great sword, surely too heavy for him to wield, in his right. His right foot rested upon the garland that was the base of the statue, while his left toyed idly with the severed head of Goliath, as if it might be a ball for the game of *calcio*. The plumes of the giant's helmet reached up to caress the boy's inner thigh. She knew at once whose work this must be, for now its twin in miniature stood upon the chest in her chamber at Castel' Valenti. She stood for minutes before the fountain, letting its fine rain fall upon her upturned face, before she shook herself out of her reverie and drew back beneath the arcade to walk and try to think how she might take advantage of signor Tarquinio's existence.

It was obvious that he would only continue his interest if he thought she might become his mistress. Perhaps she could invent some other cavalier, even a fiancé, properly betrothed, to prevent this happening in Florence? And then she might hint that in Venice—? Such a deception might succeed. But what would happen after, somehow, she had persuaded the signore to take her to Venice? There were worse things than giving oneself to a man of good looks and noble birth. *"Che será será,"* as Vanozza often said. At least it would be by her own choice—more or less.

She had progressed no further than this when the subject of her conjectures, yawning and flexing his muscular arms, wandered drowsily out into the waning light of the courtyard. He stood for a moment contemplating the David with obvious enjoyment, himself very nearly a clothed parody of the pose, hand on hip and weight on one foot, stubbing absently with the other at a loose flagstone.

"Signor Tarquinio!" she made her voice low and inviting as she called from beneath the arches.

"Is that you, Madonna?" He came toward her, peering into the gloom where she sat.

"I felt so much better in the open air, I decided to stay here. It is a beautiful evening, is it not?"

Tarquinio threw a hasty glance at the deepening blue ceiling provided by God for the courtyard of the Palazzo Medici, then cast an eye in various other directions to discover if they were alone in their appreciation of it. It seemed that they were. A few servants might come and go perhaps, but they would mind their own affairs.

He sighed and drew Tulla back toward the rustic bench she had chosen in a satisfactorily dark part of the cloister.

A past master of the golden opportunity, he seized her in his arms at once, precluding any disposition on her part to protest, by fastening his mouth firmly and greedily upon hers. His kiss, he had it upon several excellent authorities, was the only aphrodisiac needed to arouse a woman to an ecstasy of desire, even a woman of birth and breeding such as this. However, naturally such a one would expect to be the recipient of a good number of polished phrases, well-turned verses, and a scattering of small jewels at the very least. Well she should have them all in good time, but his experience up and down the echelons of Italian society had taught him that no woman was averse to the reminder, at the outset, that whatever the accompanying flourishes might be, their main business together would be physical. Give them a taste of what was to come and the interim would be the more delicious. Of course it was all the better if there were no interim—and as for this one, he could hardly wait! His trunk hose were well nigh bursting for her! To distract her attention from this fact, he raised his lips from hers and took her hand and laid it on his heart. She was panting a little, and her eyes widened in slight shock at the contact with the cold metal of St. George, an exemplary contrast to his wearer.

"Signore!" she managed when she got her breath, "you are too hasty!"

He raised her captive hand from his breast and kissed it. "But not, dare I hope, unwelcome? Madonna you have lit a fire in me that all the waters of the earth could not quench! Have pity! Say that I may hope." He played the cavalier for all he was worth.

"I would not for the world dash hope in any man," she murmured modestly.

"To speak the truth, signor Tarquinio, I have a certain hope of my own—if you would—" Her words were engulfed by the renewed assault of his lips. Too late she realized that she might have chosen her words more carefully. His fires were stoked and ready to rage into a veritable furnace. He pressed her back against his supporting arm and forced his mouth upon hers so that her lips numbed and her neck began to ache abominably. Her attempts to gain air were misinterpreted as passion, and Tarquinio was carried dizzily away upon a rising crescendo of lust. He pulled the lace from her shoulder and crushed her naked breast in his hand, moaning at its perfection. And then the crescendo diminished, and his touch became gentle, his lips caressing; his tongue tracing the outline of her mouth and teasing her lips until they trembled, his fingers knowledgeably stroking where before they had compressed. He was not about to be ambushed by his own haste. Tulla made a desperate move to rise, to be free of him. She succeeded merely in thrusting her lips more firmly against his, and her body writhed in his arms as lasciviously, it seemed, as he could have wished. He congratulated himself on an excellent choice and transferred the attention of his lips to her breast, lowering his hand to raise her skirts. For half a second, though her lips were at liberty, her voice seemed imprisoned in her throat. Her cry of "Allah, no! I beg you, Signore!" was weak, by no means strong enough to deter her manful lover, now earnestly seeking among her petticoats.

"Who is this that calls upon the name of Allah, the compassionate, the merciful? Oh daughter of Islam, how have you fallen? Or have you not, as yet?" A dark figure loomed in the archway behind them, the suggestive voice floating lightly along the cloister.

"Who's there?" Tarquinio spun round, his hand upon his sword hilt. Tulla, her heart turned to lead, put her dress to rights and prepared to be thoroughly embarrassed. She would have thanked Heaven on her knees for any rescuer at that point. Any, that is, other than Leone da Valenti!

The prince came forward at his easy, unhurried pace and leaned upon a column to survey his catch.

"Signor Deodati? You surprise me. I know at least one lady who would be heartbroken to learn that already you, whose ring she wears, are paying your—er—respects elsewhere! However I heartily commend your choice—though not yours, Madonna." The righteous tone was maddening.

"I must confess I thought my cousin would comport herself with more dignity. Perhaps Florence is too heady a wine for you, my dear. It might be as well if you were to confine yourself to Montevalenti."

Her whole body seemed aflame. His words danced about her unwilling ears like little scarlet devils, taunting and humiliating.

"It was not," she said with a dull hopelessness, "as you think." She sensed, through the darkness, the raised brow, the pained mouth.

"We will not speak of it. Nor, I am certain, will the Signore." The overtone of feline amusement was gone. "I need hardly direct you, signor Tarquinio, in the matter of a lady's reputation. Suffice it to say that what touches her, touches a member of my family—and therefore myself."

Tarquinio had been struggling for words and a place to put them. "I assure you, Prince, that your cousin has come to no harm at my hands. But, as you may imagine" (He calculated his chances. Nothing thrown, nothing gained.), "I have been gravely affected by the beauty of the lady. Even to the point of the madness that you have, so unfortunately witnessed." The eloquent hand was again upon St. George, possibly for luck. "There can be no sleep for me until I have made restitution, in the only way which honor can recognize." He drew himself to his full height, his breast swollen with new born righteousness. "I have the honor to ask your permission, Prince, to pay my addresses to Madonna, your cousin!"

Tulla gasped. The man was incorrigible.

"What do you say to that, little cousin?" She knew that he was smiling. "Shall we invite the Signore to Montevalenti and make the condottiere jealous?"

Her voice came to him with the soft hiss of a well-aimed arrow. "Go to hell!" she said.

Leone shrugged, unaffected. "It seems, signor Tarquinio,

that you had better leave us. I am desolated." His bow was dismissive and perfunctory.

"But Prince—!"

"The matter is simple, Signore. Either you depart, or I throw you into the fountain. You may choose."

Tarquinio bit his lips. His dignity had suffered quite enough for one night. He brought his heels together sharply and bowed with perfect punctilio.

"Excellence! Madonna!"

It should not be said that even a prince could display better manners than a Deodati.

His receding footsteps rang heavily across the stones of the yard.

"You are detestable!"

Her voice raked him from the darkness.

His sigh was one of ennui. "So you frequently seem to tell me. Perhaps you would prefer to have been left at the mercy of your tender companion? Do you usually shriek for divine intervention as a prelude to making love? If so, I have made a mistake. I apologize."

"Now you are ridiculous."

"And you, Madonna, have been foolish. Also your behavior is distasteful in a member of my household."

"Hypocrite! If it is distasteful behavior when I give what is mine to give where I wish, what is it when the master of Montevalenti, he of the sensitive palate, demeans himself to take by force that which I would not give?"

Her words echoed unanswered for a moment, resounding emptily among the columns. Then Leone spoke quietly and calmly. "I have not forced you, though it is my right if I so desire. I would remind you that what you would give to the lusty Signore is not yours to give—but mine. I am content enough to call you my cousin, if it pleases Il Magnifico's sensibility, but must also claim the duty that accompanies the relationship. A Valenti does not hold herself so cheaply as you have done."

"And how if I proclaim freely that I am no Valenti, but a slave bought and paid for in the marketplace—one whose inferior position in the world allows that any man, be he prince, courtier, or condottiere—may take her when he will?"

"Then," the deep voice allowed, "you will merely insult the kind, stimulate the gossips, and be sent instantly home to warm my bed! Make up your mind, Tulla. Who is it that you wish to be?"

It seemed fruitless to try to goad him. He inhabited a citadel of pride and cynicism that was as inpregnable as his accursed castle. She could not reach him there. When she spoke again her voice was dull and tired. "If only it were permitted that I might be myself."

He came nearer and stood looking down at her. He could just make out her features in the dimness. "You are a daughter of our enemy, taken in war," he said gently. "It is neither possible nor meet that I should give you back your fortune and your titles. But I have given you a place in my palace, a place not without honor, one for which you are fitted and which you can make your own. It had seemed to me that you had found some pleasure in it."

"I enjoy the company of children," she said flatly.

"Your voice is sad. I am sorry." The gentleness persisted. "This is a foolish outcome for your visit to Florence. Come!" He offered her his hand. "Let us see if this palace does not hold something to cheer you." The hand remained outstretched. She rose but did not take it. Leone sighed and ushered her out into the starlight. A thought striking him, he chuckled. "Tell me, have you examined Donatello's work here in the courtyard?"

"I have looked at the 'David.' " As always her tone with him, in her own critical ears, sounded querulous.

"Donato di Niccolo Bardi was, for me, our finest sculptor," he said conversationally as they approached the indistinguishable mass of the second fountain, subdued rather than lit by the first moonlight. "Lorenzo's grandfather Cosimo was so taken with him that when Donatello died they buried him next to the old man. He deserved the honor. He gave the Medici some of his best work. What do you think of this? But you can scarcely see it! Hola! Bring us light!" he roared suddenly, setting the stones ringing right up to the loggia on the second floor.

A liveried servant, tired ears attuned to the voice of command, hurried out with a dark lantern.

"I'll take it. You may go." Leone adjusted the sliding window of the lamp. "There, now you may see. I think the subject is one which will greatly appeal to you." As he directed the beam, the irony of his words was lost in the shock of perception. The lamp illuminated two figures, locked

205

in a relationship so terrible that Tulla cried out involuntarily.

"It is Judith, the chaste widow, with Holofernes, the general she has vanquished."

The woman stood like the angel of death, the great curved scimitar uplifted in her right hand to finish the dreadful work she had already begun. The man was seated at her feet, his head turned outward, held up by its hair in her left hand. There was a great gash across his throat. His neck was broken. The second blow would sever it.

Leone held the lantern closer to her face. "Whom do you pity there," he asked, searching it closely, "the woman who is so relentless as to do such a deed, or the man who must suffer it at her hands? He had desired her. She had betrayed him."

She did not shrink from the light but gazed back unblinking. "It is no betrayal to kill a great enemy, but an honor," she said. "I pity neither. It is not a matter for pity."

He lowered the lantern, seeking for something at the base of the statue. "Then you will approve the inscription." He read it out with an actor's bravura. " 'Kingdoms fall through luxury, cities rise through virtue; behold the neck of pride severed by humility.' What a tragedy it is, oh relentless daughter of the Infidel, that there is not a scrap of humility in your character."

"You would have me sever your neck?" she asked, surprised.

"No, I would have you learn pity," he replied. "A woman without compassion is an unnatural creature."

He rested his gaze a little longer on their bronze companions and then swung the lantern around to light their way inside the palace.

In the torchlit marble hallway, swaying on feet that had stood to attention throughout the evening, was the servant who had brought the lantern. Leone sent him for two of the Valenti guards.

"To escort you safely to your room, Madonna—and to insure that none try to enter—or leave it," he added firmly.

"It is not necessary. I have nowhere to go." She knew he would leave her no hope.

"Signor Tarquinio is noted for his persistence in romantic affairs. An excellent trait—in other circumstances. Madonna Tulla," his manner became abruptly softer, surprising her so that she did not protest when he took her hand and brought her round to face him. "We have each one come to the other's rescue this day, and I think, for all your complaints, you are as glad of it, as I was?" He did not wait for an answer. "Let us declare a truce between us, on the strength of it. I am not your 'great enemy', Tulla—and never could be."

He raised her hand to his lips with simplicity unadorned by courtly phrases and held her eyes for a second. She stood transfixed by the warmth and directness of his gaze, and neither noticed when the door to an opposite room was flung open and the Princess of the Valenti prepared to cross the hall.

Alessandra paused before continuing her passage. The sound of her guard's booted footfalls were enough to turn Leone's intent head. He loosed Tulla's hand and strolled, smiling, toward his wife. "What, retiring so soon, my dear? Does the dancing not amuse you?"

"I have had my fill of it," the princess remarked coldly. Then, with the good manners required of the Medici palace, even toward her husband, she added, "I give you good night, my lord. Much of the company remains, should you care to join them." She acknowledged his bow and ignoring Tulla, swept past him toward a staircase, her impeccable carriage inexpressive of the thought that preoccupied her. "I wonder if he has discovered yet that the slut has been violated?"

Leone turned to Tulla with a look of dismay. "I fear," he said, "that neither of us will be in my wife's prayers this night."

Disdaining to reply, she marched off, head in the air, before her guard, not at all sure that one of them had not sniggered.

"Alas, it seems that neither lady desires any more of my company," Leone confided to the remaining servant, standing staunchly back at his post.

"However," his face broke into its innocent and charming smile, "there are several left in the salon who will desire it for as long as I may care to give it."

It was beyond any doubt, especially that of a servant, that he was right.

ELEVEN

During the first days after the return to Castel' Valenti, Tulla found herself apt to greet the Donatello David in her room with an early morning scowl. The dreaming adolescent features naturally expressed no pique at this circumstance; he was, it was understood, merely a surrogate recipient of ill will.

When she had been back for a week, finding that she could no longer bear the restlessness, disappointment and self-reproval that was the corollary of her day in Florence, she threw herself and the bewildered children into an orgy of learning as a means of consuming her abundance of frustrated energy. Although privately agreeing that too much work was preferable to Madonna's recent ill temper, Bernardo and Lucia very much hoped the present state of things would prove to be temporary; it was after all nearly high summer.

"Why don't our brains fry when it's so hot?" Lucia demanded hopefully as she attempted to commit to memory the poem of Guido Cavalcanti upon the months of the year. Her wide-brimmed straw hat gave her little relief from the mid-morning sun of the herb garden.

"We should work better, perhaps, if we were to go inside," Tulla replied obliquely.

"I only wanted to know," said Lucia hastily. "Please let us stay."

"I think it's our hair that keeps them cool," offered Bernardo who was lying on his stomach, frowning into the oregano over Julius Caesar's British campaign. "And our skulls are pretty thick—especially Lucia's!"

"You may make this the subject of a special study, since

you have progressed so far," said Tulla severely. "You, too, Lucia—it was your question."

They agreed somewhat dolefully. There had been several special studies lately. Mona Tulla made them work so much that she spent all morning reading their papers and had no time left to answer questions.

The temperature seemed to drop by a noticeable amount when they spied, with deep relief, the welcome figure of their Uncle Franco enjoying a slow, scented approach to their corner. They could count upon at least a quarter of an hour's respite from their tussle with the dragons of knowledge, perhaps longer. Uncle Franco's presence seemed to exert a pleasantly relaxing effect upon their newly stringent tutor. The conversation was general and unimportantly pleasant for a while. Then Franco said abruptly, uncertain of his response, "There's a thing you might care to know, Madonna. The constable's office in Florence, have taken a man they believe to have been one of the troop of musicians we were seeking. They have sent him here for questioning and possible justice. He is one of the traveling gypsy clan."

There came the swift image of darkly arrogant eyes across the miller's table and the recollection of a cracked and cynical voice talking of the Black Mass.

"La Sventura!" she cried as the separate memories comingled into a single, inescapable suspicion.

"She was there with Stefano Bossi, the day that poor Giana died by poison! And Atroviso spoke of her with Zorza when they talked of their plan for the tournament. It cannot have been mere chance! She must be their instrument."

Franco nodded gravely. "The same thought had occurred to me."

"But you have this fellow, this musician. What has he said?"

"Nothing," was the rueful reply. "He is as stubborn as they come. He has not spoken a single word since he was taken, the lieutenant told me. But in time he will speak. My officers are engaged in persuading him."

"And then?"

He shrugged. "That depends on how much he can tell us. He may not know from where his orders came, not ultimately. If he speaks against Zorza, of course, then matters are simple."

"You will arrest him?"

"Certainly."

She smiled and nodded approval, not that she was con-

209

cerned in any way that the enemies of the Prince of the Valenti should be brought to justice, but it would give her considerable pleasure to think of Zorza behind bars.

"And the astrologer?" she asked.

Franco shook his head. "Atroviso, however you may dislike him, is both patient and clever. He will not have involved himself in any manner that can be traced. Besides, I doubt if he would profit by my brother's death. His position relies not upon Leone, but upon the cardinal." He studied her rather unpleasant expression with understanding. "You must be satisfied with Zorza, I think," he said with gentle amusement. "*If* we can extract enough information from our prisoner to satisfy Leone of his guilt!"

"The word of his other prisoner being that of a mere foreign woman of hysterical and overimaginative character!" she flung at him bitterly.

He was saved from the necessity of excusing his brother yet again by the timely appearance of Silvestro Biscaglia. The cardinal made his way toward them with the unhurried, flowing movement peculiar to him. Bernardo had once remarked that it made him look as though he were on wheels like a saint's image on a cart.

The normal courtesies were briefly performed and the growing heat of the day disparaged. Then Lucia, after a muttered conversation with her brother, interrupted the desultory talk, "Will he be tortured?"

"Who?" Franco demanded with an apologetic glance at his father in Christ.

"That man, the gypsy!"

"If necessary," her uncle replied reluctantly.

The cardinal frowned. "I hope your guards will remember their Christian duty in this matter. The Church does not look with favor on the infliction of pain upon the body unless it be for the good of the eternal soul."

"I am aware of that duty, your Eminence. The man will be given every chance to make his confession without the aid of violence."

Silvestro inclined his head, his faint smile indicating approval. "It may be that I shall visit this gypsy myself," he suggested. "The appearance of a prince of the church might be more of a persuasive shock to such a one than that of prison bars—to which, no doubt, he is already more than accustomed."

Franco laughed. "It is well worth the attempt—if your Eminence is willing to use his time in such a fashion. Indeed I thank you."

"It's nothing, my son. And how is our young instructress?" he turned his attention to Tulla, awakening a healthy alarm in her that was, for at least the third time that week, to be more than justified. It had become the cardinal's embarrassing habit to use her precipitate action in saving Leone's life as an object lesson in the Christian virtues, to be delivered to all and sundry. The children had already been greatly impressed by it as had all the servants. She distinctly did not wish to hear it again, particularly in the presence of Franco, who could not fail to be aware of her own ambiguity of mind on the subject. There did not, however, appear to be any choice, so she looked the count in his innocent amber eyes as he listened and dared him to smile.

The shepherd of the souls of Montevalenti, mindful of the precept he had quoted to Count Franco, considered that it might be best if he were to interview the imprisoned gypsy at an early point in his captivity, prison guards being notoriously careless about the amount of pain they caused during their otherwise laudable attempts to extract information. It would not do for him to arrive too late.

He thought of something he might need and having reached the lower depths of the castle, where the cells were thoughtfully placed, he paid a prior call upon his family's longstanding dependent and servator, Atroviso. He found him busily occupied among his charts, jars, and bubbling copper vessels.

"You honor me, Eminence. I was just making myself some soup. Would you care for some?"

The refusal was polite but definite.

They talked of various matters that concerned them. The astrologer offered the weather report for the coming feast of St. Pancras, when young men of the city would hold a procession in honor of the martyred Roman soldier and the cardinal would celebrate a special evening mass in the Cathedral of San Jerome. The unfortunate events of the tournament were also discussed. It was sorrowfully allowed that, upon occasion, unforeseen human behavior can effect even the best-aspected of life's moments. It was not the stars that were unpredictable, the astrologer grumbled; one knew precisely what *they* were going to do. It was unpredictable humanity that was at fault.

The cardinal, within the limits permitted to him, sympathized.

The astrologer, vindicated, brought the subject down from the stars. "There is a small matter which troubles me, Excellence. Of little importance, perhaps, but I will feel myself more secure in my duty if I relate—" He allowed his hesitation to express a delicate reticence.

*"Ergo—*speak, man!"

"It is La Sventura, Eminence. A woman of great skill—but not always reliable! The princess has insisted upon consulting her privately." A certain amount of professional chagrin was sensed. "Considering it to be my duty to protect the mistress's interest at all times—" he hesitated again. The cardinal looked irritated, so he hurried on, "I demanded of La Sventura what it was that the princess wished of her. She was not willing, but she was persuaded to divulge the fact that what was required of her was—a love potion!" Atroviso's repulsive face was alight with curiosity. Silvestro allowed his noble one to show a lordly disgust for this.

"I thank you for your dutiful delving into what does not concern you," he remarked drily. Then, with no evidence of any great interest in his sister's passions, "You had better carry the information to messer Zorza. He will doubtless take it upon himself to be much flattered!"

Atroviso chuckled. "I congratulate your Eminence! You have a rare humor."

Accepting the compliment, Silvestro prepared to leave upon his errand of Christian mercy further on into the bowels of the castle. His face, as he glided between the sputtering and evil smelling torches fixed to the drizzling walls, was more thoughtful than it had been all day. When he had done his business here, he would visit Alessandra. They must have a long, intimate talk together.

The Basilica of San Jerome, raised some two hundred years ago to the glory of God and the Valenti by the same generations of unsung but imaginative masons who had created the castle, possessed the additional credit of having been thoroughly modernized in the day of Leone's grandfather, by the great Florentine architect Brunelleschi. This resulted in a bright and spacious interior, which, viewed down the nave from the entrance, provided a harmonious perspective, the lines of which—the columns, mouldings, string courses, outlined chapel steps—repeated each other's form and proportions, carrying the tranquil eye toward the same vanishing point. A place, appropriately, of deep peace, it had also seen several bloody struggles and had been reconsecrated three times; the laws of sanctuary are not always observed, nor is the sanctity of holy service. Its walls, however, were stout enough to absorb such aberrations when they occurred.

Not that anything of the sort was expected to occur upon the feast of St. Pancras. This had always been a popular holy day in the city, particularly among her young bloods, who seized upon the attractive opportunity to dress themselves like Roman soldiers and carry out fake executions at street corners, to the shivering delight of the female population and the profit of the sellers of red paint. The early evening was dedicated to the hearing of mass, at which, for the last four years at least, Cardinal Biscaglia had been the celebrant. The city was honored. Few such insignificant states could claim a cardinal's interest. Naturally, every inhabitant of the castle above the rank of menial was honored to attend. The Prince of the Valenti, his family, and his dependents behind him, occupied the right-hand section of the fine mosaic floor with its pattern of Valenti lions lying down with Christian lambs. The princess and her train, naturally, stood upon the left. At her elbow, his upright stance and air of grim rectitude providing an aura that must cause unsavory rumor to hide its head in shame, stood Andrea Zorza. His eyes, fixed in proper humility, never left the cardinal.

Behind their lords, the people comingled, moving about and talking in suitably low and pious tones, of the day's amusements and the terrible price of Florentine dyes. From time to time they crossed themselves and muttered an Ave or two. More than one merchant drove a shrewd bargain during the less sacred parts of the mass; being made in the presence of God and His priest, it was more likely to be kept. The youths of all ages who considered this day to be theirs, swaggered about in their feast-day clothing, with something of the mock military still in their manner, swapping stories and ogling the girls. Among them, their swagger less exaggerated but more convincing, stalked the black-clad bravos of the Biscaglia guard, their numbers gratifying in view of their reputed godlessness. Tulla, standing near the front of the

213

crowd with the children, found the noise and movement reprehensible. Such impiety would have been unthinkable within the precincts of an Islamic mosque, the sensible members thereof having taken the trouble to design their churches with an adjacent courtyard for social purposes—for use *after* prayer, as was fitting. She reprimanded Bernardo most hardily when his attention was caught by the antics of two pigeons who were trying to find their way out through whatever ornamental orifice they had entered.

The service itself seemed very long although the cardinal's dignity was beyond dispute as he went through the graceful, time-honored motions, fluid and dramatic in his brilliant robes. Yet the ceremony lacked some quality that was necessary—one that was always to be found, Tulla reflected, in the small family chapel at Castel' Valenti where Father Ambrogio, the prince's Franciscan chaplain, presided with his assistant monks.

She was glad when at last the "Ite Missa est" was pronounced and the worshippers spilled out thankfully into the still sunlit square where they could exercise both their tongues and their legs without the bridle of holiness. Though nowhere as large as the Piazza Santa Croce, the square of San Jerome, guarded by its two stone lions crouched on either side of the church steps and beautified by the fountain of Neptune in the opposite corner in front of the handsome building of the woolguild, represented the beating heart of its city in much the same way. Always the center and base point of any pageantry—such as today's play of Santo Pancratio and Santa Agneta played out upon a cart before the doors of the basilica—it was also the rallying place in time of war or other trouble and the daily resort of all citizens in search of recreation.

This evening the crowd was already large when the church disgorged its contents and was further swelled by the numbers of those whose livelihood was drawn from such gatherings; the jugglers, tumblers and tightrope walkers; the itinerant musicians, the quacks with their universal remedies, the sellers of fragrant roasted meats and pastries, the painted, bold-eyed harlots, the soft-footed, magic-fingered thieves. Once again, as she descended the steps, a child secured firmly by each hand, Tulla's senses suffered the onslaught of the anarchy of sound, scent, and color that was Montevalenti in festa. In Florence, she thought regretfully as

214

she lost Lucia to a throng of small children in a roaring, dancing chain, there had always been a certain sense of decorum—the decent distance between one citizen and another that permits the striking of the elegant pose, the noticeable grace of movement—she was conveniently forgetting for the moment the uproarious press that had guided them to and from the protection of the Medici banners. She arrested her descent midway, attempting to keep Lucia in sight, Bernardo hopping excitedly beside her.

"Let me go too, Mona Tulla! There are Mario and Ercole from the Abacus! Please, I won't be long."

She was about to refuse when her attention was distracted by a shout from behind. Turning quickly, she let go Bernardo's squirming hand.

"Hola! You, Messere! A word if you please!"

The voice, pitched at a note of cold command, belonged to Francesco da Valenti who stood to the left of the open church door from which Andrea Zorza was just emerging, his eyes creased against the light. The count moved to block the way of the condottiere who stopped short at a yard's distance, his hand homing to the sword he never left off, whether in Christ's house or his own.

"Do you prevent my passage, Count?" He was coiled like a spring.

"For the time it takes to answer my question, if you will be so good?" The courtesy was nominal.

Zorza took a single step down. "No law requires me to answer your questions."

Franco stood his ground. They were almost eye to eye. A hush began to fall about them as those behind and around them noticed their gamecock postures.

"The matter touches your honor!" The challenge rang out clearly. There being no longer a possibility of leaving, the soldier drew himself up superbly and regarded Franco as if he were an unpleasant but persistent smell.

"Have you gentlemen purchased the right of way here or may anyone pass?" Leone, seemingly unaware of any altercation, swung cheerfully through the door, his wife, for the edification of the populace, attached as lightly as possible to his arm.

"If you would do me the honor to remain, Prince," suggested Franco with a formality intended to alert his brother to the prevailing mood.

"Certainly, if you insist. Messer Andrea, you don't look comfortable. Pray be at ease. There is no need to stand at attention in our presence." His air of benign amusement brought Zorza's blood to a dangerous heat, but he caught the princess's warning look and thrust down his reply.

"I will not keep you a moment," continued Franco with quiet perseverance. "Messer Andrea—we have in our custody a member of the tribe of *Zingari*—a man who was taken after the attempt on the life of the prince." A sudden buzz surrounded them, as those who knew, or thought they knew, informed those who did not, of the disgraceful doings in Florence.

"What is that to me?" Zorza presented the epitome of polite indifference. Franco, with forbearance, smiled. "The gypsy is a companion of the woman La Sventura, known as a witch." The buzz became a hiss, and the superstitious crossed themselves, the newly pious condottiere among them.

"I see you treat her name with the respect it deserves. Alas, Captain, I think you will find that she has been less considerate with yours." Franco paused long enough to sow the seeds of doubt—though he was still uncertain of the fertility of the soil. In fact his prisoner still had not confessed when he had awakened him at dawn, and his officers had nothing to report of their previous night's efforts. The gypsy, indeed, had appeared to sleep heavily enough for an innocent man, despite the undoubted pain of a dislocated shoulder and a deep burn on his thigh.

Zorza looked convincingly blank. "I regret, Count, I do not understand your meaning in this. It is not my custom to traffic with witches, if that is what you would imply." He allowed the edge of his sword to be suggested by his voice as his hand again caressed its pommel.

Franco chose his next words with great care, conscious of Leone's unhelpful amusement behind them, "I have it on good authority that you have done so—and that you have sought the death of the prince with the aid of this woman—and others." The crowd, now densely packed about the steps, growled deep in its throat. If Zorza felt any especial vulnerability in being thus accused in public, his demeanor revealed nothing of it. Rather did he throw out both his arms, palm upward to catch Heaven's witness and declare warmly, "This is not worthy of you, Count Francesco—or of you, Prince! Do you give me hospitality as a member of your wife's family only to defile her name and mine with such foul lies as these? If you seek to put me to shame before your people," one arm swept out to gather them to his righteous breast, "then I glory in the opportunity you have given me—to swear, before God and before them, that I have never sought anything other than the continued health and good fortune of the Prince of the Valenti!"

It was well done; even Franco had to admit that. A bravura performance and utterly convincing. The count was not sure for a second that he didn't believe the bastard after all. But it seems there were supporting actors to be heard. Alessandra Biscaglia now stepped forward from the porch, her proud neck taut, the crackle of frost in her speech.

"Your good will cannot be doubted, Condottiere. I repudiate utterly and with the deepest scorn, the imputation the count has found fit to tax you with! Have you run mad, my lord," she demanded imperiously of Franco, "that you sink to such a public insult of our cousin and guest? Where is your proof of such a crime? It is well known to us all, is it not," she appealed to the citizens, "that the *Zingari* are no friends of the Valenti? Why then seek further for your assassins? What has my cousin to do with it?" Her air of total bewilderment was genuine; there was no doubt of it. Only one small voice cried, therefore, that the gypsies had long been kissing kin with the Biscaglie—and he was an old man with too much wine in him, whose sons had died in the last throes of the ancient vendetta.

Alessandra turned to Leone who was standing back from the scene as though he bore no part of it. "My husband! Prince, I beg of you! Do not suffer this injustice!"

Before he could trouble himself to fashion a reply, the stage was stolen from beneath his feet by a sudden apparition beneath the arch of the church door behind him.

Cardinal Biscaglia, his crimson robes taking fire from the lowering sun, strolled forward with his arm upraised like that of an admonitory archangel, correction in every line of his countenance.

"It is I who will not suffer it further!" he boomed. The voice that could fill a cathedral dealt easily with the square. "Holy Church will not suffer it! Do you rake your midden upon Her very steps? I speak to you as Christ Himself spoke unto the moneylenders in the temple. Do not commit the sin of sacrilege!" Noting that his words had made their optimum impression upon his flock, whether engaged in the mortal sin of sacrilege or the more venial one of open-mouthed, burning curiosity, he lowered his voice to order the disputants back into the church.

"Follow me. You may finish this ill-judged business in the sacristy. The quarrels of princes are not a subject for public spectacle. I wonder at you, Count Francesco!"

"As your Eminence wishes," replied Franco equably. "But I beg to disagree. It is an excellent thing for the people to observe whom they may trust and whom they may, if they find reason, distrust. The justice of Montevalenti has always been public!"

"It is not, however, customary to try a man in public with no basis of presentable evidence," Biscaglia was brusque.

"Ah—your reminder is timely!" Franco turned at the threshold, having observed who was among his listeners.

"Madonna Tulla. Your presence would assist us, if you please?" Not the least among the curious, and with greater reason than most, Tulla's upward progress was a little too swift to be ladylike. Bernardo and Lucia, now racing happily about the neighboring streets with their friends, could not have been further from her mind.

"Softly, Scheherazade. Do not say any more than you must. I think my poor brother, for once in his excellently blameless life, has made a mistake." And Leone, the remembrance of laughter still in his face, ushered her solemnly back into the basilica.

The people of Montevalenti, more enlivened than they had expected to be upon their holy day, continued to walk and talk and await events. The betting was ten to one in favor of signor Franco, who did not have a dramatic temperament and was not therefore merely amusing himself. Those who had come in from the countryside added dark tales of the misconduct of Zorza's unemployed troops. "If they are not needed, why do they stay to plague us? Why not seek their livelihood elsewhere?" The farmers would willingly have sent them packing themselves, but, "How do you act when they threaten to rape your womenfolk and set fire to your stock if you don't give them a bit of bread and some wine?" The soldiers of the Valenti guard who mingled among the talkers, simply smiled and said nothing.

In the claustrophobic confines of the sacristy, amid the

sacred vessels and vestments, Valenti and Biscaglia confronted each other in various stages of anger. Leone, lounging by the wall, still kept aloof. The cardinal, acting as host, took charge.

"Well, Francesco, I hope you can substantiate this outrageous charge. I cannot imagine what apologies will satisfy signor Zorza if you cannot."

"Your Eminence must direct your questions to the prisoner in Castel' Valenti, as must we all." Franco looked steadily at Zorza, wishing that he did not wear his expression of injured probity quite so well.

"You would take the word of a gypsy—a tribe who serves the Devil—before that of a Biscaglia?" The princess was incredulous.

"The lord your brother asks for evidence. It is my hope that the gypsy may give it to us."

Zorza's eyes kindled. "He has not as yet done so?" he asked with a triumphant scorn. "And you are prepared, nevertheless, to subject me to this perfidious treatment?"

"I have other sources of information," Franco answered flatly.

The cardinal judged this his best moment to intervene. "I hope they are of the highest integrity, my son—for I have to relate a circumstance that may seriously damage your case. I visited your prisoner this morning, as I had already done on a previous occasion. Sometimes adversity will turn a man toward God. I regret to tell you that I found him quite dead."

There was a chorus of gasps, Zorza's among the loudest.

Franco sighed deeply. "How did he die?"

"It is not yet known. He appeared at first to be merely sleeping. However—perhaps your jailers had been a little severe in their treatment. The marks upon the body—"

"No! They had their orders." Anger replaced Franco's careful control. Best now to cut his losses. He would examine the body later.

"There still remains Mona Tulla's report. I did not intend to discuss this in company—forgive me, Madonna—but the princess is the only one among us who is unaware of this reprehensible event—"

Tulla, who doubted this, looked straight ahead and said nothing. Alessandra, her lower lip quivering with aristocratic pride, threw her a glance that should have struck lightning through her. "I have heard of the monstrous edifice of lies raised by this Turkish whore. I am amazed, Franco, at the innocence which gives them credit. The truth is that the girl, hoping to escape from Montevalenti as she has twice tried to do, threw herself at my cousin, offering her body for his use if he would take her away with him when he should leave. She became enamored of him, and when he refused her, she wove the tissue of lies to discredit him and cover her own behavior."

"Bravo, Alessa!" Leone's first words were full of admiration. His two hands applauded, cracking the heavy peace of the vaulted chamber. "It is an excellent tale—whoever may be its author!"

"What mean you by that?" Zorza appeared to choke with rage at his cousin's side.

The prince betrayed no humor as he answered him. "That I do not trust you, Messere, though it seems you have very ably taught my wife to do so. I think perhaps I no longer care to see you keep so close to her. Who knows, my dear," he bowed politely to Alessandra, "since evil tales are so easily spread, what lascivious tongues may do to you and your—cousin, here?"

Whatever had held Zorza's hatred in check was unleashed by his words. Unsheathing his sword in a single tearing movement, he sprang at the prince like a maddened dog, the point wavering unerringly toward his throat. All were transfixed except Leone himself, who, as though executing the next figure of a familiar dance, seized and muffled the wicked blade in the heavy folds of a dalmatic, snatched from its peg behind him.

Zorza, whose impetus had carried him on toward the door, now astonishingly leaped through it and bellowed at field pitch. Instantly the room was full of Biscaglia guards and the mosaic of the nave pounding with the feet of many more.

"Your day is over, Prince!" crowed Zorza, turning back to his enemy. "At my word they will cut you down where you stand!"

"Andrea, no!" Alessandra's cry was filled with disbelief.

"You fool! What are you thinking of?" The Cardinal's roar would have done justice to a battlefield.

Zorza hesitated.

"Put up your swords in this place!"

"Never! I have brooked insults long enough!" cried the Condottiere, breast heaving, his dagger replacing the lost sword in his hand as he faced Leone. The members of the guard, considerably embarrassed as to where their duty lay,

220

stood with their blades lowered and looked doubtfully from Biscaglia to Biscaglia and rather sheepishly toward the inflamed condottiere, who, reading their eyes, began to doubt.

Their orders however came from Franco. "You will take messer Andrea in charge. Condottiere—it would be best to surrender your weapon."

"Please do so," Leone entreated, "before Mona Tulla is forced to throw herself before my unprotected body. As you see, I wear no sword."

His expression of uncertainty deepening to bewilderment, Zorza slowly lowered his hand. "My lord—?" he appealed to the cardinal.

"My son, you have been very foolish," Silvestro regretted in quiet neutral tones. "I am certain the prince intended you no such discourtesy as you imagine. Am I not right, Excellence?"

Leone shrugged. "How do I know what messer Zorza imagined? I intended to let him know that I am tired of his company in my house—he may take it as he wishes—so long as he leaves us forthwith!"

Tulla, noting the sigh of relief that released Franco from a tension that had become intolerable, felt a sympathetic satisfaction. And yet—the man had offered Leone violence! Suddenly she heard herself cry, "It is not enough! He seeks your life! Will you not take his when you have the power? It is your right!"

"Her father's daughter! I apologize!" Leone's grin was inane. "No, my bloodthirsty little Turk. I shall not. He has not gouged out my eye. Why therefore should I extract his tooth?" The bantering tone dropped again to one of boredom. "I weary of the argument. Condottiere—it will be seen to that you and any of your people who remain in the city are escorted outside the walls before curfew. I want you out of my domain by nightfall."

"That is unjust!" Alessandra stopped him as he turned to leave. "He was provoked—and there has been no proof whatsoever of your brother's charges. Andrea is a Biscaglia! I demand true justice for my family. Have the Valenti become despots so soon again?" Even Tulla saw that she spoke in fierce pride of blood and true conviction as to her cousin's innocence.

Leone's look was not without kindness as he said softly, "Leave it, madam. I have spoken."

Outside in the square there was a hum of satisfaction of the

"I told you so" variety when those who waited received what they had waited for; the edifying sight of their princess's cousin (some said lover) marching solidly at the center of an escort of her Excellence's personal guard.

One or two of the vulgarly curious, pushing close, overheard but could not interpret signor Franco's interesting question to the beautiful Turkish girl as they descended the steps together. "I wonder—*how* I wonder, what made Zorza think that they would have cut Leone down upon *his* orders? Food for thought, Madonna." There was no immediate reply.

"What do you think messer Zorza has done?" Lucia asked her brother as they returned from their play. Bernardo gave his uncle's shrug. "Dunno. He's probably stabbed somebody. He always looks as though he'd like to! It's a pity, though. He'd probably have let us watch them torturing that gypsy."

At the hour before curfew Tulla stood upon the highest battlement of Castel' Valenti and watched as, a hundred giddy feet beneath her, the compact cortege of Andrea Zorza rode out to begin their tortuous descent into the valley. All wore the somber black of the Biscaglia, their silver trappings diminished at this height so that they resembled nothing so much as a small, sad group of mourners setting off for a funeral. Tulla felt only an adequate amount of complacency as she reflected that at least it would not be the funeral of the Prince of the Valenti.

Hearing sounds behind her she turned to see that she was about to be joined by that unlamented gentleman, preceded noisely by his energetic heirs.

"Has he gone? We haven't missed him?" Lucia flew to the nearest crenel and scrambled onto its ledge, careless of the height.

Bernardo, taller, could look comfortably out through the next one. "We missed all the fun in the basilica," he complained to Tulla. "We shouldn't have if you'd made us stay with you."

This unjust piece of logic confounding her, she ignored it and stationed herself behind Lucia, taking a tight hold on the child's skirt.

"Never fear, you'll be able to watch him all the way to Rocca Negra if you so desire," Leone assured them, "though I don't know what you find so interesting in the spectacle."

Rocca Negra was the last village before the road left the boundaries of Montevalenti.

"I wish I had a culverin!" exclaimed Bernardo with fierce longing, "or even an arbalest!"

The Prince smiled, ruffling the boy's hair as he stood at his side. "They'd be precious little use to you at this range, lad. You should have been swifter with the boiling tar, if murder was in your mind!"

"Murder?" Tulla's voice was pitched rather too high. "It would scarcely be termed so. The boy is right. You should have killed him."

"What a bloodthirsty household I have. Why kill him? He is gone. We shall not see him again. See how small he looks. Would you trouble to kill a gadfly when you may brush it away with your hand?"

"Look! Mona Tulla! See who's running after the condottiere!" Lucia was shrill with pleasure. "It's Atroviso! He looks like a bat with a broken wing in that old cloak. He can't get on his horse—and look at all that baggage—just like a pedlar! Do you think he's going for good, Uncle?"

Leone looked sympathetically at Tulla, "I imagine so. His reputation is not at its highest just at present."

They watched with unavoidable amusement as the astrologer attempted to mount his uneasy gelding without losing his precarious hold on the reins of a pack mule that appeared to be carrying the entire furnishing of his cavernous retreat upon its back. At last he was successful and began to beat an inelegant path after the main party, urged forward by howls of encouragement from the two children, both hanging crazily out from the battlement.

"Unmannerly brats!" Leone grinned, catching Tulla's eye. She was not so dishonest as to look reproving.

"There is one thing to be learned from this departure, Prince," she challenged, her reluctance to engage him in conversation overcome by an increasing urge to open his eyes to the world about him, "which is that the astrologer having seen messer Zorza dismissed, concluded that he too must be out of favor! Why so," she demanded triumphantly, "unless he is as guilty in this intrigue as I have said?"

Leone, who was enjoying the pleasing effect of chiaroscuro where the dying light struck ruby upon her hair, realized that she expected an answer of him.

"He is as guilty as the next man who will take advantage of

223

a fool to gain his bread," he said reluctantly. "If Zorza was willing to pay, there isn't an astrologer in Italy who wouldn't have done what maestro Atroviso has done."

She longed to call him a simpleton but was mindful of the children. "I have told you of his connection with La Sventura," she insisted steadily. "Do you see no harm there?"

"All such as he and La Sventura are banded together in league to pit their wits against the rest of us. Only so can they survive. Again I say—Zorza was fair game."

"And the attempt on your life! Were you also fair game?"

Her face, he thought, was more beautiful when it was not earnest. "There has been no proof to connect the plan you overheard with the action we have seen," he observed neutrally.

"No indeed!" she was contemptuous, "when the chief witness dies so conveniently in his cell!"

"He's caught up! He is speaking with the condottiere," reported Bernardo at this juncture. "I wish we could hear what they are saying."

"So do I," Tulla agreed grimly.

The Prince's generous laugh was heard.

"Atroviso is probably offering to say a black mass for the perdition of your soul!" She was stung beyond reason by his obvious lack of concern. "But I suppose you are quite tolerant of such practices."

Leone frowned. "Not particularly. I find them revolting. However, as they do not, in the main, involve the human sacrifices of popular superstitions, I do not feel constrained to crusade against them. Indeed the Magus will rarely deprive a man of his life. Such a habit would make for too brief a career. Sadly, the harm they do is rather to men's minds than to their body."

"You do not believe then, that such men can call up the Devil?"

He shook his head. "I very much doubt it—though I know myself in the minority. I believe that what they are really doing is furthering their own power over the weaker vessels among us by their use of the unassailable weapon of *fear*." He smiled. "Our Holy Mother Church occasionally finds it useful to employ similar methods—for rather more laudable ends, of course."

She looked at him in disgust. Had he no care for the simple minds of his people?

"They've disappeared. Gone into the trees," lamented Bernardo. "Zorza sent Atroviso to the back of the troop. Did you see?"

"They must have fallen out," Lucia judged, clambering stiffly down from her crenel. "Come on, Nardo, let's go down to the kitchen. Egrigio promised me apricot pastries. We can get them while they're still hot!"

They were gone before Tulla could complain about spoiled appetites. Besides, apricot pastries were not upon her mind. "You may find as many excuses as you will for the existence of such people, Prince, but—" surely Franco had spoken to him of this, "but I wonder you permit the commerce of your wife with La Sventura!"

He smiled at the tart edge to her voice. "Madonna, we have had this conversation before, I think. My wife no longer lives her life upon my permission. But if you fear for her," he added with perfect gravity, "which is most generous of you—I can put your mind completely at rest. La Sventura was a most devoted servant of my wife's father and will do nothing that might harm his daughter. She probably provides Alessa with the aids to beauty that women think so necessary."

"But surely you must—" the rest of her sentiment was dammed by the unexpected agency of the prince's hand pressed firmly over her lips.

"Not another word on the subject! I don't require a second conscience nor yet a moral tutor. Keep your advice for the children—though I wish you would not encourage Bernardo in his sanguinary attitudes—he has quite enough to contend with, having inherited the blood that sustained centuries of pointless vendetta."

Her head pressed back against the parapet, she realized she could not escape with dignity, if at all. She was uncomfortably aware of his closeness, of the insinuating scent of him, part warmth, part spices, and the strung bow of his masculinity which both threatened and taunted her.

"Now," he had put out his other arm gently to grip her shoulder and was turning her back to face the parapet. "I will release you from this scold's bridle if you will not speak for a while. Use your eyes, Madonna, instead of your tongue." He pressed close to her forcing her forward. "Look out upon the pleasant countryside of Montevalenti. Regard how peacefully it lies. Here a man may tend his crops and his beasts in the day-time and in the evening drink his wine, which he has made, with the bread, which his wife has made, and know himself happy because he is secure." He was silent then, and Tulla, as his fingers softly left her tingling lips, knew better than to speak.

She followed his eyes down across the hillside, through the brightness of broom and thorn trees, down the path of white rock to the silver green shimmer of the olive groves and further to the wide plains. There the cattle were gathering about their byres; their lowing floated upward with the bleak noise of the sheep and the insistent bleating of goats. A sparrow hawk circled at their own level, stretched upon the wind as though for the effortless pleasure of it, his motion leisurely embracing the valley from the castle peak to the darkening hills opposed to it.

"My father gave us that security, Madonna, and his life with it. I have repaid that debt, though I took no pleasure in doing it. I do not look for new debts. Montevalenti is at peace and has been so for seven years. I am a man of peace. Let that content you as it contents my domain."

Now she would not speak for she had nothing to say to him. Though they stood together, their minds occupied promontories that were more than valleys apart.

She kept her eye upon the hawk, intent. Leone saw what it was she waited for.

"A man of peace," he mused again in a soft undertone, "but you, I fear, though good and unquestionably beautiful, are one of nature's predators."

The hawk dropped from her eye with consummate swiftness so that she did not catch its passage again until its stoop was almost completed.

Leone heard her give a strange little gasp of shock. When the bird fell from her sight upon its marked prey it provided a marker for the eye that followed it. Out of the woods across the river, at the point where some small soft creature had died, rode the tiny figures whom Tulla had oddly forgotten by now, recognizable as men upon horses riding stolidly for the hills.

"Perhaps you have the truth of it, my lord," she answered him somberly at last. "And if it is so, I am one of a species that knows how to recognize its like."

TWELVE

The departure of Andrea Zorza and his familiar demon seemed to lift some great weight of repression from the castle. The labyrinth beneath it lost its sinister character and reverted to simple cellarage. Above there was a diminution in the swollen numbers of the Biscaglia guard, which led to an equal increase in the good temper both of the servants and the Valenti guard. Tulla, understandably, was probably the single individual most deeply relieved by their absence. She no longer went about accompanied by the watchful keeper appointed by Franco, which caused Lucia to shake her head sadly over the faithlessness of men. The only ones to miss the scowling cavaliere were the chambermaid he had seduced and left with child and the princess, who had found him more amusing than she had realized and who sensed her family numbers to be out of balance, once more, with those of the Valenti. She let it be known that she considered the dismissal a piece of dishonorable and irresponsible behavior. Her brother the cardinal remarked to her that Zorza had never known how to choose his moment. He had spoken somewhat testily.

Nobody missed Atroviso.

A fresh breeze had penetrated the ancient walls, bringing sweet summer and smiles.

As though in recognition of this, Tulla became very near to affirming the truce the prince had asked for. Certainly she did not agree with him upon any subject under the sun, save possibly the general principles by which one attempts to educate children; nor would she ever consider him less than an arrogant fool in his management of his estates; she did,

227

however, give up her practice of leaving any room that Leone had entered, of sitting with her back toward him at meal times, and of answering any remark he addressed to her with contempt or ridicule. She even thanked him quite prettily when he returned Botticelli's portrait of her in a handsome gilded frame.

She still intended, certainly, to leave Montevalenti—but she would let the moment overtake her; she had tried three times to take it by storm and it had not been possible. From now on she would wait and watch—and one day elusive chance would relent and beckon to her; she was sure of it.

Only a single member of the house of Valenti remained unsurprised when, after many days of this pleasant dispensation, the digestive peace of the venerable supper table was shattered, one night, into a thousand reverberations of the single syllable—WAR!

The sweating courier forced his words between gasps as he knelt before Leone, his eyes upon Franco at his brother's side. Fifty pairs of ears strained to hear him.

"The reports are coming in from every direction, my lords. Troops are entering the contada. The woods along the borders are alive with them. They are Zorza's men, my Prince! He is mustering an army against Montevalenti!"

There was a second of absolute silence; then everyone spoke at once as Franco's curses collided with Leone's. The shock spread in waves through the room as though a cannonball had already made its impact. Tulla, seated next to Bernardo on Franco's left, stemmed the boy's bubbling questions with an impatient hand as she leaned to listen.

"Can you estimate their numbers?" was the count's terse demand as the buzz subsided. He knew suddenly that his instinct had expected this, though he had not been superficially aware of it. He felt a quick relief. At last there was something he could come to terms with, an outright movement, an end to the slippery, uncertain schemes. He was glad he had kept the borders well patrolled.

Leone pushed the wine jug toward the panting messenger, waving him into a seat. "Get your breath, man."

"Counting's not easy, lords. The forests make good cover and night will make better. But the word is out that there are three or four hundred of them—and as many more on the march."

228

"There were nearly fifteen hundred on his last campaign," Franco regretted. "Is there any looting?"

"Some. Around Rocca Negra. Enough to scare the peasants toward the city. The word is spreading. They will all be making ready to move."

"Good. Drink up, then, and see Captain Cerruti in the guardroom. Tell him all you know. He'll start sending the escort parties to the villages."

The man nodded and swallowed his wine in great gulps before leaving them.

"How many men have we—when all the militia are called up?"

Tulla searched but could find no shame in the ruler who must beg such a fact of his brother. She almost blushed on his behalf.

"We'll be lucky if it's a thousand."

The Prince sighed sharply, unwillingness tightening his features. With brusque violence he scraped back his chair as if to put space between himself and this unwanted event. "It is seven years since blood was spilled in Montevalenti. Must all that senseless carnage begin again?"

Franco turned a hard stare upon him, his tone matching it. "Seven years? What of Rico Bossi and Giana? What about the boy who died in your place in Florence? And the gypsy player murdered in our own dungeons? Their blood was not shed, perhaps—but they died nonetheless—and because of you! This business is already begun, Leone. You must know that."

"Bravo, Franco!" Tulla cried out involuntarily. "Now surely he *must* understand!"

"Be silent!" The whip crack of Leone's voice shocked her into obedience.

Franco continued, ignoring them both. "It need not have come to this. I only curse myself for having failed upon St. Pancras' Day!"

"No!" Leone was swift to deny him. "I'll not have you reproach yourself. God knows you would have prevented this if you could." His eyes roamed his brother's face with a feral, restless glitter, the lion foolishly caught in some simple unseen net. "You think this muster of Zorza's then to be no new thing?" he continued reluctantly, curbing the anger that did no good.

The count softened his tone. "I am certain of it. This attack is the coming to fruition of seeds sown before Zorza ever entered Montevalenti. It is evident that your death was the prerequisite for an assault upon the city. The beast that lacks its head makes easy meat for jackals! When his assassins failed, twice, to kill you—thanks to chance and Mona Tulla—he lost his own head and tried it himself in San Jerome, shaken by the realization of my suspicions." He paused, annoyance twisting his lips. "It was an ill-judged and desperate attempt, but I, too, had mistimed my moment. I had hoped to dishonor him before God and the people and by this to warn off those of his followers who were with him. But I could not know that Zorza had killed the gypsy before he could speak against him. Although," he concluded with a wry smile for Tulla, "Madonna's word had been evidence enough for me."

Leone shook his head and did not look at her. He stared before him in silence, his face closed and gray. At last he looked up at his brother and nodded briefly, allowing him to see that he would find his way to acceptance, would voice no more out-of-season regrets.

"I would not have thought him capable of such a bold design. He seemed a lesser man," he said of Zorza, though with little respect. "And so, the black wheel begins to turn again. And poor Montevalenti's ears are pinned fast to its rim, to be punished once more for the sins of her fathers!" A bitterness strangely allied with tenderness now moved in him, his eyes suddenly brilliant as he said softly, "For the sake of continued peace I would almost give over my principality to this Biscaglia malcontent—if I enjoyed even the faintest hope that he would rule it in any fashion other than that of a rapacious and unimaginative tyrant." He paused, stroking his hand along the wood grain of the table before him. He looked weary, his brightness paled.

"There is no such hope," he continued flatly. "Therefore let us set about the conversion of this ancient and experienced board to her less civilized use—that of council table to men of blood."

He eyed the count with a flicker of his normal satire. "I will also attempt my own conversion into one of the latter! It will go hard against the grain!"

Franco nodded, satisfied. "We have no choice," was his grim acknowledgment. "And now, by your leave, Leone, there are immediate orders to be given." He rose abruptly and amid a battery of feverishly questioning eyes and tongues, strode purposefully off to set Montevalenti's small engine of war in motion, entreating God, as he did so, that it might be powerful enough for its just purpose.

Leone was left to make the official announcement for which his household now waited in restless quiet. As he searched his mind for words which would hearten them and lift their pride, he caught Bernardo's insistent demand, "But what will the prince my uncle *do* Mona Tulla?"

He recognized an irrepressible triumph in the cool voice that replied, "He will *fight,* Bernardo, because he must!"

Privately he unleashed a little of his anger upon her, for it was not yet time to turn it upon himself.

During the night that followed, no one slept. Those who had military or domestic duties had left the supper chamber after the prince's brief word of encouragement; those who had not, remained, by unspoken agreement, gathered about the scoured and pitted board that had endured countless nights such as this one.

Outside the city, bands of hastily mounted militiamen, led by officers of the guard, blundered about the darkening countryside in search of fleeing peasants to conduct to safety or marauding mercenaries to kill. Several were drawn by the sky's ruddy glow to the tiny village of Rocca Negra, where their comrades were battling fiercely with a company of Swiss mercenaries in the harsh illumination of the burning village. Others rode close to the whispering edges of the forest, peering through gray blackness into green blackness to count men who chose not to be seen.

Whatever they found or did not find, they sent back their scouts to the citadel, so that all night long the rooms and passages echoed the coming and going of booted feet, the chink of brigandines and the rough peremptory voices that gave orders and took them. In the streets there was a ceaseless clatter of hooves and grumble of cartwheels as the peasants poured into the city, mingled with the ring of metal and shouting as the guardsmen thrust halberds, swords, and arbalests into their eager hands and told them they were soldiers. Their wiser cattle lowed and bleated in rolling-eyed protest as they too were driven through the gates. Upon the castle ramparts the precious, lumbering cannon rumbled out, proclaiming the siege to come.

In the dining hall there was an early flutter of less martial interest when Alessandra Biscaglia and her brother entered it in response to a summons from the prince. Loosing Silvestro's

231

arm near the door, the princess moved at once toward her husband. Although she appeared calm, she was very pale. Leone was now seated between the captain of his guard and his lieutenant, pouring, head on hand, over the broad map of the contada that lay spread out before them upon the table.

"My lord Prince—?" his wife addressed his bent and preoccupied head. Tulla was not the only one to be surprised by her almost hesitant manner.

Leone looked up. "Alessandra! Sit, I entreat you. This will have been a shock." He smiled at her with a courtesy that could have passed for kindness, but she refused Franco's vacated chair.

"My lord—there is a thing I would say to you—to all of you." Her words were hurried, as though she wished the moment passed.

Leone gestured in invitation. "Speak, we will listen."

The murmurs hushed, and the assembled leaders of Montevalenti turned curious faces toward her.

"Gentlemen, I will interrupt your deliberations only briefly." The high, proud ring had returned to her voice. "It gives me joy to find you preparing so hardily for an event which none of us could have foreseen." There was a pause as she scanned their faces. "I am a Biscaglia," she stated, her tone rising, "as also is the man who marches against Montevalenti." She felt their interest pressing against her as though they touched her. "I am proud of my name," she declared unequivocally. "But I have wed your prince and am no traitor to his house." Again she canvassed their eyes without pleading. "If, at any time during his stay in Castel' Valenti, I had conceived even the slightest suspicion of my cousin's treachery, I would myself have delivered him over to your swords."

There was a rumble of muttered approval, a cry of "Bravo!"

"My lord!" She turned luminous eyes upon Leone. "Upon other occasions you have heard me offer excuses for Andrea Zorza. Now I must offer them for myself." She still carried her head at its proud angle, but she chastened her tone to one of directness without humility. "It was I who brought the enemy beneath your roof. I am heartily sorry for it."

About the table men shifted uneasily at hearing that imperious voice express contrition. They made no sound but waited until her husband should speak. After such an act of self-immolation, the prince himself could be no less magnanimous. He stood to honor his wife's words, at first with the most superbly executed bow, and then by coming swiftly to her where she stood, taking both her hands in his and carrying them to his lips.

"*Principessa,* there is no man here who would have demanded this of you," he told her ceremoniously. "You have overwhelmed us with your graciousness." Alessa flattered him, in turn, with her wintery smile.

Tulla, watching, was aware that she witnessed a dramatic example of palace protocol performed by experts. Certainly the princess had not enjoyed this public repudiation of her cousin, nor, perhaps, had Leone taken it at the value of its fair-seeming face. Nevertheless, she had spoken of her own free will, and he had received her words as though he believed her. When, her only business among them thus despatched, Alessandra permitted her husband to lead her to the door, even Tulla would have admitted her behavior worthy of the applause that followed—judged as it was upon its surface; though Leone's wife, she knew, was not a woman who dealt in surfaces.

But her brother too, it seemed, had a claim to lay upon the general interest. There was no hesitation here; the cardinal had only to move from his chosen ill-lit obscurity near the door toward the end of the great table, had only to lay down both his hands flat upon the board, to lean forward and fix them with the cold furnace of his eyes, for all present to sense themselves in his cathedral and look up to hear him pronounce.

He let his gaze travel over them one by one as his sister had done, but slowly as though marking down their thoughts that could not be concealed from him. He spoke quietly, letting his beautiful voice roll over them in warm, reassuring waves.

"You have heard the princess my sister's words, and you have shown her that you, also, gentlemen, can be generous. I too was born a Biscaglia" (There was none of Alessandra's high pride in the tranquil statement.), "and I give thanks to Christ, by whose precious blood we come to our salvation, that it has been given to me in my lifetime to see the Biscaglia joined at last with their ancient enemy the Valenti in a single, righteous cause!" He drew himself to his full magnificent height, his crimson robes flashing in the candlelight as he stretched out both arms as though before the

233

altar. "My Prince! My friends! Is this not, truly, the beginning of victory?"

They cheered him. They could not help themselves. What upstart bastard with his venial troop of mercenaries could stand against the championship of Christ Himself, represented in His servant, Silvestro Biscaglia? They welcomed him warmly into their circle, giving him a place at the center, next to the prince.

"Truly, your Eminence has a voice and manner that speed home more keenly than the swiftest arrow," murmured Leone amicably as the red silk encroached upon his own satined arm. "If only it were as lethal, we might save on the artillery!"

"Your Excellence is pleased to be merry. I am glad you have the heart for it. It seems that even the grim visage of Mars has no power to make you frown."

Leone accepted the finely-edged reproof with a mock bow before they addressed themselves to the map.

"Will the cardinal fight, too?" Bernardo asked, forestalling Tulla's latest attempt to order him to bed.

"It looks as though he'd like to," she replied as the red sleeve swept over Montevalenti. All the man's restlessness was gone as he eagerly discussed the terrain with the officers about him.

"Perhaps *he* should have been a 'man of blood' instead of a man of God."

"Why can't he be both? Saint Pancras was—and Saint Valentine!"

"Perhaps he will be. At least he is a man!" she added, glowering at Leone.

At this point Count Francesco strolled back into the hall. He wore a brigandine of tough leather and steel discs and carried his steel helmet and a bundle of papers. The hair was damp on his forehead. He had been out in the countryside. "They're moving quickly, thank God," he reported as they made a place for him. "The north and west districts are clearing nicely. They've got half the cattle in already. It's not so good in the southeast. The looting had increased and is holding everything up. My guess is that they'll attack at dawn—and we don't want anyone caught napping outside the city gates by then." He threw his helmet on the table and sat down heavily. "That's a nasty business in Rocca Negra. There's nothing left of it but a few stone walls, and there are thirty-three dead, ten of them men of fighting age." Amid the rumble of pity he noticed the cardinal.

"You here, my lord?" he remarked. Wanting no answer, he thrust his papers under Leone's nose. "You'll find these useful. These are the names and places of all our men between fifteen and fifty, the numbers and conditions of our weapons and armor, the horses, the cannon, powder and shot, the state of the walls—"

"Evidently you have been preparing for hostilities," Leone said. "Why did you not share the secret with me?" There was a tinge of his earlier bitterness.

Franco met his eyes. He smiled. "Why destroy the peace of summer before it was necessary?"

"Why tell a child there will one day be an end to childhood," translated the uninvited interpreter in Tulla's head. Her admiration went out to Franco. All these days, while his brother had taken his pleasure in the sun, he had come and gone upon the business of Montevalenti's safekeeping.

But now he had much to say, and his words were clear and hurried as he gave each man present a picture of the countryside in retreat, stabbing with his finger at the map to indicate positions.

"Our main problem is one of vicious simplicity—time!" he emphasized, stripping off the brigandine and rolling up his shirt sleeves.

"We have an excellent and unpleasant estimate of their numbers. We know their aim. And while Zorza's troops are seasoned mercenaries, ours, at present, are men such as yourselves, gentlemen, who fight for their homes and their livelihood. There is no doubt that there will be suffering but if we can hold them off while we get our people into the city, the victory will inevitably be ours at the last. Montevalenti has never been taken by siege."

A low growl of agreement applauded him.

"However, unless courage and tenacity alone should fail to overcome such unbalanced odds," he let their protests subside, "I have despatched couriers to Lorenzo de Medici, entreating him to call up troops on our behalf. He is our good friend and will do his utmost, but it will take time. He will find no free mercenaries to be employed south of Milan. Therefore we must place no reliance upon this aid but trust only in our own strength!"

During the clamor that greeted him, Tulla looked again

toward Leone. He sprawled in his seat with the wine jug at his elbow, contriving somehow not to be a part of the proceedings. He yawned and stretched and caught her eye before she could evade him. He grinned at her like a cat. She let him see her contempt before she turned away. Determinedly she set herself to study the circle of preoccupied faces about the table.

At Franco's elbow stood Pascale Cerruti, the vigorous ex-condottiere who had captained the Valenti guard since the days of Leone's father. His grizzled beard bristled like a detachment of pikemen on alert as he jutted his uncompromising chin toward the familiar prospect of war. It was plain that he welcomed it. Seven years provision of a decorative background to the Valenti at peace had sorely tried his patience, but he had kept faith with his calling by subjecting his men to as rigorous a military training as their state duties had permitted. It was not enough, but it was far, far better than nothing! And now his work was beginning to show its worth as they cleared the countryside.

Near to Cerruti sat the miller, Stefano Bossi; his lack of ease in the presence of the prince was obvious to all, but they admired the man for taking his place among them in the shadow of the deaths of the innocent Gianna and the son whose treachery he had publicly repudiated, turning away in shame from his very coffin as it had been lowered into the ground. By long-established tradition, the miller was the chief spokesman for the leaders of the militia upon whose service the prince had the right to call, in lieu of taxes, for the length of the fight—a more enlightened exaction than that of his grandfather, who had claimed both service and tax! The big man had hung upon Franco's words with trembling concentration as though he might prove his loyalty by the steadfastness of his gaze.

Ranged beside him, their faces betraying almost as much emotion as Bossi's, were the honest burghers of Montevalenti; messer Vincenti, the goldsmith said to be the richest man in the city barring the Prince, messer Buonavia, chief of the Arte della Lana, whose fine *"garbo"* and *"panna di San Martino"* compared in quality with the finest materials of Florence, close in conference with Luigi Pinacolo, the thin-faced factor of the alum mines whose adroit financial ability had earned him even Medici respect.

Across the table sat Piero Moro, the blacksmith, whose

vast forge stood alongside the river bank where he shared the water power for his great hammers with his friend and neighbor, Bossi. It was Moro who raised his deep voice to reply to the count.

"As you say, signor Francesco, it's our livelihoods at stake—and the sooner our wives and children are safe in the city, the better for everyone! But it goes against nature to give over our lands without a fight! Shall we let them burn our homes and ruin our crops without striking a blow, brothers?" He looked fiercely around the listening circle. "Or shall we ride out, before dawn and give them a taste of our swords instead of our crops?"

An energetic babble was stemmed by the wool merchant, gravely weighing each word as though it were a florin. "As Signor Francesco has also said, Montevalenti has never been stormed. By dawn we shall all be snug within its walls, well provisioned—and alive! Why take our chances on the plain? We shall need every man we can get during the siege. I say it's foolish to risk losing lives for a cheap flash of glory!"

"Glory, cheap! What have you in your veins, Messere, good Tuscan blood or puling phlegm?" This was the young swordsman who tutored Bernardo—Julio Bagno, Cerruiti's lieutenant whose reputation rumored over twenty dead men to his credit, ten of them in duels. He rose to his feet, a deservedly confident figure in his well-fitting uniform, eyes blazing with martial ardor.

"There are three-hundred fighting men in the city, more than twice as many outside the gate. If the word goes out they will converge upon the plain and drive the enemy back into the hills before he has time to pitch a tent! With surprise on our side we could sweep down upon them like the Assyrians upon Sennacherib! Can you doubt that we will be victorious? Prince," he challenged daringly, "would your father have doubted it?"

Leone, leaning back with his wine in the attitude of one who is enjoying a play, reviewed the various expressions of his commanders before replying, with perfect courtesy, "Almost certainly he would not, Lieutenant. But my grandfather might have taken pause. If it is not indelicate, one might make a timely mention of the battle of San Gianbattista's Day—"

This was the occasion, in a sweltering mid-June, when the Valenti had indeed swept down from their eyrie, only to be neatly swept up again by the Biscaglia, who had harried them through the gates and ruled the city until revolt from within had restored it to its locked-out prince. Tulla, who had heard the tale, was surprised by a grudging approval of Leone's reminder. And yet, how well she understood the need of young Julio. A siege might hold many things for a soldier, but glory was not among them.

"There is a balance in all things, my friend," the prince added gently. "I would merely point out that upon that unfortunate occasion the enemy outnumbered us in a similar ratio. The argument is open."

The discussion circled, every man adding his quota of opinion. Several of the younger men were of Bagno's mind, until it was pointed out to them that many of their comrades, even younger, would be fighting their first engagement. It was scarcely fair, let alone wise, to place so much responsibility upon inexperienced shoulders.

The summing up fell to Franco who was brief. "Thank you gentlemen, you have been succinct and clear. I think the consensus is that we align ourselves beneath the banner of wise Athena rather than that of uncompromising Mars?"

There was a harmonious chorus of assent. Only Bagno scowled and was furiously reprimanded by Cerruti. "Start thinking with your head instead of your arse, you stupid young pup, or I'll strip you down to your bare uniform again!" he growled as Franco concluded.

"There will be losses. Crops, homes, lives. But there will come a time, after you have reaped these dragon's teeth, when you will sow your own seeds again. They will take root and flourish as they have before. Do not doubt it, for one thing I promise you—upon my life and before Christ—I shall bring you to victory in this just war!"

"Amen to that, my son!" The cardinal was on his feet as the cheer was gathering, claiming them for God as well as for Valenti.

"Let us bind ourselves upon a pendulum that swings between our faith in God and our rightful cause! Let the strength of our prayers feed the strength of our arms!" He allowed the bellow to commence around him, then, arresting it with his raised hand, continued, his fine voice rolling with sincerity. "Against such invincible armor, Satan himself has now no power to harm us, let alone Zorza, that unhappy creature of jealousy and revenge!"

The walls were fairly threatened by the strength of the agreement. "Then let your cry be for Montevalenti and her prince! And may God defend the right!"

The tall figure resumed his seat, shaking his head over the prolonged ovation. He held out his hands toward Leone, smiling invitation, and the cry became a warm demand for "Il Principe."

What can he say to them, Tulla asked herself, he who has borne so small a part in this? He is their leader, yet it is his brother who leads; he is their inspiration, yet it is Silvestro Biscaglia who inspires. Where is he in all of it, the man, still half boy, who has played in the sunlight and failed to see the advancing shadows? She found herself trembling as she looked at him. She wanted to cry out to him, furiously, willing him to be half the man his father had been, for that was what his people needed of him now.

He came to his feet slowly, blinking a little as though he needed time to frame his words. He waited until the noise had subsided and began quietly and almost formally, "My friends—for so you continue to prove yourselves, I thank you all for your sound advice and for your loyalty which I shall try to repay." He did not labor the point but continued simply, "Like my wife I too must confess to you that I have lacked foresight. I did not predict the situation in which we find ourselves—though the signs were there to be read, had I had the good sense to decipher them."

Their silence waited. "My brother had that good sense, and so did others." A gilded flicker brushed Tulla's face.

"Otherwise our position would be far less secure." He was quiet a moment, and they smiled at him, puzzled, encouraging.

"We shall not be overthrown," he concluded, "for my brother has promised it on his life. I give you the same promise. But the victory will be his—and yours, alone!"

Tulla was both shocked and mortified when the rafters still rang with cries of "Il Leone!" and "Principe!"

The plain truth of his words had affected them not at all. They looked at him now, standing so modestly before them, and saw no empty, glittering figurehead, quit of a shameful confession, but the leader they needed and the inspiration they expected.

"Truly," she heard the cardinal observe as she passed

behind his chair to carry Bernardo off to bed, "God works in mysterious ways."

Tulla slept as little as any other citizen of Montevalenti that night and rose at the insistence of the same pre-dawn urgency. When she looked in upon the children, Lucia murmured a little, turning rosily into her pillow while Bernardo, flung fully clothed across his bed, was oblivious to her whisper. She left them to sleep and, rubbing at her own still-leaden eyelids, made her way up to the battlements where, already, a lively crowd had gathered in the pale yellow light to look down upon their enemy on the plain. She recognized several of the faces she had watched during the night. There was Franco, straight backed, his weariness showing only in his pallor, talking with Cerruti, their eyes straining outward as though they were to strip the opposing hillsides of their woods. The fiery Bagno, disputing still, had surely met his match in the big miller, who grinned and slowly shook his head at the boy.

And here was fat Maria, the wife of Egrigio the cook, tugging righteously at his sleeve as he leaned across a notch in the battlements. "Will you not understand that soldiers must be fed or they cannot fight! Get back to your kitchen. You have no business here!" Her pink cheeks shook with her efforts.

Meanwhile the prefectly well-fed members of the guard, both Valenti and Biscaglia, forgot for once to eye each other with their accustomed wariness, as they joined in the common speculative estimations of the enemy's power. Every possible architectural void held its spectator, craning beneath the weight of those behind them while a third layer stared over their bent backs. Only the high born were assured of any comfort; among the truant kitchen staff, indeed, a small private war seemed to be underway, as pummeled backs and bloody noses gave way to the tyranny of impatience.

There was as much noise as though it were a holiday.

Tulla, fully awakened by the commotion, crossed toward the spot where they had so confidently watched as Zorza rode away. Before the embrasure from which Lucia had peered, there now rested one of the six prized Valenti cannon. Smaller than its less efficient forebears which had fired two hundred pound stones to greater effect than the catapult-like ballista of the Romans, the gun was cast in one piece and mounted in a cunning frame so that both the angle and the elevation of fire could be adjusted. A neat pyramid of iron balls, each three and a half inches in diameter, was stacked beside the breech. Next to these stood young Alvaro Ponti, Lieutenant Gunner, his face shining with all the pride of a besotted bridegroom.

"As fine a sight as you have ever seen, Madonna!" he informed Tulla, running a possessive hand along the gray black barrel. Tulla considered. "Certainly," she allowed, "on the outside of the walls. But what service can they do you from here?"

Cannon were the weapons of the beseiger, not the beseiged.

"Why, Madonna," he began happily, preparing to deliver his lecture for the fourth time that morning; but then a little of the light left his eyes as they widened to include some larger detail behind her shoulder.

"Terror—O Scimitar of the Prophet," disclosed the suave though sleepy accent of the Prince of Valenti. "We shall strike terror and admiration to their craven hearts with the wonderous innovation of it. And then, I suppose," he murmured, "there is always the chance we might actually hit something with it?"

"Of course, Principe!" the gunner admonished, hurt, wondering whether his master were serious. Certainly he did not appear to be taking the opening of hostilities with due solemnity, if his dress were anything by which to judge. He wore one of his long loose robes of pure white cotton, more suitable for the bedchamber than the battlement.

"We shall hope to blow up their own guns, if they have any," Ponti added hastily, aware of staring, "but it is not likely, not with an army used to long marches. Cannon take too much pulling. Truth to tell, though," he grinned shyly, "I'd give a florin or two to *be* on the outside for a while—just to see how she'd handle. I wager she'd make a tidy hole or two in our walls!"

Leone's laughter turned a circle of heads toward them. "I trust your enthusiasm does not give way to any such aberration!" he chuckled at the boy who now blushed severely. Then, "Don't worry, lad. We don't need a clever tongue on you—just clever hands and a clear head."

Ponti smiled, gratefully. The prince never wished a man put down.

"The powder's good," he offered confidently, "and that's the main thing."

Leone turned from the prospect of cold iron to that of warm flesh, which he greatly preferred.

"Will you walk a little, Mona Tulla?" he asked courteously, observing her cold eye. "It will give you the opportunity to deliver whatever homily is close to your heart this morning. I read volumes of reproof in your looks last night, but unhappily, owing to my position as battle-standard, was unable to gather the entire benefit."

"It is no surprise that you should turn to me for a lecture when you most require it," she told him acidly. "I am, after all, a tutor of children, whose mind yours best resembles. However, it is time to put away childish things, my lord, or had you not marked it? Apply to your brother for advice. I am not a member of the military," she ended fiercely.

Leone looked suitably stricken. "But most militant," he regretted, "after the manner of sounding brass. Saint Paul was always the man for good advice. You trumpet your defiance most bravely, my dear, for one in such a precarious state of protection. But, as I have remarked before, I would hate to think you one of those who have not charity!"

"Be damned to you and to Saint Paul! An army sits at your gate, and you play with quotations! Look out there! It is reality that stares you in the face, not a book or a picture!"

"Do not raise your voice. And please cease to point in that determined manner. My people will think you invite me to cast myself from the parapet as some form of sacrifice."

"An excellent idea!" she muttered, lowering her arm.

Last night she had almost pitied him, she realized suddenly, as he had admitted his lack of wisdom before his commanders. Now, as the dawn fell bright upon his butterfly's garment and lighted the unconscionable humor in his face, she had nothing left for him but her original contempt, together with a growing anger upon his brother's behalf.

Surprisingly he took her unwilling arm and drew her toward the crowded rampart, where a guard attempted to clear a space for them.

"Days ago I showed you Montevalenti at peace," he said equably. "It is just that you should now show me war. You have proved a dreadfully efficient Cassandra," he added without noticeable irony. Then he spoiled it. "I may yet play Hector and gain your good opinion."

"Hector came to grief at the hands of Achilles," she reminded him, moving toward the place he offered her.

"He was all they had, poor Trojans," Leone said softly. "Let us hope Andrea Zorza is no Achilles."

"Should he be so, Francesco will discover his heel."

"Ah. So Francesco is to be Paris—and live on after my death," he remarked drily. "But this, I think, is where the comparisons must end. We appear to lack a Helen, the root and cause of the tragedy."

"Why not your wife?" she asked without thinking.

"Because that would be to put her upon the wrong side. If we are Trojans—Helen must be a Greek, in order that she may be carried away."

Tulla held her peace. She had no answer that did not insult Alessandra, whose stock was high just at present. But, Greek or Trojan, Valenti or Biscaglia, which was the princess in truth?

"And there it lies—the Greek camp—with the addition of modern artillery and, it is to be hoped, better discipline among its commanders."

She gazed after his pointing finger over a landscape whose alteration appalled her. Everywhere she looked, spread out upon the plain, tiny human creatures were moving about between colored pavilions, with the apparent dedication of the soldier ants they resembled. A few wore the definitive black and silver of the Biscaglia clan; some were in buff jerkins and shirts of mail. Chiefly concerned still in pitching camp, they were engaged in an intensity of activity that fascinated and repelled her. The notes of hammering and of the clangor of metal reached upward like those of badly-cast bells. Their weapons lay about them like the half-meant display of a casual boast.

"Culverins, arbalests, crossbows," Leone catalogued. "No lack there. I can see no cannon, however. Ponti will be disappointed. But they have some light field guns—see, over there." He guided her sight. "Those larger ones take two men to fire them. The smaller ones can be carried, though the marksman takes the risk of blowing himself to perdition. I'd sooner be a bowman myself. See there they are, those fair giants from Germany—the longbowmen with their Saracen shields. They can hit their mark at two hundred and forty yards!" The boyish excitement that had tinged his voice fell from him as he looked. "A hundred yards farther than an arbalest, which will burst your rib cage or tear out your throat at a hundred and twenty!" he continued bitterly. "And over to the left there, where they have finished making camp and are all sitting round singing and checking their brigandines for holes, you have the hack-and-thrust infantry—the halberdiers, the glavers, pole-axers, and oxtongues—the lads who would carve the carcass if it was ever brought down! Meanwhile they will make themselves useful as sappers and bombadiers, assisting with those remarkable pieces of artillery you see lined up along the river banks."

For once, Tulla had no quarrel with his tone of voice, for she felt a similar disgust as she gazed upon the ancient weapons that had threatened stout walls since times before Troy itself was built.

So had she once stood upon her father's tower and looked down upon the destruction of all that had been his life. Vertigo smothered the memory, and she swayed, white as milk. Leone, as he supported her, smiled a little again, thinking how angry she would be for her weakness. For had she not set herself up as his muse of war?

He signed, glad that she too could show weakness, and drew her close to him, giving her the warmth that the sun still withheld from the day.

When she raised her head, bemused, it was to find that the world made even less sense than when she had lowered it. Not only was she in Leone's arms, where ten oxen could not have dragged her, but there was a great tumult of shouting about them that threatened her eardrums as well as her wavering senses.

She tore away from him and instantly saw what was wrong.

Down on the plain, just before the edge of the forest, a group of terrified peasants scurried, on foot, ungainly burdens on their backs and swinging from their hands, driven toward the outskirts of the camp by a whooping, laughing band of horsemen, who swung their swords around their heads as they shrieked like demons riding without haste behind their desperate quarry. Even as they watched, a boy tripped and fell, his fallen bundle coming apart into a pathetic collection of household articles; clothing, pans, a blanket or two. Two of the riders wheeled around him, redoubling their blood-curdling cries, closing in as he lay, face upward, too terrified to move. Suddenly one bent low in the saddle and swooped toward him, his sword held high over his head. As he passed the small figure, he brought it swinging down to sever the air above the defenseless throat. There was the exhalation of many breaths along the rampart as they saw that he had missed. The boy half raised himself upon one elbow, looking dazedly at his tormentor, then, at a shout from behind, he turned his head as the second rider spurred towards him, sword at the same overhead angle. Again the weapon flashed close about the narrow shoulders, but not close enough.

"They do not mean to hit him! They are torturing him!" cried Tulla harsh with pity and horror, the memories crowding in upon her.

"It is for this that some men go to war," Leone said gently. No longer disguised by custom, weariness and distaste were in his face. He had known, when they were seated about the ancient table, making speeches about glory and victory, what it was that waited for them—the thing that was epitomized by the small, ignoble death taking place before them. They had all known. But only he had refused the shell that a man puts on with his brigandine—that self-deceptive protection which was second nature to him and which gave him immunity to the horrors of war, reflecting only its dark glories in the hollow shining armor.

The first rider wheeled in again. The boy cried out as though he knew. It was over. He lay dead across the ribbon of his blood, his head severed.

The prince looked at Tulla and thought, almost whimsically, of Goliath. An unsuitable image. He saw her angry tears and thought that he had been wrong to tell her she was without compassion.

A sudden snarl of trumpets recalled his attention. In front of the enemy camp a brief procession was riding forth, bedizened with brass and banners. A swift canter brought them up the hillside to within a hundred feet of the walls. Along the rampart, fingers itched at bow strings and triggers, but the trumpets proclaimed the visitors as heralds, beyond honorable attack.

Within hailing distance they reined in and grouped themselves behind their leader who carried the banner of the double-headed wolf stiffly before them on a gallows-shaped frame that required no breeze to furnish forth its bloody-tongued message.

He looked up and made a bullhorn of his gauntlet.

"Prince of the Valenti," he began, his strong tones carrying without difficulty, "for so I am bidden to address you, though for the last time—be it known to you that the Magnifico Andrea Zorza, of the noble house of Biscaglia, gives you leave of his clemency, in view of the immensity of the numbers he brings against you, to surrender your person—together with that of the princess, your wife, the count your brother and all members of your household—into his care. Be assured that no harm will come to those who have not deserved it and that the surrender of your person and the government of your state into his most just hands will guarantee the lives and the liberties of your subjects in as much as they shall show a willingness to give their loyalty to their true Biscaglia Lord."

A howl of anger and derision was his answer as Montevalenti hurled its contempt from the ramparts. Someone's finger slipped and a crossbow arrow whined past the banner of the wolf, causing it to flap in the disturbed air.

Leone, finding his brother and his herald at his elbow, grimaced at the one and nodded briefly to the other, a weathered courtier who had sustained twenty years in his post. Disdaining the aid of a trumpet, he let his words roll forth unheralded, hallowed by the repetition of years of Valenti-Biscaglia strife.

"The Prince of the Valenti thanks the Condottiere Zorza for his pleasant jest and begs to remind him that the illustrious family whose blood he claims have long acknowledged the rightful ruler of Montevalenti. Would he take up arms against his cousins, the Princess of Valenti and his Eminence the Cardinal Biscaglia, the only legitimate heirs of that family? What justification can he show, after seven years of peace, to the people of Montevalenti?"

Both the cheering along the battlements and the roaring upon the ground prevented any attempt at a vocal retort. Zorza's herald, however, was well satisfied with a single piece of mime. It was voluminously expressive. He had simply turned and pointed behind him, allowing his arm to sweep across the panorama of the plain.

The activity beneath them now appeared to become a frenzied chaos of noise and motion only to dissolve with an improbable swiftness into the impeccably drawn up lines of a well-drilled and confident army. More trumpets brayed defiance and were answered at last by a mocking fanfare from Guiseppe Murano's versatile players. The besieging force was growing second by second as a huge detachment of infantry of every sort broke out of the trees that fringed the plain. They marched in broad ribbons until they were parallel with the river, filling the eye and making the brave garrison of the city seem suddenly and unreliably small.

"Christ!" a gunner's voice floated beside Tulla. "Will you *look* at their numbers! They keep on coming out of those trees as if they were spawned there! Thank God we didn't opt for Julio's crack-brained attack. It would have been a massacre!"

"Still could be," came the lugubrious reply. "Have you looked over there?"

Tulla followed his pointing finger to the brow of the road that led to luckless Rocca Negra. Over it someone appeared to be driving a herd of the immensely strong white oxen common to the district. There were a great number of them.

"So they *do* have a bombard!" Leone exclaimed.

Perplexed, Tulla strained her eyes with the rest of the defenders of Montevalenti, who waited with as much interest as its intending attackers while the herd of oxen resolved itself into a string of about forty beasts, lined in double harness and drawing slowly behind them a monstrous tunnel of metal. Near 2 feet in diameter and capable of propelling stone balls 370 pounds in weight, the great "gonne" had already crumbled the walls of more than one pasha's stronghold.

"We'll have to make sure they never get it near enough to fire," said Franco grimly.

Leone's reply was an unexpected laugh. "Have you seen what they've christened it?" he asked. "Most appropriate!"

It was the custom to give these giants some affectionate title such as "Thunderer" or "Invincible."

As the 9-foot barrel of Andrea Zorza's bombard rolled slowly into view, those for whom its 370-pound, hand-cut, stone balls, were destined could just make out the words, painted in red upon its dark iron hoops, "Il Bastardo."

"Well, my friend," Leone continued, clapping Alvaro Ponti upon his shoulder as the gunner stared darkly toward the newcomer, "do you think you can blow him up?"

Ponti crossed himself with a professional fervor. "It will be my constant aim, my Prince," he promised.

"Excellent," Leone approved. "It only remains for the rest of us to concentrate upon the other one."

Ignoring his brother's levity, Francesco gazed thoughtfully

out at the exceptionally well-equipped panoply before them. "There most be upward of a thousand men out there already—their horses are fresh, their weapons good, their provision tents are bursting. Tell me Leone, by the sword of St. George—how did he come by the money to pay for them?"

Leone shrugged, "A Condottiere makes a rich living."

"Maybe." Franco was not convinced. "But not as rich as that."

He remained for a time, continuing to assess the force that faced them, greater by perhaps thirty percent than he had expected. Then, since it was clear that the day would be dedicated, as was usual upon the first day of the siege, to the hurling of insults from above and shows of strength from well within a safe range below, he left the ramparts to the gunners and to the guard and followed his brother down to join his officers at the council table.

There was an idea he wanted to discuss with them.

THIRTEEN

During the remainder of that first day, all of Montevalenti attempted to flatten itself into a single dimension facing the plain. It seemed to Tulla, whose memories of warfare were brief and brutal, that the citizens regarded the enemy camp much as they would have done a passing show of mountebanks or the New Year's fair. They crowded the walls and ramparts until the military were forced to be unpleasant to them; they sang insulting songs about the Biscaglie; they played various instruments with rude accomplishment; they brought their lunch and wine to wash it down. Two men became so drunk that they fell off the wall and provided excellent entertainment as they were chased to the gate by a couple of good-natured mercenaries who happened to be strolling that way, making a casual reconnaissance of the defenses. They even allowed their quarry to spew behind a bush and were rewarded for their humanity by apples and peaches thrown down by the inebriates' grateful wives.

For Bernardo and Lucia there was no question of school work, and Tulla knew better than to attempt it. She contented herself with shuttling between her charges. Lucia was glued to the rampart in the responsible company of the prince's Roman dwarf, with whom she shared both her size and her predilection for pastries; and Bernardo was seated gravely between Franco and Cerruti as the prospects for the siege were discussed, with a certain amount of gloom, at the council table.

The day's unrest disturbed her as much as any. This fact surprised her; she had not realized how even had been the tenor of her days despite her resentment at captivity. She found herself tense with expectation, unable to settle for long or even to eat. When, once, she looked around the ring of concentrated faces at the great table it came to her suddenly that those who were setting out to fight for Montevalenti were no mere cardboard soldiers such as guarded Bernardo's chest, but men who were known to her, among whom she had lived a season of her life. Franco, who was her friend and comforter, would lead them; the big miller, whose private tragedy she had witnessed, would follow him; as would the proud young men of the guard whose faces she knew as she had known those of her father's janizaries—Pascale Cerruti at their head and fiery Lieutenant Julio at his elbow. She remembered all those brightly dressed men and boys whom she had seen peacocking in the streets on their day of festa; the day was coming when they would have to wield their swords in earnest, a life for a life. And then there was Leone, their Prince of Pleasure, his dream of peace dispersed, an irrelevancy in the changed world upon which this day's sun had risen. An inexplicable anguish came to her when she saw how he still smiled as carelessly as the most bestially stupid of his citizens. Franco had been right when he had said that the prince had not remained a stranger to her. One is neither anguished nor angered by a stranger.

She was rescued from these unprofitable apprehensions by the realization that the count, who was now addressing the

249

board, was suggesting to them a stratagem that contained elements of both danger and daring.

"The merits of the plan are these—first, the action will provide a cover by which many of the peasants who have been prevented from entering the city will be able to do so—and second, we should be able to decrease the enemy numbers under circumstances that will place a great strain upon their morale—and upon their credulity," he added, smiling briefly. He looked about him. Had he their support?

"And so I move that we plan the sortie for this very night. There is everything to gain by speed. Zorza's troops are still resting after their march. They are not yet up to full strength, but the longer we wait the more of them will have arrived. At present they are tired, relaxed, a little bored. They expect to make the first move in this siege when they have blasted our expectations with the strength of their numbers. The last thing they will expect is any movement by us. Give me one hundred picked men, Cerruti, and I can guarantee to disembarrass us of twice as many mercenaries. With surprise and night on our side we cannot fail!"

Was he mad, Tulla wondered? To risk his hundred best men at the outset by sending them against ten times their number! The darkness would have to be that of a tomb and the surprise that of the last trump!

But already the accolade rose about him, and they ate from his hands which in all probability held out death to them.

What would Leone, their standard, their eagle, say to this harebrained scheme? Would he accept the astonishing reversal of their brotherly roles and for once, inject some sound sense into the proceedings?

Certainly he shook his head. And did not smile at all. But all he said was, "Are you sure?"

Franco nodded, irritated, eager to be at the details.

"Then I am with you," said Leone quietly.

Gods! Were all men fools but her father? If she stayed among them, she would have to speak. She would not be able to help herself.

Not even Bernardo noticed when she fled back to the battlements.

The day had tired her more than usual with its conflicting and bruising emotions and despite her misgivings on Franco's behalf her sleep that night was deep and exhausted. She was not best pleased therefore to be summoned out of it by a clashing of steel and voices that suggested the Harrowing of Hell was at hand. Cursing and fearful, she struggled into her robe and set out with her single still-burning candle to trace the source of the cacophony. A great deal of shouting seemed to be coming up the stairwell from the entrance hall but there was also the muted clash of weapons and the cries of men in pain or anger from outside the castle walls.

Her first thought was that the enemy had somehow effected an entrance to the city, and she almost expected to see Andrea Zorza himself striding in triumph, sword drawn and bloody, across the clamorous, half-illumined circle of the hall.

As she reached the stairhead this particular horror receded, and she saw that, although most of the men who stood below wore swords, none was out of its sheath. They were fewer than their noise had predicted. Franco, fist on hip faced Cardinal Biscaglia at the center of a group of assorted soldiers and servants, ringed by flickering torches. Their words, like their shadows, leaped up to her, augmented by the immense vault of the dome.

"May the Devil damn them to eternal perdition for this, my Lord Cardinal—for they'll get no forgiveness of me! I want the whole demon-infested pack of them out of this city as soon as we've rounded them up. There's no room in Montevalenti for such stupidity—if indeed stupidity is all we may level at them!"

This was a new Franco, a thousand furies riding his words, his face pared to the bone by anger.

"What do you mean?" The cardinal, robed in gilded purple and flanked by attendants bearing extravagant candelabra, was a paragon of moderation in tone at least. "What other fault is in them, if indeed the fault is theirs alone. You must forgive me if I have my doubts on this. My men have served me long and well and are dear to me, as you must know. I cannot relinquish their good name with such intemperate haste as you are willing to do."

Franco drew breath as if through a heavy grating, dropping his next words like stone shot.

"I will make my meaning quite clear, Silvestro. This ill-conceived brawl between the members of our respective guards had dealt the death blow to our hope of surprising the enemy. The noise of their quarrel would have awakened them had they been camped twenty leagues from here! Why, think you,

251

do they find it necessary to crow so loudly, if not, like the cockerel, to wake their kind!"

"Then you must account your own men equally to blame."

"I do not believe that to be the case!" Franco found Biscaglia's calm outrageous in the face of their blighted plans.

"Why so?"

"I have had the report of my captain."

"Naturally. So have I. It is obvious that the reports differ. Who then is to be believed?"

An uncomfortable silence was becoming strained when footsteps and laughter sounded in one of the adjacent corridors. There issued forth the prince, his princess, and several of her train. Tulla drew back a little from the balustrade.

"My dear Franco, my good Lord Cardinal," Leone began, handing Alessandra into the comfort of the candlelight, "there appears to have been some mismanagement!" Franco's set face apparently held no warning for him. "I was enjoying the pleasant game of chess in which my lady had invited me to while away the hours before our prospective sortie, when into the apartment—her *private* apartment—bursts the captain of your Eminence's guard, his uniform lamentably awry, and bleeding most prodigally at the shoulder, calling witness to the dying caterwaul you may still hear from outside and howling 'traitor' against young Julio Bagno! Swearing that you, my Lord Count, had ordered the whole Biscaglia troop into instant exile without the gates!" An airily wafted hand indicated bewilderment.

"And are they gone?" demanded Franco brutally, impatient. Leone blinked.

"Indeed they are not, my lord!" Alessandra now added her reproachful note. "Nor shall they go—for they are no traitors! It was your own men who started this quarrel—set on by that high-stomached Bagno and his followers. It was their cries that first split the heavens."

Franco flung round as though in the grip of pain. "You may believe it if you will, Princess. I do not. Whatever may be the truth of it, I am resolved that this night's work shall not be repeated. Therefore, Prince," he appealed to Leone in word only, his tone demanding agreement, "I ask your permission to expel the members of the Biscaglia guard from the city. They showed friendship enough to Zorza when he was among us. They will doubtless find a welcome on the plain."

"You must not! They will be massacred. And they are

innocent!" The princess, clutching her robe at the breast with one white knuckle, cast her imploring hand not toward Franco but to the prince. Tulla, watching above, thought her remarkably like a figure from some tragic *"tableau vivant"* such as actors sometimes performed. Leone was speaking now. Quietly, for the rumpus outside was diminishing steadily, she descended further, the better to view the play.

"I believe you may be right." The prince's spirits were lowered somewhat. "I cannot take such a risk, Franco. Punish them if you will—but both sides equally—and let the Biscaglia guard remain. I cannot believe them traitors. The two have never been eager bedfellows as any man knows, and the prospect of a siege in each other's close company may not delight them. But their quarrel rises from this and not from premeditated treachery. I am sure of it. Your Eminence is a powerful man. Loyalty apart, what would they have to gain in leaving you for Zorza?"

"In their estimation, perhaps the winning side!" Franco made no effort at courtesy, less at respect. "I beg you to reconsider—take the advice of the council."

"And have them argue it from here 'til Christmas? I thank you, no. Leave the matter. That is best. You'll find the guards much chastened by the experience. Henceforward they will be exemplary soldiers, I promise you. Now, my lady, shall we finish our game in peace?" He took his wife's hand and led her, smiling serenely, back toward the corridor from which they had come, enlisting several of the servants for extra light.

The cardinal too was smiling as he laid a sympathetic hand upon Franco's stiff shoulder. "He is right. It would have been an extravagant gesture and one we cannot afford. We need our men, Count, our loyal men—for such they are, in Christ's name I assure you of it."

Franco sighed, unmoving still. "You may be right. It is not impossible. But I do not think so, and my doubts are a new and undesirable burden, Silvestro. Promise me that you will talk to your men, sift this matter out—and try to find the truth of it. Your subtlety may achieve what my rage could not."

Silvestro let his hand rise and fall again upon the straight shoulder. "You have my promise. Put this trouble from your mind."

Then, summoning his torches with a gesture worthy of the

Creator Himself, he swept in rustling silk toward his own regions.

Franco, having waved away the remaining servants, stood with a single candle, the still, unquiet center of the darkness that they had left to him. On the stairs Tulla watched, from her own thistledown of light, sensing the loneliness which he must feel at this moment, when all but he seemed determined against any course of wisdom. She felt an almost maternal instinct to part him from some of that darkness, if only to set it at bay.

She called out to him softly and ran down the remaining stairs to the hall.

Their two candles became one illumination in which each saw the other clear and whole.

"Tulla?"

"I heard them. They are fools, sleeping when they should be most wide awake." Her words echoed as though in a tomb, so thick was the dark about them while above them the great dome waited for the dawn.

"No. Not fools. Just that they are unable to believe the worst of men upon whom they wish to rely. It is a common fault in time of war. Soon, if I am right, all will be made clear to them."

"*If* you are right?" He *must* be right. No stupidity could be so great as this would have to have been—to warn the enemy of their one chance to lessen the odds against them.

"Had they been loyal, they would have quarreled in whispers," she assured him scornfully. "Zorza has bought them. Remember the cathedral? They were less brave then. Their time had not come." Entreating him, she caught at his right hand. "Believe me, Franco, you are right!"

He gripped her hand in friendship and then, the mood swiftly altered, carried it to his lips in fervent salute.

"You put new heart into me, Madonna! Your conviction shores up mine. I shall seek out the roots of this contention, and tear them out of our soil. As for the traitors—whoever they are—tomorrow I'll set them a trail that shall find them out!"

He kept her hand a little longer, holding his candle high and searching her face for something she sensed he did not find. Then he smiled once, a peculiarly shy and chary smile, kissed her fingers a last time, and receded from her, his face pale beneath the modest light, his smile lingering until he turned at last and rounded the entrance to one of the passages that led away from the hall.

Now it was Tulla who was left in loneliness.

She shivered and stood still a moment, feeling the blackness into which he had gone press up against the boundaries of her own tiny circle of light. It gave way before her as she turned and climbed slowly back up the long staircase.

The next day interest was divided between the continued surveillance of Zorza's preparation (during which more discouraging substances than fruit were deposited upon those unwary enough to approach the walls), and the chill tribunal that sought to establish the root cause of last night's brawl.

It proved, however, that neither Franco at his cursing worst nor the cardinal at his brimstone best could budge any single member of the Valenti or the Biscaglia guard from his entrenched conviction that it was the opposite faction who had raised the rumpus and that their own lips had been sealed throughout.

Leone, unimpressed by the heaviness of the occasion, suggested that Andrea Zorza should be called in and, in the manner of Solomon, be given a sword and the opportunity to cleave one of the embarrassed captains in twain. Cerruti, beet-red with mortification (or guilt), pointed out that the condottiere was as likely, in this pleasingly hypothetical situation, to choose to silence his spy as to let him live. The Biscaglia captain duly noted his opponent's fear aloud. Swords were set rattling in their scabbard, and the whole to do was in danger of immediate repetition.

Franco, knowing himself beaten, had recourse to his other tactic. Although the enemy were now on their guard and their numbers hourly increasing, they had still not begun the attack. This meant that it was probably planned to begin at the next dawn and that, accordingly, tonight they would need a good night's sleep. They would be as surprised, therefore, as they might have been upon the previous night, to receive visitors from the citadel.

The sortie was on again—for the night to come!

The same picked men would be used, headed by both the discomforted captains and numbering slightly more of the Valenti persuasion. Franco was to be their overall leader and Leone, against his will, was to remain inside the castle.

"Should her general be killed, Montevalenti will have double need of her prince," Franco smiled, adamant.

"Better the prince were killed," Leone retorted, "for Montevalenti has far greater need of a general!"

They waited until the very pit of night, moving out of the southeastern city gate like their own ghosts, their boots muffled, stripped of all that could make a sound save their voices and their swords. For any slip of the former they guarded each other like enemies, whether Biscaglie or Valenti; as for the swords, they would advertise their presence only when they entered the unprepared flesh of the enemy.

Those who tried to follow their progress through the trees and brush beyond the gates soon released their eyes from the strain. The moon, undecided whether to reveal herself in full or to retain the modesty of a layer of decorative scudding cloud, gave only teasing assistance.

Even the trained watchers on the ramparts, who knew precisely where to look, saw nothing and were well satisfied.

Among them was Tulla. She had purportedly come there for Bernardo's sake. The boy now slept, it seemed, only in the early morning. She knew him safe enough alone, however, and it was anxiety for Franco that had brought her there to stretch her eyes and wear out her slippers in constant nervous walking up and down the leads, while the boy harried the watch guards for descriptions of what could not be seen.

"Madonna. The ramparts have become your chosen home. Does the lack of a roof make the world seem less your prison?"

The prince, cloaked, the hood up so that his face was a vague whiteness hanging above her, stayed her pacing, his hand on her wrist. Like her he carried no lantern. The infrequent torches set along the interior walls of the terrace gave the sparse light that was considered necessary for the nightwatch.

"The world is everyone's prison, my lord. God grant that for your brother and his band it may remain so."

"If your first remark had been less wry, I might almost imagine you had made a valuable personal discovery," Leone told her, equally wry. "And for the rest—a resolute amen! But have no fears on Franco's account. For all his preaching on the safety of *my* sacred person, he'd not put his own life seriously at risk so early in the game. That is not the work of a good commander."

"I like your argument. But I find it does not cure my concern."

His small chuckle *was* obscurely comforting. "And most of all you like my brother. Tell me, bella donna, if it were I who moved out there in the darkness, would you still pace the ramparts with such an anxious step?"

She tried to match his lightness, seeking relief in the small pretense.

"More so, my Lord Leone—since you would be less likely to find your way back."

"Now where's the compliment in that?" he wondered, peering out over the plain that was pitch black save for the tiny campfires where the sentries sat, dreaming comfortably of a tap on the shoulder.

The question was halfhearted, and she knew then that his tension equaled her own.

A sound caught her ear. From below, or merely the troubled slumbers of Montevalenti?

Again. From the plain, certainly this time. Leone had heard it too. "Look to the right, just west of the mill," he cautioned her. "They have begun the attack. The first of the guards have died."

If there was no regret in his voice, there was no triumph either. He might have spoken of cattle slaughtered for the table.

The sounds came more certainly now, and in concert, though very faint at such distance. To the extreme right a campfire flared up suddenly, and Tulla thought she saw the figures of men standing in its brief aureole. Then it was gone, and there were screams—no mistake there. Other fires blazed up while some were put out altogether. The noise spread as the right wing of the camp awakened, an indeterminable, muted fracas.

"What is happening? Why are they waking? I thought all was to be done in silence—"

He did not minister to her alarm, scarcely noticed it. He was staring hopelessly across at one particular fire—at the meaningless jumble of black figures, or trees, or ordinance, or horses, made luridly cryptic by its dull orange glow.

The rumor had spread in a semicircle upon the right, following the line of fires that were stoked and dampened and stoked again almost as if in some sort of signal. Although they were not precisely seen, there was a sense that many men were busy.

Her distress broke in upon her. "Something's wrong. I know it." She turned with a sudden savageness upon Leone. "If only you had listened to him—and to me—long before this—there would have been no need to place this risk upon him!"

Justice was the least of her interests at this point. He saw it and ignored her words, turning away from her and from the indistinct sights and sounds of the plain. They had driven him further than she could have hoped to do.

He did not bid her farewell as he set off to look for his brother.

The prince's mounted party met the first hard-pressed stragglers back before they were half way down the hillside. Most were wounded, some crawling painfully on their knees through brushwood that reared like a forest in their lacerated path. Their tale was brief and bloody.

"It was no good, my lord. They were on their guard." The man lay on his belly, weak and bleeding from a wound at the thigh.

"All seemed well at first; we stole upon them easily enough. There were few guards, and even they seemed half asleep. We marked our men, and my lord count gave the signal. Blood of a dog! It was as though it were *their* signal not ours! It was only a whistle, very low, a bird call he'd fixed on. When it came they leapt up like dead men recalled to life and set about us, two or three to one. It's like to have been a massacre! We fought—some of us are still fighting—but Lord Franco cried the retreat almost at once. He hadn't meant to risk losing lives, only to kiss and run, if you follow me—"

"Lord Franco? Where is he?"

Abashed, the man revealed interest in the methods of the soldier who was bandaging his leg. "I don't know. We lost sight of him." Reluctantly he looked his prince in the eye. "He'd not be the first to run, now would he, Excellence?"

Leone reined away from him and plunged down the hillside. As he reached the plain he encountered Cerruti, who had acquired a horse from somewhere and was attempting to inject order into the limping retreat. He rode singlehanded, his left sleeve tucked in at his belt, the upper arm dark with blood. His grimace for Leone was discouraging.

"The news is not good, my Prince. Your brother is taken. Alive."

"No!" He felt a thickening in his throat, a dislocation of breath.

"They have him at the mill where Zorza has set up his standard."

"What's their price?"

Cerruti shook his head. "I spoke with Zorza, but he would not talk of ransom. He charged me to tell you that you would hear from him at dawn." His grimness softened as he saw Leone's sick look. He had taught this boy to fight as he had taught the one he had been forced to leave behind. He had little time for this one these days; a popinjay singing on a branch, nothing more. But he had loved him as a boy and had once seen him fight like the old lion, his father, the day he'd thought they had leveled the Biscaglia trash forever. And for the sake of the past and because the popinjay's branch was shaking under him, he would not be niggard with hope, the only gift he had, "Ney, lad, don't look so green at me. 'Tis not long till dawn. Doubtless the bastard only means to make you wait. It is the mean manner of man he is."

Leone recovered himself. "God send you are right, Pascale! And the men—are many lost?"

"I estimate we may lose at least a third of them, perhaps more. Lord Franco was swift to call us off, but there have been many deaths." He considered his next words carefully, his eyes seeking Leone's. This time the questioning was his. "It was almost as if they expected us."

"Go on." Leone remembered the first man he'd met. "As though it was *their* signal—"

Cerruti moved his good arm impatiently. "Oh there's nothing solid—just a sense that—well, they couldn't have defended themselves better if they *had* known!"

Oh God. Leone stared ahead, sensing present ghosts. "If you'd listened to him—or to me—"

For an unreasonable second he wished time to turn.

"Get that wound seen to. I'll continue here," he ordered Cerruti. Then as the captain seemed about to demur, "At once! Get going, man!"

Pascale tried to make his smile approving, even a little grateful. The boy would have the sense not to be taken—and perhaps he needed to feel again, even in so slight a cause, what it was to command men.

* * *

It had taken very little time, none of it measured, for Leone
to seek out and shepherd in the remains of Franco's ill-
starred troop. At the end he had been aided by Julio Bagno,
who had come shrieking across the plain on the heels of some
poor wretch of a German whom he had executed swiftly and
neatly when he caught up with him, yards from the prince's
rallying point on the river bank just beyond the bridge.

"He killed my companion in arms," he explained cursorily,
seeing Leone's frown. He wiped his sword on the grass. "They
have the count. You know already?"

"But will not keep him long, I trust."

Bagno pulled a doubtful mouth. "I'd not trust the bastard."
He weighed his chances, then grinned.

"What say you, my Lord Prince—shall the two of us go and
take him from them? Now, at once? That way there'd be no
doubt—and no ransom to pay!"

"Except our lives!" Leone regarded him stonily. "And don't
think the idea doesn't appeal to me. It does. To my stomach.
And to my heart. My brother is very dear to me—but we
should not succeed. This escapade itself should have taught
you that, Julio."

"But my lord—"

"No argument. Go up to the fork where the Lightning Oak
stands. You'll find Alvaro there with horses. Take one and
come back here. You can help me marshal them in. We'll
take up the worst of the wounded to safe ground."

Bagno glowered at him, mutinous.

Leone looked at him bitterly. "You think I prefer my life to
his? I assure you, at this moment, that is far from being the
truth. Now go!"

Bagno obeyed.

Between them they saw every man safe home.

Thirty-seven of them had not crossed the river.

It was after this that they began to measure the time; for
now the waiting must begin.

Although many voices had counseled sleep and many more
had agreed upon the good sense of it, few save the wounded,
released by camomile or precious opium, paid heed. Gathered
once more about the ancient table, Franco's officers paid him
the tribute of their sleeplessness.

With the dead weight of Bernardo, whose years had succumbed against his will, slumped in the chair beside her, Tulla also kept her vigil.

It was Gian Carmaggio who had brought her the news. Underage and gone forth without permission, he was one of the first to be wounded and was sent back by Cerruti with burning ears to balance the pain of a shameful sliced buttock. He had proved a better courier than he had a soldier; his mother, at least, would have been delighted.

When Leone returned, therefore, Tulla had stretched the fabric of her fear for his brother to a quivering tissue of rage and blame.

When he had stopped by her chair to give her his own curt affirmation of the capture, she had clung to its wooden arm until the cedar bit into her hand in an attempt to control the palsied shaking that possessed her. She had not known it was possible to support such anger.

He had passed on, regardless of a reply, before she had mastered herself sufficiently to speak. Her voice cracked under its constriction as she hurled words like knives at his back.

"So—your care for your kin and your country has been such that now you will have to buy the let of the one with the life of another! Will that be the way of it, Prince? Or do you value the man more than your mountain top? How will you live, on the flat plain as small men do who are not princes and know how to guard their little futures with their heart's blood?"

"Madonna?" He had turned and was clearly at a loss, his bonetiredness coming between him and the sense of her words though he had read her fury in her looks. "I cannot—"

"No, indeed, you cannot—and therefore have to pay the price when Zorza asks it! Merciful God, man! Do you know what you have done? They will bargain for Montevalenti with Francesco's *life!*" She drove her words into him; if only they could make him bleed.

Leone wavered slightly, steadying himself upon the table. He smiled, almost wistfully, at the room full of attentive faces, most turning away from him in mortal embarrassment. When he spoke to her it was without rancor or reproof.

"Do you think so? I do not. There is, after all, the simpler solution—and one that will have a far greater appeal for signor Zorza. They will exchange my brother for myself—and then use *my* life to bargain for Montevalenti."

261

Several men gasped or swore and Tulla's heart gave a sickening jar. She stared at him, dazed, knowing that he had judged his man, he was right.

"All will eventually be well, Madonna," Leone continued, this time not without an edge. "For I shall ensure that the bold condottiere is thrown his quarry. I doubt," he added ironically, "if he will then raise the siege, whatever he may protest. But Montevalenti will have her finest leader once again—and the city will not fall to him. And then soon, Lorenzo may come to her aid bringing all to a satisfactory conclusion. Well, Madonna Thalia—is *that* comedy more to your liking?"

She would not lie to him so said nothing.

The waiting stretched out endless as Lachesis's thread. As the minutes passed Tulla began to know that it was partly this insupportable tension that had caused her outburst. Many of the soldiers were looking at her askance. Cerruti, Bagno, others.

It was the grizzled captain who made the suggestion that was in all their eyes. "If I were you, Madonna, I'd go to bed. You're plainly overwrought, and there's nothing you can do here. You might think, when you reflect, that you have already done too much in giving words to what should remain unspeakable—until that possibility is no more."

She deserved the chastening and felt it accordingly. She was suddenly aware of Bernardo, awake and bolt upright beside her, a prey to God knew what misery and confusion.

She rose impulsively and went to Leone, now seated before the table, chin on hands, staring wearily between his fists.

She had never once touched him willingly but now she reached out her hand to touch his shoulder. "I am sorry, my Lord Prince," she said in a low voice. "It is myself I have demeaned with my words, not you. Your brother has been a good friend to me. This night's work has exiled me from my wits for a space. Please do not mark my words. I am certain you will not, for they are unworthy either of notice or contempt."

To her surprise, shock almost, he picked up her hand from his shoulder and twisted his head to kiss it lightly and impersonally.

"That was certainly a prettier speech, my lady. And surely you are forgiven. I wish you could as easily forgive me for that of which you accuse me, or that I could easily forgive

262

myself. You have held up a mirror, Madonna, and the image therein is not what I would wish to see."

She did not know how to reply. She shook her head and moved away from him. She left the hall then, to wait out what was left of the night outside on the cold rampart.

After it seemed that the castle had waited for a dozen such nights unrelieved by a single dawn, the sun did indeed rise, a gray-yellow disc behind shifts of mist, a wan face spiritless and veiled. Almost at the moment it showed above the eastern treeline, the watchman ran in to say that a rider was approaching from across the river. The chamber was alert at once.

"A herald?" Whoever he was, he would be of no account to Andrea Zorza.

"I can see no emblem, my Prince. He is heavily muffled."

The rack of time demanded a little more from them as they waited until the messenger should gain the gate. Cerruti was dispatched to supervise its opening.

At last there came the sound that snapped the thread of that protracted night, a beating upon the iron door beneath the barbican, a deep, hollow, repeated note with the resonance of a great bass bell. The sound was carried clear across the bailey, thrust through thick glass windows, reverberated among the stones of stairs and passages and clamored in their ears.

Jesu! But it was welcome!

The herald went at his work with a will, and the blows continued to fall. There was a marked regular rhythm to them as though a drum was beaten rather than a door.

"A lad with no belief in the virtues of patience! Enough man! In Heaven's name why does Pascale not open?"

They listened more carefully, ears cocked to catch the clatter as the bars fell from the door.

The hammering continued on its even beat.

Leone leapt to his feet. "Is this insult—or is Cerruti struck deaf!"

The relentless, almost smug note continued, mocking the heartbeat of their exasperation.

When it stopped they remained taut for a second, still expectant, then slumped like rumpled puppets where they stood or sat, the tension flowing from them in a relief that was too sudden, that they knew to be premature.

They heard the bars fall and then silence.

After, there came a man's cry, from the bowels, dolorous, afflicted with pain that was not physical.

Leone was first among them as they rushed for the stairs.

The empty circle of the hallway greeted their descent, its great double doors gaping open, derelict of guards.

Across the bailey, clustered about the barbican gate, the crowd of the castle's people were gathered. Despite their numbers they made little sound. They held fast one to another, a hand on a shoulder, a hand in a hand. They shifted to open a path for the prince, but he saw that they turned their eyes from his question.

Beyond the barbican another crowd faced him, equally mute. They had surrounded Zorza's horseman on three sides but none had come within a yard or so. He stood, his face ashen, as though within a magician's charmed circle. His hands, though he tried to control them, were shaking. He saw the prince and made an impulsive move toward him, betraying a certain small relief and an even greater apprehension.

Leone cried out to him, urgent, dismissive of protocol.

"Speak, man. What are your terms?"

The man trembled.

Behind Leone another voice spoke harshly. "There are no terms, my Lord." It was Cerruti. "Only this—"

Head spun with body as the loathing in the tone instilled foreboding. And yet, though his reaction was instant, instinctive, it seemed that this single turning took many seconds to accomplish; the air became heavy about him, viscous, filled with currents that worked against him, while his body was mere insubstantial wrack, cast against the tide by invisible hands—a thing without impulse or volition, whose only purpose was to obey. As he clove through this thickening of his element he dreamily noticed the presence of the Byzantine. She was kneeling upon the ground, covering her face with her hands.

Afterward, remembering this moment, he recollected the sorrowing curves of that uncharacteristically abandoned figure as both the premonition and an accusation for himself. He knew too that within the infinity of that time out of time, he dwelled upon her for as long as he could—so that he might not have to lift his eyes and make them follow Pascale's pointing finger.

If his body was deprived of its musculature, his eyelids had, under the same dread enchantment, turned to lead. And yet they had both seen, and known, before he wished it.

His cry was one that wolves would have run from. Its agony lanced the swollen silence of the crowd and set free their lamentation with the belief they had, until now, too willingly suspended.

The thing that was nailed to the castle door bore no resemblance to any part of a man. A shapeless, bloodied, carnal token, its smallness almost ludicrous, its slaughter-house aspects obscene, it glistened and dripped against the iron-bound óak like the miraculous, bleeding relic of some saint, as before it the citizens of Montevalenti sank, moaning, to their knees.

It was his brother's heart.

For a long time he stood and very simply wished it were his own. There was an abyss of loneliness, an echoing chasm of self-hatred. He hurled himself into it. It was what he deserved.

It was Cerruti who made the first move, seeing that shock had deprived the prince of speech and motion and having himself an overwhelming need for both; though his face was seamed with tears for his commander, he suffered the soldiers' automatic necessity when confronted with death, to affirm that life will continue. Clearing his throat with a low growl, he muttered, "Sancta Maria, miserere nobis!" Then snatched the dagger from his belt and began to use it as a lever to remove the first of the nails.

"Hold, I command you!" Leone had unstopped his voice, unable to bear this crude, necessary act. Mistaking his meaning, Cerruti nodded roughly and raised the brass clarion of his own voice, rolling it above the heads of the kneeling people as though to challenge the listening plain.

"You look upon the heart of Francesco da Valenti," he cried, "torn from his breast by the hand of the traitor Andrea Zorza, would-be usurper of this principality!" Appealing to Leone and through him to all of them, he continued without the suggestion of a tremor, "Court Francesco has given that heart for each one of us here, for it was in our cause that he rode out. Shall we then be so niggard of gratitude as to deny his gift—take it down from the gates of our city and clothe it in velvet, to lie unheeded in a golden casket—or shall we accept it with a warrior's pride, overthrowing even our sorrow, and let it remain where you see it, where it has ever

265

been—inseparable from the fabric of Montevalenti in love and in loyalty! Let it be a talisman and a strength to all of us in the struggle to come!"

The roar of agreement that followed banished simple tears, and people got to their feet, cheering and waving their fists.

Leone felt a terrible nausea. Somehow he should have prevented this, but since he had not, he must let it stand. The bewilderment and fear had left his people with their pity.

"My lord! Is it true what Pascale says? Have they killed Uncle Franco?"

Bernardo was pulling desperately upon his hand; what he sought was denial.

Abstractedly Leone stroked his hair, trying for his sake to come back from his distance. "It is true."

Bernardo gasped and tears flooded from him with the suddenness of childhood. "God's curse on the bastard! Oh I will *kill* him! I will *kill* him!"

Seeing the small fists flailing at space, Leone's own sense of impotence was hideously increased. He hardly noticed when Tulla came to lead the boy away from him. She did not want to speak to him, did not trust the depth of her pain. Yet neither could she remain speechless. "Cerruti's words were brave," she said abruptly as she took Bernardo's hand. "But you are the one who should have spoken them, Prince."

He turned away to search among the crowd. He was looking for a carpenter. Some kind of shelter must be built around the hideous thing on the door that he would not yet let himself believe had anything to do with Franco. It could not be left open to fate and the weather until it resembled the leathern and unrecognizable substance that was all that had been left of the Biscaglia who had once hung upon these walls.

FOURTEEN

They had sent back the body later in the day, decently laid out upon a stretcher, the cloak covering the bloodied doublet. Andrea Zorza did not dare refuse this measure of the courtesies of war. Those who had related to him how the prince, his rival, had taken it, had also informed him that the Princess Alessandra had appeared much cast down by the death of the count. Zorza did not wish to give her *needless* offense. The day was approaching when she would become his wife.

The nimble surgeon had sewn together the bruised flesh and had given his opinion that the heart, thanks be to God, had not been riven, living, from the breast, but that it had been extracted after death, which was caused, in his estimation, by the deep sword wound found to have passed through the lungs.

Leone himself, in an effort to force himself back from that limbo of the mind in which he was exiled, had dressed his brother's body in the crimson and gold of their house and carried it into the chapel where it lay upon its catafalque before the altar, looking now, with the unwilled and merciless deceit of the dead, much as it had in sleeping life.

But even the intimacies of the mortuary had not brought Franco close to him, had not released his anger nor his tears. He longed to weep but could not. He felt himself alone, barely existing, in his void. It was as though he walked in his sleep and knew that he did but could by no means wake; as though he were condemned never to wake. He kept his vigil without rest in the chapel. He was as well there as anywhere and his brother's face was peaceful to look upon. He was angry when they tried to take him to the council chamber, angrier when, countering, they brought the council to him.

"They're bringing up the cannon, Magnifico. The bombardment will soon start." Cerruti's murmur was insistent.

"Today! Will he not leave us to mourn a single day in peace?"

One or two of them muttered in agreement, but the old soldier gave him short shrift for that. "It may be unmannerly, my lord, but it is good tactics. He knows we are stricken by grief—and hopes that we are also unmanned by it. He shall find differently," he added so firmly that Leone knew himself reproved.

Pascale wanted him roused. He supposed they all did. It was even necessary that he should be; he saw that. Only he seemed unable to connect this necessity with any action he might take, any word he might give.

He looked at Franco and wondered if indeed he too had died and they were now both in limbo. No. If that were the case his brother would not lie there and let him still be lonely—

He was alive, but in some muted, far-off fashion that had cut him off from Cerruti and the rest. They would soon see it and leave off their importunities.

What was it the man wanted? Something about the battlements.

"Very well, Pascale. Do as you think fit."

"Will you not see for yourself, my Lord Leone? It can do no good to remain here. His Eminence the Cardinal has ordered perpetual masses to be sung for the soul of Count Francesco. He will not be left alone, my lord." He fumbled the air in the direction of the body.

"Not he, no. It is I, I who am alone. Whoever that 'I' may be, for there seems no substance in it. I will come presently. Leave me now."

A hasty consultation of worried eyes, and he was obeyed. No company now save the high, pure intonation of the prayers for the dead as before him on the altar, Silvestro's priests offered up their seamless requiem.

When the cardinal passed by the kneeling figure on his way to the altar, he received no sign that he was seen. Observing the preternatural stillness, the fixed and dreaming gaze, he did not stop to make himself known but waited in prayer before the candle-ringed image of St. Jerome in its tiny side chapel until it was time to take his place as the next celebrant of the mass. It was plain, from that mask of a face, that the Prince of the Valenti was in as great a need of prayer as was the soul of his brother.

Alessandra Biscaglia, come to pay her respects to the dead, and to hear the cardinal's mass, was not afflicted with any such delicacy. Her husband's needs were very plain to her and they did not include prayer. That they were of even the faintest interest to her was something that she regarded in herself with the ironic detachment she was accustomed to confine to externals. The world had changed. She, it seemed, was to some extent changing to accommodate it. She approached Leone, undeterred by his obvious absence from the scene in all but physical fact.

"My lord." Her gown of soft gray-green wool washed across the mosaic before his knees, forcing him to shorten the focus of his wide-eyed gaze. He blinked and found the imprint of a cross upon his retina; he had been staring, without knowing it, at Silvestro's somber back, the black chasuble with its stark gold threaded symbol of crucifixion.

"You have had no sleep, Leone. Nor have you eaten for many hours. I have refreshment in my rooms and there is quiet there. They are bombarding the southeastern wall, beyond the gate, but you cannot hear it there."

Her words reached him, a pricking in his mind like the patch of green that itched at his eyes.

"Thunder, it was thunder."

"It was not thunder, my lord. They have brought up their bombard and have fired it twice. Young Ponti is trying to blow it up, but so far his aim has been unlucky. There is a crack in the wall, but it still stands. Cerruti has the masons working on it now."

What was she talking about? "Alessandra?"

"Yes?"

"Franco is dead. My brother is dead."

For a moment she thought his senses possessed.

"Come away from here, my lord. You will return when you are rested. And rest you must if those who need you are to get any good of you."

His head was dreadfully heavy; she was right. But it was not a weariness that rest might cure—only death could end it, death that should have come to him instead of to Franco.

"Those who *need me?*" His dry laugh shocked her in this place.

She looked at him with her old disdain. "You are not your-self or you would not speak so. Come. Leave these morbid thoughts and take food and wine and let sleep restore you." She hesitated. "Believe me when I say that I too sorrow for his death. Your brother was a man I could respect."

When he did not reply, she put out her hand to shake his shoulder slightly. "Will you not come with me?"

He brushed her aside and rose to his feet.

Before the altar the cardinal turned and saw his sister's solicitude. He marked it down among other things of impor-tance. Alessandra was the one being in this world whom he truly loved. He deeply desired her happiness. However, she did not always know what was best for her. It was the way of a woman, but at times it could be irksome. He turned again and knelt before the shrine of his God.

"I thank you, but I will not trouble you," Leone told his wife. The heaviness on his spirit was even greater than that upon his eyelids. He could deal with neither unless he could be alone.

And yet the woman did not go. He supposed she meant to be kind. She had taken to showing him courtesy of late, of which the last night's game of chess had been witness. He had wondered at it, but did not do so at this moment. He concentrated all his will upon wishing her away.

But it was not to be. "Leone, I have wondered—the men are talking—" there was a pregnant hesitation in her delivery.

He raised a brow, mostly in irritation.

She took it for encouragement. "It seems certain that Franco's sortie was expected. There must therefore be some traitor—within our walls."

There seemed some reluctance in her voice. Did she, he wondered, half amused, think him capable of suspecting herself? Or, if not he, others? Was this the root of her new-found ability to bear his company? Was it reassurance she sought from him? The bitterness of his smile seemed to please her.

"It is possible. I think not likely. It is far more credible that they were simply on their guard as such a company should be. A professional mercenary soon learns to sleep lightly, or his career will be as short as his sense."

Her doubt was plain. "But to be so swift and so silent in dispatching our men—it was beyond the natural. Your own leaders say it."

How much longer would she trouble him?

"I know that Cerruti is unquiet on this, my lord—"

"So?"

"Will you not seek out the traitor?" Her voice was high, though she tried not to reveal her outrage at this seeming carelessness of events.

"Let him look among your Biscaglia guards if he will—if in doing so he does not provoke another dispute."

He looked at the ground not at her, and she sensed he wished her gone. She hesitated, traced the terazzo outline of the sleeping lion with her foot, aware of her brother's voice raised in the "Kyrie eleison."

"It was not of my guard that I was thinking, but of your Venetian houri."

"What, still? I should have thought events would have quenched all fears on her account. And now, Alessa, I must beg you—"

She spoke quickly, before he could ask her to leave him. "You would do well to think again, Leone. She is not what you think her, nor yet what Franco thought her. And even you, my lord—"

"Well?"

"You must know that she was no virgin when first she came to you. Did it not occur to you that she might be Zorza's mistress?"

His brief crack of laughter sounded strange, even in his own ears.

"Alessa! You cannot have it both ways. First you claim that the 'cousin' who has proved himself so worthy of his bloodier forebears in fact refused Mona Tulla's offer of her body, thus causing her vengefully to accuse him of treachery. Now you would have her his mistress!"

"Wait. It is not so foolish. She has remained within the castle has she not? How if she accused him only so that she could remain without suspicion after his expulsion? And act as his spy within our walls?"

Her eyes and voice made demands that his weariness could not counter.

"How if she has delivered your brother to his death?"

He groaned. "How if the truth should be simpler than that—that Zorza is the only traitor and that his only relation to Mona Tulla is that of a would-be ravisher?"

"Would-be?"

271

She repeated her earlier words. This time he would be forced to hear.

"I have said that she was no virgin. It is not a subject I wish to discuss with you at length." He could not have known her part in this—and the golden eyes, sunken in their sockets, told her nothing.

"How do you know such a thing?"

She smiled thinly. "My cousin was wont to boast," she lied.

Leone was conscious that somewhere there was an ache in him. It did not seem to be associated with either bone or sinew; perhaps it was merely a bruising of the mind.

"Alessandra," he said with infinite gentleness, "there is no place here, any longer, for such thoughts as these. I entreat you to put them from you. I assure you that the girl did not betray my brother. Please, let that content you."

She gave him a shrewd look and murmured, almost with submission, "If it so easily contents *you,* my lord."

His answering sigh ghosted among the walls and pillars. From far off there came the muffled rumble of "Il Bastardo's" heavy fire.

She made a private resolve to have the girl watched. She did not know whether or not she truly held the suspicion she had voiced. But there were other things she did not know. About the girl. And about her husband. She could no longer exert the hold over the slave that Atroviso's presence had provided, but her powers of invention were fertile and were, perhaps even now, circling about the truth. Andrea had not boasted, far from it. He had been secretive. And she had felt that the girl had been some part of his secret.

She glanced covertly at Leone's exhausted face and chanced new reproof.

"You were wrong once, my Prince. I beg you, do not, for the sake of some—personal feeling you may have toward this girl—put the fate of your province in jeopardy."

"I will not bear this!"

The heat of it surprised her. She had thought him too apathetic to be cut so quickly. "I crave your pardon, my lord," she said hastily. She became grave and quiet, awaiting her punishment.

"Oh God!" He brought down his fist upon the unfeeling marble of the catafalque. The pain came and went in his face as he stared at her. "You are the only woman who could hold

272

such a conversation before a corpse! Will you not go now, and leave me and my brother in peace!"

She bit her lip. She had gone too far. "My care is for the living. I can do nothing for the dead."

Again his wild laughter tore across the stillness of the nave. "And what will you do for me, sweet wife? Will you warm my cold heart so that I can tell the difference once more between myself and *him?*"

His pointing finger accused her and she turned away; now it was he who came close to the mark. Tears filled her throat, and her relief was immense when she saw that her brother had left the altar and was approaching them, his black vestments a further reproach to her gracelessness.

"My sister, good day. Prince, you have watched too long. Will you not go now and rest? There are but three hours until the burial service."

He had heard most of their conversation, all of the latter part; his mass had been a thing repeated by rote as he listened. He had finished it some minutes before and had chosen this moment to step between them. He did not want Alessandra to damage her small new launched ship upon the rocks of her own nature. That was something that Leone was, surely, subtle enough to appreciate, even at this time. He smiled at him restrainedly and was accorded a brief tightening of the lips that reassured him he was understood.

He took the princess by her arm and drew her toward the sacristy. She did not look at her husband again and was therefore spared his further grimace of relief.

Once inside the incense-laden chamber, Alessandra leaned back against the heavy open door and allowed the accumulated tension of the last half hour to drain from her. She had never been able to relax in Leone's presence, since those dead first days of their marriage, but never before this war had started had she sensed such a stiffening and wariness of all her being before him.

Silvestro took her hands, all solicitude. "You are weeping. You must not."

"No. It is nothing. It is a sad time for all of us."

"Yes. Certainly. Franco's death is a tragedy for Montevalenti."

He kissed her hand and held it still, stroking it softly.

"Leone—can he?"

"He will take his place in time. Do not distress yourself

273

with these things. All will be well at last. Only wait, my dear. Wait."

She pushed herself away from the door and fell naturally into his arms, feeling the black folds of the chasuble close about her, the harsh gold of the braid against her cheek.

"Dear Silvio! Without you, I could not bear my life here." She lifted her face and buried it in his neck, where sweeter scents than those of incense lay warmly upon beating pulses.

For a moment the cardinal clasped her to him with a greedy strength and then, suddenly relaxing, opened his arms and left her standing alone. She stood upon her toes and kissed his cheek, smiling now. "You are my only comfort."

"And you are mine, Alessandra. Never forget it." He repaid her smile, holding her eyes with his. "And now, Principessa, let us begin to prepare for the burial of the best of the Valenti."

The funeral took place against the uneven accompaniment of the bombardment. Lots were cast as to who must remain to man the walls while every free soldier and citizen followed the crimson and gold draped coffin of Francesco da Valenti to its final resting place in the crypt of San Jerome. Their melancholy singing was as much interrupted by their own uncontrolled sobbing as by the dulled reports of the impact of stone upon stone.

Upon the walls themselves the scene was one of hard, regular activity as Ponti's gunners kept up a slow but steady order of fire directed at any enemy men or machines within their range. Zorza's great bombard, for which Ponti had sworn his soul well away, remained tantalizingly outside that range, trained upon the single weakness it had already inflicted upon the sixteen-foot thickness of the citadel's outer wall. Below, the engineers worked to buttress the crack. Up aloft, the arbalesters were occupied at every notch and behind their cross-shaped loopholes, three men in a row were shooting in turn to keep up a busy stream of fire. These, together with the crossbowmen and the culverineers did their best to repay with interest the various offerings from the plain. The accurately propelled javelins of the ballistas, the streams of stone from mangonel and trebuchet, old tried and tormenting weapons which, while incapable of making any deep impression on the walls, could keep the defenders

274

hopping, destroying concentration and aim, and occasionally fracturing the castellations into murderous, flying fragments.

To walk the narrow streets of the city beyond this beleaguered shield of stone was almost to be unaware of the siege. None but the loudest sounds could penetrate their labyrinthine density. Even had they done so they would by now be canceled out by the one familiar voice that alone could dominate the town, the mountain and the echoing heavens above them—the great bass bell of San Jerome, tolling its sonorous, deep-throated farewell to Francesco da Valenti, and gathering in those who had loved him to do likewise.

Obeying it they crowded into the cathedral, their grief twisting in them like knives and offering up, together with the prayers that speeded the departed soul, others less gentle—that they might be permitted to turn those knives upon the enemy. Those who could not thrust their way in, sank to their knees in the square and remained there throughout the hour-long mass.

When it was over they asked those who came out, "What of Il Leone? How did our prince carry himself?"

"Like one who neither sees nor hears. One could not go near him."

"Domine Dio! We must pray for him also."

"And for ourselves!"

They waited for a while unless he should yet come out to speak to them, but although the princess emerged, black-veiled and subdued, followed by Vanozza Grazzi and the weeping Valenti children, and later the cardinal and Father Ambrogio with whom he had shared the mass, there was no sign of the prince.

Sadly they turned away and took their disappointment back to their homes and to the defenders on the walls, puzzled and lacking something they had thought to receive.

To reach the crypt of San Jerome one must leave the main building by the north door and cross the courtyard of the adjoining monastery. One will find oneself in the monks' rose garden, a place of beguiling scents and deep quiet, woven alleyways of flowers leading to secluded niches where sculptured saints stand smiling, to pleasant fountains and restful seats. One such alley, overgrown with small star-white roses with dusty golden hearts, brings one to the few steps, a little

275

moss-grown in the corners, that descend to the crypt where the generations of the Valenti lie buried.

It was here that Tulla came, now that the last requiem was sung, and all of Montevalenti had looked its last on his body, to offer her private valediction to Francesco's soul. She thought abstractedly, as she came through the roses, that it was a pity to feel such sadness in a place so beautiful and so clearly designed to give joy. She broke off several of the longer stems; she would take some of their light down with her into the tomb.

She descended beneath a low arch, covering her eyes to lessen the shock of blindness. After a few careful steps, she lowered her hand and realized at once that the darkness was not total. Of course, there would be lamps burning in the crypt. The body was not yet buried but still lay in state for the visits of members of the family.

She moved forward slowly, conscious of the cold and of the faint odor, dank and ancient, that underlay the more obvious perfume of incense. It was a broad, low-ceilinged chamber, cut into the rock, its surfaces uneven, following the stone formations. There were several marble tombs set in niches carved into the walls and three that stood on the floor toward the back of the vault, with perhaps two yards between each one.

It was upon the central one of these that Francesco's body reposed, still wearing the flamboyant colors of his house, the golden cloak obscuring the violet silk of the pall beneath him. Tulla approached hesitantly, apprehensive of how he might look. But the dead face, despite its final whiteness, was not that of the stranger she had feared, but Franco still, though perhaps the gentle features appeared more serene than they had in life, the characteristic small frown between his brows smoothed away, as often Tulla had seen it smoothed by music.

She bent to kiss the still face. She did not weep. She laid her roses, a last private sunburst, upon the crimson velvet breast. As she did so her eye was caught by something that glimmered on the floor beyond the sarcophagus. A dark shape—she could not make it out—a pool of denser blackness—and here and there the glint of something bright. She lifted one of the nightlights that stood at Francesco's feet and went forward, holding it.

Nothing could have prevented the gasp that was magnified

and prolonged in the echoing vault. In the small illumination the shapeless mass at once took on the relief of a man. Prostrate upon the ground, his arms stretched wide, as though crucified upon the flags, his body buried in the dark pool of his cloak, his head in the disheveled halo of his hair, was Leone da Valenti, released at last to mourn his brother as he wished.

Tulla stared down at the motionless figure, herself stunned into a similar stillness. This was a man who had abased himself unto the utter abnegation of self. With a shock of pity she saw how his hands were shaped into claws where they had torn in agony at the flagstones.

She felt a sickness in her breast. It was not fitting that there should be a witness of such grief as this. Decency did not permit it. Stumblingly she began to withdraw, replacing the lamp upon the tomb. She stood for a last moment in silent homage to Francesco, and there came a faint interrogative sound behind her.

At once she turned.

From the ground, stiffly moving his arms beneath his shoulders, Leone looked up. He saw who was standing in the lamplight, her face mapped with alarm. Behind her, upon Franco's breast, he saw the roses shining. He cursed and sat up slowly.

His look told her at once how distant was the country to which he had traveled. She had taken the same lonely journey herself after the death of her parents in Soraya. The prince's face was drawn to the bone, his eyes glittering and restless in their hollowed-out sockets. His lips had thinned to a fine line, which trembled slightly, involuntarily, so that he bit down savagely to control it.

A wave of sorrow and pity washed over her that was as strong as the anguish she had first felt at Franco's death. Overwhelmed by its fierceness, she stretched her hand toward him, as though she groped in the dark toward a friend.

He only groaned and turned away his head, with a muttered "For God's sake take your leave and let me be."

"My lord, I cannot." Her voice did not seem to belong to her. He did not speak again, and she let the silence grow around them until it became almost comfortable, a part of the darkness.

He had not moved but remained seated with his arms about his knees, his shoulder half turned away from her, staring, not focusing, toward his ancestors in their stone niches.

Tulla sat down beside the sarcophagus, her head level with its lid.

One of Franco's hands lay near to her face. She fought a sudden temptation to take it in her own and hold it, as though he might still bring her comfort. For yet, within the confines of that strange dark silence, it seemed as if Franco were as strongly present, in death, as either Leone or herself, living.

Perhaps indeed, in some sense this was so, for both of them were loathe to let him go, the one clinging to the knowledge of friendship, an easy companionship that did not judge, and the other, more complex, as much in need of the only possible confessor for the abysmal sin of omission which he now counted his past life to have been, as of the brother and counselor, whose love was as unswerving as it was taken for granted. Because they required it, therefore, they kept his presence close to them and suffered the more from the incontrovertible fact of his death.

Some sense of these things nudged at the edges of Tulla's thoughts as she sat in that ill-lit gloom, keeping company with the grief of the man to whom she was prisoner. A part of her was satisfied by the very extremity of his suffering, not because she took any vengeful pleasure in seeing him brought low, but because it revealed to her a different man. She had thought him all lightness, all surface, and now saw him in the shadows, the surface flayed, the nerve ends of pain laid raw. And because his sorrow sprang from the same roots as her own she pitied him as she pitied herself.

The silence of the tomb enfolded them.

It was not oppressive and time was unimportant, but, after a great many unnumbered moments, Tulla began to feel that there was a *waiting* within the silence; as though this suspension of life was permitted as a respite but must not be taken beyond its limit. She looked across at Leone. She doubted if he was now aware of her presence.

She knew that, for herself, the sunlight called again. She had offered up her prayers and had indulged her quiet thoughts of Franco. This death had left a wound in her, but it would heal and its scar would come in time to remind her of the gladness of knowing the man rather than the pain of losing him. That this, rather than Leone's abandonment to desolation, was the course of true mourning came to her with the quiet certainty of a revelation. She knew too, that it was something in the nature of the dead man that had enabled her to see this and she was profoundly grateful for it. Henceforth she would mourn her parents, also, in the fashion that they had deserved of her, without the heaviness of hatred and vengeance that had formerly possessed her on their account.

Would such a release, she wondered, also be given to Leone da Valenti?

On an impulse she rose and crossed the ground between them.

"My Lord Prince—will you not leave this place now? You have much to do."

It was as if she had not spoken.

"My Lord Leone—"

Again she extended her hand to him, not quite daring to touch the hunched shoulder. Only in the bright disarray of his hair was there life, as the bent head flamed beneath the lamps.

Out of her own new found peace a decision was born in Tulla.

She understood his sorrow, as Franco himself would have done. But Franco would have deemed, as she now began to do, that this present annihilation contained the seeds of danger, both for the man and for the state he governed.

Quietly and determinedly she began to talk.

"On a day I well remember, your brother spoke to me of you. I had cried out against you, and I think he tried to make me look, a little, through his eyes. He claimed for you a love of your people as well as of women and your pleasure; a kindness, an unwillingness to hurt. He told me how he had admired you when you were boys, how you were the only hero to your peers. A matchless champion in valor, accounted second to none as swordsman or archer. A paragon of learning, your wit your truer steel. Poet, painter, maker of music—all those within your province—and above these, the invaluable facility to make men love you—as Franco loved you."

She paused, seeking more words and breath. There was no indication that she was heard. She added a tinge of asperity to her tone.

"To whom was this great gift of affection, this boundless admiration given? To the creature without hope or courage who holds to these cold stones and will not rise? Is this what he would expect of you, what he has the right to demand?"

Her words echoed emptily like pebbles dashed against the side of a well.

Defeated, she turned back to the sarcophagus, almost with the demand on her lips for the help she needed. Beneath the kindly, lambent light, there appeared more capability of speech in those pale, relaxed features than in the rigidly inexpressive cloaked and crooked figure beside her.

She gazed perplexedly from the living to the dead brother. Suddenly anger was her rescuer, tearing away the gag and bonds of pity.

"God's blood, Valenti! It is your brother who lies dead, not you! Will you make a mockery of his death by this false-seeming?"

His shoulders stiffened and the bowed head came up. "Get out!" He spat the words toward the wall.

"I don't presume to degrade your grief. It is you who degrade it by the way you bear it."

He was on his feet and twisting toward her, his face a devil's mask, white, hate-filled, his hand flailing back to strike. She moved instinctively, and his stiffness betrayed him. The blow, meant to annihilate, glanced harmlessly off her arm. Unbalanced, she fell back against the catafalque, and as she steadied herself, her hand lighted on velvet and upon something that scratched. It was a rose. Horrified, she knew that she had leaned for an instant upon Franco's broken breast. The knowledge made her anger incandescent. For a moment that madness in the yellow eyes was matched in her own as she screamed, "They have riven out his heart and nailed it to your door! Is there no live heart beating in you that will make you rise up and match his courage? Has your brother given his life only for the sake of your feeble tears? For a travesty, for *nothing?*"

He seized her by the wrist and wrenched it cruelly, pulling her toward him. "Your voice is an obscenity in this place! Do you think to wake him with your braying trumpet?"

Their eyes were close.

"It is the Lion of the Valenti I seek to wake," she returned, her voice now soft. "Has he been supine so long that he has forgotten the sound of the battle array? Or is he so lapped in self-love that it cannot concern him? Your people have taken your brother's heart for their sacred talisman. They believe it

280

will make them invincible. What will it make of you—only a coward?"

"What did it make of you, lady, while still it beat strong in his breast—that you make it so much your business? Were you my brother's mistress?"

It was unforgivable at such a time and in such a place.

"Had it been so I should have been most proud!"

He laughed. It was the most unhappy sound she had ever heard. "Never fear. One Valenti, you will find, is much like the rest—"

He thrust her wrist behind her back and forced her body hard against his and forced his mouth upon hers in a kiss that had nothing in it of pleasure or even desire, only of the need to humiliate, in insult, to crush. Then as she tugged to be free of him he suddenly released and sprung her round to face Francesco's body, giving her a derisive little push toward the tomb.

"Look your last on him, Madonna, and tell him how well you understand the language of those beyond the grave, how you take it upon yourself to be his mouthpiece on earth. Doubtless he will applaud you well though he can no longer requite you as he would wish."

Choked with tears and anger she lashed back upon him. "You shame only yourself, Prince!"

Leone seemed to be drained of the passion that had possessed him, as though his demon had flown out with his bitter words.

"It is evil," he said dully, "that you invoke in Franco's name. Do you not know the evil that has already come to him is the evil that sings in the blood and delights in the sword."

Shaken, she answered him quietly, "You have no choice."

He made a faint, hopeless gesture of the hand, as though describing the sepulcher around them. "It is a resurrection you want—a miracle?"

She might have smiled then. "Not a resurrection—perhaps a rebirth."

Without further words she turned and ran quickly to the mouth of the crypt. When she emerged, unsteady and blinking, into the sunlight, the scent of roses was so welcome that she wept.

It was here, after all, as she stood amid the tranquillity of scent and light and touched the soft hearts of flowers, that she sent at last to the soul of Francesco da Valenti her true and most gentle farewell.

Leone remained for a time in the restored silence of the crypt, looking down at the corpse whose face bore such a close resemblance to his own. After a while he addressed certain words to the shade of his brother, certain others to himself. Afterward he knelt, crossed himself and prayed. When he rose from his knees he left the tomb without a backward look. A scent of roses greeted him, and he smiled as if surprised. Traversing the garden and the cloister he knocked on a door and asked for the father prior. He took refreshment with the monk and arranged with him that his brother's body should be finally committed to the tomb after vespers.

From the monastery he made his way back through the streets to the castle, walking quickly, looking neither right nor left. Those who saw him were aware of a heightened tension in him, an unaccustomed tautness in his stride, an alertness in his eye. Equally they sensed the welcome lessening of some foreboding in themselves.

On arrival at Castel' Valenti, the prince went not to his own apartments but to those of his brother. Without calling the servants he searched in the wardrobe until he found what he sought. A few minutes sufficed to make certain changes in his appearance. Then he examined himself momentarily in a mirror. What he saw caused the corners of his mouth to curl, if not precisely with mirth, with a wry detachment that did not exclude it. Satisfied, he directed his steps toward the gunnery battlement.

At first young Alvaro Ponti thought he was looking at a ghost. The figure that strode toward him, wearing the familiar breastplate and carrying the plain steel helmet, the long sword slung at the hip, wore the somewhat grim and slightly preoccupied expression that he expected of signor Franco. At the same time it was patently *not* the count. It was, he saw now, the prince, and in a guise in which his lieutenant had never expected to see him. The flowing, biblical garments had gone with the silks and velvets, giving place to practical fustian. The luxuriant hair was shorn of its lovelocks and curled about his ears and brow like that of a page. The lineaments of resolution were newly sketched upon the handsome face whose eyes no longer dreamed of the delights of the sultan's couch but were concentrated with a hawk-like intensity upon the gleaming barrels of Alvaro's cannon.

"My lord?"

Leone sensed the boy's apprehension. What new madness was this in his unpredictable potentate? He laid a reassuring arm about the mailed shoulders.

"You have not succeeded with Il Bastardo?" he asked.

"No." Alvaro would not hang his head, however. God knew how hard and how often he had tried.

"You will not while the distance between yourself and your target remains the same. Tell me, will your guns travel easily?"

Alvaro frowned. "They are heavy, my Prince, but the carriages may be pulled by half a dozen men or a couple of oxen."

"Excellent! Have them hoisted over the walls."

Ponti's eyes bulged. His stomach sank. Il Leone had indeed been driven demented by sorrow.

"Give the order to hoist the guns down on the sward. We are about to administer a severe shock to Il Bastardo—to both of them!"

Taking pity upon the stricken Alvaro, who, he saw, feared for his guns as a father fears rape, he proceeded to enlighten him further.

Precisely one hour and forty minutes after the gunner's brow had cleared and a beatific smile had replaced his frown, there came a thunder of a report that shook the ramparts, the walls and not least the inhabitants of the castle with a reverberation that rumbled its glad tidings down to the very foundations, deep in the earth of Montevalenti.

Il Bastardo, fleeing in frenzy, at the nightmare pace of a snail, dragged at the tail of her forty oxen, had been blown sky high and back again by Alvaro Ponti's second-best gun, from a vantage point some three hundred yards down the hillside. Il Leone had brought out 200 men to ensure the operation, well protected by the treacherous maquis around them and by the determined company of archers who covered them from above.

Il Bastardo did not have a chance.

FIFTEEN

When the door of Tulla's chamber opened after midnight, she turned and murmured into her pillow, half awakened by the instinct that suggested Lucia might need to be comforted after a nightmare. No childish voice accosted her, however, and it was several seconds before her sixth sense informed her that someone was standing beside her bed.

With an effort she opened her eyes.

It was the prince.

Wearing a loose robe of crimson silk he gleamed within the aura of her nightlight like the apparition of some demon in a mystery play. His demeanor did nothing to lessen this impression. If the uncontrolled anguish of the sepulcher no longer haunted his face it was nonetheless grim.

"Magnifico? Is there some trouble?"

"None. For the present."

"Then what—?"

"Am I doing in your chamber?" His lips tightened.

"This afternoon you found it expedient to speak to me of my duty as Prince of Montevalenti and my brother's heir. It was not business of yours, but you took it upon yourself to make it so. In recompense for your trouble I have come here, as I should have done long since, to make you *my* business." So saying he reached for the edge of the sheet that covered her and threw it back before she had made sense of his words.

"You sleep naked. Charming. And convenient, if a little lacking in the element of feminine mystery. However, if you remember, your body holds few secrets for me—one only, to be unchivalrously exact."

She dragged at the other half of the sheet and covered

herself as best she could, while desperately seeking a reprieve.

"You gave me a promise once, my lord, that you would not enter this room uninvited."

"You are mistaken. *I* gave you no promise. You speak of another man."

She looked at him suspiciously. Could it be that the rumors that flew about the castle were true? They said that he had lost his senses. He disabused her at once.

"It was the man of peace and simple pleasures who made you that promise, the man with all his time before him. But the man you see before you is the man you *wanted* to see, the *Prince* born again in the image of his father—and of his grandfather and the whole red-handed genealogy before them! The man of war who may ride out to his death on the morrow and has no time for the niceties of courtship and games of love."

She shook back the disheveled mass of her hair and looked at him squarely, trying to find a trace of friendship in his granite gaze.

"You have had much sorrow, my lord. I cannot think that this—meeting—will lessen it. I ask you therefore, in your brother's name, to go now and seek your sleep, leaving me to mine."

"Once again you are very free with my brother's name. Not so wisely, if you would have me gone, for I think Franco would have been happy enough to see us share a bed—he was ever generous with his possessions."

"He has not possessed me! You know it!"

"You are very fierce in your denial. That spark of anger will do very well to kindle our passion." He knelt beside her and tore the sheet from her hand. "Come, Madonna—let's to business. I have waited long enough."

Her heart thudding, she attempted to roll away from him, but he caught the shoulder furthest from him and slammed it back into the pillow, moving over her and pinning her body beneath him. He brooded above her, feeling his power, his eyes brilliant, their emotions nameless. Then his mouth came down and fed upon hers like a greedy bird of prey. Even that, she knew as she twisted and arched her back to frustrate his determined movements, was better than having to look into those unrecognizable eyes. She felt the blind seeking of his tongue as his kiss became more intimate and the urgent provocation of his hand upon her breast as his insistent fingers coaxed and cajoled her arousal. She knew her body for a traitor, and yet did not know how she might control it. She began to kick and plunge in a panic of undirected motion only to feel her strength drain to despair at the low growl of laughter which her antics inspired. Already confused by the surprise of his appearance, her reactions still slowed by sleep, the suddeness of this assault gave her no time to marshal her defenses. Also beneath the disoriented reeling of her senses there was a tired recognition of something familiar, something that diminished the fear of the moment, leaving only the humiliation.

When she was still for a second, weakened, Leone pursued his advantage and moved to thrust open her thighs. His questing fingers excited further turbulence in her, and she moaned and convulsed her limbs as she strained to be free of him.

"You will be best to lay yourself open to me, lady, for what you do not give me, be certain I will take."

He murmured the words against her ear, nuzzling it with his tongue to incite yet another unwelcome sensation, while with concentrated expedition he parted her thighs until they would accomodate his now pressing desire. As he slid himself between them the red silk no longer separated skin from skin and Tulla knew for the first time the sensation of a man's naked body against her own. Its very strangeness arrested her struggles, and a new fear entered her.

When he came into her even the fear was dispelled by the unparalleled strangeness of what he did. At first she could not believe that this was not some perverse new way of dealing death, so outrageous did it feel to have his flesh, so alien, begin its urgent rhythm within her. She tried to expel this penetration that invaded not only her body but her secret, woman's soul, but found herself bound by bone and muscle while the blazing amber eyes told her triumphantly that there was no escape. Neither could she look away. The triumph died, and his eyes became heavy lidded and hazed. It was almost as though they smiled. They stared into hers with a terrible, knowing concentration, and it was now that her body became the most amoral of traitors, as it was drawn out into a single, singing nerve that was stretched infinitely toward that which might touch it yet whose touch it could not bear. It was with unrecognized welcome that she cried out, not in fear, as at last the sword of pleasure gave her its deepest wound.

When it was over he allowed her to move away from him while he gave himself to the abandonment of the physical relief, flung out upon his stomach, lids and limbs heavy, his thoughts in abeyance save for the single, half-surprised observation that she had, after all, been a virgin.

Tulla drew back against the pillows, dragging the dark blue coverlet about her, more for a kind of childish comfort than to cover her bruised and aching nakedness. Her mind still numb with shock she noted absently that she was trembling. She concentrated upon controlling the tremor, thus giving herself further respite from the necessity for thought. Some monstrous tidal wave of emotion, of disgust or guilt or self-pity, waited to engulf her, but she pushed back the first trickle of it and would not allow it to reach her.

She was no longer a virgin. Very well. The only wonder in that was that she had remained so long immaculate. She would not weep over it, but perhaps later she would pray. For the present she did not wish to think about it.

She glanced at Leone, as relaxed as a child in sleep. She wished he would leave, but since this seemed unlikely she decided that she herself would go. She would spend the rest of the night on the pallet in Lucia's room.

Clutching the coverlet she began to ease herself off the bed.

"No. Don't go." His hand stopped her.

Catlike, he raised himself limb by limb until he was sitting close to her.

"Is it well with you? How much have I hurt you?"

She moved away from him but made no more motion to leave. "My hurts will mend—but I wonder greatly at the anger that was the cause of them. I do not think that *I* could have given *you* enough hurt for this!"

Half her mind kept back, amazed at how imperative it was that she should know the answer. He looked down, silent, and she prompted him. "You have traduced yourself. You used the caresses of pleasure to give pain."

He smiled as though his mouth were filled with bitter aloe. "Perhaps I have discovered in myself the capacity for cruelty. You should be glad of it. It will make me a better leader."

She could not allow this. "There was no cruelty in your brother."

"My brother took a step no first-class commander would

have taken. And died for it. I shall take care not to follow him." These words provoked the memory of herself at bay in the stygian passages beneath the castle.

"So there should be nothing to chose between yourself and Andrea Zorza? You will match cruelty with cruelty, and we can expect more tattered bodies pendant from the battlements?"

He shook his head as though he shook *that* sight from his eyes. "No. Never that. I want no trophies. And I wish I had not allowed them to leave that thing hanging upon our gate—" He looked up at her so candidly then that she glimpsed the substance of his former self behind the flint.

"I will offer you no lying regrets, for I have none. Nor yet thanks—for you did not give yourself willingly. If it is reasons you seek, why then I will try to requite you."

She listened and wondered again at her own calm, the need to hear him.

He did not continue at once, appearing deep in thought. When he spoke he did not look at her but straight ahead as though to admit no distraction.

"When you came to me in Franco's tomb, you were right in what you sensed in me. In all but brute fact I had joined my brother in the grave. There seemed a lifetime of rage and sorrow behind me and I had achieved some sort of peace—a cessation, a nothingness. I had ceased even to mourn. I no longer existed." He paused and the granite mask had returned. "And then I heard your voice. It clamored most blasphemously against my quiet. I loathed it, loathed both words and speaker. *Then* I might indeed have done you damage had you not fallen back upon his breast. You came down like a scarlet goad upon a man already bleeding. But that was not why I wished to punish you—"

"Then what?" He was giving her honesty, that was clear, for his words came forth slowly, erratically, as they came to him.

"It was not your attempt that I hated—but your *success*," he achieved wonderingly, distaste in every line of his proud face.

"Whether it was your words—and your contempt—alone—or whether Franco—" he broke off with a futile gesture. There were no words. He recovered and began again, looking at her more easily.

288

"At any rate, Madonna, it seemed to me that, too often, you had played Mars where I had meant you to play Venus. Tonight I have given you no choice. You demanded that I use the talisman of my brother's dead heart to spur my blood! It seemed to me a better thing to use your living body. It seems it still. If I must be goaded like a flagellant, let me at least apply the whip myself."

"And has my virginity paid the ferryman—in your desolate voyage back across the Styx? You are right, Prince. You died, down there in the dark with your brother."

He saw now that he had hurt her beyond his intention and felt the beginnings of the remorse he had denied. Suddenly he wanted to explain to her. He could bear neither her look nor her suffering.

"You have changed me, Tulla," he whispered harshly holding her eyes. "And so I had to change you. There's an odd logic in it, you will admit? And then," he added with the weary sketch of a smile, "it would have come about, you know it—if not now, at another time. It had to be. It was as you will remember, why you came here."

But in asking her to look back so far, he saw with a sudden appalling clarity how much had changed within himself for him to have engaged in this arid and joyless coupling. It was the first mating of his, he knew with shame and regret, in which there had been an utter lack of innocence.

The siege of her virginity was raised at last, but behind the walls there lay no jewels for the plunderer, only emptiness and a sense of desecration.

As he watched her turn pale face from him and tremble, after all, into tears, the fumbling intuition cumbered him, that, beneath the damaging, retributive urge to hurt her, to bring her spirit level with his own, there had slept another, delicate and unrecognized need, the necessity—after the shock of his brother's hideous and unlooked-for death—to take a little comfort where he could. Unknown to himself he had sought that, too, in her body and felt himself all the more desolate because he had not found it.

One thing he did see, very clearly: Tulla herself, who had been close to Franco, had needed comfort as badly, perhaps, as himself. And because he had done what he had done, all that they might do now was to look at each other across the vast gulf of their united loneliness.

He wondered if he might try to tell her something of this

289

and put a hand toward her, a tentative forerunner of the words he could not yet find.

Tulla tasted her own tears as she also sought words, *any* words which would make him leave her solitary. "You have had a poor bargain, Valenti. If your ducats could not buy a willing heart to match the virginity, no more could this act in any sort, repay your brother's murder. You have been cheated—of your money and of your revenge."

She had listened to him and had not heard what she had wished to hear, though she did not know what that might be. Now her bitterness welled up like poison in an infected wound. He saw how she loathed him and could not blame her. "The revenge is not yet," he told her gently, accepting her hatred as his penance.

"God's blood, will you *go* from here!" she screamed suddenly, throwing herself across the pillows to prevent herself raking at his solemn, despairing face. It was not that her blood did not howl out for his, only that to make it flow, she would also have to make him stay.

Since it was, now that they had come to this pass, the only thing he could do for her, he left her as she wanted.

Before he went he pulled the deep blue blanket over her. The velvet brushed her cheek softly where he no longer dared to touch. He was aware of an immense, protective tenderness toward her, such as he had previously felt only for the children. Driven by the irony of this, he found that he too was now able to weep.

With the occasional inclination toward balance displayed by evil fortune, the morning brought Tulla no further opportunity to deplore the events of the night, scarcely even the time to recall them, for the citadel was roused precipitately before dawn by the news that the enemy were within its walls! Although scarcely credible, this unwelcome fact was swiftly assimilated, and the funereal quiescence of yesterday was replaced hastily and indecently by a furor of action. Indeed most of Montevalenti woke up to find itself in the middle of a battle, and pulled on its hose even as it drew its sword against the grinning mercenary who hopped in through its ruptured shutters. Within Castel' Valenti itself, however, happily this was not so. And by the time Zorza's seasoned campaigners had fought their way from the postern gate through which they had entered, through several streets of incensed and outraged citizens, several of them no longer had sword arms.

To Leone the alarum came like the knife that lances the blister. Every pent-up, misunderstood emotion within him cried out for the relief of action, and, as he pulled on his brother's breastplate for the second time, his face settled quite naturally into the grimace of savage pleasure that denotes the soldier who loves his sword. There was just enough extraneous thought left in him to order that his young heirs and their governess should be taken up to the highest solar in the southwestern tower and locked in for safety. After this his whole concentration was bent upon battle, on victory, and on the most bloody revenge.

As the first wave of mercenaries hacked their way to the square at the front of the palace, the prince hesitated only to give succinct instructions to one of Cerruti's young crossbowmen before leading his own newly assembled company of mixed infantry out to meet them. Among them was the gunner, Alvaro Ponti, carrying an interesting parcel of gray cloth.

It was not an unheard of occurrence for a Castellan to lead his troops so willingly through open gates, but it was a far more common thing for him to bar his doors and lower windows, climb up to his battlements and let his quarrels, stones, and arrows do the fighting. Zorza's advance party had expected to lower the morale of the prince by the number and manner of their executions of his people before the hundred eyes of his palace; they had not expected to be given the chance of killing him or better still, of taking him back alive to their commander. As the long rush of scarlet and gold gushed toward them, they prepared cheerfully to dam its progress. They knew that in comparison with Montevalenti's doubtful thousand, their numbers were as a river to a trickle and would soon be flushing through the city gates and over its wall like Noah's own flood. Their security came from the knowledge that the bombardment was being increased to maximum ability, while the sappers, good lads hellbent on death or glory, were even now mining away beneath the bushes covering the almost vertical declivity of the western wall. The engagement was brief and energetic. Though the prince's men fought well and bravely and accounted for some dozen or so mercenary lives during the first onslaught, they soon began to give way, little by little, until they found

themselves hard-pressed back against their gates plying
their weapons with the erratic and energy-wasting desperation that might better be expected of valiant peasants unused
to close combat. The mercenaries pressed on with a will.
There appeared to be no one yet managing that part of the
castle wall, and the open doors presented a temptation too
rich to refuse. Leone ordered his men to close about him in a
dense block, afraid, the Germans thought contemptuously,
for his life. They had heard he was no soldier. Behind them,
Ponti unwrapped his gray parcel.

Suddenly there was a commotion from above as a black
line of haubergeoned archers appeared on the parapet, their
bows at the ready—drawn—released!

The Germans fell back in painful and guttural consternation. Surprisingly, their assailants did not press home this
advantage, but began, instead, with a puzzling swiftness to
withdraw through the open doors behind them. Only the
gunner remained, swinging a little lidded bucket by the
handle. He swung it faster and then faster still.

By the time the visitors to Montevalenti had begun to
understand what was happening, ten of them had been
dispatched to a better world, and many more lay groaning
and tattered on the ground, where the sand took on an
instant and alarming shade of red.

Alvaro Ponti had just enjoyed one of the further possibilities of the prince's excellent Milanese gunpowder.

Drunk with the simplicity of this success, Leone's troop left
the ragged remainder of the castle's would-be ravishers to
those of the populace who, having scuttled home with their
fingers in their ears at the familiar sight of Ponti playing
with gunpowder, now judged it safe to emerge and tidy up
their square.

The prince then hurried to the western rampart of the
postern gate to see how the other half of his hastily-conceived
plan was faring. Alvaro, still grinning with achievement,
panted at his side.

They found Cerruti engaged in a pursuit that had delighted
the hearts of the male sex from five to seventy-five, from the
days before Christ, to this year of the Lord 1475, that of
emptying flaming cauldrons of noxious substances upon the
heads of a hapless enemy.

That first intrusion of perhaps a hundred of Zorza's men
had been made through the thick concealing thorn and

292

brushwood of the almost unnegotiable slope, at whose head lay a mysteriously open postern that had not been used for a century. The citizens had literally awakened to the fact of their presence. Having, after some bewildered searching, established the site of the leak, they had gradually battened back the gate to its former state. This meant that the deceptive green and gold silences of the mountainside contained a crawling column of men, going strenuously on their bellies like serpents, who expected at least the relief of an open gate and the sight of the friendly faces of their forerunners when their purgatorial progress should be ended. By the time those at the top had realized their altered prospects, Cerruti's burning rain had begun to fall. By the judicious use of naptha, gunpowder, tar, and heated stones, and with the imaginative addition of various animal and human refuse, the sturdy forest was soon merrily ablaze. Cerruti's crack archers came close to splitting their hose if not their sides as they watched the comically busy little figures racing about below without sense or direction, trying hopelessly to avoid their well-aimed flaming arrows.

Then Ponti made them all stop and listen for a full, charged minute until, with an explosion that brought tears of gratification to his snapping happy blue eyes, a vast section of the rock face beneath them took flight for the heavens, carrying with it the charred and blackened remains of what had been trees and men, though it was no longer possible to tell which was which.

The enemy sappers had been located.

Pent-up in the southwestern solar, behind a stout, padlocked door, neither Tulla nor her young companions were able to make a great deal of sense of the morning's events; although their ears, strained to catch every nuance, told them that these were mightily interesting, they felt sorely the lack of the evidence of their eyes. Bernardo especially took their imprisonment to heart, declaring himself every bit as much a man as, for instance, Gian Carmaggio, and hammered periodically on the door with furious fists, demanding to be let out and given a sword. Lucia, still sorrowfully conscious of the loss of one uncle, was filled with solicitude for her remaining favorite and belabored the air with his name at every sound that could possibly be interpreted as bearing danger for the prince.

If it did not occur to either child that their guardian's mood was unduly quiet for such a turbulent time, it was because their own emotions were at a consistent fever-pitch and they simply assumed the same of her.

And when the sound of the final explosion thundered through the arrow slits to threaten their eardrums, so hysterical did they become that Tulla, for the first time in their excellent relationship, administered without a second thought, a couple of sobering claps across their cheeks.

Almost immediately after this they were set free and told they might go up to the battlements and watch the fun. The prince, having rounded up the last fifty or sixty of the once hopeful party of adventurers who had actually entered the city, was going to set them free and harry them down the hillside to the plain, so that Zorza and all his mercenary army might see how the Prince of the Valenti disdained the inevitable failure of their puny and overreaching attempt.

Tulla wavered, but the children, instantly forgiving her their blows, seized her hands and gave her no choice. In moments she was behind Bernardo as he thrust his way to the front of the noisy, grinning crowd that occupied the rampart. As they fell back, not for the child but for herself, it occurred to her oddly that she must somehow have won a certain respect in the household. They did not treat her as his Excellency's slave!

The promised chase had already begun. It was not so much a pursuit, however, as a running battle, for the discomfitted mercenaries were putting up a good fight in defense of their dwindling honor and were far from consenting to be driven downhill like cattle. Leone, to give him his due, had refrained from doubling or trebling the numbers of their pursurers as he might have done, but had matched them man for man with those among the guards and the militia with whom they had already been fighting in the streets. The prince himself was well to the fore, his great sword flashing about him like the circling flames of a night feast.

The action bore inexorably downward, despite the courage of the mercenaries. The prince's men were too elated, too certain of victory, for it to be otherwise. So invincible, it was evident, did they feel, that Tulla caught a look of mortified surprise on the face of the one man who died, felled by an ugly blow to the neck from the German he had driven hard until then.

Her eyes slid constantly back to the prince. She felt a great strangeness at the thought that the man whom she watched as he plunged his weapon into yet another human body, in that teaming space so far removed from her, had last night moved within *her* to a purpose which seemed to her almost as final, as world-cleaving, in some inexplicable way, as the act of killing itself. And yet it was not a death that she had felt in herself at that last, unexpected moment of physical revelation, rather its opposite; a fluttering birth, or as though some life had awakened late from a dark winter and hastened toward the sun and its fruition—

At the precise moment that she turned from these thoughts a cry of rage went up around her.

"Blood of Christ! My uncle!" Bernardo was digging desperate nails into her hand, and Lucia, shaking, had thrust her face into the folds of Tulla's skirt. She refocused at once but could make out only the top of Leone's golden head as his men milled about him like worker bees about a threatened queen.

"It cannot have gone deep! A flesh wound, surely?"

"I don't know; it looks pretty bad to me. Devilish near the heart—"

She ignored the harping voices around her and forced herself to concentrate upon comforting Lucia, who was crying quietly and fiercely into her skirt.

"Are you well, Mona Tulla? Are you going to faint? You should sit down—here, come this way! You can lean against the cannon." It was Bernardo who was now solicitous, firmly taking his sister's hand and leading both her and his gray-faced governess to the back of the voluble, gesticulating crowd where a damaged cannon lay at rest.

Had she been about to faint? It must be so. Bernardo's words had come to her from a long way off, and even now the swaying throng appeared as though she looked at them through some glass that diminished sight. Gratefully she relaxed her weight against the gun carriage. There was a scent of powder still about it.

"Don't worry, Madonna. It will be nothing, you will see. They're all saying so. My uncle will not be badly hurt!"

Suddenly she came to herself, fully and overwhelmingly as she had not done since she had been left alone at last amid the destruction of her bed. Her eyes blazing, she thrust away Bernardo's anxious arm and addressed the boy with a cold venom that, with consummate good sense, he knew was not for him.

"The Devil may care for the hurts of your accursed uncle, boy, for assuredly I do not!"

Puzzled but not quite distressed, he put his arm around his sister and spoke gently to her as she wept. He watched while Tulla stalked away across the battlement and was lost to his view as she plunged down the stairway into the dark interior of the castle.

The prince's wound was in the shoulder, a glancing blow that had failed to do any serious damage. He had covered himself in approbation by picking up the sword that had fallen from his temporarily nerveless right hand and dispatching his assailant with the left. They had brought him back screaming "Valenti!" and "Il Principe!" until they were hoarse and still would not stop.

It had been, as far as Montevalenti was concerned, a magnificent morning, a morning to remember. The prince's father, older men declared affectionately, would have been proud of him.

There was, however, one sad corollary to the "rout of the Germans" as the occasion came to be called. This was the suicide of the big miller, Stefano Bossi, who took his oldest son's way out of the world and was found hanging from a sword hook in the armory.

At first it was thought that grief for his family had perhaps deprived him of his reason, but then all was explained, even more simply and yet more miserably by a grim and shaken Cerruti, Bossi's companion-in-arms since their shared childhood.

"It was his responsibility to guard the postern gate," he told Leone, hanging his gray head, not disdaining for his dead friend's sake, a share in the shame. "He took full charge of the defense of the western wall when Lieutenant Fabrizio of the Biscaglia guard went sick. We all thought he was merely doing a favor for the lad. Fabrizio's men had given him a hand with all his gear from the mill—family possessions, furniture, the like. And then for *him* to turn traitor like this—Stefano! My lord, I can hardly believe it," he ended half appealingly.

Leone, resting restlessly on a narrow couch, displayed no emotion in particular.

"But you are certain it is true?"

"Yes, my Prince. Fabrizio is absolutely certain."

"Which is by no means," Leone mused, "the same thing. However—of one thing we can be sure—and that is that there has been—perhaps still is—a traitor among us. Whether it was poor Bossi—"

Cerruti eyed him curiously. "You think perhaps not?" He held his big hands wide. "But he has taken his life."

"He is dead. May he rest in peace. And from now on, Paulo—"

"Excellence?"

"You are to oversee all the exterior defenses personally."

His captain bowed and left him, even more distressed than when he had arrived.

A traitor. Always traitors, treachery, the hidden hand working in the darkness.

Most of them would be satisfied that it was Bossi, he knew.

Perhaps he too should be satisfied. It was feasible, certainly; a whole family dedicated to his downfall. He suddenly remembered that day he had spent in the hills, "hunting" with Lorenzo and Sandro Botticelli—remembered the sweet game he had caught—Antonella, the dark-eyed miller's daughter. Bossi's daughter.

He wondered—could *that* be one of the reasons? Was Antonella bearing him a child and had Bossi thought it shame?

Then he shook his head and laughed, paining his shoulder. Never. It was no shame to bear a prince's bastard.

He must look deeper than that for his reasons—if he must look at all.

Alessandra, at least, had been wrong. She had been so sure that the key to all treachery was Tulla, so ready to believe Zorza's empty boast of having made her his mistress. Poor Alessa. He supposed he should not have brought the girl to Montevalenti. But she had been so beautiful, and so contained, so perfectly at home in her own olive skin, despite her terrible circumstances.

He had wanted that beauty; but perhaps, even more, he saw now, he had wanted that containment, that ability to retire into her own strength that he had seen at once—and had seen again, even last night.

Had he damaged her? He did not think so. He had not

imagined her physical response. He had known that she was capable of that, and of far more—and all for him. His blood had known it, as with so many others. But there was a part of this girl, this unusual and in her way, rather terrible girl, his pricking conscience, his scarlet goad, that was recognized not by blood but by—what? His soul? His spirit? He didn't know. Needless to give it a name. Sufficient that it was the better part of him.

And yet—with what a hideous contrariness she had seen fit to call out, only yesterday, all that was worst in him, in his blood, his family, the history of his small, indomitable realm. True, she had not known her risk, not seen the dangerous simplicity of the fact that lion sleeping and lion salient, lion rampant are one and the same beast.

Well, the beast had awakened and had turned on what had provoked it. Unwilling or not she had been magnificent! He would not seek to humble her again, for it was not within his power, neither was it any long in his heart to wish to do so. He wondered if she knew that he had in the end felt tenderness and regret; if she had understood at all his halting attempt to explain why he must punish her.

He sighed and directed his thoughts toward the siege. Thinking of Tulla served only to increase his loneliness.

During the following days the fury of the bombardment increased in portion to the depletion, amounting in numbers to some two hundred men and in pride approaching the decline of hubris, suffered by Andrea Zorza. A demon of impotent rage had possessed him as he watched his men driven down the hillside like a pack of pariah dogs. The worst thing had been the sight of that flamboyant golden head at the center of the fight. Every sinew within him had strained toward that tantalizing aureole. At one point, he would have flung toward it and cloven through twice the numbers who struggled there in the dawn light, if only he might come at his quietus by delivering death to the prince. But they had held him back, and he had known they were right.

His time would come.

It was early evening. Leone, whom the little doctor had ordered inactive with both threats and poultices, lay resting his wound after a strenuous spell on the ramparts. Consciously seeking a peace which the sensual provocations of his own rooms could not give him, he had prowled endlessly for some time before hesitantly entering his brother's study. Here the welter of books and papers, so deceptively disorganized, recalled Franco to him with a closeness that was sudden enough, at first sight, to make him gasp with a pain that perhaps he should have expected but had not. The reminders were everywhere: the books that they had read together with their tutors; the beloved Dante still open at the tale of Paulo and Francesca; the lute that he had loved to play when he was alone, having no taste for the display of his own accomplishment; his pens with the silver knife he kept to sharpen them; the monstrous ledgers, heaped up on the desk, that gave witness of his love, proved in hours of laborious computation, both for the city of his birth and for the feckless, work-shy, empty, and posturing peacock that was the brother of his blood.

Leone roamed about the chamber, touching familiar objects gently and reminiscently. Then he lay down upon the old dark brown sofa and covered his eyes with his hand. After a while he noticed that the evening was filled with bird song. It came to him freely through the open window to the loggia, and the remembrance of Franco's pleasure in such simple things was almost more than he could bear.

He did not know how long he lay there, half victim, half prey to memories and bitter regrets, before the door was quietly opened to admit his wife.

She was quite alone and wore a simple dress of warm, deep blue that both enhanced the elegantly sensual curves of her body and reflected color into her clear pale eyes. She had chosen it carefully.

"Does the wound pain you less now, my lord?" she inquired serenely, moving to the center of the room where she stood and smiled at him like any wife solicitous of her man's well-being.

"I thank you, yes." He waited warily. She must have taken considerable trouble to establish his whereabouts. It would not have been out of a simple care for his welfare.

"I—will you not have the musicians play in the passage, Leone? The noise of battle must be wearisome to you." It was a false start. She was not quite ready. The courage was there, but not the certainty of her reception.

"I have not heard it since I have been here. Only the birds."

She smiled again, unsure whether or not she should send for maestro Murano.

He saw the hesitation in her, the diminution of her mannered hauteur. He noted the dulcet blue of the soft-bodied gown. Dispassionately, he was curious. Courteously he returned her smile.

Alessandra did not find his mien very encouraging, but she had reason to suppose he would warm to her in time. If he did not, the woman La Sventura, in the now unlikely event that they should ever meet again, would feel the princess's whip across her back. Leone had been given the filtre at least three times to her certain knowledge. It could only be a matter of time—

And then, she had a great deal to offer him.

She wandered dreamily to the casement and stood, her back half turned to him, in apparent appreciation of the nightingale whose song was paramount.

"Since you have come back to yourself," she began quietly at last, "your conduct of the siege might have been inspired by St. George!" He grimaced inwardly at her estimate of what was "himself."

"None would deny this, and doubtless your good generalship will continue—but," she turned to him in direct appeal, "not even St. George could alter the fact that while Zorza's numbers will increase daily, ours can only diminish."

"The present ratio is one of two hundred to thirty," Leone remarked dryly. "If it continues it should prove an expensive experience for your cousin."

"How if it were *not* to continue? If the siege were to come to an end. At once?"

"Then we should all sing Hosannas and give thanks for a miracle."

"I do not speak of miracles." The time had come to loose her bolt. "Merely of a truce. I want you to let me go to Andrea Zorza. I do not think he would do me harm. He has a—fondness—for me, as I'm sure you are aware. But it is not only to him I would speak, but to his officers, the men of the Biscaglia guard whom he took with him, men who have been loyal to my brother and to me before Andrea suborned them. I do not know what promises he made them, but they were well satisfied with their lives in Castel' Valenti before now—and there is not one of them who will have felt anything but horror and repulsion at your brother's death. They

300

are not mercenaries but my father's liege men. And I think, now that they have learned what manner of man it is who leads them, they would be only too glad to return here. They are few, I know, but they are his captains. And in addition," she paused, catching the scandalized refusal in his face, "why should *we* not buy off his hundreds, even as they came to join him? It is often done and it is the best savior of blood of all. God knows a mercenary fights only for gold, and if he can have the gold without the battle he is even better pleased. We have gold enough—between us. My lord, will you not consider it?" She sighed a little at the end. It was over and not so difficult after all.

Leone looked at his wife as if he were suddenly unsure of her identity. He was habitually a quick thinker, but he needed time to absorb *this* new turn of the feminine mind. The first thing to become clear to him was that what she proposed required tremendous personal courage on her part. The second was that it was not, viewed with disinterest, a foolish proposal. But more than anything he asked himself *why* she should make it. Three years of frost and snow had left him ill-prepared for such a sudden, melting summer.

"It is a brave offer, my dear. But as for your going yourself to Zorza, it is impossible. There can be no doubt that, whatever his fondness for you, it would not prevent him from seizing so valuable a hostage."

He was wrong. *There,* ironically, she could be sure enough of her physical dominion. But she let him continue.

"Please don't think me ungrateful, Alessandra." He rose from the couch and walked about the room as he spoke, looking at her now and then to gauge the effect of his words. "Perhaps once—before Franco's murder, I don't know—perhaps I would have considered such a truce. I have no wish to shed the blood of my people. But now," he stood immediately before her, every line of his body decisive, "there is no possibility. I cannot consider it. I will be satisfied only with the death of Zorza, at my own hands."

"But you may have his death—and without bloodshed. He will be easily captured when we have taken away his army."

"How if he were to run, to escape? And leave me with Franco's death nailed into my heart as *his* heart is nailed to my door? No, never. That is no way for *princes*. I want no hollow victory, bought with dishonorable gold. I want the blood I am owed!"

301

She took a brief, sharp breath, half-sigh, half-gasp. She had long since ceased to hope for such words from him. She felt a swooning in herself toward him, her lips parted; her eyes became glossy.

They stood close now, and Leone's certainty again gave way to puzzlement. He felt disoriented suddenly by her presence. Her mood was extraordinary. She even *looked* extraordinary.

He saw how she gazed up at him, panting a little, her face warm and filled with expectancy.

"What *is* it that you want of me, Alessa? Why would you put yourself in such danger for Montevalenti? You have never loved it."

Her lids fluttered down then. He was too near. Too soon.

"It is my home," she murmured. "And I cannot think," she raised her head again with a smile that was almost shy, "that I should love Montevalenti any better if it were ruled by Andrea Zorza."

The puzzled eyes challenged her. "Not even if he were to make you his wife? You seemed to like his company. Better than mine." he added with a truth designed to make her blush.

She did no such thing, however, but gave him a straight unclouded look that much resembled innocence.

"Seeming is one thing, truth another. And yes, I did enjoy my cousin's company—but that was when I did not shrink to *call* him cousin. My lord—as I have said to you publicly, I feel much to blame for all our misery. I long to do what penance I may."

"My God, Alessandra! I don't know what to make of you."

She seemed to sway toward him, her eyes brimming with meaning. She was changed, womanly, even vulnerable as other women are. Seeing her thus he was reminded forcibly of their wedding day, and of the night that had followed. She had worn this look then, in response to his sensual and delicate wooing—for although the marriage was one of convenience, forced upon them by his father, a further witness of the subjection of Biscaglia to Valenti, Leone had seen no reason why they should not be happy. They would look to the future, not, with the awful old men, to the past.

And, for a time, they had been happy. She had loved him then and he, her, as he had loved all women.

It was this generosity of the senses that had been their

302

downfall, of course. The Biscaglia pride brooked no rivalry, however lighthearted. And Leone was not the man to play the courtly lover, languishing after a single rose, when a whole garden lay warm for his plucking.

He sighed and touched a hand to her cheek in reminiscent tenderness. They had been so young—

For Alessandra it was as if all the flickering, half-illuminated thoughts and shadowy, uncomprehended instincts of the past weeks suddenly coalesced into a single, bright flame of certainty. Perhaps she had begun to know it when she had first seen the Byzantine girl hold up her head in pride beneath this roof; perhaps when she had sent for the witch and began to learn the mysteries of herbs and simples; most certainly when Clarice Medici had spoken of children; and piercingly when she thought that he had followed his brother to death in battle.

Without conscious motion she fell forward upon his breast so that he had to catch her in his arms.

"Make of me your wife, Leone. That is all I want," she said.

Only a man of iron would not have kissed her then with all the riches of her body in his hands.

Her lips were as smooth and as sweet as he remembered, but no longer as cool. Moist, fervid, and demanding, they trembled apart and softly assaulted his own, while her hands remembered his body with the careful searching and dwelling movements of the blind. Her breasts and thighs pushed against him urgently as though begging his touch, and he found her tears upon his cheek and in his mouth.

It had been too long, and she had too far to fall from her hard-won pinnacle of ice. She wept as though demented but not for a moment did she give over her fierce kisses or her wooing of his body. When he unfastened her bodice she moaned and clasped his hand to her breast, biting into his lips until she tasted his blood. He sank down with her upon the couch and prepared to give her what she sought of him, his own veins pounding with the same desperate necessity.

She was quite naked, he nearly so, when the door opened once more.

Leone looked up with a face of apocalyptic fury as he hung above the white, expectant body.

It was Tulla who stood in the doorway, her hand frozen upon its handle still, its fellow flying to her lips to stem the cry she might have made.

303

It seemed as though the moment repeated itself over and over again like the wooden movement of a mechanical toy—forever and ever the door would open and he would raise his head and see her there and eternally her hand would travel upward and cover not her lips, but her eyes, her damning, truth-filled, utterly wounded eyes.

SIXTEEN

Alessandra felt the desire drain out of him even as the command and the strange curse broke from him. She knew at once that she had lost him. Her own lust died as abruptly, extinguished by a flood of foreboding that set hammers pounding in her heart. She had seen nothing, only heard the door open. She had not needed to see.

"It was the Byzantine." Her voice was a whip cracking ice.

He was astonished. How could she know? "It doesn't matter who it was," he muttered. But he shifted his weight from her. She did not look at him again but gestured toward her gown, a quiet pool on the floor. He hesitated. She felt his gaze, waited for his words. But then he reached for the dress and put it into her hands.

After a long silence he spoke her name. The kindness in his voice set her trembling with anger. She called back to her the control she had relinquished for his sake.

"I would be glad if you would leave me." She wrapped herself in the gown and remained upon the couch, her eyes cold as glass, her passion had left no mark upon her. It was as if it had never been.

"If I should come to you later—?" he began.

"Perhaps."

But he would not. Or even if he did—

304

After he had gone she lay staring at the ceiling, seeing not the huntsman and horses of the aging fresco, but that dying of desire in his eyes. So sudden, so swift and so final. And all for the opening of a door.

He had rejected her.

After some time she dressed and smoothed back the disordered fall of her hair. When she was sufficiently mistress of her appearance once more she left the chamber. Without thinking she made her way to the cardinal's apartment.

Only her brother's arms about her could help to heal the stunned and bleeding Biscaglia pride that must face the enormity of that rejection.

As for Tulla, she too had sought the region of the castle where she felt most at home and was seated in the corner of the herb garden where Botticelli had sketched her portrait. There she had found the cat Annibale asleep in a favorite clump of catnip and had clutched the acquiescent but ever dampening bundle of white fur to a heart now in the throes of a new emotion—perhaps the most painful of all—one that often breeds disastrous consequences.

It was to this retreat that Gian Carmaggio was dispatched, as was so often the case, to fetch her. This time the summons had a novelty about it that both appealed to him and, to a greater extent than he would have admitted, alarmed him. For it came from a most unusual source.

"You are to follow me, if you would be so good, Madonna."

"Not if you will not tell me who sends for me."

"I may not. But I am to say that it is neither Valenti nor Biscaglia."

She raised an irritated brow, hoping her despicable tears had dried without trace

"Oh very well." Curiosity was better, at least, than what she had undergone this last half hour.

To her surprise, the boy led her steadily down to those subterrain regions she had not entered since her terrifying captivity by Andrea Zorza, halting outside the very cell that the discredited Atroviso had occupied. Tulla drew back, but the boy shook his head and rapped upon the door, pushing it open immediately.

Inside, her strong features cast into high relief by the half dozen candles branched before her on the table, La Sventura sat among the remnants of the astrologer's possessions.

She looked very much at home.

"How have you come here?" Tulla's amazement evidently pleased her, for she showed her fine teeth fleetingly as she indicated the chair opposite.

"I said, did I not, that we should meet again?" was the unsatisfactory reply. Tulla sat down, conscious of Gian's swift melting away and the click of the latch as the door closed upon them.

"You take your life lightly—to enter Castel' Valenti."

"There is no danger here for me." Her eyes were like jet, hard, brilliant, taking the light into themselves, revealing nothing of mood or intelligence as they assessed and judged.

"If Gian should reveal—"

"He will not. He is too much afraid."

"You have threatened him?"

"I did not come here to discuss the servants."

"No." It seemed suddenly entirely credible that she should be here at this disturbing woman's behest. A sense of something falling into place, something waited for, came to her. The gypsy offered her wine from a flagon at her elbow, and she accepted, almost reassured by that knowing, regal smile.

"You are a woman, I think, who wishes to be mistress of her fate?"

It was hardly a question. Aware of the irony, Tulla's reply was acid. "Unfortunately, I do not possess your powers to make this possible."

"Neither, I see, do you believe in them. But you will. You are more fortunate than you suppose. I have come here to offer you the power you require."

"Like a djinn from a bottle. How convenient."

La Sventura did not frown. It was pleasant, for once in a way, *not* to be feared.

"A bottle is involved, certainly. And it holds, indeed, as among the tales of your people, the secret key to your fortune—or in your case, your freedom."

A trickle of cold descended Tulla's spine, and she felt a premonitory quickening of her already erratic heartbeat.

"What can you have to do with my freedom?" Her voice seemed not her own, strained and oddly pitched.

Now there *was* a bottle, a very small one, between the brown, elegant hands.

"I am a woman who has always had the welfare of women at heart—you have only to ask. They fear me, but they seek me out when it is a matter of an unwanted child or of a man who is desired. And then, you will know that I do not love the Valenti?"

"And yet he lives." Tulla's voice in her own ears was stranger still.

"It is not my habit to act as executioner." Reproof sang along with high pride.

"You make others your instrument. I have seen how their darts can fly," was Tulla's tart retort.

"You saved him then, would you save him again?" The question homed as the dart had done, and not even the darkness could conceal the spasm of hatred to which it stung its ambushed victim.

"Never. I wish he had died then!"

Sweat prickled on her brow, and her breath came unevenly, fast and shallow.

La Sventura smiled and reached out her hand.

"Then give him this."

The small phial glinted sulkily, made of dullish yellow glass.

"In food or drink. It doesn't matter. It is tasteless and will not be marked."

She withdrew the hand, and the bottle lay on the table in front of the long quiet fingers.

"What is it?" Tulla shivered. She had forgotten how dank it was down in these dark cells.

Black-clad shoulders shrugged imperceptibly. "Its name would mean nothing to you. It comes from China. First there is paralysis. Then death comes swiftly, there is no pain."

Beads of silence were threaded slowly between them.

"I *can* give pain if you so wish?"

"No! I don't—" She snatched up the bottle.

"Then all is well. It will not fail you."

It was a dismissal.

Unable to bear or to understand the flock of black, misshapen images that flapped about her brain, Tulla scraped back her chair and fled, conscious only of the smile that followed her along the dripping passages and still did not leave her when she reached sunlight, trembling, sick and weeping once again, the hateful little bottle thrust deep into the breast of her gown.

La Sventura poured herself another cup of the excellent red wine that Tulla had hardly touched. She waited relaxed and content, for she would have another visitor. She wondered idly if the girl would save them trouble as they hoped. If she were to administer the poison she would provide an admirable scapegoat; all Montevalenti would mourn its prince, none more than those she served. She thought it most likely that it would be so. The Byzantine had been so hot against Il Leone that she had not even thought to ask why she should have received this summons so conveniently to her own innermost desires. But then, the witch supposed, her superior knowledge allowing her an emotion akin to pity, that she could not be aware that the way of her deflowering was known to them, as also was her discovery of the prince in the arms of the wife who had not been kind to her.

La Sventura sighed and ran a distasteful eye around the eclectic accoutrements of the departed Atroviso. It was all one to her. If the girl used the poison, she would make an excellently publicizable assassin. If not, they could wait. There was time.

Alone in her chamber, unable to face the world at supper, Tulla put to herself at last the questions that should have come earlier to mind. The whirlwind of her thoughts had settled, and one by one, like blown leaves, they danced before her, mocking the little bottle that stood beside the night light on the table next to her bed.

How had La Sventura entered the castle? The city itself? Who had sent her? For it was obvious that she did not work on behalf of Alessandra Biscaglia. It must be that she was in Zorza's pay, for he had more cause than any to wish Leone dead—

And then, the last and most important question of all—why had the gypsy come to *her?* What had made her think that *she* might—she pushed away the thought of murder. An *execution,* La Sventura had called it. And so it would be, for there was no doubt that, in her own country, Leone da Valenti's execution would have been most public and most painful for what he had dared to do to the daughter of Quara Rashid.

She seemed to see again those flint-lit and unfathomable jet-colored eyes. She found she could not now remember what had been said between them. It was almost as if the gypsy had possessed the power to empty her mind, and then to fill it with her own dark dreams, that would lie in wait, somewhere below the level of her consciousness, until she herself should sleep and set them loose. She sat upon the edge of her bed, unconsciously rocking herself to and fro, staring at nothing, plucking the velvet pile of her coverlet to blue nudity.

She did not want to sleep for fear of the dreams that would come. Neither did she want to remain awake in the company of such black thoughts.

An executioner. Was that to be her destiny?

She remembered the night when she had walked with the prince in the courtyard of the Medici palace, how they had gazed at Donatello's "Judith" by the light of his dark lantern, saw again the sad, gashed throat, the woman's look of cold triumph. "Whom do you pity there," he had asked her, "the woman who is so relentless as to do such a deed, or the man who must suffer it at her hands. He had desired her. She had betrayed him."

She felt her judgment dissolve and waiver as she remembered other things. How he had accused her of lack of humility, of compassion; how he had that night saved both her pride and her person from the foolish cavaliere, and her own more foolish stratagems. How he had said he was not, and could never be, her enemy.

But *then* he had only desired her. He had not taken her, not torn down the entire, fragile edifice of the pride once rescued in obscene sacrifice to the monster within himself that he had last night accused her, *her*, of calling into being.

She rose from the bed and walked feverishly about the room, passing and re-passing the lamp at the bedside, more and more aware of but not able to look at the yellow phial that stood beside it.

A single conception began to grow inside her, as monstrous as the thing that bred it.

If Leone had now become Holofernes, whom should she be but Judith? His executioner.

She picked up the glass phial and stuffed it between her breasts. The lamplight had warmed it a little, and she did not shrink at the contact.

To quiet her mind she took up the volume of Plato that she had taken from Franco's library and often read at night when sleep evaded her. She had reached the chapter of the *Republic* that deals with the concept of justice. The great philosopher reveals Justice to be nothing more nor less than the state of cosmic harmony ordained by the Heavens, in which every part of creation has its function, an eternal order that man seeks to alter only at the peril of his soul.

Upon a scrap of paper clipped to the page, written in Franco's painstakingly beautiful script were the words of another philosopher, Anaximander on this subject.

"Into that from which things take their rise they pass away once more, as is ordained; for they make reparation and satisfaction to one another for their injustice, according to the appointed time."

So far was she from finding this helpful that she threw the book from her with unusual violence and resumed her pacing of the floor. A doctrine of divine order in which man nor woman may intervene did nothing to dispel the repeated images that tempted her now—the pure features of Judith swimming, serene and implacable, above the profane and decadent face of Leone da Valenti, bent in a mocking triumph of sensual conquest above her own, or—and this was where she must delve deep into the dark places of her soul, dragging the unwanted, the repudiated, the blasphemous emotions to the surface and ruthlessly exposing them to the light—above the naked and lubricous form of his wife.

What she saw was something that must not be permitted to exist.

There was a sense of the rushing of wings inside her head when the waiting, that she had not recognized as waiting, was over at last and the prince's messenger came to her door with his master's delicately phrased request for her company.

He received her in the small salon, the most impersonal of his private rooms, its furnishings rational enough to include a desk, albeit a scarlet fantasy of oriental lacquer, several cases of books, both printed and inscribed, some comfortable chairs and a decently severe sofa in mellow umber.

Like his visitor, Leone had been pacing his chamber. A half-eaten peach was in his hand.

He was not sure why he had sent for Tulla, nor what he would say to her when she came. He felt simply, as he had not felt until this time, that there was something he wished to put to rights between them. There had been a feeling of a similar order, that night, before he had taken her, but it was not precisely similar in nature. He had not brooded on the differences; as always, he would be guided by his instincts where his understanding would not take him.

When she came into the room he looked at her searchingly. That desperate look of pain and loneliness he had seen in her earlier was gone. In looking for it now, however, he knew suddenly that it was that look, as she had stood in Franco's doorway and seen him with Alessa, that had made him send for her. He could not have expected to see it still imprinted upon her face; no such foolishness. But now that it was gone, replaced by a very distant self-possession, its message for him was also gone, so that he found himself in a position of one who had been expecting the answer to a question that he could not even begin to formulate. It was very puzzling.

He put down his peach and gave her a subdued greeting, dismissing the servant. He felt oddly at a disadvantage.

"Please be seated, Madonna. Will you take wine?"

She accepted and saw an instant mirage of the mind whereby she would drop the poison in her cup and slyly exchange it with his after the manner of dramatic villains. At the same time the distance between her chair and himself and his cup seemed as negotiable at this moment as were the Alps on foot in winter. To speak to him at all would require resources of humility she feared she did not possess; to speak *easily*, as though he were any other human being; to roam the room; to make any kind of mental or physical attempt to engage his concentration—these were impossible. She sat like stone and waited for him to speak. She wished she had not come.

"You were not at supper. Have you eaten?"

She shook her head, fearing the strangeness of her voice.

"Then I will send for something."

"No. I'm not hungry."

"Some fruit then? The peaches are good—and the apricots—"

"Nothing."

She sat before him like a doll, so quiet and pale. He missed the spirit in her, the ascerbity, the humor, even the anger.

He wanted to bring them back, to demolish the distance she had brought with her and set down between them, confounding his own tentative purpose. Mere courtesies, however well-intended, would not do it. He considered whether he should perpetrate some monstrous clumsiness that would force her reaction; if he were to touch her, to come behind her and let his hands slide down that alabaster shoulder that the lamplight flattered so warmly, to cup that known, delightful breast. But no. In her present isolation, she would simply

311

freeze further and leave at the first opportunity. Besides he had no wish to humiliate her.

There was a path less fraught with hazard, one which conveniently, involved the only subject she might find it possible to discuss with him temperately.

"I have asked for your presence here on the children's behalf," he lied, his expression grave and elderly. "No one, however wise, may predict the outcome of this siege—though naturally *all* are doing so with the utmost confidence. And I would rest easier in my mind, therefore, if I was persuaded that my heirs, at least, might be sure of surviving it. We may be certain that Bernardo and Lucia are among Zorza's marked targets. I have decided on that account that it might be best to send them to the Medici in Florence, for safekeeping. I would be glad of your opinion on the matter."

At first he thought she would make no reply so long did she keep silent.

Then she said quietly and with no perceptible expression, addressing the air immediately to the left of his shoulder, "Has not your brother already sent more than one courier to Florence, to ask Lorenzo's aid?"

"It is so."

"And no reply has come?"

"No."

She gave the ghost of an irritated sigh. "Then I should think the possibilities of getting the children and their escort through to the Medici are so remote as to be discounted. They would suffer the same fate as the couriers have evidently done."

"We have no means of knowing what has happened to the couriers. It is not likely that Lorenzo could have organized an army by this time. He may do so yet."

"You would take such a chance with the children's lives?" Even now her voice remained colorless, abstract.

"I don't know. It is something that should be considered."

It was true that he had been toying with this idea, and unlike Tulla he knew of a way in which it could be managed. There were secret ways out of the city, immemorially old, beneath the mountain, but the plain was Zorza's. It would mean taking to the mountains to the north at the back of the city and doubling back, avoiding the plain. It would be a long journey but only ordinarily dangerous, if the escape could be made from the city.

312

"Wait. I have a map that will show you the possibilities—"

Incredibly he was gone, striding into the adjoining chamber, leaving her shaking on the edge of her seat, ambushed by the unexpectedness of the opportunity she had not yet begun to plan for.

Now was her moment, now, now!

She had only to rise, walk to the table where he had left his cup, take the phial from between her breasts—it would take no more time than it had already taken to think of it.

Why, then, did her feet cling like clay to the floor, why was her entire body suddenly made of lead? Oh quickly, quickly—it took but one stroke for Judith!

But that was with a sword and honorable.

And has not *he* dishonored *you?* Does he not deserve to die as much as Holofernes? Do you not want him dead?

She rose upon the thought and went quickly to the table, her hand to her breast, her heart hammering into it.

Just one little action and he would be dead. Dead as his brother was dead. The lithe, elegant body, the restless intelligent mind. The insolence, the humor, the culture and the kindness. All dead.

And she would be free. Free of him. She would never have to be in his presence again.

"Here it is, Madonna. Perhaps this will change your mind. It reveals the secret heart of Montevalenti."

She was standing by the table, her hands at her sides. How pale she looked. Perhaps the wine would bring back her color. He filled up both their cups and lifted his to encourage her. Then he laid out the map across the table.

It was more like a child's drawing than a true map. A section was shown, as though cut through the mountain looking from the north; the *campanile* of the cathedral, the castle towers, the roofs of the Arte della Lana were all recognizable as they perched upon the hilltop like pastry figures upon a pie crust. Below, in many-colored inks, were displayed the passages, the cisterns, the dungeons, the underground streams, and the hidden mysterious ways that penetrated the bland white rock upon which the city was set.

"You see? *Here!*" His finger lighted upon a spot that must be well within the dense woodland that covered all that side of the base of the hill.

There was a swift movement and a slight, definite crack as her own hand hovered near his. Then it was gone and a small, clouded yellow bottle stood upon the spot that marked the secret entrance to the underworld.

"What is this?" Half surprise, half curiosity.

"It is poison."

"And its use?" The voice level, betraying nothing of the thundering descent of the heart. He breathed in, slowly.

"For you. To kill you."

Just as slowly, he exhaled. The sound was deep and harsh like the rale of a dying man. He might have been a dying man. He nodded as though she had clarified some obscure point. He did not ask her why. But another point occurred to him.

"How did you come by it? And what is it?" He was surprised to be thinking so clearly. Both of them were still gazing at the map, their heads bent as though they actually saw it, were even concentrating upon it.

"It was given to me by La Sventura. I don't know its name."

"That witch!"

"She was here in the castle; may still be here."

He noted that and returned to the only thing that concerned him.

"You did not use it?" This time he was asking her why.

She managed to reply calmly and steadily as though she had not made a discovery that made nonsense of her own existence.

"I found I did not wish you dead." The question therefore remained.

He found the grace to smile. The moment was the strangest in both their lives. Neither was equipped to deal with it. We give such equipment only to gods and heroes. Leone took refuge in the surface of things, as he had managed to do in all matters save that of his brother's death. He said, as lightly as a slight tremor in his throat would permit, "I seem to be constantly indebted to you for the gift of my life."

Tulla, whose refuge, equal and opposite to his, was her own inviolable depths, replied, "That is not mine to give, nor is the taking of it. Such choices belong to God alone."

He looked at her shrewdly. "Vengeance is mine, saith the Lord? It was the fear of mortal sin that prevented you? Fear for your soul. You would not burn in hell for me. I can only applaud your decision. I am not worth such a desperate price."

"It was not that." Her honesty spoke before thought. "I gave no thought of God."

"Then why—?"

"I did not wish you dead," she repeated with a stubborn lack of emphasis as though she had let a fly continue to live.

"Despite the fact that I have given you what some women might think to be reason enough?"

"Despite that." It was obvious she would say no more.

"But why have you told me this? I need never have known of the poison, of your intention or your dismissal of it."

She looked at him now, her face clear and thoughtful. "To warn you, perhaps."

He laughed. "Against yourself—or against La Sventura?"

"I don't know. Both perhaps. I could have done it. I almost did. And La Sventura will find another instrument."

"I am surprised to find *you* ready to act as such an 'instrument'."

She fought off shame. "It was an opportunity. Slaves do not often receive them. Especially—at such times as they are most welcome."

"Dear God!" he groaned, striking his fist into the table, "how you goad me still with your terrible honesty!"

For a moment it seemed that he must give himself over to shame and self-hurt, but with a sudden turn of mood he drew himself up and looked down at her almost threateningly, a new demand glittering in his eyes.

"And yet it seems to me that, despite this confessional need to lacerate me with the truth—there is still much that you keep concealed—perhaps from yourself. I would remind you, however, that there are some things it is impossible to hide." He saw her eyes begin to snap and continued determinedly, ignoring her flushed face.

"You have told me things with your body, Madonna, that you would doubtless repudiate with your tongue—though I would prefer it if you would *not* speak for the moment—for God's sake! I comprehend your pride, but we may die tomorrow, despite the life you leave me today—"

Her carefully schooled blankness of expression told him his words fell fallow and therefore he had done with words. He dragged her impatiently into his arms and closed her mouth to both truth and falsehood. He held her fast but did not move his hands about her body, only clasped her tightly to him as though to force them into the one flesh they had once been.

315

But this time, and he knew she sensed it, it was a thing of the mind, despite the crushed lips, the steel embrace. Quite soon he let her go and stepped back from her. Inside him something burned, bright and certain, and he knew a sudden rush of happiness that made him laugh aloud. He saw that her eyes were dazed and full of shock and question. This satisfied him. It was enough for the moment.

"We will meet soon, and I will tell you what I have decided about Bernardo and Lucia," he told her steadily.

She was surprised. She had forgotten.

"Where, precisely, do you suppose I might find La Sventura?" he asked. "I would like to see yet *another* sunset, if you will not consider this a deplorably insatiable appetite for life!"

She forced her thoughts into some kind of order. "I met with her in the cell which Atroviso once used—but—"

She shook her head, and he saw that her cheeks were wet. He sighed and turning from her took a dagger from the drawer of the desk. Placing it in his belt he smiled and made her a helpless, masculine gesture, explaining nothing, for he had no explanations to give, and withdrawing on a Venetian salute, his hand most gravely upon his heart, he left her, very thankfully, for the dungeons.

When he had gone Tulla sat down at his scarlet desk, put her head in her arms, and wept as she had not wept since leaving Soraya.

When Alessandra Biscaglia had fled, earlier, along the marble passages toward the brother who had always been her comforter, she had fled too, down the corridors of her childhood to the one fixed and immutable fact of her divided life; the certainty of his love. It had been the pivot of her young days. Her warrior father had been to her a dragon figure who occasionally breathed fire in her direction; her mother a gentle, abstracted woman who had prayed a great deal when he was away from home and even more when he was present. Only Silvestro had taken her into his arms and his heart so that she had worshipped the towering young brother who wore armor as lightly as he wore his liturgical vestments and who lived his days as fiercely as though there were no tomorrow. At first she had wished he were not destined for the church. But as she grew older she became appreciative of the fact that he would never marry. His many mistresses did not disturb her. She knew with an instinctive certainty that he did not share his love with them as he did with her.

Now, as she wept her tears of rage and pride within the circle of his crimson sleeve, letting the bitterness flow from her as she never could have done with Leone, she felt again the closeness of their blood, the strangeness of all other minds.

She would not tell him precisely how it was that she had suffered; her pride was too great for that, but she made it known to him that she had tried to make up the long quarrel with her husband and had found him intractable.

"I thought, perhaps, that when this siege had ended, it could be between us again as it was once, at the beginning—but it can never be. When we have beaten Andrea from our gates, Silvio, I want to leave Montevalenti. There is nothing for me here but old age and emptiness. Will you go with me? Will you take me to Rome?"

Silvestro smiled thoughtfully, not breaking the regular rhythm with which he stroked her soft hair as he held her close. He bent to kiss her cheek; it too still had a child's softness.

"Little one," he murmured, "what if there were no necessity for such a desperate remedy?"

"What do you mean? I cannot bear my life, Silvio. Leone does not love me. I do not love him either," she added quickly, "but neither does he show me the respect that might make my days supportable. Even when I offered to intercede for him with Zorza—"

The cardinal's arms dropped from her so that she almost lost her footing. She told him of her plan for a parley with her cousin, though not of her desire, through that plan, to find favor in Leone's eyes. That must be locked forever in her heart, together with the alien passion that had conceived it. And yet, as she thought of Leone, of his beautiful body hovering over hers—her loins contracted with desire even as she hardened her heart to a resurgence of hatred.

"I thought it my—duty, as a Biscaglia," she said mechanically. "I would not have them call me traitor."

Silvestro led her gently to a daybed and made her sit down, drawing up a footstool at her side where he sat with his arm in her lap, her hand held fast in his.

The time had come for him to acquaint her with many things. Events had drawn toward this moment irrevocably

317

and naturally as he had known they must. It was excellent. Most pleasing. And yet they had come together to a crisis of the most delicate nature, and he must step more carefully with his sister in the next few minutes than he had ever had need to do before.

"Alessa—" It was easy to make her name a caress. "You are right to say that Leone does not love you. Nor could you wish it. For in your deepest nature, you know, as I have always known, that there can be no love between a Valenti and a Biscaglia."

"Silvestro? What are you saying?" He saw the trouble rising in her face and hastened on, his fine voice narrowly edged with severity.

"When the prince's father married you to him, you accepted it as a child accepts its fate. But I did not. I have never accepted our family's defeat by the Valenti, nor their accursed spilling of our blood. I swore when they killed our brother that with God's help I would take back all—everything they had wrested from us. There were only two of us left, Alessa—one man in holy orders and a girl in love for the first time. Oh, don't think I blame you for that. Leone was always the most attractive of the Valenti, but it is long past. You do not love him now." This affirmation struck a coffin nail into any last remnant of hope within her, as he had intended it to do. "Only two, against the whole principality of Montevalenti," he continued, a subdued violence investing his tone, "and so I knew that I must wait—wait and plan until one day God would place the weapon in my hand. He has given me that weapon, Alessa, in the form of Andrea Zorza—"

"Stop, Silvio, please stop. I can't—"

"You can understand me very well, my dear. I am telling you that the Biscaglia will rule again in Montevalenti and that this time we shall put an end to the Valenti, forever." She felt the dry burning of his lips as he kissed her hand and the wrist above it then raised his passionate face to meet her wondering, awakening look. "Is it so much of a surprise to you, my sister? Did nothing whisper it along your veins, hint at it in the depth of your dreaming? In your secret parts, did you not long for it also?"

She gasped, pressed thus hard in a direction that was new to her, and yet she did not find it shocking as it should be, but both exciting and exhilarating in ways that were also new.

"All is prepared. All is coming fast to fruition. All you will

318

need is a very little courage." His smile was especially gentle as he watched her breast rise and fall with her quickened breathing.

"And yet not even that—for I am here to be your protector, as I will always be."

"Silvio, beloved brother. But why have you not told me of this? That you could have taken Andrea Zorza into your confidence and have left me in ignorance—"

"I have given Zorza just as much of my confidence as he will need to play his part, nothing more. His role is almost over—he need not concern you unduly." His eyes slid away from her. "Although I would be glad if—in the nearer future, you could find it possible—however, we need not speak of that just yet." His fingers lingered upon the inside of her wrist where he had kissed it, and the sweet tingling brought a flush of shame and delight to her pale cheeks. He was looking at her closely now as though searching her face for signs of doubt in him. She did not pull her wrist away but gripped her brother's arm with a sudden determination so that they sat locked, wrist in hand, like companions at the outset of some great enterprise.

"Then you don't mean Andrea to rule here?"

"No. At least—only at first. Then it will be Zorza who seems to conquer—Zorza who has already devastated the countryside—Zorza who brings his foul horde of mercenaries into Montevalenti—who deposes its prince and puts both him and his heirs to death—oh yes, they must all die, you must see that—Zorza who forces you to become his wife—"

"Never!"

"For no time at all," he reassured her. "You need not submit to him." He transferred himself to the edge of the daybed and took her into his arms once more, his lips in her hair.

"As though I could bear to let the bastard—but to the people of Montevalenti, our overreaching cousin will seem a most self-imposing villain. Don't you see? So much blood at his door—the prince, the two innocent children," he felt her flinch and clasped her closer to his breast, exulting at the fluttering of her heart so near to his own.

"And of course the little Turkish girl—I believe you have no love for her—will be identified as the traitor who first let Zorza's troops into the city."

"But I have heard that Bossi—" she began uncomfortably.

319

He sighed. "I needed an early scapegoat. Bossi had allowed himself to be maneuvered into a most unfortunate position by La Sventura, an excellent woman in many ways. But her interest in the old religion often leads her, and those who serve her, beyond the bounds of the church's approval. Stefano stood in fear of trial for heresy. He would do all she—or I—asked him, poor man. But I did not choose well. There was a weakness in that whole family as we have seen." Suddenly he frowned deeply and terribly so that Alessandra herself was afraid of him.

"If only he had been efficient in his treachery, we should have found our task so much the more simple!" His fine voice was thickened by hatred, a venomous sibilance injecting his words. "He is hard to kill, the scented sybarite whom they gave you for a husband."

Now truly alarmed, Alessandra pulled back from him, stammering with shock, "You cannot mean that *you*—no, Silvio, it is horrible!" Leone's last gentle smile haunted her as though she had never known how to hate him.

"More horrible than our brother's death, crushed beneath the stones that built our castle? More horrible than our father's—split on a Valenti sword—dying upon a curse without time for even one prayer? More horrible than the corpses hanging on these walls?"

But this only served to remind her of something else.

"Franco! Oh it was not necessary! It cannot have been necessary that *he* should die."

He shook her then, in rage and disappointment.

"They must all die—all the Valenti! You know it! Do not make me ashamed of you." Then more quietly, "He would have died later, that is all. He was a good man. It is a pity."

She bowed her head. She was trembling now, her world more awry about her than she could have conceived to be possible.

Silvestro saw that she would weep shortly and opened his arms again, showing her his most kindly expression.

"It is not easy for you to accept all this in one moment, I know." He sighed and fixed his gaze upon the darkening skies beyond the level of the opened casement. "It has not always been easy for me. No less as a man than as a cardinal." He did not need to simulate his earnestness as he continued, "It was not I who chose to enter the church. It was never a vocation. It was our father who wanted to make me a cardinal. It did not occur to him, I suppose, that it would not make me any less a Biscaglia. And so you see me now—with blood on my hands to match the color of my robe."

Now the storm of weeping broke over her as he had foreseen. He made no attempt to stem it, but let her sink her head onto his shoulder until she had worn herself out with tears. Her grief tore at his heart as nothing else could do, but he knew, equally, that only he held the means to comfort her.

When she was quiet, her trembling over he began to stroke the loose, bright tresses of her hair. It was warm beneath his hand like the feathers of a falcon covering its small, vulnerable body. She did not move and he thought after a time that perhaps she slept. He continued his stroking, following the long strands wherever they fell, upon her back, about her shoulders, and before them onto her breasts beneath the soft blue gown. She was not asleep and shuddered at the sudden intimacy of the touch but did not move away.

"I want you to understand, my dear, all that I have done, all that I have still to do. It is for you, Alessa. For us. You must not judge me more harshly than God. For I know that He loves me still—can you believe that, my dearest."

She nodded, her face still hidden in the ruby silk, and he drew her still closer.

"All is for God and the Biscaglie. Our noble family must not die out but must go on from strength to strength, taking back all that is ours. But our blood must be pure, Alessandra, pure—not sullied by a bastard strain such as Zorza! You understand, my love?"

There was no reply though he felt again the quickening of her heart. He began to caress her hair, but when he touched her breast the second time, he did not sweep lightly over it as before but made a sudden fierce sound in his throat and dragged her gown from her shoulders so that it lay exposed to his touch and, at once, to his ravening lips. When at last he raised his head, he did not look at her but sank on his knees to the floor at her side. He buried his head in her lap and stretched out his arms in a conscious imitation of crucifixion.

As still as though he worshipped indeed at the altar, he waited for her sign.

SEVENTEEN

Down in Atroviso's stale, deserted den, La Sventura waited also, drinking her wine. She had hoped he would find a way to come to her. She knew he would take pleasure in what she had tried to achieve with the Byzantine girl and that he would reward her for it, both with gold and with the exquisite attentions of his body. Silvestro was a far more imaginative lover than his father had been so that her loyalty to his house was now partly a slavery of her body. She found an especial, esoteric gratification in the knowledge that in taking the seed of the cardinal into her willing and impious flesh, she was cheating the Christ, whom she and all her tribe so hated and feared, of a celibate priest. Her richest hopes outstripped any mere sins of the body, however. She had begun, with the assistance of the intelligent and resourceful astrologer, to lay claim upon the Biscaglia for her own lord and master. She had already had some slight success with the princess and would improve upon it gradually; from love philtres to more effective potions, from the *dream of flying* to the *abomination of the mass*. A cardinal was a far greater matter—the greatest of all possible prizes. She did not expect either a swift or similar conversion there; but Silvestro was ambitious. She knew his desires—more of them, even, than he would have her know—

But he would not come now, and she must not stay here.

She pulled her hood up and over her face and made her way quickly to the inhabited part of the castle. Then, in common with a great many other bent and black-clad women, she went to offer up her prayer in the ever-open cathedral. Once

322

there she shuffled unobtrusively into the empty sacristy where she shook off her cowl and moved toward the tryptych of Saint Jerome that hung upon the south wall. Covering the saint's drear companion, a grimly laconic skull, with her right hand and one of the least interesting rocks in the landscape with the left, she waited a second until, with a whirring and groaning reminiscent of the mills of God, she was admitted to the underworld.

Leone, finding no sign of the gypsy among his dungeons, retraced his angry steps toward his wife's apartments. She, at least, he knew to have had some traffic with the accursed creature. Perhaps she could explain how it was that such a known enemy could so easily penetrate his walls.

The few guards that remained within doors, young pages in overlarge uniforms, knew nothing of the woman although they crossed themselves energetically at the sound of her name. The princess was not in her rooms. Perhaps she was with his Eminence her brother?

Cursing roundly, Leone flung off in the direction of Silvestro's chambers. He doubted he would find the witch now, but she had always been a Biscaglia minion and he was in no mood for a polite overlooking of her latest misdeed. She may not have sought his death before now, but most certainly she had sought it tonight and he intended to exact a death for a death.

The banners of the wolf stretched insolently above him as he entered the cardinal's chambers. For the first time he found it an impertinence that the bloody-tongued blazon of their greatest enemy should hang in the Valenti palace. Once it had afforded him a cynical amusement. Apart from a few pairs of bored guards, playing chess or cards to compensate for the dull watch indoors, the somber rooms seemed as deserted as those of the princess. He crossed the reception chamber and entered the grand salon, wrinkling his nose as he so often did at Silvestro's taste for the majestic mixed with the macabre. In the context in which they had been placed, the Biscaglia colors, the sable, the silver, the scarlet that flared and gloomed about him could only represent the black certainty of death, the livid flash of the sword's fall, the bright splash of blood as it was shed. An immense Crucifixion hung upon the narrow northern wall. The figure of Christ, the flesh luminously pale, attenuated, bleeding, pierced with wounds and thorns, seemed to rise out of the dark, nebulous background toward the watcher as though pleading for an end to pain. The tortured fingers clawed toward him, the cracked lips mouthing how he was forsaken; the crazed and disillusioned eyes conscious only of betrayal, the eyes of a man in the extremity of suffering, a man without knowledge or hope of the Resurrection.

The other walls, where they were not swathed in dark-hued velvet that caught no light, portrayed scenes of the martyrdoms of saints. Katherine, Ursula, and Lucy were naked and nubile young girls, in various stages of distress at masculine hands, while Sebastian, John and even the staid Jerome, seemed in their half-clad and exuberant masculinity to be more fitted to provide the ladies with husbands in this life than to join them in heavenly chorus in the next. A jeweled skull, to be used as a drinking cup, stood upon a silver and onyx table. It was that of one Jacopo Marni, an enemy of Silvestro's late grandsire. A candle burned before it as though it, too, were the representation of a saint. Indeed, the branched and jeweled lamps suspended from the ceiling burned so low that this one candle drew the eye at once to his grisly illuminatus. Leone's lips tightened as he passed on toward the more intimate chambers. With such a sensual appreciation of death within him, his brother-in-law should have been born a Spaniard.

The smaller salon was also in near darkness, its silver appointments gleaming coldly in the emptiness, though a faint sweet-sick scent of roses suggested a recent occupant. The prince was about to abandon his search when he thought he caught a murmur of sound from beyond the closed doors which led to the cardinal's dressing room. They opened soundlessly at his touch and invited him into a richness of color and texture that was as far opposed to the public apartments as is life to death. The walls glowed in apricot velvet; the ceiling gloated with nymphs and satyrs in explicitly bawdy bacchanalia; garments of silk and damask, primrose, indigo, crimson, lay scattered over perfumed wooden furnishings in profuse disarray. Somewhere incense burned, its heavy, provocative odor far from that of sanctity.

Through the open door opposite the threshold came the soft, indulgent sound of a woman's laughter.

Since he recognized it to be his wife's and found it, therefore, somewhat unusual, Leone moved toward the sound, hoping that his presence would not precipitate too sudden a fall in her spirits.

They did not hear him as he came into the doorway, being deaf, as they were blind, and in every way insensate to all the world save that circumscribed by the spreading base, the exquisite carved posts and the triumphant golden tester of the cardinal's silken, sleek-sheeted bed.

Alessandra's white body lay sprawled in an extravagance of open, nerveless limbs that betokened an utter voluptuous lassitude. Her face, where the lamplight colored it softly through the tall Venetian jug of wine upon the side table, was roseate with completion, her lips wet and parted, her eyes wild and yet heavy as though she were drugged or intoxicated. Between her long thighs, his vermillion robe covering them both a little, her brother lay, his dark head upon her breast, one hand loosely telling over the gold of her streaming hair. It was as if the prince looked upon an old, familiar picture as they lay there in the wine-light while he stood, arrested, himself framed by the doorway, until his stumbling understanding should keep pace with his eyes—a strange psychic canvas that showed him, in all the cruel colors of his age, not only the incest of a cardinal, the adultery of a wife, but the fount and base of Silvestro's terrible patience, of Alessandra's flawed and restless existence, her incapacity to love beyond her blood—

But she had seen him now and rose at once upon her elbow, eyes wide not with guilt but with *accusation,* an absolute denial of his right to intrude his presence here. She made a sound like a growl of some small animal, and Silvestro sprung up at once, red silk spilling about him as he turned to where her face bid him look.

He saw the prince come toward him with a dagger in his hand.

"Leone—"

"Silvio." Not, "My Lord Cardinal." Death is an intimate moment.

The red silk shrieked as he whirled to seek a weapon. There was nothing. He seized the jug of wine and threw it in Leone's face. Most of its contents sprayed across the foot of the bed in a gaudy premonition of blood. The jug crashed to the floor and splintered upon the mosaic. The prince shook wine from his dripping hair as Silvestro dived for a jagged fragment of the glass, and his eyes were still clenched against

325

its sting as the fractured shard was dragged hard across his wrist.

Despite the pain he did not drop the dagger as the wine mingled, burning, with his blood, but drove it swiftly into Silvestro's breast, sinking it in close to the shoulder. Instinctively Silvestro pulled back and the blade parted from the flesh with a curious sucking sound. The wound was deep enough to cause a momentary hazing of his vision, and he staggered back upon the edge of the bed, where Alessandra caught him in her arms, moaning his name in terror.

The hateful weakness passed, and he felt the knife pricking at his throat, her arms clinging desperately, heard her pleading.

He cursed her obscenely. "Beg not my life of *him!*"

"You do right to tell her so," Leone said, "for it is not on her account that you die—she had no honor worthy of defense—but for the name of Valenti which you have dared to defile in her."

Silvestro laughed. His certainty did not desert him even now. His success would live on, in part, though he himself would die.

"The name of Valenti will soon be dust and ashes, a mere memory in a book of hours, turned over and forgotten again by the generations of Biscaglia bastards who will have your inheritance, Prince! What though you kill me and kill her too—you cannot prevail over the army of Andrea Zorza. He will put an end to you and yours irrevocably as I have ordered it. As it was with Franco, so will it soon be with you."

At the sound of his brother's name upon those blasphemous lips Leone felt as though his veins ran freshly with a stream of pure hatred, as sweet and, it seemed, as uncorrupt an emotion as had ever come to him. He knew without any shadow of doubt or reluctance that he would shortly encompass this man's death, but he would not do it in the heat of anger. And there were things he would know. Flattering the cruelty that loves to boast, he said evenly, "God does not give the ordering, even of so small a universe as Montevalenti, to such as you, Biscaglia."

Silvestro smiled, his arrogance still perfect despite the increasing pain in his chest. "Does He not? Then why does He set such willing and excellent instruments to my hand? Why has He sent Zorza to be your scourge? Why does He beset you with traitors? Above all, my dear brother, why has He made

326

you a fool who could see nothing but his own face in the glass?"

"So you have turned others traitor, Silvio, as well as your sister, my wife?" He did not look at her, only at the serenely smiling face of the fallen angel beside her, so that her voice surprised him with its harsh control as she swore, "I am no longer any wife of yours. It was a madness in me to think I could be."

"And *this?*" the prince cried, goaded at last, "is this not the greatest madness of all?" The point of his dagger wavered dangerously and Silvestro drew in a sharp breath. She shook her head, a sudden fierce radiance in her face as she wound herself more closely about her brother so that he might take her under the scarlet wing of his robe.

"This is the end to which I was born. We cannot escape our fate, Leone. There is no doubt in me," she said. "If I was ever a traitor—it was when I married you. Then I was a traitor to my blood."

The simplicity of it made Leone shudder. Shifting his grip upon the knife, he lifted Silvestro's head with the other hand and slit his throat across.

Although the blood was unspeakable and Alessandra's screams most terrible to hear, the thing that he would never be able to forget was Silvestro's look of surprise.

He had not, even as he bled at dagger point, with Leone's wife naked in his arms, truly expected to die.

Tulla had not returned to her chamber that evening but had remained in the prince's apartments. At first she had stayed because she was weeping and because she did not care where she might be. Later, when she had admonished herself severely for such weakness, she had sat staring ahead of her at the lacquered desk and tried to put her thoughts—and more difficult, her emotions—into some sort of order.

One thing was clear to her already. Her tears this time were not those of ill-usage nor even of any great unhappiness. They had flowed partly out of relief that she was not, after all, to be a murderess—or an "executioner"—and partly—and here she met the thing, that was so hard to recognize—

And yet, he had already forced her to recognize it, not an hour since; and this, too, had been a relief almost too great to bear, and was chiefly the reason why she had wept.

For she had discovered that she was the prince's slave in earnest, no matter how high her birth or her pride. She knew now that what she felt for him, after all her attempts to fly from him, after having come near to taking his life in order to escape him, was that which, if it was to flourish and grow strong, must make a gift of freedom—

She did not think she could speak to him of these things; she could not even bear to contemplate them herself for very long; but she would remain here in his room until he returned and it would be in some little way a sign for the things she could not say.

It seemed a very long time until she heard a sound outside in the corridor and then, when she realized that there was shouting and the noise of running feet, she sped, herself to the door and threw it open.

She was standing in the passage, holding a candle high, when he came toward her. He walked very quickly, almost staggering. She saw at once that he was covered with blood, that his face was deathly pale.

"Leone, my lord! You are hurt!"

She set down the candle and ran toward him, her face filling with fear. He waved her back, some part of him noting her care and wanting to be glad.

"No. It is not my blood." He almost choked, then added with seeming irrelevance, "Is there still one candle then, in all the dark? Take it up. I have great need of it."

She followed him back into the room, disturbed no less by his words than by his appearance.

A clutch of worried servants hurried after them their faces strained with curiosity.

"No, please leave us. I will serve the prince." They stared at her in amazement, but they obeyed her. The daughter of Quara Rashid is obeyed without question.

"You may bring fresh water," she called after one of them.

Leone stood before the window, his back to the room. He lifted his hands and carried them to his face.

"My lord, there is much blood," she said gently. "If you will tell me where I may find fresh clothing?"

It did not seem strange that she should minister to him. Had she not waited for him, he would have gone to her. But it was not clothing he needed; it was comfort.

He told her where to find his wardrobe.

She brought him a robe of dark wool then unlaced his

doublet and pulled the streaked shirt from his body. Seeing the soaked and spattered garments hanging limp over her arm he shivered involuntarily, and though the sight harrowed his very soul, he could not turn away his eyes.

The servant timidly brought water and was instantly dismissed again.

She offered him the basin and the sponge.

"Pilate's gesture for Pilate's deed. I have become an executioner," he said. He was still trembling slightly. He washed his face, hands and arms; the water changed its color. His last word mocked her own half-simulated calm.

"Should Pilate trouble over the death of a gypsy?"

It is the power that she held in life that has disturbed him, she thought.

"I have not killed the gypsy."

"No?" She waited for him to tell her, forcing her concentration upon the bandaging of the gash she had found across his wrist.

"I have killed my brother-in-law."

"The cardinal!" Her mind reeled; for a moment she thought him mad. Then the mocking words came back to her. "And this was an *execution?*"

"Most deservedly." He wondered if he would be able to tell her. Then, knowing that there would soon be others, many others whom he must tell, he gripped tightly upon the hand that held his with the bandaging, stopping her movement, forcing her to look at him while he spoke, as temperately as he could, of what he had seen and done.

After a first brief, horrified, protest, she spared him her reactions to his words, which fell with the violence of hot pitch upon shrinking flesh. In the end she was surprised only at her own lack of surprise as the dark heart of Montevalenti spilled its poison and ceased to beat. She felt relief, as though a fabled monster had been slain; relief, and pity for the slayer.

When he had finished she began again to wind the linen about his arm. It was now quite steady. Not so her thoughts.

"You spoke of Pilate," she said neutrally at last. "But I see only sorrow in you, without trace of guilt. The tetrarch had condemned an innocent man—"

"And I have killed one as guilty as he is surely damned. He died without a prayer. It is a terrible thing to have sent a man to eternal damnation."

"He was a cardinal," she said ironically. "He must have spoken as many prayers as there are stars. His sins have been the greater infamy for that. Yet if there is forgiveness for him, God will offer it without the price of a dying prayer." Her tone hardened. "But I do not think there can be forgiveness for such a one."

"We are what we are," he said dully. Suddenly he had realized how tired he was, weary to the bone, he could no longer be bothered with meanings. "It's better he is dead, for Montevalenti, even for—Alessandra. If only—"

She knew he thought then of Franco, and she heard again the beautiful, unctuous voice that had urged him to lead Montevalenti to war and afterward had intoned his funeral oration. Silvestro Biscaglia had died too late! It was useless now, however, for Leone to reproach himself upon that score.

"His death will avenge your brother—and cleanse the city," she said firmly. "It will bring them new heart to know that the greatest traitor of all is overthrown."

He did not answer her. She had finished the bandaging and now touched him lightly on the arm and indicated that he should rise.

"You need sleep now. Come." Now, while he swayed before her with exhaustion, before his overstretched mind could begin again to rehearse the terrible scene he had described to her, could torment him with that slaughtered, impious body, the naked woman raving in her brother's blood.

He let her lead him, childlike, to his sleeping chamber and lay down without demur, consciousness already slipping away from him. He flung out one hand across the pillow in a groping, half-determined action, the fingers lifting a little as though seeking direction. She knew what it was that he sought and gladly gave him her hand.

It was many hours later when the prince awoke to find a light still burning at his bedside, vying with the dawn and Tulla, her hand still curled about his own, sleeping, clothed upon the coverlet, her features as pure and serene as one of Botticelli's madonnas. His movements must have wakened her, for she shifted a little and opened her eyes. He watched as memory flooded in upon the peaceful features and molded them in its image of horror and pity, then caught his breath at the sudden changing sweetness of her fully awakened smile.

330

"Strange, my lord, to wake at your side," she said shyly.

Stranger still that happiness could strike with as swift a lightning as tragedy.

"Stay at my side," he said with equal simplicity. "Be my candle against the dark." He carried her hand to his lips. His look was as grave and as clear as though the events of yesterday had never taken place. He had set them aside so that he might have space in his mind for *her*. Seeing this, and recalling all of those events, she was seized by remorse.

"But I might have brought you death!" she insisted.

He smiled. "You may believe it, but I do not think so." He threw back the sheet that covered him and knelt over her, purposeful and determined. "If you wish to do penance for that—you may now assist me to celebrate life!" His eyes kindled, golden and exultant, stabbing her with the reminder of his green and careless days. It was as though he shook a spear in the face of the evil that snarled over Montevalenti and proclaimed the ultimate triumph of the right; as though he would outwit the bloody wretchedness of the night by this early morning joy which he begged her to share with him.

She saw that her feeble design to take his life was already quite discounted, scarcely even worth his forgiveness, and that therefore she might begin to forgive herself, saw too that since that very design had denied her any further right to maintain her pride before him, she might now allow herself to admit freely that which he had last night compelled her to recognize—the desire of her body for his. Above and beyond these selfish considerations, she knew as she lay looking up into his beautiful, careful face, was the fact of his present need for her, the necessity to have his brave affirmation of life confirmed in the face of all their possible deaths. It was this need that opened her arms to him so that an even greater happiness was suddenly hers—the reassurance that this was not, and perhaps had never been, a love of the body alone. As he moved over her and upon her and into her, his lips, his hands, his whole heatedly sensual young body provoking the sweet, wild, ungovernable responses that she had never yet wholly set free, she heard herself cry out as if at some great victory; with all her strength she held him fast to her, her kisses soon outdoing his in their possessive, almost predatory fierceness. With the knowledge of love, as often with great joy, came pain—the terrible fear that she might lose him, that the evil would prove too strong for them after all.

Leone only half understood her tears at the climax of their loving though it was made sweetly clear to him that they were none of his fault.

To disperse them, and perhaps to calm them both after the storms of passion and revelation, he fetched his lute from the seat where it lay and played to her softly and with loving expertise, one of the courtly love lyrics of Machaut set to a tune of his own making. Plaintive and amorous, it told her, as though their existence were bound forever in some distant bower of roses, beyond all troubles and all years, that in his eyes she was the one "fairer far than beauty and kinder than kindness," the sole object of his desire and cause of all content, whom he sought only to love and serve forever. His voice was calm and resonant as a bell and his face, as he looked at her over the lovely, full-bellied instrument, showed a rueful attention to the verse which, she sensed, he had not given in any previous performance. The prince's loves had been frequent and fleeting. It was his custom to love well but not for long. But this woman, with her nobility and her courage, and the honesty that would give itself no quarter, was not one whom he would soon be able to leave with a companionable kiss and a fine present—perhaps, never, now that he had found whatever nameless thing it was that he needed of her and she had found the grace to give it.

The sun began to steal into the chamber as though Leone's music, note by note, were calling up the dawn. Bird song had long been his accompaniment, and the sound and the light and the look of him, the knowledge that for this little hour at least, he was wholly hers, brought her new content to a pitch almost beyond bearing. The fancy came to her that they inhabited one of the delicate apple-shaped spheres of glass that the Venetian blowers fashioned merely to prove their virtuosity, small, scintillating globes of crystal, so fragile that even a breath, it seemed, might shatter them to atoms.

In any event, it was not a single breath but many that put an end to their idyll. There came the tramp of feet, a rapping on the door and the stern, unsurprised figure of Pascale Cerruti advanced upon them granite faced and without apology.

"My Lord Prince, there is grave news. It is feared we may have plague in the city!"

There was a crashing discord as the lute was swept to the floor, and Leone harried his valet to dress him in seconds.

332

Three other officers confirmed Cerruti's report, each having the evidence of his eyes for proof.

"The woman seemed at first to suffer only from a rheum. Her eyes ran and she had the fever. But when she raised her arm to leave her pallet she cried out in pain and it was then I saw the bubo—blue and swollen beneath her arm. I only looked in through the window," he added hastily as several servants gasped and covered their mouths. "I have taken no infection. I am certain of that."

"And there is another matter, Principe," Cerruti offered in a low voice as his officers departed and the valet buckled on Leone's brigandine. He hesitated.

"Go on, man."

"La principessa," he began, then stopped again, his weathered face reddening. "I regret it deeply, my lord, but my lady has disappeared. There was a guard at her door, as you ordered. They swear they did not sleep—and I believe them, my Prince. But this morning, when her maid went in to her, she was gone." He shrugged uncomfortably and shifted his feet, embarrassed and defeated and plainly irritated by this strange turn of things.

"Have your men look for her. She cannot be far away. I told her women to look after her—"

"I know, my lord. They say she would not have them near her. She was in such great distress—"

"I know! I know. Leave it. Just *find* her, Cerruti!" Only too glad to make no reference to the events of the previous night, the stalwart captain saluted and left him, and he turned at last to Tulla, quiet and still upon the vast bed, his robe wrapped close around her for comfort now that he must leave her. He made a gesture of regret, showed her a brief, sweet smile that meant much, even more briefly caressed her head.

"I know," she said and watched him go.

Plague! The agonized cry whose reverberations had rolled in terror across Europe time after time, in place after place for over a hundred years; God's judgment upon the unjust and the Devil's torment of the just; Death stalking black-robed in the streets, skull-face cowled until he should knock on your door and look you in the eye.

Rumor spread with the rising dawn, and by the time the sun was fully up panic raged about the city. The apothecaries were dragged in all directions either on pain of death or on offer of rich reward, according to the fortune of the patient. Anyone who could be even faintly suspected of infection was immediately boarded up in his house by his neighbors, the ensuing close conditions insuring that if he *were* contaminated, his family became the next victims. And who should blame the neighbors? For, if the plague were present, all within would be dead within a week, when their bodies and their possessions might be burned. If it were not, any man might survive for a week without leaving his house—and at least he'd be safe from the chance of *catching* the dread disease. So ran the belief of all intelligent persons. The same persons also favored other beliefs—as for instance that the main breeding ground of the plague was the air about them, which became thick with the atomies of the pollution and hung about the town or village much as a swarm of black bees about a hive. If this dense air could be set in motion, the grave argument went, then the danger would disperse and all would be well. To this laudable end every bell in Montevalenti was set to ring without ceasing, musicians were entreated to play at a furious pace, women and children encouraged to bellow their lungs away, and any man who possessed any kind of firearm was exhorted to fire it off constantly for the greater disturbance of the invidious ether.

All this in concert with the babble of human fear and the renewed, morning vigor of Zorza's bombardment.

The prince held a council of war at which the little dottore was a feared and respected speaker. Having gravely confirmed the worst, he offered the advice of his experience. Being a much-traveled man, he had observed several previous examples of the scourge. The fact that he had survived them put much heart into his listeners.

"*Can* there be any good property in this cacophony?" Leone enquired at the outset, as their ears rang, sang and burned with the orchestrated torture that no walls could keep out. The physician shrugged, his hair scandalized about his untidy cap.

"It can do them no harm—if their eardrums are healthy. It gives them something to do other than sitting suspecting themselves of having the plague. It was unfortunately been my observation that there are three things about this disease that are unchanging whatever the circumstances of the outbreak. They are, firstly, the speed with which death may follow the initial attack—generally within three days, sometimes in twenty-four hours—secondly, the velocity with which the contagion spreads and reaches its peak, and, thirdly, the level of mortality—which must always be more than half of those infected. It is a sorry truth and saddens me to deliver it."

There was little consternation; these things were known; there was, however, much discussion. "What are your remedies against infection, doctor?" voices called out, more truculent than hopeful. Many believed the causes of the plague to be supernatural so that human precautions could not be coincidental to avoidance of it; however God helps those who help themselves, and even the Devil can be foxed on occasion; as yet no one in the castle displayed any symptom of the disease so they would join with those who considered it a natural malady in making what preparations they could to stay free of it.

"The best preventive medicine for a healthy man is to follow the saying 'Pronto, lontano e tardi!' " was the forthright opinion of Julio Bagno. "But in our case we don't have the option."

"Go swiftly, go far and stay long" was advice not intended for the besieged.

"Don't despair, Lieutenant Julio." The doctor smiled slightly. "A young man in his prime has every chance of staying healthy if he is sensible. He will naturally, avoid all infected places or persons, indeed all places where people congregate in numbers—such as the taverna, the gaming house and (if you will forgive me, Lieutenant) the bordello." Sheepish grins accorded him wise.

"I personally believe the odors of certain pungent herbs to be efficacious in keeping contagion at bay—wormwood, oak leaves, lavender, and laurel and the fir, even the humble marjoram. At any rate, their scents are pleasant. I do not, however, concur with those who think that the fouler the stench the greater the deterrent to infection! I counsel you therefore against the burning of leather or horn, or of the ordure of men or animals and the tethering of goats and cattle indoors. To my mind such noisome filthy practices can only increase the danger."

Some laughed while others looked dubious, and the latter were relieved when Father Ambrogio, his normally optimistic features still shadowed by the duties he had recently performed in the Biscaglia apartments, added his universally acceptable quota of advice.

"There is nothing in this world so efficacious as prayer—if the learned doctor will forgive me—and *my* counsel to you and to all the city is that you make yourselves as spiritually pure as you may. Go often to confession, and pray more frequently then you have ever done. Unless you are truly wicked or unless God wants you for his own, he will not suffer your faith to go unrewarded. But your faith must be strong." Here Leone looked as though he would have spoken, but shook his head and kept silent.

"Even should you or anyone near to you be taken, there is no reason to suppose that death is inevitable—"

"No! Only fifty percent inevitable!" cried an impious spirit somewhere near Bagno.

"By no means," Father Ambrogio hurried on, "for we have the best of intercession in Blessed Saint Luca, himself a physician." He glanced slyly at the doctor.

But Leone had heard enough. He cut off the priest with profuse thanks and moved on to matters of a purely practical nature concerning the conditions at the hospital attached to the monastery, the places where grave pits might be dug, the arrangements for the transport of the sick and the dead.

He ordered an immediate council of every physician and apothecary in the city and charged the dottore with its management. The sick were to be isolated as soon as their symptoms appeared; when the hospital was full the hall of the Arte della Lana might be used. The main problem would be to persuade his fearful and recalcitrant citizens that such isolation would be the best course both for themselves and for their relatives.

"Julio Bagno has already reminded you that being thus penned inside our walls," Leone said, "the disease will spread more quickly than would otherwise be the case. We have most of the peasants in the town, causing the crowded conditions in which the plague thrives! Therefore when I have agreed with the physicians upon the ordinances we shall give for public hygiene, I want those ordinances imposed as though they related to the worst of crimes. Any family found guilty of disobedience shall be isolated instantly—if we can find anywhere to isolate them."

The edicts were few and simple. No physician or surgeon who attended plague victims was to attend any other sickness. The infected blood that they drew was to be thrown over earth not into the common sewer. All who had survived the plague or who had in any way come into contact with it were to wear a white band upon their arms. It was forbidden to remove goods and property from the houses of the plague dead until the epidemic was over. Every citizen was to wet down the road outside his house twice a day. The streets were to be kept clean of refuse and the sewers clear of blockage. In addition to these private admonishments, all public buildings, including the baths, were to close—except of course the churches, but only those whose households were without infection might enter these.

There were to be no more spectators upon the beleaguered walls; the defenders themselves were given a stringent rule to follow which insured that no man had more contact than was strictly necessary with any of his fellows. There was lively argument as to whether or not the soldier should be allowed to fire the clothes and bedding of dead victims among the enemy as a discouragement to close offensive. The younger contingent were strongly in favor of this, knowing the terror and consternation that the discovery of the plague would cause, but Cerruti preferred to keep their misfortune secret as long as possible so that Zorza might not realize their increasing weakness. He knew, however, as did Leone, that it would be next to impossible to prevent Bagno and his friends from carrying out their intentions.

Tulla felt it to be almost disgraceful that, under the attack of such troubles as they now suffered, she should possess the consolation of a deep and sweet personal peace.

She sensed it to be very much a payment for this disgrace therefore when Leone himself swept away that peace with a single, determined sentence.

He had come to her himself, in the little, book-lined chamber where she taught the children, with whom she was at present engaged in disposing of several of the various forms of precaution against infection with which Vanozza Grazzi felt it her duty to surround them.

Bowls of fresh milk and bread warm from the baker's oven confronted them on every threshold; these were supposed to be excellent absorbers of the plague poison. So, ludicrously and unfortunately, were small living birds and spiders, so that Lucia had driven herself almost to a frenzy of concern for the dozens of quails and sparrows that now flew desperately about the castle chambers, alternated with hysterical outbursts at the sight of the bowls and vases containing black and tangled masses of hostile spiders, to which she was less than partial at the best of times. In addition to the food and the wildlife, the entire palace was pungent with herbs and lavender, while the more opportunist among the servants went about selling those objects that purported to supply a holy or a magical remedy—for the nobles, a bezoar stone or a portion of unicorn's horn or an amethyst; while lesser men would be well satisfied with a piece of toad skull, the tongue of a viper, or a hollowed-out hazel nut filled with mercury. Father Ambrogio's monks did a roaring trade writing papers for those who could neither write them themselves, nor read. Upon them were the Holy Names of God and his Blessed Mother and certain specified prayers. The papers were either pinned to the clothing of the believer—or, even more efficaciously, folded seven times and eaten daily before breakfast. Tulla had already had great difficulty in persuading the tearful Lucia to part with one of these papers, to which she had thoughtfully added a large helping of apricot preserve; what with that and the spiders, it was not the easiest of her days.

And now, just as with Bernardo's ingenious help she was beginning to reestablish order—he had removed the spiders, driven the birds out of the window and generously exchanged an amethyst pendant (for the duration of the plague only) for the jammy prayer paper—the prince had dispersed their hard-won seeds of calm.

They were to leave Montevalenti that very evening.

They must travel to Florence where they would be safe. They would use the underground path he had shown her on the map, and messer Simone Buonavia of the Arte Della Lana would be their chief escort.

"I must have someone in Florence whom I trust and who is respected enough by the Medici and by Montevalenti herself, who will be able to return some day and take charge of her fortunes if—this war should have a disastrous outcome. Messer Buonavia is accustomed to government. He is honest and will do his utmost to see that Bernardo comes into his heritage."

Tulla's heart sank as she listened and seeing this, Leone added with a smile, "But be assured, my dearest, that it will not come to that."

"Then why cannot I remain here and fight at your side?" demanded Bernardo staunchly.

338

Leone took him by the shoulders and regarded him with studied gravity. "What is the reason for this war, Bernardo?"

"Andrea Zorza seeks your throne," was the instant reply.

"And I am resolved that he shall not have it—or, if by some mischance he does—that he shall not keep it. Therefore I cannot have its heir falling dead of the plague before the outcome is decided. And besides, I have a duty for you in Florence."

"What is that, my uncle?"

"To beg aid from Lorenzo—and so make *sure* of the outcome."

The boy nodded reluctantly but a last hope sprang. "Can't messer Buonavia do that?"

Leone shook his head, his smile tight, and Bernardo knew that the issue was closed. But not so Tulla. She sent both children down to their beloved kitchen, after counseling them not to accept *any* plague precautions that might be eaten or drunk unless they should bring them to her to be pronounced digestible.

"I am in complete agreement that the children should leave," she began when they had left the room, "but there can be no possible need for me to accompany them. Clarice Medici will give them the most loving of care and the best of tutors. They could be in no kinder hands. I do not wish to leave you, my lord. Do not ask me to do so," she finished with a little lift of the head meant to remind him that she too was of noble blood and accustomed to make her own decisions.

His reply was to demolish her dignity by seizing and kissing her soundly. "Do not make it more difficult for me," he said as he let her go. "Those children have come to love you dearly and no Medici care can replace your own. And your possible death at enemy hands can do them no service." Behind the lightness of his tone she sensed that his resolve was absolute. It would do her no service to persist in trying to shake it. She quietly agreed that she would go and turned her attention to the point that had worried her when he had first suggested this escape.

"We have no proof that it is possible to reach Florence; no word from your couriers or from Lorenzo—while La Sventura, and who knows how many, like her, in the service of—" she hesitated, seeking the least painful title for that dead evil, "the cardinal come and go within your walls as they wish.

Who can say that the passage you propose to trust is not already under enemy surveillance?"

"What will you have me do?" His words burst the thin membrane of his control. "You know how fast the plague will spread. We'll have it here in the castle tomorrow!"

He would not say to her that, with the prospect of losing over fifty per-cent of their fighting men, there was little chance of their holding out against Zorza. That would be too cruel. He had denied himself the luxury of her death at his side; indeed he would take the strength he needed for the next decisive days from the knowledge that she, with the children, was safe, would live, perhaps with *his* child in her belly.

"You speak the truth—but all other truths, at the present time, are equally unpalatable. I beg you, Madonna, to do what I ask of you and not talk of it any longer. We have little time to be together," he ended astutely so that she gave a tiny cry and threw herself into his arms again.

Their time was indeed brief, its tenderness laced with the pain of parting and its passion the whiter flame.

Again he surprised her with his ability to create, despite the red-tongued howling of the wolves and furies around them, his own affirmative moment and space. Tulla had already begun to know what it was to love him; now she began to feel what she must lose in leaving him. She did her utmost not to show him this, sensing, though he would not speak of it, that he shared her sorrow.

They spoke little, and he did not speak of love. The time was not yet—and if it should never come, he wished to leave her free.

When they parted, she did not see him again until it was time to leave.

EIGHTEEN

To the north of the city of Montevalenti, the ground fell away
with inhospitable suddenness into a density of primal green
forest, an area familiarly known to the inhabitants as "il
fondo verde," the green backside of the city. It was through
the rock beneath this fundamental jungle that the proposed
passage to safety lay. When Tulla, who did not care for
underground ways, inquired tartly whether they might not
just as well descend through the trees, she was cordially
invited to try it for herself if she had several days to spare
and could command a stalwart party of strong men with
machetes. Indeed these impenetrable depths represented the
town's best means of defense upon the northern side, and
only a skeleton guard was needed to patrol the ramparts
above it.

The passage opened from the enclosed garden of one Giorgio
Nadda, a dyer and fuller by trade who was much overcome by
the presence of the prince among his humble fruit trees—or
so, at least, it appeared from his behavior which was nervous
to the point of imminent collapse. He had worried his finger-
nails into rags before they had been there ten minutes, and
his continuous bowing and scraping gave the impression of
an uncontrollable twitch rather than of good manners.

The truth was that he was in an agony of indecision over a
promise that he had recently made. For this was the second
occasion on which his trees had been privileged to shelter the
doings of great ones. Only two nights ago, well after midnight,
he had been roused from his bed by no less a person than the
fearful witch, La Sventura. She had extracted his pledge of

secrecy upon pain of the most terrible of curses and then had commanded him to reveal the opening of the passage. At first he had not dared, for fear of aiding a deserter from the walls, but the witch had fixed him with her basilisk eyes and begun to murmur of such exquisite and intimate tortures to be conjured from Hell especially for him that he had given in. He had escorted La Sventura together with another lady, heavily cloaked and masked, to the overgrown entrance to the passage and had moved away the obscuring boulders, sweating, with his own hands.

The sight of his earthly lord and master was enough at present to drive him near to apoplexy but not, in the last resort, enough to drag forth his clandestine knowledge. However this time he sweated even more profusely over the boulder, despite the assistance of the half dozen men-at-arms who were to accompany the party who were leaving.

Dismissed, he did not hear the farewells between the prince and his young heirs, but noted that they were brief and that Il Leone bent his magnificent back over the hand of their lovely young governess as though she were the highest lady in Italy.

It was true that their private parting was already accomplished; nevertheless Tulla found it very hard to school herself to this quiet and courteous public farewell, reduced as it must be to a few well-nigh meaningless pleasantries as the children raced adventurously forward between their guards, and messer Buonavia satisfied himself for the last time that he carried safely the prince's money and his letters, both to the Medici and to the friends who would provide them with hospitality and with horses for their journey.

She could feel no sensation of his hand in hers: even though it might be the last time she would touch his flesh. The numbness seemed to spread throughout her being so that she could only manage the travesty of a smile as he kissed her wrist and said softly, "If you do not soon return from the Underworld, my Eurydice, be sure, that like Orpheus, I shall come to seek you."

He turned her gently about and made her enter the cavernous opening in the rock, holding her lightly by the shoulders so that she could not turn to watch him go.

It was only as she heard them begin to roll back the boulders, tomblike, at her back that she remembered how the legend of Orpheus had ended.

Someone thrust a lantern into her hand, and though her thoughts lagged behind in the moonlight she went forward slowly to begin the stifling and hazardous descent.

The passage seemed half natural, half hewn out of the hillside. For the most part it was a low-roofed, close-walled tunnel, its floor sanded but strewn with fallen stones and very uneven, full of potholes; these became full of water as they came further down the incline. Their progress was slow and careful, the guards testing out every step before allowing the excited children to press forward. The air was cold and damp and lay heavy upon the spirit, but Tulla, despite her loathing of such close confinement, found her circumstances less oppressive than her anxious thoughts. She gave no consideration to what lay before them; if all went well she would thank God. If not, she would face what came. Her anxiety was all for Leone.

The cardinal's death had rid him of his greatest enemy, but Alessandra Biscaglia was still not to be found, either within the castle itself or in the city outside. It must be presumed that someone was sheltering her, though the search had been most thorough. Leone had said that she had taken the death of her brother very ill and was, perhaps, near demented. He had not known, nor had he seemed to think it was necessary to know, how far his wife was also his enemy. It seemed to Tulla that if she was so far within her brother's influence as to commit both incest and sacrilege for his sake, then she might well count vengeance for his death the only felicity that life could still hold. The cold thought claimed her that the princess must be waiting, hidden, somewhere near to Leone so that she might plunge a dagger into his breast or drop poison into his cup; she shivered, knowing how easily that might be accomplished.

And the woman, La Sventura, who had wanted him dead—did she desire his death for herself or for another? In either case would she not, having once ill-chosen her "executioner," choose again more surely? With the cardinal removed, there no longer remained the necessity for Leone's murder to appear to the people of Montevalenti to be the work of a jealous woman or a passing mountebank—anyone, indeed, other than a Biscaglia. Andrea Zorza would employ no such politic subtleties in the event of his subjugation of the city.

All in all, Leone's life might not be expected to last the

length of another candle; if he did not die by private violence he might well do so while directing the defense of the city; if neither of these, then by the plague. It was a prospect of despair for Tulla, and more than once her stumbling progress was halted by an instinct to turn back. The soldiers would not hear of it, however, and she had no choice but to continue, naming herself coward with every step.

It took them an hour to negotiate the tunnel, after which time even Bernardo and Lucia were weary of its damp declivities. The floor gradually became less steep and began to level out, much to the relief of their stretched muscles. Then, suddenly, they rounded a bend and were faced with what appeared to be a solid wall of rock, built up of boulders of every size, piled upon each other in a mortarless but impenetrable barrier.

"Im'sh'Allah!"

Tulla heard messer Buonavia's dry chuckle at her side.

"Don't distress yourself, Madonna. It is only that we do not wish to make the passage a public one." He nodded and the soldiers began to pull away certain specified stones until very soon they had uncovered a space large enough to admit a man. They passed through this one by one and found themselves in a cave, about the size of a rich man's bedchamber, filled with the sweet welcome of fresh air.

As the men replaced the boulder, messer Buonavia took a noticeable interest in their task.

"This tunnel is frequently used by the guild upon errands that we do not wish to publicize. It has been invaluable, but its worth depends upon its secrecy—even as it does tonight."

When the stones were replaced none would have thought the back of the cave to be other than a potential avalanche of broken rock, best avoided.

The point at which they must emerge onto the lower hillside was more easily recognized where the black darkness of rock changed, just perceptibly, to the green darkness of the thick foliage that obscured the exit.

One after another they extinguished their lanterns, and Tulla took Lucia's hand as their escort held back the curtain of vine and thorn to let them pass, half blind, into the late moonlight.

The air was cool and scented with mint and myrrh. They were among the low trees and close-woven thickets where the hillside began to level into the valley.

344

Messer Buonavia laid a finger on his lips, warning them to silence as, between two parties of guards, they ghosted their way downward, every crack of a twig or rustle of foliage stopping their hearts.

When they reached the valley floor, there was over half of mile of rough walking in front of them. The summer villa of Astorre Gravini, a Florentine nobleman and the prince's friend, lay secluded upon the opposing hillside to the east. There they would exchange their guard, whom Montevalenti could ill afford, for an armed escort of Gravini's servants and ride at once to Florence, circling well to the north and east of the Valenti lands so that they would soon be well beyond any danger from Zorza's patrols. It was here, at the foot of their mountain, that the danger lay, along the valley road where such patrols made frequent reconnaissance. As the going was somewhat smoother upon the south side of the valley, they would not cross the road and the narrow river that preceded it until they reached a position approximately opposite to that of the villa on the northern slope.

They set off with as much speed as the undergrowth permitted them, the guards still leading the way. They had traveled perhaps 600 feet when their leader froze in his tracks, his hand flung up in warning.

They all halted, hearing their own labored breathing as they stood among the thinning trees—and, as yet, nothing more.

Then Tulla made out the distant grumble of hooves that the guards' trained ears had already caught.

"Flatten yourselves!" the leader ordered, and they fell upon their faces among the brush.

"It prickles!" Lucia complained, and Tulla covered her mouth with a swift hand, praying to Allah and the Blessed Virgin in turn to protect them.

The seconds were spun out like silk from the cocoon as they lay and listened to the horsemen approaching. The thread tightened as they drew level, seeming to pass by interminably, making no sound save that of the hooves and of the steel with which they were clad; for these were indeed Andrea Zorza's mercenaries, their dark figures impossible to distinguish either from their horses or from each other, clothed as they were in the Biscaglia black from which the moon had also hidden her face. There must have been about a dozen of them. Their headlong speed had not slackened, and Tulla felt light-headed with relief when she rose and shook out her skirts and gently admonished Lucia for allowing a sound to escape her.

"They couldn't have heard me from the road," was the reproachful and justified response. Tulla smiled, glad that the child was spared the fear that amplifies every sound.

They picked their way steadily forward until they reached the point where they must cross the valley. It was a narrow basin, the little river no more than a stream at this time of year, and easily fordable; one would scarcely wet one's feet.

Perhaps it was because her eyes were precisely upon her feet, as she stepped from stone to stone behind Lucia, that Tulla had no inkling of their danger until it was all but upon them. She heard one of the guards suddenly grunt with surprise, then the air resounded with curses, and messer Buonavia cried out "Misericordia!" and clutched her arm, caring nothing for the water in which he walked. She raised leaden lids to the road as it stretched back toward the west, almost knowing what she would see.

The mercenary patrol was coming back. Riding swiftly, their heads close along the flying manes, the sound of their hooves growing triumphantly louder once more, they would reach them in minutes.

"Run! We can but try for the villa! Keep close, and don't look back!"

They splashed frenziedly for the river bank and raced across the pasture for the road, crossing at a right angle so that they should not give the patrol a chance to cut them off from the wrong side. By now Lucia was whimpering with fear as she clung to the shoulders of the guard who carried her, and Tulla could hear Bernardo, pacing ahead with the leaders, crying "bastard! bastard!" rhythmically as he ran.

There was little hope.

They could not match the speed of mounted men. The guards plunged gamely into the wilderness of the hillside once more, however, and Tulla followed, cursing her recent lack of exercise as the blood pounded in her ears. Just before the greenery closed above her head, she looked upward and saw, flush in the first light of dawn, the rosy, characteristic Tuscan tower of the Villa Gravini rising above the trees, more it seemed, in the spirit of mockery than of encouragement.

They ploughed forward, giving every ounce of strength to

346

the effort, but they had made little headway among the hampering broom and briar that clustered about the foot of the hill making it almost impassable. The path they would have sought vas some way farther east, and here, it seemed, no human foot had trod for centuries.

In an agony of frustrated haste they heard the patrol skid to a noisy halt on the road behind them and dismount and tie up their horses in a gale of curses and laughter. The thorns tore at their clothes and at their arms as they worked frantically to force a path, the soldiers and Bernardo using their knives while messer Buonavia hacked fiercely about him with his dagger, and Tulla employed the totally inadequate scissors that hung in her chatelaine, viciously regretting the lack of the tiny, jeweled dagger she had worn in Soraya.

It was a matter of moments before the mercenaries caught up with them, with shouts of loud and exaggerated gratitude for their preparation of the way. The first cry must have come not five minutes after they had begun their hopeless task. Tulla turned to see the two guards behind her desperately engaged by three, then four sable-clad assailants. Even as she rushed toward them, brandishing her scissors as though they were the deadliest of weapons, her companions were felled and dispatched where they lay, their throats slit like cattle slaughtered.

The others fought bravely, but must have known that they faced certain death. The leader gasped a prayer as he went down beneath the blades, and after he had died, the last to do so, the tangled glade fell very quiet.

The attackers cleaned their swords upon the grass, then motioned their prisoners back down to the road. Their leader was a young lieutenant, one of the members of the cardinal's guard who had defected with exiled Zorza. He had recognized Simone Buonavia and treated him, from custom, with respect, assuring him that no harm would come to himself, to the Valenti children or to Tulla if they bore themselves sensibly and obeyed orders. The bodies of the prince's soldiers were left behind among the bushes; if some fellow Christian discovered them they might be given decent burials; if the wolves did so first, at least they would not become carrion.

Tulla tried to look unafraid as she lifted Lucia onto the neck of the horse where she would ride in front of a soldier.

"Will they kill us too?" the girl asked, tears falling.

"Not you, my pretty! You're much too valuable!" Her escort cheered her, and even in these straits, Tulla blessed him for his good nature with the child. Bernardo's behavior was unfortunately far more truculent; he knew what was expected of a Valenti in the face of his enemies and treated the mercenaries with a frigid pride and open contempt based upon the memory of his grandfather. He had to be cuffed and lifted, struggling, from the ground before they could get him onto the horse he was to share with the lieutenant. The latter's grave courtesy affected him not at all; he bit the hand that held the bridle and was at last abandoned to the less pleasant care of the grim stalwart who had accounted for at least two of the Valenti guards.

Before taking her own pillion seat Tulla approached the lieutenant. "Do you take us to Zorza's encampment?"

He shook his head. "To the Villa Nero, the Magnifico Zorza's headquarters away from camp."

"And what do you think will happen to us—to the children?" she demanded in a low voice, in the shelter of his tall bay's flank. He seemed an honest enough fellow, for one of his trade, and would perhaps not lie to her.

But again his reply was negative. "I cannot say, Madonna. I am not in the Magnifico's confidence."

He would have answered her more positively if he could, but he had recalled the manner in which Andrea Zorza had treated his first Valenti captive—the lamented Count Francesco.

He nodded at her curtly and ordered a man to hold her stirrup as she mounted. Then they were off at a gallop, skirting the mountain toward the east.

The early morning sun flattered the gardens of the Villa Nero into a sensation of scent and color; neither sun nor moon could in any way improve upon the dour complexion of the house itself. Built of dark, dense blocks of a rare granite of unpleasant appearance, it had been christened rather for its black looks than for any suspicion that one of Rome's least prepossessing emperors might have slept there.

Inside the house stalked the living memory of cardinal Silvestro Biscaglia. His preferred hues of scarlet, silver, and sable covered walls, ceilings, and furnishings, while his somewhat eclectic taste in works of art veered, in this more private of his possessions, toward the mythic and exotic rather than the religious. Most of the protagonists were naked, as were the figures in his Valenti apartment—but none of them were saints; anything but, to judge by their occupations, most of which exposed an adventurous disposition toward sexual novelty.

Alessandra Bascaglia had had the pictures removed from the room she now occupied. The princess had presently ensconced herself in the small room that overlooked the formal part of the gardens, and it was here that she discussed a matter of supreme importance with an honored guest, her rescuer from Montevalenti.

"You are certain that it can be done? It is a most unnatural thing." The regal voice was unsteady.

La Sventura bowed gravely. "It has been done."

"And there can be no—other consequences—no hideous birth or monstrous disease?"

The gypsy wore her most reassuring expression. *"Mi' Principessa*—I would have not have told you of this thing unless I could place my greatest confidence in the method. The only possible outcome, other than a natural success, in the fullness of time, is failure. And we shall not fail if we have the body in time."

"Do you think he will give it to us?" The wavering voice was doubtful.

"If he does not, there are ways and means of procuring it—but I think that he will. He will not wish to honor it himself."

"That is true—but supposing my brother is already buried?" Despair racked her.

"He is not."

"You are sure?" She caught at hope again.

"I know. I have informants who come and go like worms within your prince's white mountain."

Alessandra had not eaten since they had taken Silvio's blood-drenched body from her, only sipped at wine. She was prone to giddiness, a little drunk, and more than half out of her mind. La Sventura found in the princess an excellent prospect for the future. The gypsy had already conquered her own rage and (for one of so perfectly controlled a nature) her considerable pain, upon learning of the cardinal's death. Although she deeply regretted losing the *man*, she had swiftly come to realize that his sister, especially in her present

349

extremity, could be turned into an instrument well fitted to her hand—and *that*, Silvestro could never have been.

It had taken her very little time to discover the illicit love of the two Biscaglia—and to know how to use it. She had already done all that was necessary with Alessandra. All that remained to be secured was the cardinal's body, containing the precious seed of the Biscaglia—and a form of insurance policy, should her extraordinary method not succeed. She would be certain of both within the next few minutes.

"My lady—since the matter is so urgent perhaps you would allow me to speak to Andrea Zorza on the matter of your brother's body? It will save time if I reveal to him the ways and means of removing it from Montevalenti, should this, sadly, be necessary."

"Do as you will. Yes—give him my orders." Alessa seemed to have fallen into a fit of dullness. She plucked absentmindedly at her black gown. "Only do it at once!" She hissed with sudden venom.

In the marble hall with its black-veiled statues the witch explained delicate matters to the bewildered condottiere. Zorza was already somewhat distracted by the loss of his leader, also weary and irritable from unprofitable attacks on Montevalenti. The news of the plague had cheered him greatly, but it had been quickly followed by the first bundle of stinking rags to be catapulted from the ramparts onto the heads of his healthy, shrinking soldiery.

And now this Egyptian witch came to him with a story so outlandish that he didn't know whether or not he believed it.

He crossed himself to be on the safe side and, like his mistress (if only in title), demanded anxiously, "Are you sure such a thing can be done?"

"Perfectly sure," replied La Sventura patiently. "Nevertheless we *cannot* be sure that the seed will bear fruit—*certo,* we can *never* be sure of that!" she chuckled ribaldly. "It is even less certain when one of the parents is a dead man!" she added with a suggestion of dryness. "Therefore if we want to be certain that the Biscaglie—and, when you have conquered the prince— the Valenti, *shall* have an heir—well you must go to work yourself, my lusty condottiere. Have I made myself clear?"

Zorza grinned, though not altogether comfortably. "Very clear. You have, as you know, given words to my dearest heart's desire."

La Sventura's black brows wrinkled slightly. "Yes. Well—you may not find the princess quite as charming as she has been in the past. She is more than a little disturbed by her brother's untimely murder. Her behavior may seem a little strange—but do *not* let that discourage you. You hear me? It is of the utmost importance."

It was Zorza's turn to frown. "I hear you," he said unwillingly, wishing this upstart gypsy would show herself more conscious of his rank and station, especially now that these had ascended to such unexpected heights. He was, after all, the last surviving male Biscaglia. But that, of course, was precisely what she had been telling him—

The opening of the outer door terminated their mutually useful conversation. Through it marched the lieutenant in charge of the reconnaissance patrols for the northern section, looking conscious of his own virtue. The reason for this immediately became obvious as his men trooped in behind, escorting four prisoners, all of whom were well known to Andrea.

"Well!" he smiled, "what have we here—the babes in the wood—and their careless guardians?" He clicked a disapproving tongue and shook a sorry head. "You really should take more care of them." His eyes kindled appreciatively as he looked at Tulla. "But I won't say that I am sorry to have visitors. You must understand, however, that my time is limited. I am not here often. Indeed, I must leave you even now." He came close and bowed derisively, then straightened and fingered her breasts, lingering at their tips and looking deeply and insolently into her eyes. "But when I return—believe me, Madonna, I shall make the most of your delicious company." Sickened, she thought of no reply as he strolled toward the door, throwing out commands as he went.

"Take them first to the princess! If she does not give you other orders, keep them confined separately. The children may stay together. The woman can have the small chamber two doors from mine!"

His officer grinned and saluted him as he left upon his urgent errand—that of seeking a parley with the present Prince of Valenti.

Tulla meanwhile exchanged a look with the wary and shaken Buonavia, which contained both surprise and relief. If Alessandra Biscaglia were here in Zorza's villa, then at least she could not seek Leone's death with her own hands.

351

"What is my aunt, the princess, doing here?" asked Lucia doubtfully.

"She's a traitor, fool!" her brother informed her tersely. He had listened a good deal about the palace in the short time after the cardinal's death. He did not know how his aunt, whom he disliked, had offended, but was sure that she had done so.

"I expect she'll lock us in the dungeons," he said.

"It's too small here to have dungeons."

"The cellar then, it's all the same," the boy muttered as they were hurried up the staircase to the room that contained Alessandra.

Tulla, following with heavy foreboding in her heart, wondered yet again at the facility of children for accepting whatever fortune comes to them. She did not wish to see them fearful, but constantly expected to do so. The funereal aspect of the villa weighed on her spirits like a prediction of evil, and she did not expect an interview with Leone's wife to improve matters.

It was clear to her at once that the princess was not herself. Her white face gleamed intensely out of a welter of black veils, its planes as pure as bone. Her carmined lips were shocking against her pallor. Tulla was put in mind, disturbingly, of the bloody jaws of her family emblem, the wolf.

"Come here!" the voice was cruel. "No, not you messer Buonavia. Take him away! I have no interest in him."

"But Principessa—" the merchant began, thoughts of ransom prompting a quavering tongue.

"Lock him up somewhere!" The poor man was taken away at once, without dignity. He hardly minded, if truth were known. His embarrassment at the changed position of his sometime liege lady was too great for him to know how he should behave.

"You have done well, Lieutenant," Alessandra told their young captor with a gracious inclination of the veils. "The Valenti's heirs and his whore in one package. I am well pleased."

The lieutenant bowed respectfully. Then he hesitated. "What is your Excellence's pleasure regarding the prisoners," he hazarded. He was a man of normally humane instinct and would be happier when he knew what might be the fate of his charges.

"This is a matter to which I must give careful consideration," his mistress replied thoughtfully, almost dreamily.

He did not like her smile.

"For the present you may take the children to the south wing and secure them safely there. But before you do so," again the smile, charming and carnal at the same time, "be so good as to lend me your whip, Lieutenant."

The long horse whip, which he rarely used, was tucked beneath his arm more as a badge of office than a cavalry implement. Uncertainly, he presented it to her, wondering what new vagary had seized her. He had already contended, in an off-duty hour, with her demand for three hundred crucifixes, which he had collected with difficulty from the army; soldiers do not like to be without the image of their Savior. The sight of the crosses, displayed, black-draped, about the villa, was unnerving.

Tulla had known what must happen. She had seen the dead gray eyes become alive again with hatred when she had entered the room, seen them travel restlessly until they lighted on the whip. She wished that they would have taken away the children first. Even that was not permitted her.

"Let these children see what punishment is meted out to whores. It will be a salutary experience for them," the frozen voice continued. Lucia only looked confused and frightened, but Bernardo spoke up boldly.

"Mona Tulla is not a whore!"

His aunt was on her feet, her breast heaving, her eyes those of a mad woman in that terribly altered face. "Is she not? There you are wrong, boy!" And she brought down the whip upon Tulla's shoulders.

It was the shock that made her stagger; the pain came afterward. She heard the cries of the children and the gasp of a man as they turned her around and uncovered her back so that Alessandra could whip it until it was raw.

Even when they had taken Tulla away, and she had told the soldiers to guard her well and do what they liked with her, Alessandra found that she had not, not yet, erased the memory of the man who had rejected her body because this filthiness from the quays of Venice had entered a room.

She had done what was right. Silvio would have told her so.

Leone had not been surprised at the request for the cardinal's body. Nor had he been astonished to discover the present whereabouts of his errant wife; his own problems and those of the city were such that it could only be a relief to him to know her gone.

He had communicated with Zorza through their respective heralds, determinedly cutting off the torrent of rage and the need for revenge that shook him as the erect figure rode up to his walls between the Biscaglia banners and the flag of parley.

He had sent out the body at once, decently laid out and covered in black. It had lain in the cold cellars of the castle, being no longer fit to enter the precincts of the cathedral. As La Sventura had guessed, the prince was glad to avoid the necessity of burying his enemy within the city he had tried to bring down.

The business had been done swiftly. Zorza had begged the body courteously, on Alessandra's behalf and reported her safe and well—should Leone care to know. He had been thanked in the floreate language known only to heralds and within minutes the gate, still bearing its grisly token, had opened to dismiss Silvestro Biscaglia forever from within.

As he turned away from the departing cavalcade, Leone wondered fleetingly how far Alessa had known the deep drift of her brother's mind. It seemed to him that her recent behavior toward himself had not, however dispassionately reviewed, been that of a woman who assumes desire in order to deceive. She had wanted him again; he was sure of it. And, with the lust of a man whose body is easily wooed, he had wanted her, had even briefly dreamed it to be enough for himself and for Montevalenti.

He bore no ill-will toward Alessandra. Later, if he survived, he would divorce her. The pope would be willing enough to save a scandal. So be it; it was finished.

Andrea Zorza remained—the bastard overreacher—Franco's murderer.

At least the hopeful condottiere was a soldier, one accustomed to do his work in the daylight. To overcome him would give Leone pleasure, vengeance, exhilaration even—and there would be none of that sickening of the soul that had attended him at Silvestro's death.

The prince did not deceive himself that this was the most probable outcome of events. The city was now in the first fierce grip of the plague. Many of those who were not laid low by the disease itself were rendered almost as useless by fear.

The dread apparition of the Plague Virgin had been seen in the streets. By now, at the end of the first week of the pestilence, it was not only those with sickness in the house who were boarded inside, but whole healthy families who thought thus to escape the grim lady and her gifts. Superstitious Vanozza Grazzi, grumbling at her fellow citizens for shameful irreligion, had made the soldiers' duty more difficult by barring every door of the castle against the Devil, whom everyone knew to be the true bringer of the blue-black bloodspots filled with poison. Each door now carried a weighty deterrent in the shape of a wooden cross, inscribed with the Holy Names, stretched tight across the frames both laterally and horizontally. This did not make for easy access and Leone was forced to dare her anger and remove them. Her prayers and grief were an awesome spectacle.

Already several of his fighting men had gone down with the fever. There had been a loss of perhaps an eighth of their strength. The doctors were doing their utmost to contain the disease; those who had died had been instantly burned. But while the sick were all too pleased to be isolated, they preferred it to be within their homes, believing that those who went into a hospital rarely came out again. The summer heat, now near its height, also worked against them, as did the inescapably crowded conditions. Every household sheltered at least one entire family from the contada, more if there was room. The streets and yards were full of animals; cattle, dogs, pigs and goats, even sheep; they were not permitted to roam freely, but those who tended them were hard put to shepherd them.

And in such circumstances as these, despite the prophylactic precautions laid down by the prince, the plague could only spread.

Even as he attempted to guide his increasingly discouraged, skeleton army through the sporadic hostilities of the siege, Leone was aware that the only true hope for a small, enclosed city, harboring the plague, was that of the complete evacuation of those who were still well.

If that city were besieged, this was impossible.

If the siege were to be raised, however, all things became possible.

It seemed to Leone, as he daily discussed the whys and wherefores of their predicament with the invaluable Cerruti, that what they were asking was a purely philosophical question.

"If we want to evacuate we must raise the siege. To do that we must beat Andrea Zorza. To beat him we have to face him on the open field—no one can conquer an army from inside a city wall. If we attack them on the plain, no matter how greatly they are surprised, their numbers will always be greater than ours. There is no answer, Pascale."

There was. Just one. And it was not encouraging.

"If you do not attack them, my prince, *our* numbers will continue to decrease—just as *theirs* will continue to do the opposite. I saw the banners of Siena arrive shortly after dawn. Who knows who will join him tomorrow?"

Leone lifted his chin and frowned very slightly. It was an expression habitual of his father when under pressure. Cerruti, recognizing it, waited for the order he knew he would receive, and wondered how he could ever have thought the boy a mere popinjay.

NINETEEN

The cell into which the soldiers had carried Tulla was very small, perhaps eight feet long, not three wide. Meant to serve as a cellar, it took light and air through the narrow tunnel in the thickness of the outer wall that led to a tiny, round window, densely barred.

Mercifully she had been left to recover from her injuries; shock had induced sleep and it was not until she awoke, agonizingly stiff and sore, that she realized their full extent. Alessandra had laid on the whip with the strength of insanity, and her back was a mass of dried blood and striped gashes.

Upon first wakening she had been much in fear of her guards, but she soon discovered that this, at least, was something she might discount. One of them had brought her a rough meal and water for washing, both of which he had shoved hastily through the door without himself entering. He did not speak, and she saw that he held a linen towel over the lower half of his face.

The reason was not far to seek. He knew that the prisoner he guarded had recently come out of the plague city. Trembling with relief, she permitted herself a smile and offered a prayer of thanks to Saint Luke. Then she ate the bread and did her best to tend her own wounds.

It was mid-afternoon when the door was unlocked to admit a visitor who appeared to pay no heed to the possibility of infection. She climbed slowly to consciousness out of the half sleep into which she had fallen again to find the ugly and unmistakable visage of the late cardinal's astrologer hovering over her.

"Atroviso!"

"Madonna. I am pleased to see you, though I appreciate that for you, it is not under the best auspices. However, perhaps there is something I could do to make your rest, at least, a little easier. There is almost as much of the physician in me as of the astrologer."

His curious eyes, little, black, and shining like the shells of small beetles, caressed her in a way she remembered too well, traveling busily about her body, reminding themselves, making themselves promises—

"Have you no fear lest you take the plague from me?" she asked abruptly, hoping that her slight fever was noticeable.

"No," he said. "I have had the plague—it must have been some twenty years ago. I have never heard that any man who has survived it has taken it again. Now if you will lie face downward, I will apply this wintergreen unguent. You will find your hurts much improved by tomorrow."

She did not want his hands upon her, but there was no choice and the smell of the ointment, at least, was reassuring. When he had finished treating her back, Atroviso allowed himself the small reward of sliding his hand down under the rags of her gown to the pleasant rotundities it concealed. He dreamed momentarily of pleasures forbidden by the church and then withdrew his hands, clicking his tongue in soft self-reproach.

"You do not look to me as though you are going to have the plague," he observed, releasing his unhealthy breath in his unfortunate smile. "And in a day's time or so you should be able to move about without too much discomfort. I will visit you again—and we shall see."

It was evident what it was that Atroviso wished to see—but all that Tulla could think of was that her scars had given her a day's reprieve. At any rate the old scoundrel was disposed to be pleasant. She might therefore ask him a question that much occupied her.

"Tell me, Messere, what has the princess done with the children?"

Atroviso wiped his oily hands upon his gown and smiled indulgently. "Be sure they are well looked after and in the best of health. A little bored, perhaps, but that is the way with children." He hesitated, the dreamy and delighted expression reappearing upon his simian face. "I am going to find them most useful, yes, most useful—"

"What do you mean?" Tulla was alarmed.

"Nothing that need concern you, Madonna. You should simply concentrate upon becoming quite well." He did not think a description of the part the children would play in his black mass would do much to aid her recovery.

Try as she would she could get no more information out of him. He would speak only of her wounds and of the necessity for her to eat everything she was given. When he had bowed and scraped his last and scurried away, she reflected with weary irony that she might have *known* that he, of all men in the world, might have been chosen by Satan to survive the plague!

Her spirits plummeted as she drew for herself a brief and brutal outline of her future. It was something best not contemplated if she wished to retain her sanity, especially since sleep was now no longer necessary or possible.

She had reached a point rather over halfway in an exhaustive attempt to count the stones that comprised the walls of her prison, when she became aware of a sound from outside those walls.

It was the relaxed and generous sound of a girl's laugh.

She was still listening.

Words followed the laughter and still more laughter after that. There were two of them, both young girls. They must be somewhere close outside the window; the tunnel, about level

358

with the top of her head, which led out through the six-foot thickness of the wall, brought every word to her as clearly as though they stood beside her.

"It isn't that I don't *want* to see him again. I do. He's one of the best-looking young men I've ever had—and fair to middling well-off, too!"

"Well then—what are you making all the fuss about? He's asked you, and he'll be there waiting. So will Luigi, and *he'll* not be best pleased if I'm late. I wish you'd hurry up and make your mind up. I don't see what the problem is!"

A couple of maids or perhaps girls from a nearby village— Tulla knew the villa was well beyond the bounds of Monte- valenti—their voices rough with the vivid accent of Tuscany, discussing their hopes for an amorous evening.

If she jumped up a little she could see the grille which covered the aperture. A swift impression of green beyond it; that was all.

Her mind raced. There must be some use to which she could put the presence of these girls. She determined she would try to climb up to the window and attract their attention.

She turned her pallet upon its edge and stood it against the wall beneath the tunnel. It was less than an arm's length high but it enabled her, after a strenuous and painful strug- gle, to scramble into the narrow tunnel. It was only just wide enough to admit her and she had to inch herself into it slowly, every jar an insult to her damaged flesh.

She lay panting, just able to support herself on skinned elbows, her face close to the grille beyond which lay freedom—or one of its many changing faces.

The girls were still disputing whether both of them should keep their assignation.

"If I were you I'd find it flattering! If he spends so much time in doing *that,* it must mean he thinks you well worth looking at."

"Yes, but—he spends nearly *all* the time doing that—and only ten measly minutes at the most in kisses and the like. I don't know what to make of him, surely I don't!"

"Saint Peter's Parts!" exclaimed her companion, now richly impatient. "I'm off, that's what, my friend! Now—do I tell Sandro Botticelli you're coming after me, or not!"

Tulla's cry rang out almost before her mind had grasped the words.

"Botticelli! Oh wait, wait I implore you!"

There was a gasp, a cry, then silence.

She became aware of their breathing, so close to her head. They must be standing just beside the grille.

She called again, an agony of pleading in her voice.

"Please—I beg you. Don't be afraid. Draw close in front of the grille, where I can see you."

The silence continued, then there was whispering.

"Who can it be?"

"I don't know. Come on, let's go! Likely 'tis a spirit or a demon!"

"No!" Tulla howled, demoniacally enough, "I'm a friend to Sandro Botticelli—and he will not thank you if you leave me!"

Another moment's whispering brought them to her at last. Two apprehensive faces, round-eyed and apple-cheeked, pressed against the grille.

"Deo gratias! I thought you would go." She reassured them with the most comfortable smile she could manage.

"Madonna, who are you? What are you doing there?"

The bolder of the two, a robust girl, ox-eyed and beautiful with a heavy fall of dark hair, questioned in low tones.

"First, tell me, who is it that you serve?"

"Maria is a servant here. As for me, I serve no one, now that my father is dead." She tossed back the hair with a proud, conscious gesture. "He served the Prince of Valenti all his life."

"Then will you help me? I am of the prince's household and a prisoner here."

The girl peered at her closely, so near to the grille that they were almost eye to eye. She made her decision with a characteristic speed for which Tulla was grateful.

"I will aid you, Madonna. A friend to the prince is a friend to one of my family. Tell me what I should do."

"You will see Sandro Botticelli tonight, you and Maria?"

The other girl blushed and nodded.

"Then tell him that you have spoken with Thalia, daughter of Quara Rashid and that she entreats him to go at once to the Magnifico Lorenzo de Medici, and beg him to send as many men and horses as he can muster to aid the Prince of Valenti!"

She described the straits in which Montevalenti found itself as coherently as she might at such speed and swore the two young women to secrecy. The one who had taken Botticelli's fancy, shy and fair, more slender than her companion, still looked afraid.

Tulla reached toward her hand through the grille. "You will not betray me, will you—even though you serve here?"

The girl shook her head. "No, not I. Anyway, like 'Nella I serve none living. This was Cardinal Biscaglia's house. And then too," she giggled suddenly, amusement conquering shyness, "I shall be very glad I do not have to spend another evening with Sandro sitting all glum before the fire—without drinking, without talking—thinking only of his dreary old brushes and inks, never touching me, never kissing me—but only sketching my naked body!"

"Come, little idiot. We waste time," her friend ordered abruptly, returning Tulla's swift smile.

Then, raising her right hand in both contract and farewell, Antonella Bossi went purposefully off to uphold her father's allegiance to the house of Valenti—not to mention her own which was warm and reminiscently personal.

Inside Montevalenti a satanic symphony of noise intended to drive away the plague had reluctantly given over, as was only hideously just, to a subdued silence, broken only by the ragged chanting of penetential psalms and funereal plaints, and the mournful complementary bells of the body-takers and the churches. There were no funeral parties as such; all public gatherings were sternly under the prince's interdict. But stricken families and their unwanted guests would intone the muffled offices for the dead as best they could, standing in the next room from the body, their faces covered against contagion. Then they would huddle away from the door as the carter came by to collect his terrible and pitiful burden. They were spared, at least, the spectacle of a cart piled high with bodies; this too was against the edict of the prince and his physicians. The empty ground where the young men had used to play *calcio,* being the only space large enough to serve, had become the public burial ground.

There was little beyond bone for burial, for Leone had flown in the face of Father Ambrogio and his assistant priests by ordering the bodies to be burned.

"But my son," the little cleric expostulated, "how if a man shall not have his body whole to be delivered back to him on the Last Day?"

"If God can make a man, he can make him a new body," was the terse and irreligious reply, tempered out of respect for the priesthood.

The situation was now such that the prince and his captains had made every preparation necessary for forcing upon Zorza the surprise and shock of open battle. Every citizen, as much as every soldier, knew what his duty must be should the signal be given. The signal itself was to be the tolling of the great bell of San Jerome, in a pattern of three repeated notes, in honor of Father, Son, and Holy Ghost.

It might come at any time.

Meanwhile the dead were disposed of as quickly as was decent, sometimes more quickly—and the sick were exhorted either to get well or to die but to hurry up about it, whichever it was to be.

It was drawing toward noon when, up on the rampart, Gian Carmaggio, never to be found far from his latest idol, the prince, reported that his sharp eyes had discerned the approach of another cavalcade toward the castle.

"If they want any more bodies," remarked Julio Bagno coarsely, "they can have what's on the plague carts!"

It was not, however, a question of bodies. The party of horsemen was very small, consisting of two heralds, both bearing the Biscaglia banners and two of the riders, not as yet recognizable.

Behind them, the enemy camp seemed to be organizing itself into some sort of order; hoisting flags and straightening cannon, putting their weapons into open display. It was not battle array but rather an exaggerated show of their possible strength, a shaking of their spears in the face of the beleaguered city.

Gian hung over the battlement, screwing up the eyes that his mother supposed to be those of an artist not a soldier, and soon called out in amazement, "My Lord Leone! If I'm not mistaken it is the lady your wife!"

And so it proved to be.

Alessandra Biscaglia rode a white charger, accoutred for battle in the colors of her house. Its head and body were completely obscured by a black mantle, the edges and eyeholes scarlet rimmed; the harness was scarlet tricked out with silver. Alessandra's spurs were also silver and she carried a tall, naked sword, damascened in silver and gold.

"Diavolo! She has a look of her father," muttered Cerruti, much impressed.

"She rides under her father's banners. My wife displays her true colors at last," was Leone's cool reply.

"What can she want? They carry no flag of parley."

"I think," Leone said, "that she wishes to show me her hatred. It is a custom of her family to ride beneath the enemy's walls and hurl filth—verbal or otherwise."

"We in Montevalenti have our own customs regarding our enemies and our walls," Cerruti grinned, nursing pleasant memories.

Alessandra had reached the balding greensward before the gates. She wheeled her mount and halted, looking up at them, the sword standing uncompromisingly before her.

Her heralds called upon the Prince of the Valenti. Leone gave her no greeting, waiting for her to speak. Her expression could not be interpreted from such a height, only the oval of her face seen, deathly white, wrapped round with a black cap.

"I wanted to bring you my challenge in my own voice, Valenti!" The voice was unlike itself, deep and harsh. "It is I who now command my brother's army. Andrea Zorza is my good right arm, as he was always his! Look behind me and read your fate! See how many men have joined in the cause of vengeance against the tribe of Valenti thieves and murderers!" She paused, panting, her hand wandering to her brow. She was suddenly troubled, as she so often was, by visions of Silvestro's death and had to fight for continued control. Those upon the rampart took it for grief but could not share it.

"There is one certainty that gives us joy beyond all things except one more—and that is your death, Leone." Now indeed she showed him her hatred, the white face a mask of fury as she forced herself to go on and not to dwell upon the sweet, savored circumstance. "It is that you are the last of your accursed line!"

Upon the battlement the nature of the silence became changed.

"What—have you nothing to say upon the death of your heirs! Do you not weep for them—and for the Turkish whore who served them?"

Her triumph was unmistakable; it crowed and swelled in her throat and vibrated along the sword which, in the growing passion of hysteria, she shook toward the prince.

"There is a fever of madness upon her," Bagno whispered, aghast.

Leone said nothing. He turned from the battlement and strolled away to his own apartments. Neither had his face told them anything.

When he had gone they hurled their pent-up loathing in the blanched face of his wife, who only laughed at them the more and rode away, exultant.

In the quiet half-darkness of his room, Leone knelt at the foot of the bed, head bowed, and grasped the coverlet in outstretched hands as though so meaningless a contact could have the power to aid his struggle for the command of himself, so that he, in turn, might command others.

His soul howled within him at Alessandra's cruelty. But though he sorrowed gently and with true and bitter tears for the brief, barbarously ended lives of Bernardo and Lucia, it was for the death of the woman that with a final, desperate and almost blasphemous prayer, he arose at last and gave the signal for the bell to begin to toll.

Then he laid his brother's sword reverently down in its scabbard and took up the yard-long butcher's weapon that had been his father's.

When he took his place again before the chosen best among his army as they stood ranged before him in the courtyard and beyond it, he appeared to his men to have been translated by fury.

Words flowed from him, hot and foul and full of venom, crying death to the Biscaglia and every man, woman or child who served them.

Gian Carmaggio had fought for and won the inestimable honor of arming him. The suit of fine Milanese armor was laid out on a red cloth upon the flagstones. All about them, similarly, men and boys prepared to lace each other into the medley of steel plates that covered the yard like the shells of sleeping sea creatures. Last night they had stayed up with the moon while they had cleaned the steel of the marrow from the leg bones of goats that kept it free from rust, and then sanded and burnished it till it mirrored their own eager faces and would do the same for the enemy they would meet.

Each man wore what he could afford. Montevalenti's principal armory could clothe the officers and men of the guard, but the militia had to make do with what they had inherited—if they had not sold it—what they could buy—if a soldier would sell it to them—and what they could devise with the help of the blacksmith. Most at least possessed some sort of brigandine.

The prince first put on his arming-doublet, toughly padded and armed with linkmail at collar, skirt and sleeves, to protect those parts not covered by plates. Over this went the cuirass; this consisted of waistlength back and breastplates with lower flanges affixed to cover the belly and thighs. These were all joined as one, hinged on the left and strapped at the right. Then came the leg harness, cuisses to cover the thighs, articulated with the poleyns about the knees and the greaves about the calves, attached to shoes of mail. When Gian had added the vambraces to his arms and the pauldrons to his shoulders and handed him his mail gauntlets, it only wanted the helmet with its visor to make Leone into a faceless monstrosity of steel, a buckled and plated metal machine for making war that no longer bore the faintest resemblance, except in parodied outline, to a man.

The whole was covered by a silk tabard in singing crimson and gold that leapt with lions no longer resting. This would make him a clear rallying point for his own men in battle and would distinguish him from his officers who wore short red cloaks attached flamboyantly to the backs of their cuirasses.

As he began almost immediately to sweat beneath his load of nearly seventy pounds of steel, he envied the archers who would travel lightly, favoring only breastplate, helmet and gauntlets, with their bows flung at their backs, swords and knives in their belts. An armed cavalryman is a wondrous blunt implement, but he requires a constitution as strong as that of his horse.

In under an hour every man was armed and armored and had taken up the position from which he would leave the city. The great bell still sounded its sonorous alarm above and around them, its slow and heavy pulse, in their fancy, the very rhythm of Montevalenti's stout heart.

The prince gave a brief address to his captains and to every man who could crowd into the outer bailey before the barbican gate.

"Citizens and soldiers of Montevalenti—we had not thought to go into open battle, but we do so with a glad heart, for in doing it we may hope to take back our land and our freedom with one brief hour of blood—the blood of the bastard of Biscaglia and of his servants!" They roared and cheered him. He looked every inch the fighter his father had been, a steel

365

man over two yards high, broad-shouldered and upright in the sunlight, his yellow head flaming like a beacon.

"You all hear the bell of San Jerome that bids us wait no longer! Andrea Zorza hears it also as he has done this hour past. He knows that we have the plague among us and knows also that the tolling is to signify death. What he does not know is that it signifies not our death, but his own!"

Again the deep-throated roaring made the air ragged and a great surge of forward motion seemed to pass through the massed ranks where they stood locked man against man.

It was time.

"Then let the cry be Saint George for Valenti! Andrea Zorza is mine!"

He had not spoken of his wife, nor did any man expect to see her in the field. There was nothing of the Maid of Orleans in Alessandra Biscaglia—apart that was, from witchery and treachery.

Expectant as their weapons they rasped in their breath like one man as Leone raised his sword.

Then it came down like a judgment and they were released!

To the two thousand or so men who were desultorily polishing their weapons or exercising their horses on the plain, even more to those engaged in firing the numerous ballistas, mangonels and trebuchets drawn up dauntingly before the cracked but uncrumbling castle walls, the sudden appearance of Leone's troops must have been like some fearful vision of Hell let loose upon mankind. Scarlet figures swarmed where there had been blank stone, spilled from every orifice, shinnying down ropes and flowing through gates and guttering, while overhead came the first thrilling-deadly knock of the arrows as they were loosed by the forefront of the archers, followed by the vibrating whistle as they homed toward the hapless, gape-mouthed siege engineers. Many of these died where they stood. Others took to their heels as though they ran from the Devil indeed.

Knowing that he could match the enemy two men for one, Zorza was sanguine enough of the outcome of this unexpected confrontation, but his pride suffered at the surprise of it. He had not understood that the plague had taken such a grip on the city, for only that circumstance, he was sure, could drive the prince to such a desperate course. As his well-greased and often-used machine for killing rolled slowly toward action of its own, his dark face relaxed somewhat and took on the grim half-smile with which he was wont to greet the arena of his skill.

He had neither time nor any inclination toward speeches. With the condottiere's ancient cry of "Carne!" he sounded his trumpets and urged his hungry horde toward their feast.

Upon the ramparts of Castel' Valenti too, trumpets sounded, the harsh note of the clarion discordant with the low, golden oliphant and beneath them the voluble beat of the tabors and the big drums. For Giuseppe Murano there would never be another such concert in all his life.

The prince had deployed his forces for the maximum mobility and, it was to be hoped, survival. Zorza, knowing that every second was of the utmost importance to Montevalenti and therefore expecting, and seeing, the prince's cavalry begin the charge downhill at once, was laying out a line of pikemen with their eviscerating weapons at the ready to impale the horses who would be hurled onto them by their headlong impetus. He also had his gunners hurl a couple of hundred caltrops in their path, the small, spiked instruments that could sink deeply into an unwary hoof.

What he had not expected was that Leone, besides his two hundred cavalry (plus a hundred doughty militia on their own plough or carthorses) had sent down his archers at the same time, where they might usefully begin their fire. Thus Zorza's pikemen, and bows massed behind them, and the enormous weight of the Swiss and German mercenary cavalry behind *them,* found themselves the victims of a hail of bolts and arrows before their own archers could properly take aim. They kept up this stream of missiles while the cavalry, far from stumbling over the caltrops, parted suddenly into two separate wings, still scarcely within range of Zorza's fire, and galloped off toward east and west across the river where they harried the archers and gunners on the enemy flanks. This left the infantry to move toward each other at their own speed, the archers and arbalesters shooting at will, while the men-at-arms, with halberds, glaves, and pole-axes, moved inexorably toward each other and the eventual carve and jab of the melee.

As Leone pounded downhill at the head of the horsemen, the jarring rhythm of Brigante's hooves became somehow inextricably mixed with the drone of the great bell behind them, together with the jangle of smaller bells and the shrill martial music. The whistle of arrows and the whine of quarrels about his head seemed mere added percussion until one flew past his ear so closely that he felt the lifting of his close-cut hair. Warned, he crammed on the helmet he hated, half-blinded with the clumsy effort. Galloping beside him, Cerruti gave a grim nod of approval, himself lying as close along his stallion's neck as its own black mane.

It came to the point where they must separate. Both saluted and inwardly wished each other well, then wheeled their unhesitating mounts to right and left, flying for the river beneath the whining torrent of missiles and worse, the hideously accurate fire of the first of the field guns.

Leone knew that he had lost men already, but they were not many and most of them had ridden the slower, peasant horses; some of these were thankfully seized by men whose horses had been shot under them.

As he had hoped, Zorza's right flank was in disorder, with the cavalry milling among the men-at-arms to get to the attackers, while the archers and gunners were forced to hold their fire to avoid killing their own men. It was only moments before both guns and crossbows would have to be abandoned and every man turn his hands toward the barbarism that was the melee.

As he spurred Brigante toward the congested right center, his way was challenged by a glaver who came at him from the left, aiming low at the thigh. He deflected the blow, right-handed with his sword, wheeling the horse on ground space for a florin. The man went down beneath the gigantic plates of the horse's hooves; they came up as ruddy as they had been on the blacksmith's bench. First blood to Brigante; but Leone bloodied his sword in the next second as, from the right, another horseman swung at him with an axe, bellowing, "To me! To me! Biscaglia!" In order to avoid the murderous blow to his head Leone had to ride over a man who crawled, a scarlet slime of blubbered flesh and moaning, animal noise, across his path. As he whirled to give the axeman his quietus—a brief, sideways stab to the kidneys with his short sword—he thought how strange it was that he should hear one man's groans among so many cries of agony and anger, amid so much screaming of men and horses, the clang and clamor of steel, the crack and snap of bone and blow. Raising his head once, like a swimmer taking breath, he looked about him for Andrea Zorza.

Just then he heard a warning shout of "Il Leone!" and looked down again just in time to prevent Brigante being hamstrung by a swarthy little fellow with a short sharp dagger, most often used after battle to put the dying out of their misery. He beat him down almost without thinking and sliced his blade across his throat.

After he had been killing and butchering men for some time, it began to seem to him as though all movement became endlessly drawn out and slow, like that in a dream or the long measure of a dance—the stately sarabande of dealing and avoiding death. He would move toward an enemy as if toward a partner; they would engage, the blood would flow and a man die. That man was never himself, though he did not suppose he would sense the thing even if it occurred. There was a red haze before his eyes, red beneath his feet. The ground had become slippery as though they rode over a slaughterer's unwashed yard. He heard his own voice shouting his name and that of his brother, leaping jagged and coarse like a ragged banner above the rout.

His men were all around him now, forming an unsought wall against all opponents. He saw the plunging of their horses, rolling-eyed, nostrils distended as they carved a magic circle about their leader. And by God and St. George—there was Cerruti—he had hacked his way through the center of the mob, wielding his great, heavy blade that could shear through steel plate and bone as easily as a woman's tooth through a sweetmeat. And he brought good tidings.

"Zorza," he roared, pointing with his sword back toward the center. "Fighting like the wolf he is!"

The prince spurred to an almost impossible gallop, bursting through the carefully contrived defenses of his men and did not stop for horse or man until forced to do so by the sheer press of flesh around him.

It was hot as the Devil's cauldron. He raised his visor and blinked sweat-blinded eyes, broiling and sodden inside his armor. But he was well enough now; back there he had felt for a moment that he would lose his senses, his lungs bursting with his efforts, his sword arm well nigh useless—but now suddenly it was as if a cool wind blew upon him and he could breath easily, the weight of steel mysteriously lightened.

A man challenged him from a big chestnut beside him. He felled him as though he were brushwood and reined forward, his eyes sulphurous.

He had found Andrea Zorza.

The condottiere, dismounted, was engaged with one of Ponti's gunners, a lithe, quick-witted boy, by no means out of his element with the sword. Zorza was pressing him hard, however, and Leone saw that the youth's left arm hung broken and useless, dashing numbly against his side as he parried his opponent's monstrous double-headed axe. Even as Leone dismounted, flinging his reins to the nearest unoccupied infantryman, he saw the lad go down beneath the sweep of the blue blade as it knocked the breath from his breast, cratering the steel that covered it. Zorza stepped close and wrenched back his head, tearing off the helm. There was a strangled half cry, then blood gushed toward Leone's feet from the boy's efficiently severed neck and head.

"Zorza!"

The condottiere spun around at the hated, welcome voice.

"A Biscaglia!" he cried and gripped his bloody weapon more firmly, the left hand feeling for the sword at his waist, as he circled, testing his ground.

Leone moved toward him slowly, his own sword at the ready. They were mismatched in that, while the prince was encumbered with full armor, Zorza fought by preference in helmet and brigandine. This not only gave him greater mobility and speed, but also the precious *balance* upon which the armored man must hang his life when he fights upon the ground. While Zorza's main intent was upon felling his enemy, Leone's must also be that of supporting the heavy shock of the axe's blows and staying upon his feet. He let himself become the center of Zorza's circling, tensed and bent forward a little, into the blow that would come. A glaver brushed against him, eyes fixed greedily on Zorza, then fell back as he saw who had claimed him first.

The prince's aim was death. He knew as he trod around the slippery ground that it would be given to him. A cold and impersonal exultation was in him that he remembered from the first time he had killed in battle; then he had done penance for it afterward, ashamed. Now he recognized its steadying usefulness. As he moved to keep his enemy to the fore he realized that Zorza was increasing his speed, beginning to spring about his own slow and careful lumbering as a clown will urge a bear to dance. His blood flushed hot beneath his carapace, and the will to end it swiftly almost overpowered his careful stance. If there was to be mockery it should not be from Zorza! The first blow came, and he leaned toward it, taking it full on the flat blade of his sword. He felt the ground shake under him with the shock—or perhaps it was merely the tremor of the thousand hooves that thundered about them in the throng. He wavered faintly but did not lose his balance. Best to take no chances however; once it was lost he would soon follow the young gunner's fate. He let Zorza continue his mocking dance, parrying or avoiding the vicious blows, which seemed to increase in power as he used his energy in absorbing them. Then he leaned in suddenly as Zorza drove down the axe toward his breast, turning and beating the blow onto his hip, jarring and surprising his whole body with pain. All but paralyzed, he retained just enough of his purpose to drive his own sword into Zorza's groin as he drew back from the blow; he heard his own grunt and Zorza's blasphemy at the same time; then the condottiere staggered and fell back, dropping his dagger, to staunch the wound.

Leone pressed toward him as he made an effort to regain the short sword, misjudged it and went over beneath the prince's blade.

The strange coldness persisted in the prince's brain as he surveyed his enemy, wounded and powerless at his feet. He brought down his blade almost thoughtfully upon the hand that still held the axe, so that it dropped from the numbed and dinted gauntlet.

Beneath them there was a roar of fury as the mercenaries saw their leader go down. But try as they would to come to him, they were prevented by the equally determined press of Valenti men-at-arms who had followed the prince's fortunes as closely as they might in anticipation of such a moment.

There was nothing Leone wished for so much as for the death of Andrea Zorza, but first there was something he must know. His blade held steadily above the pulsing throat, he met the agony of rage and shame in the eyes.

"My wife—where will I find her?"

Zorza looked round wildly. How in Satan's name had he come to this pass? And where were his aides? He had had the prince at the end of his blade, dancing to his will and now—this! His own impotence unnerved him, yet he could not believe he had come to the end, not yet.

"Let me rise. This is not honorable."

He was conscious of the *virtu* of the professional soldier.

371

"You have not been an honorable enemy. You should not have mixed your fate with that of your family—there is better blood in you, whoever it may belong to."

The slender blade above his throat did not falter, and Zorza knew with the appalling solitariness of despair that he would not be permitted to rise.

"Alessandra," Leone persisted. "Where is she?"

Andrea shook his head. "I will not betray her."

Leone looked at him consideringly and drove home the crueler of his weapons. "She has betrayed you—she had never meant otherwise. When I killed him she was naked in her brother's bed."

He watched as the black eyes, all he could see of Zorza's face, fought through the cloud of pain toward comprehension and a terrible, shamed outrage. So it was he, all along, it was he who had been the dancer to Silvestro Biscaglia's will. They had promised him sweet fire and would have given him nothing but cold ashes.

He groaned and turned away his head. Now indeed he sensed himself defeated.

"She is at the Villa Nero," he said. It was just, he was not the only one she had betrayed. Then, "I don't wish to be taken prisoner." His eyes appealed; he fumbled at the strap of his helmet. Leone nodded, then knelt to unlace the helm. They had no more words for each other.

Zorza turned away his head again, and Leone took his dagger and gave him the coup de grace. As the blood flowed from the open throat a brief wave of pity passed over him for the man who had allowed his mind, as well as his soldier's body to become another man's mercenary.

Abruptly he became aware again of the turbulence about him. Leaving Zorza's body to those who would care for it, he plunged back into the hacking press of infantry, intending if he could to reach Brigante, whom he saw his man had mounted and ridden toward the edge of the fray where he might do plenty of damage with his flailing hooves, but avoid the worst chances of being brought down.

As he battered his way toward them, the prince heard a new clamor go up toward the left, strong cheering mingled with bellowed curses. He thought he caught the word "Medici" and disbelieved his straining ears. He stood stock still a moment while flies buzzed about the blood that was upon him. Then he turned and pulled the nearest cavalryman, protesting, from his horse, so that he might stand in the stirrups and gaze with all the disguised hope of his disbelief, toward Florence.

It was true, by God, it was true! There they were indeed. By no means near, but approaching, first the horsemen, perhaps two hundred of them, coming at a gallop; behind them a close column of infantrymen marching strongly. They carried the blue and gold banners of the City of Flowers, and their meaning was life to Montevalenti.

He threw a brief, loving gaze toward the hillside which his city crowned, set on fire by the red-gold burning of the broom. His exultation became warm and whole within him, and he cried out with joy as he fought his way back to Brigante and the banner of the lion.

TWENTY

It was a short time after this that one Gunter Alberich, a commander of cavalry, sought out the prince beneath the flag of truce. With the realistic eye of the true mercenary for the main chance he offered to transfer the allegiance of his company of two hundred and fifty trained professionals from the service of Alessandra Biscaglia to that of her husband. With his general gone and the Florentine *bargello di contada* approaching fast, it was a bold move. However, it would mean the battle would be over far more quickly and many lives saved.

Leone, with equal realism, accepted the offer, if Alberich would be contented with half pay. His might hope to recoup the other half from the princess after all was done. The bargain was struck and a few dozen Valenti pennants hastily borrowed so that the prince's men might recognize their new allies.

During the decreasing enthusiasm of the fighting that followed, as Zorza's partisans learned of his death and feared for their pay, having already noted the Florentine approach and feared for their lives, Leone found that his own, brief flame of joy had also died. As he rode mechanically up and down the lines of his men, gradually shaping them into containing blocks that might hold until the Bargello reached them, it occurred to him with a sudden simple force that he was as fitted by nature to be a soldier and a leader as he was to eat bread. Throughout the course of the strenuous and bloody battle he had killed and mutilated without any thought save how it might be done most efficiently. He had left pity behind him, discovering it to be a purely civilian emotion. He had felt no fear to speak of—only heeded his body's warnings when it was most in danger. His being had narrowed to make this field his universe and he had neither thought of nor wanted for any other. His concentration had been a complete and perfect thing. His men now cheered him wherever he went. He had been the commander they had wanted. He had become, in fact, the man he had never wished to be—the true heir of the awful old men, inspired with the old lust to drain all there was to drain of Biscaglia blood. He had never expected to be the victor. Although he had spurred his troops as a leader must, he had ridden out that morning like a sacrifice. And now God had placed the victory in his hands and rather than taking to Himself the last of the Valenti, offered him also the last of the Biscaglia.

With Alessandra dead, there would be no more Biscaglie. And no more of the brutally stupid wickedness of the vendetta they had sanctified for generations.

And Alessandra would die—

When Atroviso had entered her cell upon the morning after her encounter with the two peasant girls, Tulla at once surmised his intentions and prepared herself for a protracted struggle; he was elderly and might, she tried to hope, have insufficient wind to satisfy his desires.

She was surprised and relieved therefore when, gloomily, he ordered her to follow him out of the cell.

"It is a pity," he murmured deprecatingly as they climbed

374

stairs. "There was nothing I could do—and anyway," he shrugged, "she will die—my poor mistress—"

"The princess? Why so?"

He sighed, rubbing his hands together in genuine distress. "She has taken the plague—she did not leave the city soon enough." He saw that Tulla had come to an astonished halt. "She insists that you are to nurse her," he added. "I did what I could—but—" Another eloquent shrug.

"My thanks," Tulla replied, doing her best to assimilate the news and to determine whether anything personally might be hoped to come of it.

"The children?" she inquired next.

"Well."

For some reason she believed him and was reassured. "Then by all means, let us visit the princess."

Atroviso, scurrying at her side, found himself once again admiring the spirit of this slender girl. What an acolyte she would make if her conversion were at all possible. She walked so coolly toward that pestilence-infested chamber—as though she had never known how to fear.

The princess's room was in near darkness, the windows shrouded with black velvet, the air close as in a tomb. And that it would soon be, in fact, a tomb, seemed apparent as Tulla moved toward the black-veiled bed and looked down at Alessandra Biscaglia. She lay supported by a heap of pillows, her deadly blue pallor leaving no room for doubt.

It was clear that her feverish aspect had been as much that of illness as of the madness Tulla had suspected.

Beside the bed, scarcely distinguishable in her own black garments, sat La Sventura busying herself with bottles and dishes upon a nearby table.

Alessandra raised herself a little more, holding her arms wide of her body. Her armpits were beginning to pain her.

She smiled at Tulla's approach. "Come closer. Bring your face next to mine."

Tulla hesitated.

"Do as you are bid!" La Sventura ordered threateningly.

She lowered her head until it was level with her enemy's.

Alessandra met her eyes. In that brief look she saw cruelty mixed with question, hatred with a pure puzzlement.

Then the eyes burned and the carmined lips were fixed insatiably on hers in a long, hideously intimate kiss.

"That is for my husband—the last you will have," the

princess sighed with satisfaction. The justice of it pleased her. This girl she so hated would die of the plague in her place, while La Sventura would bring all her skills to bear and her patient would soon walk in the light again—to live and thrive and bear her brother's child.

"You shall stay and nurse me diligently," she told her prisoner, "until you are no longer capable of it. La Sventura will give you your instructions."

And so Tulla took the gypsy's place beside the bed, to wipe the damp forehead, to give potions and herbal teas; and always, unless she must move away from the bed, Alessandra kept her hand a rigid captive in her own. She did not loose it even when, in response to a strong draught of poppy seed, she sank into a disturbed and sweating sleep.

An hour passed, slowly.

There came an urgent knocking at the door. La Sventura rose and left the room.

While the princess still slept, Tulla, with the temporarily admitted relationship of those who cannot avoid it, exchanged a look of impatience and curiosity with the astrologer, who was seated near a crack in the curtains, pouring over a bundle of charts he had produced from beneath his gown.

When the gypsy had been gone for perhaps a quarter of an hour, Atroviso began to look uncomfortable.

"If Madonna will excuse me?" he said with revolting courtesy and followed La Sventura out of the room with sideways haste.

Had he been investigating what the future held for himself, rather than for the surviving members of the families of Biscaglia and Valenti, he might well have left the Villa Nero long before now.

As it was, things were beginning to look very disquieting. He had made certain readings that today appeared capable of a rather different interpretation from the ones he had previously put upon them. They had, of course, been largely the ones he had been paid to make—but they had also seemed quite possible—even, more importantly, probable.

He had become more apprehensive when he had found no guard outside the princess's chamber. In fact he did not find a single guard anywhere in the villa. There were, however, several of the late cardinal's servants ransacking his private study, their arms full of goblets, jewels, and other precious objects. Several others were doing the same service for the pantry.

It needed only the single piece of information that one of them was pleased to toss him, to ascertain that Atroviso, with the self-protective wisdom shared by La Sventura, would not return to the darkened chamber of his mistress. He was on his way down the front steps, his pockets well filled with the cardinal's jewels, when he fell into the appreciative hands of the Prince of Valenti's men-at-arms. They were led by Leone himself, though he was scarcely recognizable to his ertswhile unappreciated guest, armed, bloody, and grim faced as he was.

The astrologer's expression became one of fawning servility. "Excellence! I was just hastening to put myself at your Magnificence's service. I have just discovered a most wonderful conjunction of Mars and Venus in your present horoscope! A true miracle of the heavens—"

"Where is the Princess of Valenti?" Leone demanded, his voice as savage as a blow.

"She is in the main bedchamber—but you should not visit her—she has the plague!" was the instant, hopeful warning. Atroviso did not like the prince's aspect and was eager to begin his good behavior.

Leone, however, either did not believe him or did not hear him and was already running through the doors, leaving the despairing astrologer to the far from tender mercies of his troop.

"Our greatest poet, the divine Dante," remarked Gian Carmaggio, who had insisted upon joining their number, "placed all such sorcerers in the fourth ditch of the eighth circle of his Inferno, with their heads twisted so that they could only look behind them—as their reward for the heresy of predicting God's intentions with man. Would it not be a fitting end to this malicious astrologer," he asked amicably of his companions who stood suitably transfixed with awe at his education, "if we were to twist his wicked old head into a similar position?"

They all agreed that it would.

The prince ordered the few men who had accompanied him into the house to make a thorough search of it. Meanwhile he would enter his wife's chamber alone.

Although he doubted that he had come so far to be leveled

377

by the plague in this stage of his fortunes, he covered his face against infection with a piece of lace that lay over a table in the anteroom.

He did not believe the sight that met his eyes when he had flung open the bedchamber door.

There were only two people in the room. One was his wife, tossing in feverish sleep in the great bed, the other Tulla, seated close to her, holding her hand as though she were a beloved friend.

Tulla, who was dead, but was not dead!

She looked up at the noise of his entrance and met his incredulous shout.

"My lord!" she cried, with a disbelief almost as strong as his own. Pulling her hand from Alessandra's she flew toward him, and he threw plague and care to the winds to clasp her in his arms.

"But what are you doing here?" he muttered staring past her at the shrouded bed. "It is dangerous to be so near."

She shook her head. Explanations did not seem important. Only the one that would reassure him.

"I have had the plague," she smiled, thinking wryly of Atroviso. "Long ago, when I was a child. I will take no harm from her. She is dying, Leone," she concluded softly.

He betrayed no pity. "It is well, for I had come to take her life." Then abruptly, "The children? Are they still alive?"

"I am told they are."

"Then my men will find them." He let them go then and went to the bedside to stand looking down on his wife. Alessandra's sleep had been constantly disturbed, and now she opened alert eyes as if aware of some change in her surroundings.

"Alessandra. How is it with you?" He spoke without emotion.

Triumph glowed in the white face. "Leone! So they have taken you also. I am glad. Now it can be finished."

She raised herself a little and offered him a livid smile of terrible and ironic sweetness, holding out her arms toward him, blue-white against the black drapery.

"Will you not kiss me, my husband. Your whore has already tasted my lips. Come, Leone—will you too not embrace the Plague Virgin."

Then harshly and with a malevolence that almost had the

378

power to make Tulla afraid, "There are far worse ways to die, as—if I wish it—you will discover!"

"It is you who are dying, Alessa," he said quietly. "Is it your wish that I send for a priest?"

But she had fallen back, panting, and it was clear that his words held no further meaning for her. She caught at the last phrase however, her eyes suddenly flooding with tears.

"Yes—send for my brother, for Silvio," she whispered. "He does not know that I am sick—tell him he must come to me and then it will go better with me." She twisted her head upon the pillow, her eyes glassy, her pain obvious.

"And tell him, tell him," she gasped, dragging at Leone's hand, clearly no longer aware who he was, "that the child will be born in May with the spring—promise me—"

He turned away from her, sickened with his own thought.

Her head fell limp on the pillow, and her eyelids fluttered shut. She was not dead, but the end was very near; she would not survive the coming crisis.

Tulla held the opium mixture to her lips, tilting it carefully until she swallowed a little of it. Then she wiped the wet hair from her forehead and passed the cold cloth across her face.

"Leave her—I will send others to her," Leone murmured, his hand on her shoulder willing her away.

"Since she must die, there is no reason to let her suffer more than necessary. She has great need of the priest," she added, but she would not tell him why, though she knew from Alessandra's ravings of her terrible pact with the witch.

"I will see to it myself," he said, giving way to her compassion, and left the room to send one of his men for a priest. There would be many to be found upon the battlefield.

The men-at-arms, having completed their search of the house and grounds, had found no one left to face the victors except two or three frightened servant girls, all of whom had hidden in one clothing cupboard—and Bernardo and Lucia, whom they had found wandering cheerlessly in the corridor after the discovery that their guards had left their door unlocked before making their own escape from the wrath of the Valenti.

The prince watched Tulla's radiant face as she held both children to her on the shadowed terrace, and a strong sense of what his future would be released the severe lines into which his face had tightened during these last days.

He resisted, before his men who were now crowding onto the terrace also, the impulse to fall upon his knees and thank God for his care of them all.

Then Gian Carmaggio ran up to him, and he found he was able to greet the boy with the smile he longed for.

Gian proceeded proudly to give his prince a full account of the literary death of Atroviso, and Leone was bound to admit it a most fitting end, though he was not to be persuaded, to his esquire's deep disappointment, to view the body, which had been trussed in position head to tail and slung over someone's horse.

"I have seen cadavers enough for a lifetime today," he remarked. He realized that Gian himself must have done so, too, and marveled at the difference ten or so years could make in a man's appetite for corpses.

It was Tulla who thought to ask just as they were mounting to leave the Villa Nero, "What has become of La Sventura? I don't see her among your prisoners."

"We've not seen hide nor hair of her," a soldier replied. "You are certain, Madonna, that she was here?"

"Certain."

She shivered. She could have wished *that* evil, above all to be laid to rest; she did not know why it had been so, but that woman, above all the Biscaglia, had caused her soul to shrink in fear.

She would have been considerably more comfortable if she could have watched the tall figure, scarlet cloak flying above the black mare, ten miles distant upon the road to Milan.

La Sventura had no companions. She needed none but her talent and her power over the weak minds of men. She would find friends in Milan. The Sforza noblemen were at daggers drawn for the dukedom.

There was always fertile soil in Italy where evil might flourish and prosper.

As the prince and Tulla led a small cavalcade up the steep track that led back across the sad, battle-strewn hillside of Montevalenti where the broom that was not broken still flamed optimistically above the shattered ordinance and ragged rocks, the blood-rusted grass and the desolate weapons, their thoughts were somber and separate.

Leone felt the city reach out to him like a stricken child, bringing all its hurts for him to cure—its deaths, its plague, its desperation and confusion; the widows and the orphans, the work without masters, the master without workmen. He knew there was a weight there offered him that he would wear forever about his neck as the ox wears the yoke; sometimes it would be too heavy to bear, but he would bear it.

He no longer had Franco—but perhaps he no longer had so great a need of him.

Tulla, riding close at his side, glad of the silence that lay between them, had cast her mind back to the first time she had ridden this way, with Gian Carmaggio prattling at her heels—as indeed he still did, some yards behind them among the men-at-arms.

She remembered how the beauty of the city, at that first sight, had pierced the apparent calm that concealed her frightened, alien, ignorant youth. Remembering, she looked toward the man whose beauty pierced her now—and thought how she had closed her heart to his every kindness—had locked herself in the isolated tower of her pride, making herself her own prisoner as much as his.

Now, she knew, he would give her freedom, freedom to leave the city or remain with him.

As the track rounded out toward the greensward beneath the castle wall, they looked up, each at the other, at precisely the same moment, each catching the dying hint of gentle, private irony in the other's eyes. They smiled then, though they were still content to ride on without speaking.

The castle gates had long been open for them, and as they came nearer they saw that there were many friends waiting to greet them.

Too many men had died and would die yet, for the citizens of Montevalenti to give their prince a triumphal return upon any scale that the Romans would have recognized, but those who were able to do so had come out to welcome him home.

At their head was a stooping figure in a familiar rusty black gown, who came forward limping a little, with his arms outstretched. It was Lorenzo de Medici who had ridden with a courier's haste behind the small but totally successful army he had been able to raise, literally overnight, among the Florentine militia and the invaluable bargello.

"Leone, my friend! You waited long enough to ask my help. I was almost too late! But now you are victorious and I offer you the congratulations of my heart!"

Leone dismounted and clasped him heartily, kissing both his cheeks. "It was not I who summoned your aid—though

381

Christ knows I tried hard enough! If it had not been for Mona Tulla, the day would have gone hard for Montevalenti."

Sandro Botticelli, hearing them, stepped forward bashfully from the crowd. "Magnifico—my message *did* indeed come originally from Mona Tulla and by a most unorthodox route. However, I thought it would save time for everyone if it appeared to come straight from the prince."

"Bravo, Sandro! A most excellent judgment! Your knowledge of men equals your knowledge of beauty," Lorenzo applauded, his eyes narrowing slightly. It was true. He would have hesitated far longer over a woman's word, even that of his own most respected wife. They were inclined, in general, to exaggerate. However, as he looked up at the pure and collected countenance of the girl whom Leone was now helping down from her horse, he was bound to admit that there could be exceptions.

Madonna's expeditious message had enabled him to perform a small human miracle for his friend, and he counted himself as much in her debt, therefore, as Leone himself.

He limped toward her, cursing the family bane of gout and bowed low over her hand. Behind and above them, covering the sward and hanging from windows and ramparts as gladly as they had done before the siege, Leone's subjects made her resoundingly aware of their gratitude and their approval of his salute. The cry of "Mona Tulla!" blasted the ear almost as loudly and as often as that of "Il Leone!" or "Lorenzo!"

Looking up and smiling, shy acknowledgment of their tribute, she caught sight of the dark hair and flashing eyes of the voluptuous Marcellina, who was hanging from an embrasure of the barbican, her wares displayed to the usual tempting advantage. Laughing up at her, she gave her a companionable wave and was rewarded by an overblown rose, thornless, which plumped softly onto her shoulder.

There would always be a Marcellina. That was a fact with which she would have to come to terms.

Sandro Botticelli hesitantly claimed her attention; first he too must kiss her hand. Then he said happily, "I am overjoyed that all has come to this happy pass—Madonna, I am your slave!" She began to try to thank him for what he had done but he would have none of it. "It was nothing Madonna," he disclaimed gently, but she realized that he was scarcely listening to her words, so intent was he upon gazing at her face.

382

"Sandro?" she queried. He had moved a little to the right and was now staring at her with a decided squint.

"Eh? Oh, excuse me, Mona Tulla! It is just that—Madonna you must sit for me again, *very* soon. It is imperative! Something has happened to your face."

She clapped a hand to it in pretended alarm.

"No, no—it is a new thing in it—a softness, a *willingness* toward life—a kind of *freedom*. I cannot explain it—but I can paint it for you."

She smiled and pressed his hand, promising that it should indeed be soon. She wanted to weep, for he had touched her deeply, but here was Vanozza Grazzi hurrying forward to envelop her in the warmest welcome of all. With all the proud dignity of the peasant whose family is as ancient as her lords, she enfolded Tulla to the black-clad vastness of flesh that covered the vastness of her heart. "Beloved mistress—I thought they had killed you! Praise be to God for this deliverance!"

Rocked in the warm reality of this motherly embrace, Tulla felt her tears begin to spring, beyond her control.

She was saved from them by the sudden appearance of Luigi Pulci, sprung from the crowd like harlequin from a box, who threw himself dramatically upon the ground before her feet.

"Bellissima!" he exclaimed. Then, swiveling towards Leone who stood close by with Lorenzo, "Principe! Your citizens have empowered me to be the spokesman of their thanks and their loving welcome on this, your day of victory. I would do so in verse," he added disarmingly, "but there has not been time. I will merely add to the glad praises that now assault your ears and the heavens my own salutation to the beauty and bravery that has saved Montevalenti from the Sins of the Lion!"

Leone, who had caught Tulla's eye in amusement, looked slightly taken aback.

"The Sins of the Lion?" Was it so clear to them, then, to what his indolence might have brought them?

Then he remembered; again that day Dante was the chosen authority. Heresy and violence were the Sins of the Lion—and these indeed had all but brought Montevalenti down. The heresy of a man of God who had dared to put himself before that God—and the violence, to God, to men, and at last to Silvestro Biscaglia himself, into which that heretical pride had led him.

Letting Pulci's oration clatter about him, he turned his eyes and his heart upon Tulla. It was right that they should give her their thanks, as it was that he should give her what he would make of himself.

He stepped close to her and let his smile tell her what he would never say to her, unless it was with the aid of his lute.

Tears threatened her again as she met his warm appraisal and saw in it the blessed promise of all that she could need—a little ordinary happiness.

Then he placed her slender, capable hand firmly upon his arm and moved toward the gates.

The iron-bound wood was empty of its archaic talisman.

It was time to enter into his city.